DEA

A flicker of motion
warned her to sway
that came stabbing
but only grazed it,
caught a glimpse of cross-hatched leather strips
that wrapped his forearms. She entertained an
instant's notion to simply kill the whoreson who
held her, but even that second's work could be
fatal. Her desperation left her one option: She
drew her lips back from her teeth and gave a
piercing whistle. The assassin at her back never
saw what hit him.

As he leaned over the wall to stab at her, Graegduz
slammed into his back like a thunderbolt. The
impact of the wolf's leap sent both of them tumbling into a scrabbling tangle at Barra's feet. The
wolf rolled away, scrambling to get upright; the
assassin had time only to look up and see the edge
of Barra's broadaxe an instant before it was buried
in his skull.

The other assassin stared wide-eyed at his companion's shuddering corpse, and made a gagging
sound.

Barra hefted her bloodstained axe, and smiled at
him. "Now it's just you and me."

IRON DAWN

IRON DAWN

MATTHEW WOODRING STOVER

A ROC BOOK

ROC
Published by the Penguin Group
Penguin Putnam Inc., 375 Hudson Street,
New York, New York 10014, U.S.A.
Penguin Books Ltd, 27 Wrights Lane,
London W8 5TZ, England
Penguin Books Australia Ltd, Ringwood,
Victoria, Australia
Penguin Books Canada Ltd, 10 Alcorn Avenue,
Toronto, Ontario, Canada M4V 3B2
Penguin Books (N.Z.) Ltd, 182–190 Wairau Road,
Auckland 10, New Zealand

Penguin Books Ltd, Registered Offices:
Harmondsworth, Middlesex, England

First published by Roc, an imprint of Dutton Signet,
a member of Penguin Putnam Inc.
Previously published in a Roc trade paperback edition.

First Mass Market Printing, April, 1998
10 9 8 7 6 5 4 3 2 1

Cover art by Keith Birdsong

 REGISTERED TRADEMARK — MARCA REGISTRADA

Printed in the United States of America

BOOKS ARE AVAILABLE AT QUANTITY DISCOUNTS WHEN USED TO PROMOTE PRODUCTS
OR SERVICES. FOR INFORMATION PLEASE WRITE TO PREMIUM MARKETING DIVISION, PEN-
GUIN PUTNAM INC., 375 HUDSON STREET, NEW YORK, NEW YORK 10014.

For Robyn,
for giving me Barra

The author gratefully acknowledges
Robyn Fielder, Paul Kroll, H. Gene McFadden,
and Charles L. Wright for many hours
of reading, advice, and role-playing.
Thanks, guys. I couldn't have
done it without you.

Prologue

Dear Chryl and Antiphos,

This will be the last letter of this packet, I think; if we can make Tyre before winter shuts down the trade, you should be reading this before the Turning of the Sun.

As you might be able to gather, the last three months have been a bit lean. I've managed to be more-or-less steadily employed as a marine, especially since I hooked up with this Athenian, Leucas. But with the surge in piracy breaking up the trade—particularly here in the East—and stiff competition from Akhaian veterans driving the wages down, we've managed to do little more than support ourselves. These Akhaians, half of them seem to have left their brains in front of the walls of Troy along with the corpses of most of their friends; they hardly seem to care if they get paid or not. If business doesn't improve, I might have to go back to scribing contracts in Knossos next year instead of dealing for myself.

Don't worry, though; there's rumors of trouble in Tyre, and I'm sure to find profitable employment.

Leucas' thigh is healing nicely; all the infection seems to have subsided. There's a lesson for you in what happened on Kypros: when hunting boar, especially man-killers who've been hunted before, keep your spear grounded and never try to deflect the boar's charge. It was his own strength that almost killed him, you see. He was trying to shift the beast over toward me for the death blow when the spear shaft snapped. If Kheperu—my newest partner; he's Egyptian, and you know how they are—hadn't managed to blind the boar with one of his powders, it would have certainly savaged Leucas badly, maybe killed him, before I could get there and sever its spine. Another lesson: when facing a boar with an axe, come at it

*from the side and strike for the back of its neck. It's almost
impossible to penetrate a boar's skull—the bone there is
like armor—and if you hit the spine farther down its back,
it can still turn and rip you good using just its front legs.*

*I may be traveling with these two for some time, by the
way. Even though Leucas and I have been together for
only a couple of months, we seem to make a pretty good
team, even more so now that we have Kheperu. I still don't
trust him much—he's far too clever for his own good—but
Leucas is steady as a rock (he's not really bright enough to
be treacherous) and he helps me keep Kheperu in line.*

*King Demetor was very grateful for our help. He gave
us some lovely gifts—I'm sending the bronze sword for
Antiphos, and the silver cup is for Chryl. He also paid us
in Athenian coin, sixty large weights apiece, which will be
enough to support us in Tyre for many weeks, buy a nice
gift for your Uncle Peliarchus there, and have some left
over to bank at Knossos.*

*I think I should be able to return to the Isle of the
Mighty next summer, in time for the Midsummer Festival.
In the meantime, tend your lessons—Abdi is a good tutor,
and expensive; if the Phoenikian this letter is written in is
too hard for you, he'll read it for you, I'm sure. You obey
Coll, now—I gave her enough trouble when I was little,
she needs no grief from her grandsons; trouble her too
much and your great-grandmother Maeve will turn you
both into goats. Give my respects to Llem, and tell him the
tin trade should be very good next year, and I hope he's
having no more trouble with his underkings. And if your
grandda Ouendail should visit from Eire, tell him to keep
his shaggy butt away from my mother.*

*I love you both very much, and with the favor of the
gods I'll see you in summer.*

> *Take care,*
>
> *Mother*

Barra trimmed off the soggy end of her reed brush and returned it to her pencase made from a bull's thighbone. The
whistling, agonized cries of one of the wounded sailors had
faded into silence, and she supposed she really ought to be

up helping to dig his grave. The other wounded sailor only gasped, and occasionally roused himself to ask for water; he'd taken a pirate arrow just below his navel, and Barra figured they might as well dig both graves now. The second sailor'd be filling one soon enough.

The orange glow from the campfire flickered across her face, and the faces of her partners, who drowsed nearby. Trees leaned close around overhead, of the same pine that made the campfire pop and spit. Barra could smell the sea, even through the bitter scent of the burning pine, and hear the low splash of waves on this windless night, but she couldn't see it; the days of making landfall camps on beaches were long gone. She missed it, really, missed sitting on the sand and watching the moon paint silver across the ripples, but these days a campfire on the beach served as a beacon for pirates.

And there was at least one band of pirates, out there maybe even in the darkness tonight, that would be looking for them.

They had come out of the east, a pair of long, low ships rowing hard around a wooded point. She and her partners, trading their skills for passage on this ship, had barely time to arm themselves before the battle was joined. Their captain had tried to run, but their ship was a broad-beamed sea-goer, wide and sturdy to ply the passage from Thrace to Kypros to the Phoenikian coast, and even with every crewman straining at the oars, it had no chance of outracing the sleek pirates. Kheperu's firepots had sent one pirate longship burning toward the bottom of the sea, but by that time the fighting was hand-to-hand. Pirates from the sunken ship swam to the trader and clambered aboard, to join howling pirates from the other ship, that already ranged among the oar-benches, hacking down sailors with short bronze swords. These pirates were Akhaian renegades, probably themselves veterans of the Siege of Troy—skilled fighters, they cut through weary sailors with ease. All that had saved the trader's crew was a desperate counter-board led by Barra and Leucas and Kheperu; with the sailors scrambling behind them, they had abandoned their wallowing trader, captured the pirate's longship with hard fighting, pulled away, and left the trader in the pirates' hands. They'd escaped with little more than their lives and the clothes that they wore.

Barra shook her head as she rolled up the papyrus scroll and returned it to its bone case. In her letters home, she never wrote of how bad things really were, here around the Mediterranean. She rarely mentioned the pirates, the way nearly everybody with thirty friends and a boat seemed to have gone into piracy, these past five years—if they don't have a boat, they become bandits and prey on inland towns. Outside of Egyptian holdings, the only really safe places left were Knossos, Argos, and Mykenai; even the Hittite Empire could no longer summon the strength to put down the Phrygian tribes that pressed on their eastern and northern borders. She certainly wasn't going to tell her young hero-worshiping sons that she was dead-broke—all her silver, all the gifts from Demetor, all the money she'd saved since her last trip to Crete, all had been left behind on the trader; the cup and the sword that she'd written of she'd found under a bench on the longship. She'd only barely managed to save the bundle of letters and the pencase, which now bore a bright scrape where she'd used it to block a pirate's shortsword until she could open his skull with her axe.

She bundled together the scrollcases, tied them with a leather thong, and tucked them into the drawstring bag that held the cup and the smallsword. Fifteen years around the Mediterranean, more than ten of them spent spilling blood for pay, and here she was, burying sailors at a furtive camp on the Hittite coast, barely owning more than the axes that weighed down her belt. She shook her head and got up; she carried the bag over to where Leucas slept, and laid it close by his side— none of the sailors would dare risk disturbing the giant Athenian. If anyone had pointed out to Barra the irony of guarding her few possessions against men that, only hours before, she had very nearly given her life to defend, she would have only shrugged. Sailors are thieves, and that's the whole of it.

Well, she'd only have to deal with this lot for another day or two; Kheperu had done a divination before he'd retired for the evening, and he'd predicted clear weather and hot for the next three days—plenty of time to make Tyre.

She picked her way quietly inland to where the captain sat on a stone outcrop and watched a pair of his men scratch a grave into the stony soil. He acknowledged her approach with a bare nod, and she squatted beside him.

"I'd give him a hero's pyre, if we could risk the light," the captain murmured. "Instead, we must stick him in the ground like a peasant."

Barra said, "Why are you only digging one grave?"

The captain looked at her with raw and bloody eyes. "Paxo is going to live, that's why."

"No, he isn't. He may breathe till morning—may—but he'll not see another nightfall. I can smell the bile from the wound." Barra's nose was as keen as a wolf's; there was no chance that she was mistaken.

As if called by her words, the wounded sailor moaned raggedly behind the trees. The captain turned away from Barra's level gaze.

"He'll live," he murmured.

"If wishing could make it so, he will," she said. "But if wishing could make it so . . . well, many things would be different."

They sat in silence for a time, and watched the sailors scratch at the earth with tools meant for shipbuilding.

Finally, Barra said, "What will you do, now?"

The captain shrugged, and let out a long, slow sigh. "Most of the boys, they're hired only as far as Tyre. I'll likely pay them off, and get a new crew . . ."

And go pirate, Barra finished for him silently. What else could he do? Unless he had hoarded wealth enough to build a new ship, crew and supply it, and buy a load of trade goods, his only resource was this long, low, sleek pirate ship, useless out of sight of land. It had no room for cargo, barely any for supplies. This man would never captain a trader again, unless he took it by force.

Barra's foster-father was a Tyrian shipmaster; her two foster-brothers were trader-captains, with ships she herself held a part interest in, an investment made after a particularly fat year; she hated pirates more than anything else on land or sea. There should be money waiting for her in Tyre, a return on that investment—unless pirates had hit her ships and killed her brothers.

And yet, she could not bring herself to say anything to this man who would be a pirate in months to come, this man who blinked through fat and rolling tears as he watched two of his men dig a grave for a third. He had sons of his own.

In her mind, she flashed a vivid glimpse of herself, in the spring of her fourteenth year, as she stood at the high-curved

prow of a Phoenikian trader and watched the green shores
of the Isle of the Mighty recede into the mists. She'd done
her duty, fulfilled her obligation to her brother and her
gods: she'd given birth to a son, a squalling red-faced baby
boy fathered by a traveling prince who'd had a taste for
girls at the brink of womanhood. Chryl, she'd named him,
Golden, after the color of his father's hair; another heir to her
brother's throne in Great Langdale. After that birth her child
had seemed hateful to her, as did her life, her family, the very
air that carried the oaken scent of the Isle. She'd given her
son into the care of her mother, and boarded that ship for
Tyre, and she'd stood in the bow and watched the shores
of her home fade into moist greyness, and she'd dreamed
of coming home someday with a fleet of ships to carry the
fabulous wealth of the East, and heroic tales to tell of earning every piece. She'd sworn she'd come home richer than
her brother would ever be; she'd come home as a real Eastern
princess, with servants and exotic pets—unlike her sisters,
who were only chapped-cheek shepherdesses and broodmares.

   Now, fifteen years later, here she was: on the Hittite coast
without a shekel in her purse, her own cheeks scaly and
peeling, nearly as rough as the callused palms of her hands.
She scraped her hands together and looked down at the hard
muscle of her thighs and thought, *Well at least I've still got
my figure.*

   And, ignoring the pained, incredulous look from the
grieving captain beside her, she laughed out loud.

PART ONE

The Job

CHAPTER ONE

The Bear

The sun is the hammer, Barra thought as she swung down to the beach from the high-curving prow of the captured longship, *and I'm the bloody anvil. Kheperu surely called the weather right enough.* She used both hands to wipe sweat from her face back into her tightly tied hair. *Be cold come nightfall, though.* "Leucas! Kheperu! Come on, shag it!"

A rare south wind had brought the smell of Tyre to last night's landfall: cinnamon and pepper in the cedar-laced pine smoke, sharp young wine and close-packed sweating humanity, smoldering hemp and horse piss. She'd been out from Tyre more than a year, broken only by one single-night stopover on her way from Thrace to Pharos six months ago, and those scents brought her blood up like a tired horse in sight of her paddock. Now she was home, or as near to home as anywhere in the bloody burning south could be. No matter that her purse was as flat as a little girl's chest; her foster-father Peliarchus would be holding her share of the profit on the pair of ships she jointly owned with him and her foster-brothers. It wouldn't nearly equal what she'd lost to the pirates, but it'd be better than a sharp stick in the eye.

She'd take the morning to wander the Market, meet people again, take the pulse of the city—remind herself how much she loved this place. And, perhaps, the afternoon as well. Leucas and Kheperu both had a few coins left; surely her partners could stand her a meal or two here, seeing as she'd be putting them up at her foster home tonight.

Tonight, she'd be home, and eating Tayniz's cooking—she'd likely roast ducks with currant sauce, and fry mushrooms in butter, and bake fresh barley bread—and then her own bed in the room that had been hers now for fifteen years, a real feather mattress, not one of these bloody piles of rugs and fleeces that the Akhaians pretended were so comfortable.

The thought of so much sheer self-indulgent pleasure brought a sting to her eyes. In between times, she could make a great fuss over Graegduz, the young grey wolf who was her only friend from home, to apologize to him for having left him here in Tyre for so long; and she had a full wagon load of stories to trade with Peliarchus while they sat around the fire, in the courtyard under the Tyrian stars . . .

About half the surviving sailors had debarked, muttering among themselves and giving dark looks to the beachsiders that streamed toward the longship. The *Pelican*—the captain had named her so, for the way she'd scooped them all from the sea—was the first ship in this morning, and the beachsiders pressed curiously around to catch first glimpses of what cargo she might carry, and perhaps to snag a piece or two if no one armed was looking. They appeared more interested than disappointed to find that there was no cargo at all. The captain stood amidships, looking out over the gathering crowd, and Barra read on his face, clear as if the words were burned there, the determination that the *Pelican*'s next landfall in Tyre would be different. He met her eyes, and quickly looked away.

She folded her arms and held herself still in the sunlight to wait for her partners; patience was not in her nature, but she could fake it. The beachsiders took in the look on her sunburned face and her vivid red hair, then the hard muscle of her shoulders and arms left bare by her leather tunic, and finally the wickedly sharp edges of the three stone axes she wore, two small ones of flint tucked behind her wide boar skin belt, and the big basalt broad head that looked like it belonged in a slaughterhouse strapped to her right thigh, its haft in a smallsword scabbard; they wisely gave her a wide berth, muttering among themselves of "damned lunatic foreign women."

Their wariness gave her no satisfaction; on the contrary, it stirred a powerful impulse to raise knots on a skull or two—particularly one big strawheaded guy with a leering smirk on his stupid face. Barra spent a brief, half-smiling moment calculating the profit of the pleasure she'd get from smacking that smirk off his face with the flat of her axe against the possible loss of offending one of the Great Houses. This fellow was tall enough to have been born into nobility, and his hair was too clean and his clothes, though old and somewhat shabby, fit him too well—he could very well have been a Mursuwallite purchasing agent dressed down for bargain-hunting.

On the other hand, he looked more Akhaian than Hittite, and she could always plead ignorance. . . . His smirk grew wider and wider the longer she thought about it, and his stare became ever more insulting: that made up her mind. Among the Picts of Great Langdale, a stare like that is an invitation to bloodshed.

"I can understand why you keep your lips together when you smile," Barra said in conversational Phoenikian. "Eating shit can rot your teeth."

His grin got wider; his teeth were perfect. No beachsider, then. "Don't come all hostile," he said easily, his Phoenikian carrying the rural burr of the Akhaian peninsula. Corinth, maybe. "You make your living with that hardware?"

Barra switched to perfectly accented Athenian Greek. "A girl's got to keep *something* hard with her, these days; I keep meeting men like you, who don't know the meaning of the word."

He shook his head and chuckled, and responded in the same tongue. "Where'd you learn Language? You look like a barbarian—and civilized women don't carry weapons, little girl."

Despite being from a family known for the size and strength of its members—her brother Llem could hoist a full-grown man in each fist—Barra had suffered through a youth and adolescence of japes about her height: she was a full hand shorter than any other woman in her family, and a finger or two below average even down here among the smaller Mediterranean races. It was still a sensitive subject—one among many, as even Barra would admit, including this insulting tendency of folk down here to refer to her people as savages.

Barra's lips drew back from her teeth; she fought to make this reaction look like a smile. "You probably wouldn't know a civilized woman if she knocked you on the head. What do you say we try it and find out?"

His grin began to fade. "A man could get real tired of that mouth on you."

"You think so? Why don't you go find one and ask him?"

"You little whore," he said, reddening. "I ought to break you in half."

Barra made the long-practiced move with her right hand;

before the man could blink, the broadaxe was out and cocked back over her shoulder. "Try it. See how you like being able to breathe through your forehead."

A looming shadow blocked the sun from behind her left shoulder. "Barra," Leucas rumbled softly, "why are you about to kill this man?"

Barra kept her eyes on the Corinthian; the Corinthian was speechlessly staring up at Leucas, all nineteen-and-a-half hands and eighteen stone of battle-scarred veteran, dressed in the Cretan style, bare-chested, wearing only a kilt and sandals. Barra said, "I don't like the way he stared at me."

"Mmm-hm."

The Corinthian recovered, and drew himself up. "It's a good thing you got here when you did. Your woman needs to be on a leash. You should muzzle her like a bitch."

Leucas slowly lowered the huge bundle of armor and weapons from his shoulder to the sand. When he straightened, the top of Barra's head came just up to the nipples on a lean, scarred chest layered with deep muscle that looked as hard as a bronze breastplate. In his youth, Leucas had stolen away from his family home in Athens to drive a chariot at Troy. Like so many of the men who'd survived the ten endless years of war, he'd returned to find his home changed beyond recognition; to him, Athens was now just another city, where he'd once lived for a while. Barra had met him only two months before, while they'd both worked as marines on board traders that plied the coast of Sicily, and had already come to rely on him more than she'd have liked to.

Leucas lacked the vicious temperament necessary to make a living as a bandit, or a pirate, as did so many of his former comrades; the profession he practiced when mercenary work was not to be found was proclaimed by his ruined face, a face in which every bone had been broken once or more by fists wrapped in leather and sometimes weighted with bronze in the boxing circles of every Greek-speaking land. Some of the damage was hidden by a short-trimmed black beard shot through with streaks of white, but nothing could conceal the lumps of scar tissue that made up his sharply bent nose and flattened ears. The only feature that had escaped damage was his eyes; eyes that appeared as though they could sparkle with deep amusement, but now fixed on the Corinthian with a look as cold as grey winter ice.

"Barra is not my woman," he said slowly, "and I don't believe I was addressing you, sir."

The Corinthian swallowed. "I only wanted to make a business proposition, that's all."

"He called me a whore," Barra said, her voice flat and hard as the side of her axe.

Leucas winced, then sighed. "Well," he said heavily, "I'm sure you called him worse than that. Didn't you?"

Barra lowered the axe. "Maybe."

"Now, do you want to listen to his business offer, or do you want to kill him?"

"You're asking the woman?" the Corinthian said incredulously. "What kind of a man are you?"

Leucas gave him another considering, long grey look. The Corinthian took an involuntary step backward. Leucas looked back to Barra, and waited.

Barra shrugged; remembering her current poverty shredded her temper like smoke before the wind. She slid the axe haft back into its scabbard. "Why not? It's what we're here for."

The Corinthian coughed his throat clear and patted down his coat, his hands unconsciously reaching toward his shoulders for something that wasn't there. *These aren't his usual clothes,* Barra thought. What was he reaching for? Straps that would hold a breastplate? Shoulder pieces of a corselet?

"How many in your company?"

Barra shook her head. "You'd best start with your name and what you're paying."

"I'm Chrysios," the Corinthian said. "I need about five men who can handle themselves and don't mind a little red work."

"Men?" Barra asked mildly. "Do I count?"

Chrysios shrugged. "That's a nice move you have with the axe, little missy—just for show, or can you swing it, too?"

She was about to show him, but Leucas laid his heavy hand gently on her shoulder. "Wait, Barra, he hasn't yet said how much he's paying."

"It's not enough," Barra growled, irritably shaking free. "A nomarchy in the Delta wouldn't be enough."

"Fifteen silver shekels," Chrysios said. "For one night's—" His eyes glazed over, and he turned his head and coughed harshly: Kheperu was approaching from upwind.

Even in Tyre in late autumn, when fresh water was scarce—

the nearest river that runs year-round, the Litani, empties into the sea more than an hour's ride north of the city—and bathing was considered a luxury reserved for those with no better way to use their time, the stench that emanated from Kheperu's person could strike the unprepared like a physical blow. This was more than the goaty reek of the old sweat that caked his robes; the chemicals and aromatic herbs that the stubby Egyptian carried on his person added a sinus-piercing overtone. Barra glanced over her shoulder at him and moved to one side—standing downwind of Kheperu for a few breaths could numb her nose for hours.

She smiled to herself as he approached; Kheperu was doing his Fat Old Man act, leaning heavily on his stout oak staff, disguising the weapon as a walking stick, the same act he'd done that day he'd introduced himself on the Paphos beach on Kypros. He'd come up and asked their help in the swindle that later became the Kyprian Boar Hunt; the swindle, and the hunt, had worked exceedingly well—it was only bad luck that had brought them afoul of pirates before they could get away with their money. In their brief association, Barra had learned that Kheperu was greedy and treacherous, a whiner and a practitioner of a bewildering variety of perversions; he was also a former seshperankh, a Scribe of the House of Life who had been banned from the priesthood and exiled from Egypt for some unnamed crime, and he claimed to have the entire *Book of the Secrets of the Laboratory* committed to memory. This was almost certainly a lie, as were most things that came out of his mouth, but he did know a great deal of alchemy and a bit of magic and was, on occasion, capable of acts of astonishing bravery.

He wheezed loudly as he labored over the sand, mumbling in a plaintive undertone about the heat. He was only a hand or so taller than Barra, but outweighed her by nearly four stone, his rotund bulk enhanced by the stiff leather armor that he constantly wore beneath his stained, fraying robes. The scalp stubble around his topknot was salted with grey, and only the squirrel-bright glitter in his eyes belied the overall impression of incipient senility.

"Great Mouth," Chrysios gagged. "Doesn't that man ever wash?"

"Best hope he doesn't," Leucas murmured. "It's worse when he's wet."

"You know him?"

Barra said, "He's our third partner."

"Disgusting."

"Tell him so," Barra offered. "He loves compliments from pretty Greek boys."

Chrysios scowled. "How many more?"

"That's all of us."

He looked at Leucas, then at Kheperu incredulously. He said to Barra, "Don't tell me you're *his* woman! How do you stand the smell?"

Barra sighed. It was endless, this automatic assumption that she belonged to a man. In Langdale, the only people who belonged to other people were debt-slaves, and then only until their debt was paid. She tried to be tolerant of the East's barbaric customs, but most of them wore on her, and none more than this one. "I'm tired of you, Chrysios. Go away."

The Corinthian blinked. "My offer still stands—"

"She said," Leucas rumbled, "go away."

The Corinthian looked up into Leucas' cold grey eyes, and decided he'd received valuable advice. He turned with forced dignity and stalked off along the beach.

Kheperu finally trundled up. "Who was that?" he said in bad Greek.

"A job," Leucas said, watching the man's retreating back. "Barra didn't like him."

"Pity. He was lovely."

"Yes, he was," Barra said sadly. "Why are the pretty ones always such jackasses?"

"Your mistake," Kheperu said in a tone of world-weary wisdom, "was in talking to him. Greek men are always more attractive with their mouths tied shut."

Leucas hoisted his bundle back up over his shoulder. "Don't make me hurt you."

"Make you?" Kheperu leered. "I'd *pay* you. Speaking of that, there's an inn in the Greek quarter, run by an old friend of mine—Lidios, his name is—he has the most extraordinary whores—"

"We're broke," Leucas said, frowning down at him. "He'll let you screw on credit?"

"Well, you know," Kheperu patted his robe near his heart, and a muffled jingle of silver was audible. "In Egypt, we have a proverb about eggs and baskets . . ."

"Later," Barra said. "We're going to the Market. We need to drum up some real work."

The Market of Tyre is the centerpiece of the city, an enormous expanse of close-fitted flagstones around which Tyre radiates like a tangled sunburst. Open to the west, toward the sea, the balance of its arc is walled by the golden al-tobe facades of Tyre's oldest buildings, broken only by crowded street-mouths of hard-packed earth. It had been paved more than a hundred years before, by the Hittites, in the days when Great King Suppiluliumas of Hatti had contested with Asshur-ballit of Assyria for the rule of the Phoenikian coast. The days of Hittite rule were long past; Tyre had been an Egyptian holding, part of the Canaan District, since not long after Ramses the Great had smashed Muwatallis' cavalry at the Battle of Qadesh nearly fifty years ago. Over this century and more, these flagstones had been worn in curving paths by the wheels of wagons and war chariots, by feet of sunbaked Kushites and pale Picts, boots of Bottlers from Iberia and the sandals of Indusians from the Far East, pads of dogs and housecats and the occasional captive lion, hooves of fine-boned Arabian horses, of asses and thick-muscled mules.

From the stone islands around which these pathways weave, rise clusters of tentstalls, ranging from simple pole-and-rope shrouds of linen to semipermanent frames of hard northern cedar, with real doors and framed windows hung with folds of translucent silk. The sites of these stalls, even more than the stalls themselves, have often been in the same family for generations, passed down from father to son as the clan's most precious birthright, and are guarded as jealously as a miser guards his gold. One can judge the success of a Market vendor by the number and equipage of his guards. Even a relative newcomer often has several young men, usually his sons, lounging nearby with knotted sticks in their hands, ready at the instant to drive off with shouts and blows any of the ubiquitous "bedrollers"—transient vendors, usually poor, who carry their wares in blanket-bundles—who might be bold enough to spread their displays too close by.

For Barra, the Market was the heart and soul of Tyre. Tyre was without doubt the most cosmopolitan city of its age; the original inhabitants of this coast, the small, olive-skinned Kena'ani, were outnumbered perhaps four or five to one by the descendants of the Egyptian conquerors and the Hittite conquered, the remnants of the earlier Assyrian occupation, the wealthy Cretan refugees who'd fled Theseus' sack of Knossos, and the steady stream of immigrant fortune seekers from across the known world, for it was well-known that a man could make something of himself, here in the trading hub of the world, that here wit and guts counted for more than did any accident of birth. Of the five Great Houses that controlled most of the trade, not one had existed a hundred years ago.

And so the immigrants came, by ship and by desert caravan, on horseback or afoot along the Coast Road, and they huddled together each in their own loosely bordered ghetto— it was only natural, to prefer to live with those who speak your language, who remember how the air smells and what the sunsets look like back home—but the Market was the leveler, the mixer, the welcoming arms that gathered them all in. The Market was where they all came together.

In the early years of her self-imposed exile from her brother's lands, Barra had lived for the days she could slip away from the home of her foster-parents and bury herself in the surging, shouting crowds. It was here that she had learned the value of money and the arts of bargaining, here that she sharpened her Phoenikian and Greek, became fluent in Egyptian and the Canaanite spoken by the Amorite princes of Kena'an, studied Akkadian cuneiform and picked up her smatterings of Hatti, Minoan, and the liquid Iberian of the Bottlers. Here she had learned to judge men by action, since words usually lie; here she had learned that a quick punch buys more than a soft word. It was here, in a twilit alley nearby, that she had first fought for her life.

More than the house of Peliarchus, more even than the huge hall of her brother in Langdale or her father's great fortress of Tara, this was home.

The energy of the Market was contagious; after only a few minutes even silent Leucas was animatedly haggling with a vendor over a saw-toothed spear with an intricately carved haft, even though he had no money with which to buy it. Kheperu was already deep in his third shouting match, dark eyes alight as though he'd been sampling his own drugs, shrilling insults and imprecations as he bargained for a pound of cinnamon bark he didn't want.

Barra moved silently through the crowds, keeping within sight of her companions—an easy task: Leucas stood head and shoulders taller than any man in the Market—exchanging greetings with the occasional merchant who remembered her, complimenting this one or that on his wares or the additions to his stall, dodging the occasional knots of the Egyptian garrison troops. Even while enjoying the warm nostalgia of looking over the places where she'd spent her adolescence, she was attentive to the mood of the marketplace, to the slight shift of eye of a sweating vendor, the conversations muttered in urgent undertones. As she had told her companions when they'd reached the Market's western verge: "Now, look, let's stay in sight of each other in there," she'd said, gesturing into the Market. "For now, I only want to shop around, but keep your eyes open. Talk to people. Even you, Leucas; plenty of people around here speak Greek. I've heard rumors of a trade war brewing, and that means people will be looking for guards, at the very least. For the real money, we'll have to hook up with a Great House, and maybe do a little dirty work. And for that, we need to get their attention—you don't just walk up to the gate of a Great House and ask for a job. Maybe we can start with some guarding, and work our way up when people find out we don't mind getting our hands bloody."

Kheperu'd asked, "Well, what about that fellow on the beach, then?"

"He wanted red work—he wants us to kill somebody."

"So?"

"So he was only paying fifteen shekels. Five apiece. I don't blow my nose for five shekels. Come on, let's move. Tyre is a pricey place to visit, and I want to leave with more money than I brought."

"It's always money with you," Kheperu had complained with feigned despair. "What about good food, and straight sweet wine? What about companionship? What about *sex*?"

"In Tyre, they all cost money. A lot. Come on."

Now she was sure the rumors she'd heard in Kypros were correct: some trouble was brewing in Tyre. That Corinthian on the beach had indicated he was looking to hire mercenaries; this had been a good sign, even though he was an asshole-biter. She noted an unusual number of beggars asking alms, many of them doing it poorly enough that they probably weren't professionals—that was another good sign, a sign that business was down all over the city; the Great Houses might be feeling the pinch and getting antsy. The Egyptian regulars she passed here and there uncharacteristically wore their quilted armor in the heat of the day, and they stuck close together in groups of four or five: this was a better sign. She figured that if she and her friends could keep their eyes open, they just might catch sight of some serious profit.

She sensed a shift in the crowd, people starting to drift northwest, toward the central plaza, near the wells. Any disturbance in the Market caused the crowd to flow like sand falling into a sudden sinkhole; when people noticed those nearer to the disturbance moving toward it, they naturally—even unconsciously—followed.

Barra drifted along with them. A simple syllogism: A disturbance indicates an unusual occurrence; Barra and her partners made their living dealing with unusual occurrences; therefore, something might be happening on which they could make a profit. She caught Leucas' eye and nodded him in the direction of the drifting crowds. He returned her nod, shouldered his bundle, and moved off. She stopped along the way to collect Kheperu—she couldn't get his attention, so she marched up behind him and hauled him along by his topknot, ignoring his squealing protests. When she finally released him, she wiped the grease off her hand onto her breeches.

"Thank you," Kheperu said, all seriousness. "That bastard would have taken me for everything I own, plus a year of indentured servitude and my firstborn son."

She shook her head, chuckling. "Didn't I warn you about Tyrian traders?"

"I believed," he said, drawing up with vast Egyptian dignity, "that you were indulging in your usual exaggeration."

"I never exaggerate."

The gathering crowd became more and more noisy as their progress slowed; once the companions gained the central plaza, they were halted by a solid press of human backs. Leucas looked toward the center, over everyone's head.

"It's a bear. A big bear."

"A bear?" Barra frowned. "What's the fuss over a bear? Trappers bring bears through here all the time. Let me see."

Leucas helped her up onto his back. She leaned her elbows on his hard shoulders.

Five armored men held heavy ropes that attached to a

specially designed collar around the bear's thick neck. The huge brown beast made muffled grunting sounds through its muzzle of leather and bronze as the men urged it along. It seemed sleepy and docile, and ambled willingly enough through the plaza. To Barra's eye, its skin seemed to hang a bit too tight—the way to keep a bear like this docile is to starve it into submission, and it looked to her like it was a tad too well-fed for safety.

Barra squinted at the designs painted on the handlers' armor. "That's Meneides livery," she mused. "What would Idonosteus want with a bear?"

"Likely to sell it," Kheperu said, one hand on Leucas' arm to steady himself as he balanced on tiptoe. "That's the biggest damned bear I've ever seen."

"Oh, please," Barra scoffed. "It's just a baby! Where I come from—"

"I know," Kheperu interrupted tiredly. "In the Isle of the Mighty the bears graze on the tops of oak trees, right?"

Leucas chuckled. Barra answered innocently, "The top's the tenderest part, you know. Once, when I was a little girl—"

"Don't tell me—you climbed a great brown mountain, and when you got to the summit, it turned out to be the belly of a sleeping bear."

"Well, no, actually, I didn't make it that far—I'm afraid of heights, you know." She grinned at his low-voiced groan of surrender. "That's a northern bear, though, probably from the continent, northeast of the Isle. That means something like two months on shipboard. There's no way he could sell that bear for enough to recoup the cost of just *feeding* the bloody thing."

"Ramses the Living Horus keeps a menagerie," Kheperu offered. "Perhaps this Meneides fellow does as well."

Barra shook her head. "Idonosteus might fancy himself to be a little pharaoh, but he doesn't like animals—of course, he could be dead, I suppose, he wasn't all that young . . . I don't know who might have succeeded him, I don't remember if he had any sons . . ."

"Bearbaiting."

Barra could feel Leucas' rumble in her own chest, and she craned her neck around to get a glimpse of his face; the huge Athenian's expression was as grim as his tone. An ill weight gathered in the pit of her stomach, and she nodded disgust-edly. "You're probably right." She spat on the flagstones, nar-rowly missing Kheperu. "Sick bastard."

"What is this bearbaiting?" Kheperu asked.

"It's a game," Barra told him. "A vile game. They chain the bear to a post, usually down in a pit, then they send dogs against it, laying bets on how many dogs the bear will kill before it's torn to shreds."

Kheperu stared at her, eyes wide in horror. "That's revolting! I've never heard anything so hideous in all my life!"

"It's the next thing close to murder."

"Murder, nothing! They're just animals! They let that beast kill *dogs*?" Like many Egyptians, Kheperu would cheerfully disembowel a man he caught beating a dog. "Does the Gov-ernor know of this?"

Barra shrugged. "Won't make much difference if he does. The Great Houses pay about as much attention to your Gov-ernor of the Canaan District as they do their own drooling old king in Byblos."

"Someone should do something." Kheperu's outrage sub-sided as quickly as it had arisen, falling off to a sullen mutter.

"It's none of our business what House Meneides does for fun," Barra said.

"Funny that it's not in a cage," Leucas said thoughtfully. "That'd be safer."

"In a cage," Kheperu said, "one must drag the entire weight of the animal. This way, the animal carries itself."

"Mm," Barra said, nodding in thought, not in agreement. "And a bear in a cage wouldn't draw this size of a crowd. I wonder what old Idonosteus is really up to?"

Leucas said, in a distant, musing tone, "I've heard tell that Theseus once killed a bear, unarmed—strangled it, the story goes."

Kheperu snorted. "You Greeks and your stories—where did you hear this one?"

Leucas didn't so much as shift his gaze. "From Prince Demophoon—his youngest son, that is. Theseus, you know, he wasn't that much bigger than I am . . ."

"Don't get any ideas," Barra said firmly, slapping him lightly on the top of the head, and Leucas lifted his shoulders in a sighing shrug that ignored her weight on his back.

"Have you seen enough, Barra?"

She squinted at the bear, which was now becoming balky and restive at the noise and smells of the crowd, tossing its head and growling. "Not yet. I don't think these boys know what they've got hold of here. If that bear decides he wants to be free, the five of them won't be enough to stop him."

"Mm, Barra?" Kheperu said dubiously. "If that bear wants to get away, and those men aren't enough to hold him, don't you think it'd be a good idea to be somewhere *else*?"

Barra grinned down at him. "What, you're afraid of a little baby bear?"

"Baby or not, that beast's a long way from little—"

Somebody threw a rock.

It sailed out from the depths of the crowd and hit the bear's shoulder-joint with a muffled thump. The bear reared up, dragging the Meneides handlers offbalance. Barra could see clearly their expressions of sudden panic as they struggled to regain control; they were shouting something that was buried by the wash of laughter from the crowd. Perhaps encouraged by the response, the rock-thrower hurled another, which also landed, this time thumping the bear's thigh, causing it to spin with a muzzled roar, reeling in the handlers to barely beyond the reach of its claws. *Some idiot's messing with them on purpose,* she thought. From her elevated vantage point, she looked for the idiot but couldn't spot him. Now others in the crowd got into the game, pelting the bear and its desperate handlers with everything from stones to apples to mutton bones. The bear howled and twisted and turned, the men clung to the leashes, and then one of them was down and another had lost his grip on the rope, and the bear charged a third with horrifying speed, knocking him flat. One swipe of its claws tore his face off; spouting blood painted scarlet across its muzzle. It pinned its prey beneath one massive paw and looked snarling at the other handlers. Nobody was surprised when their nerve broke.

They dropped the ropes and bolted.

The crowd surged back, away from the plaza. People began to scream. The bear leaned down and nuzzled its feebly struggling victim, trying to bite. Frustrated by the muzzle of leather and bronze, it howled again and charged the crowd.

Barra shouted, "This is our chance! Let's get in there and catch us that bear!"

Leucas had dug in his heels when the human stampede began; the crowd broke around him like surf against a cliff. Barra clung to his back as he now began to breast through the surge, knocking men and women aside with great sweeps of his knotted fists. Kheperu shouted, "Catch it? You're completely insane!" but followed nonetheless in the Athenian's wake.

Over short distances, a big bear like this can outrun a horse; it reached the massed crowd long before the three companions could get clear. It was going the wrong way, northeast into the city, away from them, slashing into the backs of screaming people with its huge hooked claws. By the time Leucas could fight his way into the open plaza, the flagstones were littered with torn and bleeding people, some of them rising to run, a couple only twitching out the last of their lives.

Barra leaped to the ground and shouted, "Kheperu! Turn that bloody thing, get it coming back our way!"

"You're mad!"

"Do it!"

Muttering a short prayer under his breath, the Egyptian reached inside his robe and withdrew a small sphere of some black and sticky material; he wound up and threw it past the bear. By great good luck, it hit open flagstones instead of struggling people, and it exploded with a loud *whoosh* into a ball of white fire. The bear reared, howling through its muzzle, and turned to run away from the flames.

Barra smoothly drew one of her twin throwing axes, took half a second to judge the distance, and fired it overhand. The axe sang through the air, a perfect throw, as though it rode a taut line tied from Barra's hand to the bear's head. The flat back of the axe struck the bear between the eyes with a solid thunk. She hummed satisfaction and waited for the bear to fall.

The bear blinked and shook its head, then its beady little black eyes fixed on Barra, and she suddenly thought that this might not have been such a good idea, after all.

The bear dropped to all fours and charged.

Barra drew her broadaxe and crouched, ready to leap out of its path. "Don't kill it!"

"Kill it?" Leucas' voice was thick with crazed Greek battle

lust. His face split in a huge feral grin, and his eyes gleamed like fire. "I'm gonna ask it to *dance!*"

The bear shot toward them with terrifying speed. Leucas swung the huge bundle of armor and weapons in a tight arc and hurled it, catching the bear a glancing blow to the head and shoulder, knocking it off stride. The bear reared, howling, clawing at the air; Barra and Kheperu both watched with openmouthed disbelief as Leucas closed with the beast, snapping its head back with a swift jab that was followed by a titanic overhand right hook that crashed into the bear's skull below the ear and rocked it sideways.

Between Barra, Kheperu, and the bear, it was impossible to say who was the most surprised.

The bear recovered first. Still rearing, it towered over Leucas the way the huge Greek towered over ordinary men. It raked at him, a clumsy slash that Leucas easily ducked, but its following slash with the other paw tore open his right shoulder.

Barra snapped out of her daze and screamed at Kheperu to *do something, goddamn you!* She sprang at the bear's back, left hand gripping the collar at its neck, hauling herself up high enough to slam the back of its skull with the flat of the broadaxe in her right. It was a weak blow, with only the strength of her arm to drive it, but it got the bear's attention; it dropped to all fours and shook her off. She hit the ground rolling and came to her feet; Leucas hammered a fist downward into its head.

Kheperu had no faith in the efficacy of his staff against this monster that could shrug aside Barra's axes and Leucas' fists. A panicked glance around the plaza showed him bundles of bronze-headed spears leaning against the wooden counter of a nearby tentstall. As Barra and Leucas frantically danced around the whirling bear, trying to keep it distracted and to prevent it from concentrating on either one of them, Kheperu ran for the stall and reached in, grabbing a bundle of spears, yanking on them, but they wouldn't come clear. He looked down behind the counter, where a sweating Tyrian crouched holding the bundle with both arms.

"Let go, idiot!" Kheperu screamed in Egyptian.

"Seven shekels!"

"What?"

The vendor shrilled, *"Apiece!* Seven shekels *apiece!"*

"Fine!" Kheperu yelled. "It's a deal! It's a deal!"

He let go of the bundle, and as the vendor half stood to collect, Kheperu spun his staff end-for-end and cracked the man soundly across the face. The vendor dropped like a poleaxed steer. Kheperu grabbed the spears and ran.

The bear slashed at Barra; she managed to block its claws with the haft of her axe but the force of the blow sent her sprawling. By the time she'd scrambled to her feet, the bear had turned on Leucas, both arms swinging wide. Leucas got his arms up like the boxer he was, blocking with his forearms; for one incredible instant, he matched his strength against the maddened bear's, and held back its claws. Barra blinked, not trusting her eyes: *Nobody's that strong!* she thought—she half expected him next to lift the bloody thing over his head and body slam it like a Greek wrestler, but before he could move, the bear lunged forward and drew him into a hug, clawing at his back. Kheperu had managed to drag one spear out of the bundle, and he launched it from across the plaza.

Barra screamed, *"No!"* as the spear sailed, her mind flooded with an instant's vivid vision of the spear taking Leucas in the small of the back, but the bear twisted and the spear only grazed Leucas, its bronze head stabbing into the bear's side. The bear released Leucas and clawed at the spear shaft.

Bears have one weakness that Barra knew of, one that they share with men; sprawling on the flagstones had given her a fine view of her target. As Leucas staggered back, trying to recover his footing, Barra dove forward into a shoulder roll that brought her to a low, split-legged crouch directly in front of the bear. She swung her broadaxe in a vicious whistling underhand arc that drove its blunt back hard up into the bear's testicles.

The bear said, *"Whuff."*

It stood, swaying, its eyes glazed.

Leucas stepped up and pulled the spear from the bear's side. He gripped the spear just below the blade, touched its end to the bear's face to measure the distance, then swung it with all his might. The spear shaft splintered across the bear's head.

The bear sighed and sat down, rolling slowly onto its side. Barra and Leucas stood side by side, panting, looking

down at the unconscious bear. Leucas touched the torn skin of
his shoulder and thoughtfully examined the blood on his
hand. "This is our chance?" he said slowly. "Gonna catch us a
bear?"

"Don't look at me," Barra said breathlessly. "Nobody told
you to *box* the bloody thing . . ."

"You broke my spear!" Kheperu said as he came up, carrying the other four. "I paid sev—*ten* shekels for that spear!"

"I'll owe it to you." He looked down at Barra. "How much
is a shekel?"

Barra shook her head impatiently. "We have to get your
wounds cleaned and stitched up. And where are the damned
handlers?"

"One of them's lying in that pool of blood over there,"
Kheperu said, pointing.

Barra followed his finger and wrinkled her face. "He won't
live. Where are the others?"

Around the plaza the crowd had returned to watch the fight.
Barra looked around, searching for the handlers, and saw
wounded citizens. Three were down, knots of people clustered around them. Anywhere else she would have ignored
them—it wasn't like they were anyone she knew—but here,
the thought of walking away from them produced a sharp
twinge in her gut. She held out one of her throwing axes and
said to Leucas, "Keep an eye on that bloody beast. If it stirs,
hit it." The Athenian nodded and took her axe, hefting it
thoughtfully

"All right if I wrap my shoulder first?"

"Ay, whatever. And you"—she jabbed a finger at Kheperu—
"come with me."

She led him over to the wounded; his smell was enough to
break up the crowd. One was a middle-aged woman torn from
ear to shoulder blade, half her neck ripped away, and was
clearly dead. The other two were men, one hamstrung and
sobbing, the other with a calf wound and a broken ankle; the
second was unconscious and had blood on his face—probably
struck his head on the flagstone when he fell. "Help me bind
them up. And give me some of that salve you use."

"Are you serious?" Kheperu said. "That's expensive stuff.
Let their friends tend them."

"I'll pay you," Barra told him evenly.

"What profit is there in this? I simply don't understand why you would—"

"Because I *live* here!" she snapped. "If you need a better answer than that, I'll explain it with my fists."

"No need to be so prickly about it . . ."

It was only the work of moments to stop the bleeding. Barra beckoned to four men in the watching crowd. She told them to carry these two to the Meneides compound and present them there for physicking; placing her hand on the head of her broadaxe was all the persuasion she needed.

As they carried the wounded away, Kheperu leaned close to murmur in her ear: "How much do you know of this Leucas, our partner? Did you know him well, before we met?"

She shrugged expressively. "Why do you ask?"

He twitched his long beaky nose toward where Leucas stood keeping silent watch over the unconscious bear. The morning sun beat strongly upon his chest and his broad serene brow, brought a golden glow to his bronzed skin and highlit his beard and hair. "Only a madman would charge a bear like that, to engage it bare-handed, if you'll excuse the pun."

"Got away with it, though, didn't he?"

"Mmm, yes. Yes, he did. Just as he 'got away with' fronting the Kyprian Boar after his spear broke. One swipe of the claws tore the face from that handler—killed him outright, or near enough; he won't live an hour—yet Leucas has come away with only bloody scratches, a gash across the back of his shoulder."

"What's your point?"

"I'm not sure I have one," Kheperu said thoughtfully. "I only wonder if perhaps there may be more to our Athenian friend than meets the eyes."

"Guess he's just lucky," Barra said. "You'd have to be, to live through the Siege of Troy. Come on."

She turned her back on him and walked over to the bear, Kheperu trailing close behind.

"No sign of the bloody handlers?" she asked, and Leucas silently shook his head. Barra cupped her hands to her mouth. *"Meneides! Hey, Meneides! Come get your bloody bear!"*

"You're not going to let it go?" Leucas asked, frowning. "You're going to let them keep it?"

"Of course," Barra told him. "Sure, I hate bearbaiting and

all, but this is business. When this story gets around, everyone's going to know that we're three bronze-chewing heroes
who aren't afraid of anything—even if, maybe, they'll think
we're none too bright." She pointedly avoided looking at
Leucas. "See? Our price goes up. Meanwhile, the way I see it,
Idonosteus owes us a big one. Now we only need those handlers to take us to the House Meneides compound along with
the bear, and we can collect."

Leucas and Kheperu exchanged glances. Leucas shrugged,
and winced at the pain from his shoulder.

"I have always admired," Kheperu said warmly, "the way
your mind works, Barra."

"Have you really?" she said. She looked up into the limit-
less blue of the Phoenikian sky, followed with her eyes the
curving wheel of a gull overhead. "You want to know what
my mind's working on right now?"

Kheperu ducked his head, flinching; he recognized her
tone. "Well, no, actually . . ."

"I'm thinking," she said mildly, "that if I were to, say,
knock you over the head and tie you up, then hang you from
one of these balconies, set you swinging back and forth,
blindfold myself, and start throwing knives and axes and
whatever in your general direction, for an afternoon or so,
you might learn not to heave spears into a melee where you
have a good chance of killing one of your partners. What do
you think?"

"I, ah . . ." he coughed, "I don't think that will be
necessary . . ."

She bared her teeth. "Are you sure?"

"Now, Barra," Leucas said, "there was no harm done—"

"I'm talking to Kheperu. I have to make sure you're sure,
you see, Kheperu, because if you ever do it again, I'll feed
you this axe, understand?"

"Quite." Once again fully composed, he shifted his gaze
over her shoulder. "The handlers are coming back. We don't
want to be bickering in front of the servants, do we? You
know how they gossip."

"This bear has become an expensive proposition." Idonos-
teus mopped wine from his beard with a linen napkin of
Tyrian purple, almost the same color as the wine itself.
"Lucky that Brachmus had no family, and that he wasn't

popular with the men. No compensation, and the funeral can be cheap. You say only one townsman was killed?"

Barra nodded crisply. "Yes, sir. Three or four were injured, but were able to walk away; then there's the two downstairs."

"Lucky again. They'll be presenting themselves for compensation, of course, but if they weren't actually crippled, I may still turn a handsome profit on the beast."

The room was small but lavishly furnished. Barra and Kheperu half reclined on low couches of intricately carved Kushite ebony, piled with silk-covered pillows so soft as to be practically nonexistent. Wide double doors, thrown open to admit the noonday sun, led onto a broad gallery that overlooked the interior courtyard and led to other second-floor rooms. The walls of this room, the informal sitting room of Idonosteus' private apartments, were painted with vivid Cretan motifs of dolphins and octopi, twisting seaweed and playful nymphs. The ceiling was painted with scenes that Barra guessed represented the heroic actions of some ancestor, possibly Meneus himself, during the Sack of Crete.

With the help of Barra and Leucas, the remaining handlers had dragged the bear to the Meneides compound on an improvised travois. Along the way, Kheperu had managed to sell the other four spears for a total of nineteen shekels, despite his continued whining and moaning about the loss he was taking. Under threat of imminent bodily injury, he split these earnings with his partners. When they'd reached the huge bronze door that formed the gate in the compound wall, Barra had an instant's doubled vision: as the door swung wide now, she also saw it as she had a thousand times, passing by here on errands for Peliarchus. As a girl of fifteen and sixteen, she had looked upon these ten-cubit walls, wondering if she would ever see within. House Meneides was second in wealth and power only to House Penthedes; their compound was constructed like a fortress, warehouses full of olives and salt, exotic foods, casks of spices, local wines and Egyptian beer, and—it was rumored—a storehouse of African gold, protected by these walls.

They were received cordially enough, but Idonosteus was "engaged in important negotiations and much too busy to see them," until Barra insisted that the houseboy who'd brought them this message return to Idonosteus and carry the story from the handlers of the bear. The houseboy had bowed minutely, with a skeptical look, and vanished. A few minutes later, a sweating Meneides lieutenant who identified himself as Pharku came scampering out to welcome them. Leucas was ushered off to have his wounds tended by the surgeon, and Barra and Kheperu were led directly to Idonosteus' apartments.

Idonosteus reclined on a broad pile of cushions, and offered the Kushite couches that held similar piles with a lazy wave of his plump, soft, bejeweled hand. The other hand was occupied with a winebowl and a fistful of ripe olives that he somehow held simultaneously. An ankle-height table before him was spread with golden platters of fruit, young cheese, and strips of delicately smoked fish, as well as a pair of golden chalices of wine. The couches were strategically placed so that the table would be within reach of someone sitting on any of them, but only with effort—it'd take a long reach.

The Head of House Meneides was of medium height and round as a dumpling. His sleek black-dyed braids glistened with scented oil; his beard also was braided in the Assyrian style. His teeth gleamed within his wide welcoming smile, but his eyes were calculating and cold as chips of topaz.

"Sit, please, be at home," he said indulgently. "I am curious—Barra? Is that your name?"

Barra lowered herself cautiously onto the bench. "Yes, Lord Idonosteus."

"I am curious, you see, how a trio of scruffy mercenaries—"

"Scruffy?" Kheperu bristled. "I am so far beyond scruffy that—"

Barra kicked him in the calf and said smoothly, "Please excuse my ill-mannered partner, and please continue. I am at your service."

Idonosteus flicked a glance sidelong at Kheperu and the corners of his lips teased upward toward a smile. He went on. "The handlers were five. You, I'm told, are three, and one of you a woman. Yet they ran, while you fought."

Barra lifted her shoulders in an expressive shrug. "How better to get your attention, my lord?"

Idonosteus' eyes glittered, and his smile broadened, and Kheperu stared at Barra as though he could not believe his ears.

"You look vaguely familiar to me," he mused. "Have we met before?"

Barra ducked her head in an obsequious nod. "I scribed a contract for you once, at the Trade Fair on Crete . . ."

"Ah, yes, now I recall—you're the one who's supposed to be the exiled barbarian princess, or somesuch." He nodded and released a wet and bubbling belch. "Odd combination of trades you practice. Well, get on with the tale."

The Head of House Meneides occasionally sipped his wine, or munched olives, while he listened to Barra recount the fight in the plaza, but she could clearly see that he missed not a word. While she spoke, she watched him mentally calculate his losses, toting up the silver he'd have to pay to families of the victims. Once the total had been adjusted to his satisfaction, Barra said, "If you don't mind my asking, my lord—why did your men bring the bear through the Market? It seems to me that an indirect route would have been safer, and less costly."

Idonosteus nodded glumly. "Politics," he said. "Image. Piracy in the Mediterranean has surged in the last five years or so, ever since the end of that business at Troy. It's putting tremendous pressure on me—and the Penthedes, for that matter. We're losing ground to the Mursuwallites, Jephunahi, and Tomitiri, since they used mostly overland routes, north, east, and south. So by bringing in a cargo that could only come from northwestern Europe—"

"You're showing the whole city that your ships can run unmolested all the way from the Pillars of Herakles," Barra finished for him. "Impressive, my lord."

"Exactly; or"—he snorted—"it would have been. You think like a trader."

Barra smiled. "I was raised by one."

Idonosteus waved a dismissive hand; her life was too dull to contemplate. "You told me that you think the same man threw both of the first rocks. Did you get a good look at him? Would you know him if you saw him again?"

Barra shook her head. "The crowd was too thick."

"Someone has been stirring up trouble, and this certainly seems to have been an attempt to embarrass House Meneides. Or perhaps it was simply ill luck; there is a great deal of ill luck going around these days," he said with a heavy sigh. "It's almost as though I've been cursed. Nothing seems to go right anymore; the bloody bear will probably get a fever from that little spear-cut and die, that's the way my luck's been going—I'm tired of it, and it's costing me a great deal, as well."

"On that subject, my lord—"

"Excuse me," Kheperu interrupted, casually leaning far forward to slice off a hunk of cheese with a gold knife. "What do you intend to do with that bear?"

Idonosteus shrugged. "Oh, I suppose I'll bring it to Crete in the spring. If it lives. That's where the big gamblers go to drop their gold."

"*Savages,*" Kheperu muttered under his breath, then continued in a normal tone. "How much, mm, I imagine we saved you a great deal of *money* by our heroic capture of your bear, didn't we?"

Idonosteus' thin-plucked eyebrows lifted minutely, and he glanced at Barra. In the process of shifting her weight on the couch, she managed to tread heavily on Kheperu's foot. His eyes bulged with the effort of restraining a sudden yelp of pain.

"We'll be in Tyre for some weeks yet," Barra said. "You'll be able to contact the three of us at the home of Peliarchus."

"Peliarchus the shipmaster? Penthedes man, isn't he?"

"Yes, sir. And my foster-father. I, however, owe no particular loyalty to Agapenthes, if you follow my meaning, and my two companions are strangers here."

Idonosteus' eyes narrowed, and he gave her one short nod. "I may very well be in touch. Meanwhile, know that you have earned the gratitude of House Meneides, and *that,*" he said pointedly to Kheperu, "is no inconsiderable thing."

"The limp-prick bastard stiffed us!"

Leucas frowned down at Kheperu as the three skirted the Market on their way to the home of Peliarchus. His right shoulder had been stitched and neatly rebandaged in fresh white linen by the Meneides surgeon, and more linen wrapped his chest. He claimed that the wounds were shallow, only torn skin; he told them he should heal in two or three weeks, without even much scarring. Barra kept glancing at the bandages as they walked, but the surgeon had apparently done a good job—no blood showed through, yet.

"Not one thin shekel," Kheperu went on. "Like we risk our skins to get some dogfucking olives and cheese!"

Leucas turned to Barra. "What really happened?"

Barra smiled. "Idonosteus will hire us. I'm sure of it. And he'll pay good money, too, because I'm connected in House Penthedes. Something's going on between the Great Houses, maybe another street war warming up. Kheperu damned nearly killed it, though."

"Me?"

"If we had taken a reward for the bear," Barra said flatly, "he would have read us as low on money. Poor."

"Barra, perhaps I'm confused," Leucas said, "but we are poor, aren't we?"

"Idonosteus doesn't know that. By passing off the bear thing as hardly worth mentioning, we come off affluent. Unconcerned. Our price goes up."

Kheperu grunted. "Well, perhaps so and perhaps not. We did not come out empty-handed, though." He reached inside his robe and pulled out a gleaming knife, its broad blunt blade shining gold in the sunlight. "We should be able to sell this for enough to buy an ox or two."

Barra gasped, "Kheperu! Bloody Mother, what were you thinking of? Why would you steal a *gold cheese knife off Idonosteus' table* while he's *sitting* there?"

"Because," Kheperu explained with exaggerated patience, as though speaking to a child, "the chalices were too fucking big to hide under my robes."

CHAPTER TWO

Othniel

Othniel bin Jezer pressed himself against the sun-warmed wall at his back, and squinted along the crowded street. There he was, the stone-thrower, a bobbing head of dark hair sun-bleached to the color of dried blood, making the turn in front of Chapli's incense stall. As soon as he was safely out of sight, Othniel broke into a run toward the corner around which the man had disappeared, ignoring the sweat that poured from his brow over his round cheeks. *For a man of forty,* he reassured himself breathlessly, *I can still run—it's only these heavy robes that make me puff so.*

Othniel had walked these flagstones in the Market of Tyre since the day he could first stand upright; he had grown up here, running errands for his father, a prosperous merchant of imported wines. Later, when he'd grown into his strength, he would carry two monstrous jugs dangling from their nets upon his own back, deliver them to the waterfront inns, and return unguarded with empties and silver. Often this would take hours longer than it should; he loved to drift through the Market, stroll among the stalls watching people, greeting his many friends and acquaintances, meeting folk he didn't know. This last became less and less common over the years—it seemed that he knew nearly everyone. He knew every twist and turn, every nook and cranny of Tyre; he knew the names of every merchant in the Market and the names and ages of nearly all their children; he knew where this spice seller's mistress spent her afternoons, and where that rug dealer went for pleasures his wife flatly refused to provide. When Othniel was twenty, his father had overextended his credit with the Tomitiri, and the Great House had sent armed men to confiscate his father's inventory. Othniel had returned from his last delivery that day to find his father dangling from a twisted noose made of the carrying nets for the wine jars. He was an only child, and his mother was long dead; alone in the world, he'd drifted back into the Market in search of a living.

In those days, there had been a new trading House in Tyre, the House of Jephunah, Amorites out of the East with strong trade connections to the fading glory of Babylon. They only barely qualified for the appellation House—it was applied mostly by courtesy, out of respect for the enormous sums they had spent trying to establish themselves. Othniel, alone and beggared at twenty, with no resource beyond his strong back and his voluminous knowledge of the city, had boldly reached out to old Jephunah himself and put both at his service.

He rapidly became indispensable. Knowing who could be intimidated, who should be bribed, who must be flattered, and who could be killed without reprisal, he helped build the Jephunahi from fringe-nibbling outsiders to what they were today: a Power of Tyre, a Great House. In the process, he'd made himself into a man who wore rich brocade robes, and gemstones on every finger; a man whose smile could save a merchant's business; a man whose frown could kill.

And he'd done it by simply doing what he loved best, loafing in the Market, killing time, chattering with this vendor and that whore, getting the gossip and sniffing the wind. He could imagine no better life; he served House Jephunah with not only his mind and body, but with his whole heart; and in return, Jephunah had granted him more power than any Jephunahi, saving only the old man's sons—and, Othniel sometimes felt, more respect than he gave even them.

A week ago, a Jephunahi caravan had been ambushed in the Lebanon. The usual inquiries—and offers of ransom—to the Habiru tribes that held the mountains had produced responses that seemed honestly puzzled; more significantly, none of them had offered to sell back the caravan's cargo. Old Jephunah, always quick to sense a pattern of hostile action, had instantly assumed that one of the other Great Houses was behind it, and had set Othniel the task of determining which. Othniel had returned to his beloved Market and had relentlessly sought information.

House Jephunah was not the only Great House that had suffered recent losses, he learned. The Penthedes had lost three ships, perhaps to pirates; a Meneides wine warehouse had burned; Summilitallas, the aged Head of House Mursuwalli, had died of some mysterious wasting illness, leaving it in the hands of her son, and three of the inns loyal to this House had come under some inexplicable sorcerer's curse that slew all their guests; the Tomitiri had lost a caravan of Kushite oils and a shipful of ivory from Punt. These were only the most blatant manifestations of what Othniel had come to believe was a concerted attempt to foment war between the Great Houses. It was clear that misfortune was more-or-less equally distributed among the five Great Houses.

What he'd been unable to determine was the author of these misfortunes. He became increasingly convinced that old Jephunah was correct, that there was a Great House behind this. The resources of a Great House would be required, to sponsor the sort of powerful magic that was being used to stir things up. Even the lost ships of the Penthedes—there was a rumor that they'd met no pirates, but instead sank due to a sorcerer's curse that had been burned into their bows, a curse at which their captains reportedly had laughed. Another curse of a similar sort was said to have been found, charred and barely legible, in the ruins of the Meneides winehouse. Which of the Great Houses had deliberately inflicted a loss upon themselves, so that they might appear innocent?

Ordinarily, he'd approach such a problem by determining who had the most to gain from the ensuing war; unfortunately, any of them would gain immensely from winning a trade war, and would gain even more by letting two competitors fight one, while waiting to mop up a weakened winner.

Next, he tried to discover which Great House had *not* been recently hiring sorcerers and workers of magic, reasoning that the House behind these various curses would need hire none for defense. Again, he was frustrated. The only Great House that was not aggressively seeking even the lowliest kinds of charm-wrappers was the Penthedes: they controlled the priesthoods of both Ba'al-Berith and Ba'al-Marqod, and thus were defended by the gods themselves. They also, as the greatest of the Great Houses, had the most at risk in a general war.

Days passed, but Othniel never became discouraged; from long experience, he knew that if he kept pecking away, eventually he'd hit the corn among the gravel. Finally, when the Meneides handlers had tried their silly bloody stunt of bringing an uncaged bear through the Market, Othniel himself had been standing not five paces distant from the dark-haired man who'd thrown the first two stones. Interestingly, this man had not thrown anything else, once the crowd picked up his game—that fact alone led Othniel to keep an eye on him, even through the panic of the bear's escape and its fool-hardy but lucky capture by those three foreign mercenaries. This stone-throwing individual had drifted slowly out of the crowd immediately after the bear's capture—not as though he had someplace in particular to be, but casually, as though he had all day to loaf and wander. But, if he had all day, why didn't he stick around to watch the aftermath of the fight, to see who lived and who died? Nobody else was leaving; in fact, once the bear was down, the crowd grew ever larger and thicker.

But the stone-thrower sauntered away, and Othniel followed him.

The stone-thrower would stop now and then, turn at some stall or other, and examine their wares. Othniel could clearly see that this was pretense: the man's eyes flicked this way and that, scanning the crowd to see if he was being followed. Othniel was an old hand at this; he stayed barely in sight of the man, keeping himself screened by people between. Once when the stone-thrower turned a corner, Othniel reversed the stole he wore over his robes to show the plain white linen underside; on another occasion he removed the stole altogether and covered his head with a newly purchased burnoose. Of such small details is made success, in following unobserved. Now he was sure he'd made his lucky find; he was positive that this stone-thrower would lead him to the secret enemy. His scalp tingled, and he wore a tight but happy smile—he felt young again, as he followed this man through the Market. This was like the old days, and it warmed his spirit to find that he'd lost none of his skill.

I can still do this as well as any man in Tyre, he thought as he followed the stone-thrower into a narrow alleyway. As he peered around a corner within it, he was thinking, *Probably even better; I'm probably the best follower in Tyre* even as the fist-size leather sock half-full of beach sand slapped him precisely on the top of his head. His vision showered sparks, his knees buckled, and he pitched forward toward the dirt.

Even stunned, he understood what was happening—he'd been sapped once before, many years ago. He brought up his hands to protect his head, but the second blow crushed the bones of his fingers against his skull. The third struck him solidly where the base of his skull joined with his neck, and darkness exploded within his mind.

He must have been slowly awakening for some time, because he found himself unsurprised that he was alive. When he'd tumbled toward the hard-packed dirt in the alley off the Market, he'd been quite sure that he'd never open the eyes of this body again. The burning ache in the shattered fingers of his left hand nearly covered the dull throb from his head—the fire that lanced his fingers when he tried to wriggle them pushed a groan past his lips.

It also came as no surprise that he was bound hand and foot; not tied, but shackled to a table that felt rough but not uncomfortable through the layers of the robes he still wore. Shadows danced on a ceiling that had the creases and folds of natural rock, as though he were within a cavern. Although he could smell nothing, not even the smoke from the tripod braziers that cast this reddish light—he must have been shackled here long enough to numb his nose entirely—he could taste, when he licked his lips, some bitter tang, a faintly nauseous taste that reminded him of jugged lamb that had gone over into white webs and decay.

By turning his head, he could see other tables flanking the one upon which he lay. They were empty, though they had shackles at the corners and grooves carved into their surfaces—these looked like drains, not unlike butcher boards, and the dark stains that painted them he found alarming. And on his right hand, past which he looked, glittered the precious stones of the rings he wore on every finger.

This, particularly, was bad. If the rings had been missing, he would have allowed himself to hope that he would merely be robbed and beaten, or held for a fat ransom. But there they were, untouched. A cold, sharp-fingered hand of apprehension clutched his belly; this might be very bad indeed.

"He is awake," said someone softly, behind the head of the table, where he could not see.

Othniel licked his lips again, and cautiously tried his voice. "Come, this is not necessary." It came out a weak, ragged croak. "I'm sure you know who I am, and know that Jephunah will ransom me. Failing that, he will also avenge my death."

A stocky, broad-shouldered man stepped around the table into view. His deep chest was bare, either shaven or naturally hairless, as was his head. He wore a beard in the Egyptian style, bound in a stiff rod from the point of his chin, but his skin was as pale as cave moss, and when he spoke, his Phoenikian had the native accent of the southern ports. "Your throat is dry, mm? Here, drink this."

He offered a cup, from the rim of which hung a curving straw of bronze. Othniel turned his head away; he squeezed shut his eyes and wished with all his heart that this man had worn a mask. He wanted to live through this.

"Don't—*hrakhakh*"—the pale man coughed harshly— "don't imagine that you can refuse. Drink."

"This isn't *necessary*," Othniel insisted, face averted and eyes still shut. "The man I followed is the only one I've seen—and he can't be very important. Truly, I am less trouble alive and free."

His captor said, "Let me explain."

His broken hand was seized, his fingers forced apart. A freezing line drew itself across his thumb, accompanied by a crunching thunk, like a butcher's cleaver hacking through bone into the wood of the block; he felt the shock through the table. Something small and light struck him on the chest; he opened his eyes to see the first two joints of his left thumb, ragged and bloody, caught in a fold of his robe. The polished tourmaline set in its familiar thumb ring of gold gleamed bright and uncaring; he'd worn that ring for nearly ten years.

"Drink," the man told him, again offering the cup.

"Please, you don't *understand*," Othniel pleaded, trembling now uncontrollably. His stomach spasmed and burned the back of his throat with half-digested salt fish. He had to explain, he had to make them understand, this was unnecessary! "Don't you know who I *am*?"

The man with a Phoenikian face and Egyptian beard leaned close and said kindly, "We know who you are, Othniel bin Jezer, faithful servant of Jephunah bin Abieizel, of course we do. We know you have been asking about us. Now, you must drink, or—*hrakhakh*—or I must hurt you again."

Othniel could see now that this man's smooth cheeks were cosmetic; even beyond the kohled eyes that were common among men of rank, his face was painted like a whore's. And within the paint that caulked over the lines of age and slackness, his lips were loose and wet, and his eyes glittered remotely with the disinterested glassy stare of a fish. No appeal could reach through this utter lack of human connection and no appeal would he make: fear paralyzed Othniel's will. He took the straw with trembling lips and drank. It was wine, with a sharp, resinous bite and a sweetish undertone.

"Good, that's very good," his captor muttered distantly, as he turned to the task of binding the spurting stump on Othniel's left hand.

Now spoke another voice, from back behind the table's head; Othniel recognized that this was the voice that had spoken first. Now it spoke in Egyptian, in the aristocratic dialect of the Nile Delta. Did this man, whoever he was, imagine that Othniel, who'd spent his entire life in the Market of Tyre, would not speak the language of this land's rulers? He said, "Really, it's a piece of luck, Sim, this fellow falling into our hands. I think I shall not punish Haral at all for letting himself be observed. After all, had he not seized the opportunity presented by the Meneides' bear, we wouldn't now have our little friend clipped to the table here, would we?"

"No, Remmie," the man who bound Othniel's hand agreed. "It's luck. It must indeed be."

"Luck, perhaps. Perhaps destiny. Perhaps they are the same. The play of chance; the roll of dice, and here I am. I have been searching for a prominent citizen on which to make our next demonstration, and now one is delivered unto my very door who is known and loved by all. A gift of fate, perhaps. Yes, I like that." His rich voice had become a smug purr. "I like that a great deal. But I am curious about these three foreigners who captured the bear. An extraordinary feat, hmm? Haral thinks that they are probably mercenaries; perhaps I can hire them myself—I admire boldness. Ask him if he knows who they are, or anything about them."

While Sim unnecessarily translated the question into Phoenikian, Othniel concentrated on what he was learning: three names, so far, Sim, Remmie, and Haral. He had faces for two of them. If this fellow behind him continued to chatter in Egyptian, he might learn a great deal. He swore to himself that he would survive, that he would escape. He would carry these names to Jephunah, and exact tenfold revenge for his torture.

He answered, "I saw some of the fight. Two men and a

woman. One of the men is a boxer—Akhaian, I think—and is crazy; he fought the bear with his fists. The woman throws stone axes, and she's crazy, too. The other man, well, I don't really know, but he looks even crazier than the others. I don't know who they are, or where they are; they're foreign, though. The woman looked faintly familiar, but if the other two were Tyrian, I'd know them—they are both extremely conspicuous. They looked poor, but mercenaries often do." He swiveled his head around, trying to get a glimpse of the man behind. "Do you see that I am trying to cooperate? Do you see that I am not even asking why they interest you?"

The next question he expected—Why did you follow Haral, the stone-thrower?—he had an answer for, and for the next one after that, and after that, a conversation that spun out in his mind and led inevitably to proof that he was innocent, and harmless, and that they'd be much better off if they pleased Jephunah by releasing him. Even the throbbing of his battered skull faded behind this happy expectation; new warmth suffused the room, and brought a glow to his cheeks.

From behind his head, Remmie said in Egyptian, "Of these inns that we are prepared to curse, are any loyal to the Jephunahi?"

Sim, murmuring, "Yes, Remmie, one is," completed tying off the stump of Othniel's thumb with a dirty rag that was crusted with some cracked brownish substance. This Sim must be a fine surgeon; any lingering pain in Othniel's hand was forgotten. He struggled to contain himself, to give no sign that he'd understood Remmie's words. He'd been right all along! A single agent behind the curses! Now, all he needed was to discover which Great House these two worked for—and then to escape, of course, but that was a mere detail; he took it for granted.

Remmie continued, "I wish to make clear that Othniel is no random victim; we must demonstrate to Jephunah that we despise his paltry power. The next inn to fall under the curse shall be this Jephunahi one. Furthermore, we shall escalate these proceedings. Let us . . . mm, have a Jephunahi tax collector killed—and no sneaking about, knife in the back kind of thing. I want as many witnesses as can be gathered; I want it to be spectacular, to be the talk of Tyre for a week. Perhaps we should maim a few of the witnesses, just to give the scene more impact. Yes, I think so."

"A tax collector will have guards," Sim murmured. Now he held Othniel's chin with one hand, while with the other he peeled down Othniel's lower eyelid and peered at it thoughtfully. Othniel tried to form words to ask Sim what he was doing, but his mouth seemed packed with cotton.

Still, the warmth of his impending release kept Othniel happy; until, at least, he began to try to remember if they'd ever asked him that question he'd been expecting . . .

"Of course he'll have guards," Remmie said expansively. "The more the better. I'll put the Greek on it; he likes this sort of thing. He can hire some of the street trash, as many as he needs. And, I think, we should put the word out about those three bear-fighters. I want them."

Sim nodded distractedly, and turned away to fiddle with a tray of winebowls set nearby.

"Sim?" Remmie's voice took on a new tone, a dangerous tone.

Sim's head jerked up from the bowls, and they rang faintly as his hands twitched. "Yes, Remmie?"

"Don't you *yes-Remmie* me, you shit." The words were those of a woman, or a whiny adolescent, but the low, lethal tone in which they were spoken robbed them of all comedy. "When I speak, you *listen.*"

"I was listening! I was, Remmie, I really was."

"All right, then," Remmie purred. "What did I just say?"

"You were, you were going to have the Greek kill a tax collector, and, and something about those three mercenaries with the bear. You, er, you want them." Othniel fought back a smile as he watched Sim try to conceal a sigh of relief. "I'm—*hrakhakh*—I'm sorry, Remmie. I get caught up in my work, you know—he's ready, almost."

Who is? Othniel wondered fuzzily. *Is he speaking of me? Ready for what? Are they going to let me go now?* And, belatedly: *What was in that wine?*

"I want them," Remmie went on calmly, as though the previous exchange had never occurred, "because of the way they've entered my life. The play of chance is the hand of destiny. Haral happens to be in the Market; he stumbles across the Meneides' foolishness of bringing a bear through the crowd. He makes a snap decision to interfere. This decision brings Othniel to me, just now, when I have need of him. These three mercenaries also happen to be there, the right place at the right time. They, also, are a gift to me: a gift of fate."

"Then," Sim murmured, "you should take them. You should have them. You will."

"Of course I will. Have I ever been slow to accept the gifts of fate?" He breathed a long, satisfied sigh, like a fat man after a heavy meal. "Is he ready, then?"

"Oh yes, Remmie, I think so."

"Go ahead."

Sim looked down at Othniel and said in Phoenikian, "How are you feeling?"

"Ahll . . ." Othniel found that with great effort, he could make his tongue work. "A lid . . . liddle sstrannge . . ."

"Good, that's very good." Sim turned away from him for a moment, and when he turned back he held a long rod of bronze by its wooden handle; the other end was a molded disk of bronze that glowed yellow with heat. Othniel could smell it, the coppery, bloody smell of hot bronze, and the yellow glow seemed to flow and pulse from side to side, and drip toward the floor, and trail behind it when Sim moved it toward the tray of winebowls. He stuck the hot end into one, which caused a great hiss and a plume of steam—or was it smoke?—that drifted upward in the cavern's still air, twisting into fantastic shapes, a dog-headed man, a crocodile with human arms and legs . . .

Othniel giggled. "Frr . . . for a momen', I thought you were gonna use tha' on me . . ."

"I—*hrakhakh*—I am."

He lifted the branding bronze once again, and now it dripped pale green fire, of whatever substance had been in that bowl. He dipped it in another, and when it came up it flared blue. Sim once again took Othniel's broken left hand and spread its fingers gently, then struck with the hot bronze, searing deep into the flesh of his palm.

Othniel screamed. Sim leaned on the bronze, driving it deeper and deeper into Othniel's charring flesh as his body twisted convulsively. He screamed until his voice failed, until from his throat came only the hiss of escaping air.

It ended slowly, as contact with Othniel's flesh cooled the bronze. Sim dropped the bronze casually on the floor, reached over, and plucked Othniel's severed thumb out of the fold of his robe. "I'll have need of this."

His hand was already growing numb, and the numbness grew along his forearm, crept past his elbow toward his shoulder. "Wha' are you going to do?" he whispered.

"With this?" Sim said, holding up Othniel's bloody thumb. "I'm going to burn it. A bit, *khm,* a bit later on. It's part of the ritual. For now, though, you should be seeing shapes in the air. Tell me what you see."

The numbness reached his shoulder and surged down his chest to his heart. Almost instantly, he could barely feel his body at all. His eyes rolled in terror as absolute as his earlier confidence had been. Things were moving in the shadows, becoming more and more clear. The cavern began to fill with ghostly forms, smoky outlines of obscene shapes that seemed to enter through the stone itself and drift out again. Some of them swirled and stayed near the braziers, as though they lusted for the oil's paltry heat and glow. And their bodies, their forms seemed to have no shape at all, or rather too many shapes, and they flowed from one shape to another, and they twisted and warped, and the only parts of them that seemed to have solidity were teeth, and claws, and eyes, far too many eyes.

Sim said, "Never mind. Your face shows all I need. What you see are the Children of Apep, the divine monsters that tear the souls of the dead. Spirits, you'd call them, or demons. It doesn't matter. You see, they are around us all the time, everywhere—*hrakhakh*—everywhere we go, they are inside us, in our mouths, our nostrils, our bowels. Perhaps they are a bit thicker here, as jackals cluster more thickly around graves of the poor. They take no notice of us, while we live, nor we of them. Well, except for you, Othniel bin Jezer. You have been granted a rare gift; even I have never seen this. You can see them now, faintly, no doubt, their glory dimmed in this faint light. They'll be so much more solid, so much more *potent* tomorrow after dawn, under the gaze of Ra. You'll see them perfectly. Of course, this means that they also can see you."

Othniel's chest heaved. "Please. I beg you. I swear I won't tell, I swear I won't tell anything!"

Remmie's rich baritone came from behind him again, in Egyptian. "Tell whatever you like, to whomever you like. In fact, please do." Othniel flinched helplessly, and Remmie's voice took on a chuckling undertone. "Oh yes, I speak your filthy little pidgin, though I choose not to soil my mouth with it. And I imagine that you speak Egyptian as well. I certainly hope so. Nothing that happens here, Othniel bin Jezer, is a *secret* at all . . ."

A warm, dry hand stroked Othniel's cheek, almost a caress. "That is why I shall set you free. Oh, not now—it shall be several hours yet. Just before dawn, I think. Then you may tell anyone you like."

Remmie laughed, deep and long. "Tell *everyone*!"

CHAPTER THREE

Old Friends

The home of Peliarchus stood to seaward of the Penthedes compound. It was large, by the standards of crowded Tyre, but not ostentatious: the second floor, which had been under construction when Barra was here briefly last spring, was now completed in the same simple, unadorned style as the centuries-old ground floor, smooth straw-colored walls broken by narrow windows shuttered with wood.

Barra fought down the familiar twist in her stomach when she saw the main door. When she'd first seen this house, she was fourteen and bitterly homesick; she spent every waking instant regretting her rash decision to sail to the East. Seeing the house from the outside always brought that back to her, the despairing weight of the knowledge that her home was far beyond the edge of the world.

Before she knocked, she gave Leucas and Kheperu strict instructions to be polite, and to look cheerful and prosperous; nothing burned Barra's spirit more than coming home in need. At least she'd been able to bring some gifts.

After some moderately heated discussion along the way from the Meneides compound (Kheperu: "I stole it; it's mine!" Barra: "But if you'd been caught, we'd all have been in the shit." Leucas came in on Barra's side, which decided the matter) they'd managed to discreetly sell the golden cheese knife for five bolts of brightly dyed silk. One of the bolts bought them an array of lovely faience spice pots; another bought them a thick bundle of exotic incense from Dilmun. It cost two more bolts for the matching bracelet and belt buckle of rope-worked silver from Punt. These things, with the one remaining bolt of silk, Barra judged to be suitably impressive, and she calculated that they'd traded up the value of the cheese knife by at least a third, maybe by half.

The porter who opened the spy gate at her knock had been

opening doors and sweeping the hearthyard in the house of
Peliarchus for ten years before Barra's first arrival. He recognized her instantly and pulled open the door. "You come on in
right now, Barra! 'S improper for a young lady to be standin'
on the street alone with men, people'll think you're a whore!"

"I'm not all that young anymore, Milo," she said through a
smile as she gripped his wrist. "This is Leucas of Athens, and
this is Kheperu, and where are my parents?"

"You just wait here, right? I'll get everybody. Missis is just
back from the Market, and Mister's in his chart room, and
your bloody dog is upstairs asleep on my bed!"

"He is? Graegduz! Hey, *Graeg*!" She whistled sharply, and
Graegduz streaked down the stairs and across the hearthyard
like he'd been shot from a bow.

Four years ago, she'd spent a summer at home, on the Isle
of the Mighty; she'd made the six-week journey aboard one of
the ships she part owned, the *Skye Swift*. She'd spent the
summer reacquainting with her family, teasing her brother
Llem about the grey that had begun to raddle his black hair,
slowly getting to know the happy, golden-haired eleven-year-
old that everyone claimed was her son. She'd also crossed
the Eirish Sea to make the obligatory visit with her father at
his fortress of Tara, bringing gifts and stories of the wide
world. One of the gifts her father gave her in return was a
wolf cub, only a month old. A wolf pack had been raiding
Ouendail's flocks, and he had ridden out with his hounds to
hunt them down and kill them himself, as befits an Eirish
king. When the slaughter was done, he'd found this cub shivering silently in the hillside cave that had been the den, this
cub which he could not kill—to slay the innocent young is
blasphemy.

Barra had brought him back to the East and raised him with
her own hand. She hadn't trained him, exactly; one doesn't
train wolves as one does dogs. She'd come to a certain understanding with him, a sort of mutual respect and affection and
cooperation. She treated him as a junior partner; he accepted
her as his pack leader. But he didn't like the sea—he became
uncomfortable and snappish on shipboard, which could ter-
rify any crew—so she had left him here in Tyre for the past
six months while she sailed in search of money, and had
missed him terribly.

She staggered under his joyous rush; he was big enough to

put his paws on her shoulders and lick her face. She hugged him and kissed his nose and crooned to him in Pictish until Leucas and Kheperu began to look mildly nauseated. She went through the ritual of introducing him to her partners; he was particularly interested in Kheperu, and kept coming back to sniff him again, even though the Egyptian's reek made him sneeze. Leucas was more than a bit bemused by all this.

"I've never seen a tame wolf before," he said thoughtfully.

"You're not seeing one now," Barra said with a grin. "Graeg isn't tame, he's just respectful. Be polite to him, and he'll treat you the same way."

"He's big." Leucas crouched in front of him, gravely bringing his head to the same level as the wolf's.

"So are you."

"I think the word Leucas is looking for," Kheperu said, "is *fat*. That is the fattest wolf I have ever seen."

"He's put on some weight," Barra allowed. She patted his flanks. "How'd you get so bloody fat?"

"Peliarchus spoils him mercilessly." Paused regally at the head of the stairs from the second floor was Tayniz, wife of Peliarchus and Barra's foster-mother. She swept the partners with a gaze that made Barra acutely conscious of the six days it'd been since she'd last had a bath. "I could feed three slaves on what that beast eats."

Her hair was piled and wrapped upon her head like a polished silver helmet, held in place by a number of mother-of-pearl combs; her dress of deep Tyrian purple draped flawlessly across her ample curves. "Barra," she said warmly, descending toward the hearthyard. "What a wonderful surprise! Welcome home." It was a peculiar talent of Tayniz's, to be both sincerely welcoming and regally intimidating at the same time.

When Barra had first met her, all those years ago, Tayniz had terrified her. On first look, Tayniz had frosted her with a glare like a northeast gale—she'd assumed that this slim young redheaded savage had been purchased in the West to warm the bed of her aging husband. Peliarchus had reassured her, of course—over and over again—that Barra had been given into his care by the High King of Langdale, Barra's brother, and that she was to be treated as a daughter. But that initial freezing reaction had colored her relationship with her foster-mother forever. It hadn't helped that for twenty years

Tayniz had prided herself on being Peliarchus' first and only wife. As she and her friends aged, her friends' husbands had married again and again, bringing in ever younger girls to swell their households; Tayniz had, deep in her heart, held herself above these other women because she, alone among them, could hold a husband all to herself. After finally becoming convinced of the truth of the situation, she had cared for Barra as though Barra had been one of her own children, even loved her in the cautious, distant sort of way that one loves a half-wild pet that might at any moment disappear back into the forest, but there had always remained a core of reserve between them, an unspoken recognition of a fundamental gap in understanding. Barra could no more imagine herself living her foster-mother's life than Tayniz could picture herself opening someone's guts with an axe.

As a trader's wife, Tayniz had seen far stranger and more disreputable guests than Leucas and Kheperu. She made warm, admiring comments about the spice pots and silk, and accepted Barra's introductions of her partners with perfect grace. Within moments, the household staff had relieved the companions of their gear and led Leucas and Kheperu to a comfortable couch on which to wait for a bath to be drawn; Leucas had accepted Tayniz's offer of a bath with thanks, after Barra's translation—Kheperu, unsurprisingly but unfortunately, had demurred. Tayniz blinked, once, at his refusal, but her expression never altered. "And for you, Barra?"

"Ay, sure, draw a bath, I can use it," she said. "But first I have to talk to Peliarchus. He's in the chart room, Milo said?"

Tayniz nodded. "Doing accounts, and not to be disturbed."

"Good then, I can surprise him." Barra stood on her toes to give her foster-mother a peck on the cheek; from this close, she could now see new lines under Tayniz's daypaint, and puffy flesh under her eyes. "What's wrong?" she asked softly, holding Tayniz's shoulders. "Something's wrong, I can tell."

Tayniz shook her head. "I don't know. You know Peliarchus doesn't discuss business with me—but he's worried. And I think he's frightened. It's the times, I think. The whole city is . . . changing. Everyone is worried, these days."

"He'll tell me," Barra said, giving her shoulders a squeeze. "Then I can tell you. It'll be just like the old days." With one last squeeze in lieu of a hug, Barra slipped back into the inner house, Graegduz padding happily at her heels. At the chart room, she told Graeg to stay outside—the last time he'd been inside the chart room he'd upset Peliarchus' sandtable, destroying several hours' worth of calculations, and had been banned ever since.

When Barra swung open the heavy door of the chart room, Peliarchus nearly knocked over the sandtable himself in his rush to leap to his feet and gather her into a bear hug that left her gasping. "Great bloody Ba'al!" he said, setting her down. "Oh, Barra, I'm glad to see you!"

Peliarchus was a barrel-shaped man a hand shorter than his wife, and his sunburned scalp hadn't seen a scrap of hair since before Barra could remember. One of her earliest memories was of this man, this bright-eyed bald Phoenikian trader bellowing with laughter as he bounced her on his knee—she couldn't have been as much as three years old. Every summer his ships would put in at Langdale's western coast, and he and his men would spend a month in trade and good guesting at her brother's great hall. It was he who'd taught her Phoenikian, who'd first told her tales of Egypt and Assyria, Babylon and Ur; he was one of the bare handful of men in Tyre who could converse with her in her native tongue. As she grew up, she'd marked the years by anticipating Peliarchus' summer arrival; when she'd chosen to leave her home, there was no other man in the wide world her brother would have trusted to care for her. He was a loud and joyous man of sudden passions and swift decisions, but level judgment. Her brother Llem, a deep and silent man, described him as "steady, with a brave heart"—the highest compliment that he would bestow on anyone.

Barra and Peliarchus held each other at arm's length, each enjoying the sight of the other's grin, and traded happy barbs about their weight: from him about her skinny shanks, from her about his round and jiggling belly. She released him and looked at the sandtable, its moist surface grooved with figures of this and that, various additions, subtractions, and multiplications, but mostly dominated by doodlings of some sort of two-masted ship. "I thought you were supposed to be doing accounts," she said with a sideways glance.

He shrugged. "There's not all that much to do."

A faint echo of despair under his offhand tone warned her not to let the silence stretch out too long. "Well," she said quickly, rubbing her hands together, "the *Skye Swift* and

Langdale's Pride should make port any day now. Then we'll be able to feast and trade tales all week long—and I have a whole bundle of letters for my sons to be sent back with them. Come on out here, I want you to meet my new partners."

Peliarchus looked pained, and he laid a heavy hand on her shoulder. "They won't be making port in Tyre. Not this year."

A high, buzzing sound sang in Barra's ears, and a cold knot of apprehension twisted tight in her stomach. "What do you mean?" she said carefully. "They're all right, aren't they? Nothing's happened . . . has it?"

"No, oh no," he told her, shaking his head. "I sent letters to Knossos for them, told them to sell off on Crete and make their turnaround from there, that's all. They'll winter in Langdale as planned, and come back first thing in the spring."

Breath that she wasn't aware she'd been holding whooshed out from her. "Oh, thank Lugh," she gasped. "I thought you were going to tell me that pirates got them, or a storm, or some other . . . hey, wait. You changed their itinerary?" Her ears suddenly flamed crimson. "You changed the itinerary of *my ships*?"

"Now, calm down, girl. They're only part yours, and their captains are my sons—practically your brothers. Things in Tyre are, well, a little unsteady right now. Agapenthes has lost three ships in the past month; he can afford to. We can't."

"Shit," Barra said. She bit her lower lip and turned away, clenching and unclenching her fists. She'd been counting on her share of the ships' earnings, depending on it. "Shit, shit, bleeding *shit*. I need that money, Peliarchus. I really do."

"What's the matter? Are you in trouble? You have a bad year?"

She shook off his paternal hand and sagged onto the stool; it was still warm with the heat of his body. "No, I'm having a great year. A fucking *glorious* year. Right up to the day when a pair of bloody pirate ships made off with everything I've earned. I am dead fucking broke, Peliarchus. Outside of the stuff I've sent back to Langdale, all I've got left in the world is my share in those two ships, three stone axes and a bronze cuirass that's been mended so many times it looks like a goatherd's cook pot."

"Well, y'know, listen," Peliarchus began cautiously. He knew Barra too well to offer her money; he'd experienced her temper too many times. "I could advance you something, against your share . . ."

"No. Absolutely not," she said. "I won't do that, and you know it."

"It's only a loan—"

"Don't insult me." Her face suddenly blazed to match her ears. "I earn my own living and pay my own way."

"It's no shame to admit you need help—" Peliarchus took in the white line her tight-stretched lips made against the angry red of her face, and shook his head with a sigh. "All right. Have it your way. You always do, anyway."

Barra shrugged and looked at the scrollcases stacked on their shelves on the other side of the room as though they were suddenly interesting; while the color drained back out of her face. She said softly, "Don't tell Tayniz. I don't want her to worry."

"No fear," he said warmly. "Come on, let's go meet these partners of yours."

Introducing her partners took a bit of doing, since Leucas had no Phoenikian, and Peliarchus, though of Argive heritage (three generations back) had only enough broken Greek to trade linen for wine and the like—not to mention the familiar difficulty of introducing Kheperu to anyone; Barra really admired the self-discipline of her foster-father, who was able to shake Kheperu's hand without so much as a blink or the faintest wrinkling of his nose.

Peliarchus made appreciative noises when he was presented with the bracelet and belt buckle; he instantly put them on and found a silver mirror in which to admire them.

Eventually everyone settled onto couches around the hearth, munching on grapes and cheese and strips of smoked pork while Tayniz got the cook working on a more substantial meal. Shortly, Leucas retired to his bath, muttering sourly about keeping his stitches dry.

The first question Peliarchus had for her was how long they would be staying in Tyre. When Barra told him their plans were indefinite, they might even winter here, he looked both relieved and vaguely worried at the same time.

"Good, then, you'll stay with us"—a pained expression crossed his face—"starting maybe next week."

"Next *week*?" Barra's ears flamed, and her eyes went wide. "What do you mean, next week?"

Kheperu noticed the color of her ears, and began to unobtrusively edge away from her.

"Now . . . now, Barra, don't get mad—" Peliarchus began.

She came to her feet. "You don't want me to get mad, y'shouldn't embarrass me in front of my partners! I told them we'd have a place to stay in Tyre! You'd make a liar of me, now?"

"You *do* have a place to stay! You will—as soon as I can clear up this crap with Agapenthes . . ."

"Barra," Tayniz said, "you know that this is your home as much as it is mine and his. It's only that we're committed to these guests—it's a favor for Agapenthes, and you know that when he asks for a favor, we can't refuse."

A favor for the Head of House Penthedes . . . She was right; refusing to do a favor for the Great House that employed you could have terminally serious consequences. Barra took a deep breath, and huffed it out disgustedly. She plumped back down onto the couch. "Well, all right, fine. What's going on that I can't stay?"

Peliarchus sighed. "There's a distant cousin of Agapenthes coming in for a visit. The lord is planning to have his household so full that this idiot and his entourage will have to stay here, with me."

"Why? Who is this guy?"

"Like I said, he's an idiot. Agapenthes hates the guy, can't stand to be around him—I'm told all he does is talk, drink, and fuck, and the only one he's good at is the drinking. A letter came last week—a special ship chartered straight from Kypros—he's on his way here with seven or eight of his nobles. They might even be here later tonight; it depends on the weather."

"From Kypros . . ." Barra said slowly.

Kheperu suddenly snickered. "Do you think it could be possible?"

"Oh, no," she said, starting to laugh, "oh, it couldn't be! Please tell me we're not talking about the king! King Demetor of Kypros?"

"Yeah, his name's Demetor." Peliarchus scowled at their laughter. "Why? What is it?"

"This is a man," Kheperu said with relish, "who has more brains in his eleventh finger than he does in his whole head."

After that, of course, Barra had no choice but to tell the story of their visit to Kypros. They'd arrived the morning after an unsuccessful boar hunt—it was all anyone was talking about at dockside. Two men had been gored, one fatally—Barra and Leucas had been on the beach only a few minutes when they were approached by Kheperu. Kheperu drew laughs from Peliarchus with his re-creation of his Wandering Seer act that had all-too-easily convinced King Demetor that this boar had been sent by the gods to punish his people for their king's impiety.

"What impiety?"

Kheperu leered. "Fucking. Not enough fucking. They worship Astarte, do they not?—even though they call her Aphrodite. I told him Astarte was *verrry* angry with him because he had not been fucking."

Tayniz blinked, and Peliarchus smothered a laugh. "How'd you know?"

"He's *old*," Kheperu said with a careless shrug. "I told him that to appease the goddess, he had to futter seven women a day for seven days. He went white and began to stammer; I had him by his limp old dick. I told him not to worry, Great Poseidon would send him two heroes from the sea, a man and a woman—you see, still harping the Astarte/fucking/lovers angle—and they would be the only ones who could slay the boar. So quite naturally, when Demetor went down to the docks, he found Leucas and Barra swimming, innocently naked, in the surf."

Peliarchus shook his head, chuckling. "And did it play?"

"Hundred and eighty Athenian large," Barra told him. "Pretty good wages for two days' work. That's when Leucas and I took on Kheperu as our third partner; the whole gag was his idea."

Tayniz leaned forward seriously. "But weren't you concerned about your own impiety? Don't you think the gods might take revenge on you for taking their names for a swindle?"

"Not at all," Kheperu said loftily. "Who's to say it really was a swindle? I would never presume to actually know the mind of the gods—it's entirely possible that I was telling the truth without even knowing it. The gods often use us mortals to work out their will without our knowledge; trust me on this—it is a doctrine known by every priest in Egypt. Who's to say that Barra and Leucas *weren't* there by the will of Great Poseidon? I met them by chance on the beach; it is often said that what seems chance to us, is the hand of a god at work."

"Hmpf," Tayniz sniffed. "I still think it seems needlessly risky."

"But it worked on Demetor," Barra said. "And it's probably Kheperu's fault he's coming for this visit."

Kheperu spread his hands. "The day we left I sold him a salve, a private recipe," he said with a broad grin. "I told him that rubbing it on his cock every day would keep him hard come earthquake or hurricane for a week. So he would be able to—*ahem*—to satisfy Astarte, even at his age. I'd wager he is coming here to try it out away from the wife and kids."

Peliarchus, the old trader, answered his grin. "And you thought you'd be far away when he finds out it doesn't work."

"Doesn't *work*?" Kheperu bristled. "Of course it will work. Am I a cheat? Am I a swindler? Shit, I use it myself!"

When twilight had painted purple across the sky and there came no sign of Demetor's arrival, Peliarchus and Tayniz had insisted that Barra and her friends should stay the night. The feast had been eaten—the roast duck in currant sauce was every bit as delicious as Barra'd remembered—and the servants dismissed to their quarters. Now brilliant stars gleamed overhead and the fire in the hearthshrine had been built up with hard oak, to burn long and low, keeping off the night's chill. Pale moths, some as large as Barra's hand, fluttered around the hearthyard, circling the fire, occasionally sizzling in the flames, some falling prey to the sudden jittering swoops of a pair of brown bats.

Barra lay back on her couch, watching the bats, Graegduz's great grey head warm in her lap. She swirled the warm wine in her cup and took another tiny sip. On the couch nearest to hers sat Peliarchus and Tayniz, arms about each other's waist, quietly at ease in the late autumn silence. Kheperu had already excused himself to the room he would share with Leucas, muttering about some poultice or ointment that must be prepared before midnight. The huge Athenian lay sprawled on a couch nearby, snoring softly under the blanket Tayniz had spread over him after he'd drifted off. Leucas was unaccustomed to the straight wine of Tyre; he had drunk it as though it were the three-parts-water mix that was common on the Akhaian peninsula. Combined with the fatigue of his wounds and the heavy meal, the wine had leveled him like a blow to the head; even his snoring was only a pale shadow of its usual grinding roar.

"I've been thinking about those letters of yours," Peliarchus said. "I'll be sorry if we can't get them to the Isle before winter; I'd hate to have your boys think something's happened to you when the *Swift* and the *Pride* arrive without them."

Barra shrugged tiredly. "Tomorrow I can see if any ships are heading north for the winter. Perhaps I can pay for the letters' passage."

"Oh, you can't do that. Most Tyrian sailors'd take your coin and toss the letters into the sea. I was thinking, maybe, I might want to take them myself."

Barra sat up on the couch, drawing a whine of protest from Graeg as she dislodged his head from its comfortable spot. "You're serious? You're going out to sea again?"

"In fact," Peliarchus went on, "Tayniz and I have been talking about going out to sea together. I've been thinking, y'know, I haven't been to the Isle of the Mighty in more than ten years, since that time I had to go and tell your brother you'd run away. And Tayniz's always wanted to see it, y'know, and meet your boys, that are almost like grandchildren. And I was thinking, maybe it's time you went back for a visit yourself. Take the letters in person."

Barra stared into the flickering hearthshrine as though searching for a vision. "Are things really that bad here?"

"Moving in that direction, maybe."

"You would not believe," Tayniz murmured, "what's happened to prices in the Market. Everything's down, way down. Except for weapons and armor."

Barra nodded silently; she'd made most of the cheese knife profit in the initial trade for the silk. Gold was valuable everywhere and easy to hide or transport.

"Mercenaries are coming in from all over the Med. Nearly every ship brings a few more. Way I hear it, most of them don't have much trouble finding work." Peliarchus gave her a sad smile. "And I have a feeling that you and your partners didn't come to Tyre right now just to visit with an old married couple."

"You think it's going to be war."

"Maybe that's the best we can hope for." The shifting light from the hearthshrine painted bloodred shadows across his face. "House Penthedes is still the big dog in Tyre. In all Phoenikia. In an open war, we have the resources and manpower to wipe out any other House, maybe even any two together, and do it before the Governor can get any sizable force of Egyptians in here to stop it. We'd come out of a war with a stronger position than we have right now. Agapenthes has been spoiling for a fight for months."

"So what's stopping him?"

"He can't make the first move. The other Houses would all line up against us—there isn't one of them that wouldn't like a piece of what we've got—and we can't fight them all together." He shifted forward, elbows on his knees, fingers knotting together to pop his knuckles one by one. "I'm thinking this is a good time to take a vacation for six months or so."

"I've noticed that everybody seems tense," Barra said, absently ruffling the fur behind Graegduz's ear. "Has anything actually happened? Has anyone made a move?"

Peliarchus shook his head. "Not openly. But things are going on. Three Penthedes ships are a month overdue. So is a Tomitiri caravan. A Mursuwallite warehouse burned a week ago. You ask me, I say it's the Jephunahi behind it."

"What makes you say that?"

"They're Amorites," Peliarchus said, as though this was a full explanation. "You can't trust 'em. They've only been in Tyre twenty years. Young and hungry, out to carve off a bigger slice . . ."

"And they're sorcerers," Tayniz put in with a whisper.

"Don't start that crap," Peliarchus told her.

"It's true," she said firmly. "Everybody knows that Amorites are sorcerers. The Habiru are Amorite tribes, and look what they did to Jericho! Not to mention Beth-Horon—they have *magical powers*."

Barra smiled. "That's what the New Tribes say about us, back home, and the only real sorcerer I've ever met is my grandma Maeve—and she's New Tribes, a Gael, herself."

"What about your friend Kheperu?" Tayniz asked.

"He's no sorcerer, though he'd like you to think he is. He

was once a seshperankh, and he can do a few tricks with powders and potions; it's magic, I guess, but it's not like real magic."

"Well, what about the curse on Nicoras' public house? Everyone who goes in there *dies*! What about that?"

"Probably just his terrible food," Peliarchus grumbled.

"But Nicoras is still alive, and his family, and all his slaves. And I heard that one of his slaves tried to run away, and she got so sick that she would have died if she hadn't come back." Tayniz leaned forward and lowered her voice. "Everyone who was living at the public house when the curse was laid lived—only new guests die. And nobody can leave . . ."

Peliarchus scowled darkly. "Tayniz—"

"And nobody knows how to break the curse. Four underpriests of Ba'al-Berith performed a protection, and an exorcism, and all four of them died right there in Nicoras' common room!"

"Hush up. I'm tired of hearing about this." Peliarchus appealed to Barra. "You see what this situation is doing to people? Everybody's getting crazy, believing any damned rumor that flies into their head. I hear the bloody Governor is already on his way in from Byblos. With the full division. Nobody wants Egypt involved in this; the garrison here is no trouble, most of the officers have been here for years, and they know the tally, but . . . well, no offense to your friend Kheperu, but once those bastards leave Egypt they shed their precious civilization the way a cobra sheds his skin. The Governor himself is a well-meaning old fart, but if he takes it into his head to let the army loose on us, to 'keep the peace,' well . . ." He shook his head. "Once King Demetor is here and gone again, I think we're going to go. And you'd better come with us."

"Peliarchus—" Barra began.

"No, I've decided. We're leaving. Demetor probably won't be here more than a week or ten days, then we're gone and you're coming with us."

"I'm not."

"Barra, dammit, this is no time to turn stubborn."

"If I winter on the Isle," Barra said patiently, "I could miss the Trade Fair at Crete in the spring. One bad storm is all it'd take, then I'm screwed for a year. Maybe more; I could lose everything I've been working toward these last ten years."

"None of that will do you much good if you're dead."

"You worry too much." Barra yawned and stretched. She stood, rubbing her eyes. "It's been a long day. Help me get Leucas up to his room, will you? Between the two of us we should be able to carry him."

Peliarchus pushed himself to his feet. "Well, even if you won't go home, there are a lot of places on the coast that'll be safer than Tyre."

"Relax, will you?" Barra said with her best friendly and innocent smile. "Believe me, I have no intention of getting mixed up in any trade war." This might have fooled Tayniz; the look she got from Peliarchus said he knew exactly what her intentions really were.

By the time the sun peeked over the mountains on a clear and bright morning, the three partners were already headed back through the Market. Tayniz had prepared a huge breakfast from the leftovers of last night's feast, which Barra and Kheperu had dug into with a will. Leucas spent breakfast time leaning his head on his hands and grunting monosyllables. His one burst of language had been a heartfelt prayer of thanks to Polydeukes; Leucas' nose had been broken so many times in boxing matches that he no longer had any sense of smell, for which he was profoundly grateful. The mere sight of so much food painted a greenish tinge under the tan of his cheeks.

Conversation at breakfast was limited; Peliarchus had obviously wanted to pick up the argument from the night before, but was stopped by the knowledge of long experience: once Barra had set her heels, any further pushing would only dig her in that much deeper. She made it easier on him by chattering away on a variety of trivial subjects, but silences tended to grow and deepen whenever she stopped to chew and swallow a mouthful of food.

After some debate, and much insistence from Kheperu, they decided to take up residence at the inn of one Lidios, an expatriate Argive whose substantial establishment (eight private rooms and a staff of twenty) was in the Greek quarter on the southwest side of the city, a short walk from the beach and not too far from the Market. He charged only three shekels a day for full service in a private room; this gave Barra two days' grace before she'd need to start cutting purses for a living.

Before they left the home of Peliarchus, Barra handed over the packet of letters and left strict instructions that anyone looking for her or her friends should be directed to Lidios.

"Especially anyone in Meneides colors," she'd said.

"The Meneides?" Peliarchus grunted. "You're not mixing up with those bastards, are you?"

"Maybe," Barra had told him. "It depends on how much they're willing to pay me."

It was too early yet for the streets to be crowded with traffic, and the golden morning sun gave only a promise of the day's later heat as the three companions walked slowly across the city. Here and there the streets were dotted with half-skirted slaves carting jugs of water back from the communal wells—once Leucas stopped one with a threatening hand, grabbed a jug from his handcart, and drank it nearly dry, pouring the remainder over his head and shoulders. He paid the slave with a shrug and a copper coin, and the slave, muttering sourly, headed back toward the wellhouse. The companions walked on, past scowling merchants tying back the flaps of tentstalls and tired-eyed men who scraped the street smooth before their doors with bronze rakes. In deference to the wounds on Leucas' shoulder and back—not to mention the self-inflicted ache in his head—the bundle of their possessions had been divided three ways, and each carried their share. Graegduz padded sleepily alongside Barra, toenails silent on the hard-packed earth, while she explained in low tones her conclusions drawn from last night's conversation with Peliarchus. The prospect of a trade war seemed to cheer Kheperu considerably; he was nearly dancing as he led them through the streets, laughing and humming snatches of Egyptian songs.

"I don't mind you being happy," Leucas rumbled dangerously, "but do you have to be happy so loudly?"

Kheperu only shrugged and grinned—but he did so silently.

Barra frowned at the buildings around them and squinted up at the sun. "Uh, Kheperu? Are you sure you know where this place is?"

"Of course. I lived there for two months only a few years ago."

"We're going the wrong way."

"No," Kheperu told her with a grin that stopped just short of an outright leer, "we're going the right way."

"You're lost."

"I'm not. I know exactly where we're going. In fact," he paused at the street mouth, where it opened onto a broad avenue, and spread his arms, "we're here!"

A slight shift in the wind brought a light breeze against their faces; now she could smell the place. Barra, who never forgot a scent, would have known it with her eyes closed. Juniper and crushed amber rubbed into human skin to mask the rank smell of fear sweat, that was the distinctive note. Broad walkways circled the building, mirroring the gallery with no railing that ringed the upper floor. Brightly dyed awnings of saffron and scarlet shaded both gallery and walkway, and a third set stretched over the roof. Each wall of the building was set with a wide door of solid bronze, and above each, carved into the stone in Phoenikian, Akkadian, Egyptian demotic, and the Cretan script that served as the written form of Greek, was the simple legend: SLAVES.

Barra said, "I'm not going in there."

"What is this place?" asked Leucas.

"The Mursuwallite Slave House," Kheperu answered cheerfully. "The best slave market in the Canaan District. They have slaves from all over the world! Assyria—Skythia— dwarfs from Punt, Kushite tribals—they have *blondes,* Leucas! Golden-haired women from Europe beyond the Alps! The best part is, they don't speak a word of Language, so you don't have to listen to them *talk.* Think about it."

Leucas frowned. "I can simply walk in that building and *buy* a slave. With money, if I had any. They *sell* them, there."

"Of course. What's the matter?"

"It doesn't seem right."

Kheperu appealed to Barra, "Talk to him. I don't think he appreciates the quality of this opportunity."

Barra shook her head. "Leave me out of this."

"It's wrong to buy slaves," Leucas said slowly. "There's no honor in it, to pay with money for something that should be bought with sword and spear."

"So you're not going with me?"

"Where I come from, a slave is taken in battle. Wives and

children of defeated men. You don't buy them. You don't sell them. If you can't support a slave, you marry her off or let him go."

"Fine, you can wait here. Come on, Barra."

"I told you," Barra said, "I'm not going in there."

Kheperu threw up his hands. "What's your problem?"

Barra shifted uncomfortably. "It's none of your business."

"What, did somebody sell you for a slave once? There's nothing wrong with that; could happen to anybody. Even whatsisbugger—Herakles—was slaved once; ask Leucas."

"I told you it's none of your business."

"Oh, come on, we're partners, aren't we?" Kheperu wheedled in a weaselly tone that set Barra's teeth on edge. "We must be honest with each other. No secrets, remember?"

Barra surrendered with a sigh; even after only a few weeks in Kheperu's company she was well aware that the stubby Egyptian was fully prepared to stand here and badger her all day long. She said, "It's because every time I go into a slave market, I end up buying five or six."

"What's wrong with that?"

"You don't understand. I buy the sick ones, the weak ones. Then I end up spending all my money to get them healthy and strong. What do I need with five or six slaves? I've got nothing for them to do—and by that time I'm so attached to them I can't sell them back. I end up letting them go. A few times I've even paid their passage back to the Isle of the Mighty—and with a purse of silver and a letter to my brother asking him to sell them a little land of their own. The last time I—" She stopped herself just in time, just before saying *I adopted one.* She had no reason to tell these men about Antiphos, the broken, brutalized little boy she'd bought four years ago at Crete; she'd told them far too much already. Friends or not, she wasn't in a line of work where one advertises one's soft heart. She'd trust them with her future, but not her past. She shook her head and spat, "It's revolting. And expensive. So I don't go into slave markets anymore."

"But this time you are safe," Kheperu pointed out. "You can't afford any."

"That just makes it worse."

Kheperu eyed her, aghast. "You mean there's something in

that heart of yours beyond the clink of silver being stacked in coin? Barra, I'm shocked. Shocked and hurt. Disappointed—"

"Shut up. Go enjoy yourself. I don't know what you're going to be able to afford, either."

He shrugged, a cheerful smile on his face. "Children are cheaper—you have to feed them for a few years before they can do any really useful work, so you can get them for a discount—"

"I don't want to hear about it. Go on; Leucas and I'll sit here in the sun."

Head resting against the wall at his back, Leucas snored like an approaching thunderstorm. Barra left Graegduz at his side to watch as she strolled off into the Market; a growl from the grey wolf should be more than enough to discourage any would-be mischief-maker from bothering the sleeping Athenian or his possessions.

She wandered idly through the swelling crowds, pretending to take an interest in the wares of this stall or that. Nearly every man in the Market was armed, which was not so unusual: most Tyrian freemen carry at least a dagger as part of their normal clothing. What made it unsettling was how many of them supplemented their daggers with shortswords worn ostentatiously outside their overcloaks; there were a number of the small trumpet-faced Egyptian handaxes in evidence as well, not all of them in the belts of the quilt-armored Egyptian regulars from the garrison. Also unsettling was the number of foreigners about, many of them wearing armor of bronze plates as they sat guard near the stalls of wealthier merchants. Tall Northmen, hair shining white-gold in the morning sun, red-faced Kelts and broad-shouldered Picts— Barra avoided the Kelts and Picts; many of those from her lands who traveled the Mediterranean might recognize her— grim, sweating Hittites who likely were deserters from the army King Mutuwalli had raised against the Phrygians, and an astonishing number of Akhaian men with wind-etched faces and the flat cold stares Barra knew from seeing the look on Leucas' face in unguarded moments. These were the empty eyes of men who'd survived the ten years of endless warfare on the plains before Troy.

Barra found herself unconsciously testing the edge of her broadaxe. She gave it a week, two at the outside.

When she returned to where she'd left Leucas, he was awake and sitting up; Kheperu was seated at his side. She could hear the whining tone in his voice before she could make out the words. "What happened?" she said as she walked up.

"What happened is your damn dog almost took my leg off when I tried to wake up Leucas," Kheperu said.

"Did you, Graeg?" Barra chirped in Pictish, ruffling the wolf's fur. "Good boy!" Graegduz responded with a warbling croon.

"You know, Barra," Leucas said with a faint smile, "I'm starting to really enjoy your wolf's company."

Kheperu grunted sourly. Barra told him, "Actually, Kheperu, he likes you. He says you smell like a big pile of fresh shit."

"Does he, now? I suppose you really expect me to believe you can talk to each other."

"All animals speak Pictish," Barra said innocently. "Didn't you know that? And all Picts understand animals."

"Really? Then why didn't you tell that damned bear to roll over and play dead?"

"I did. Bears are contrary by nature, and besides, it's half-deaf. It thought I said come here and eat me. It apologized, later."

Kheperu shook his head, surrendering. Leucas chuckled. Barra said, "So what's doing with the slaves? I expected you to come out of there with at least a little girl or two."

"Ah, they have none," Kheperu said sourly. "Nor boys, either. Some rich Egyptian outside of town comes in once a week and buys up everyone under twenty. You would not believe the going price for a fourteen-year-old."

"Hard luck. Come on, get up. Let's get to Lidios' and stow our gear."

Voices of men shouting in anger and fear suddenly erupted deep within the Market. Barra grinned at her companions. "Sounds like a fight. Want to go watch?"

Leucas shrugged, and Kheperu said, "Why not? If they're not too backed up when we get there, I might get some side bets down."

But as they moved toward the disturbance, the shouting faded away to a single voice: a man's, shrill with terror, screaming barely comprehensible words. Beyond that, all was deathly silent.

Leucas looked down at Barra. "Not a fight. What's he saying?"

Barra frowned. "I'm not sure; he sounds drunk. I think he's saying something about getting something off him. Or someone off him. Other than that, it's about what you'd expect. 'Ba'al-Berith, god of my fathers, help me, save me,' and that sort of thing."

Leucas hissed through his teeth, then said abruptly, "Follow me." He set off crashing through the press of people, battering them aside with the swift ease of a chariot company galloping through a mob of farmers; Barra and Kheperu followed easily in his wake.

They broke free of the press, and stopped. The broad street was empty save for the screaming man; people watched from doorways or pressed back against buildings as he staggered along, lurching and spinning like a scarecrow in a windstorm.

Clear morning sun struck brilliant splinters of light off rings on every finger when he lifted his hands to beg for help or to bat at the air like a man caught in a cloud of stinging flies. A bloody rag was bound around his left hand, and his face was smeared with blood that had splattered a gleaming crimson trail back down the street; patches of blood darkened his striped overcloak and dyed his ankle-length robe. He screamed until his voice cracked and danced his aimless whirl; the crowd watched in silence.

Kheperu spat on the ground. "Just a damned lunatic. What's wrong with these people? Don't you have lunatics in Tyre?"

"He's no lunatic," Barra muttered grimly. "Look at his clothes. That's a rich man."

Leucas moved cautiously toward the screaming man. "What is it, sir?" he called in Greek. "How can you be helped?"

"Shut up, are you *crazy*?" Barra hissed. "Do you want to catch what he's got?"

Leucas looked back over his shoulder at her, frowning, uncertain. The screaming man had seen him, though, and he rushed at the huge Greek, clawing at him desperately. At Barra's heel, Graegduz crouched, holding his head low and snarling.

"Kill me!" the man croaked, his voice gone. "For the mercy of god, kill me! Don't let them take me!"

Leucas held the man's arms, supporting him like a child. His ruined face twisted into a mask of helplessness. "What's he saying?"

Barra was at his side in an instant. "He's saying he wants you to—*Loving Mother!*"—she whispered in sudden awe.

Even as she spoke, the flesh on the side of the man's neck tore and his blood spurted across her face. She reeled back, arms up to protect her, gagging.

The wound was small and curved: like a bite.

The man convulsed with shocking strength, tearing free of Leucas' grasp. His bowels and bladder voided themselves into a pool at his feet, and he fell back, screaming and writhing in his own waste, wisps of steam rising vividly in the bright sunlight. His back arched, and his feet hammered the hard-packed earth. The three warriors watched in helpless horror as his convulsions quieted; the last of his life fled.

The street was still and quiet, sharp-shadowed as an Akhaian fresco.

Barra said hoarsely, "I know this man. His name is Othniel." Graegduz bent his head to the body, sniffing at the blood. He sneezed abruptly and backed off, whining.

Kheperu knelt beside the body, parting the robes to examine it. "Friend of yours?"

"Not really," Barra said, wiping his blood from her face. "I just knew him from the Market—he's a fetchit for the Jephunahi."

"Look here," Kheperu said, holding the robe aside. "All these wounds, they look like bites of some kind, like manbites. But the robe isn't torn above them. And do you smell that?"

It was a strange, bitter scent, like that which sometimes rises from hot springs. Barra nodded. "What is it?"

"Burnt sulphur; that is, brimstone."

Leucas shuddered, sharply, only once. "This shouldn't happen by light of day."

Kheperu spread the clenched fingers of Othniel's left hand, and pressed aside the crusted rag. "Someone cut off his thumb, and not long ago, either. And look at this."

On the palm was a fresh brand, the flesh red and angry at its edges:

"You know this sign?"

Barra shook her head. "Egyptian glyph; I don't read it. Contracts are written in demotic or Akkadian cuneiform."

"It means," Kheperu said grimly, *"Behold."*

Barra and Leucas looked at each other, and at the curious Market crowd, now pressing close around. Hundreds of people had watched Othniel die, and hundreds more joined them even now and got the story in a rising buzz of frightened voices. This tale would be all over Tyre before sundown.

"Behold," Barra repeated. "Well, we did. Everybody did." She looked down at her hands, smeared with the blood she'd wiped from her face. She rubbed them together, and the blood scraped off in half-clotted little wormlike threads. "Let's get out of here before some Jephunahi asshole shows up and decides this is our fault."

CHAPTER FOUR

Murder

Lidios wiped his hands on his blood- and grease-stained smock as he stared critically up at the breaking clouds. He nodded sharply, his chins echoing the gesture, and turned away from the doorway, a small smile of satisfaction buried between his massive cheeks. "The skies are clearing," he said to no one in particular, muttering in his native Greek. "We might get enough sun this afternoon to bake off some of the mud."

He waddled back into the common room and grabbed the ear of a passing slave, giving the boy a list of goods to bring from the Market, and a coin purse barely the size of two doubled fingers. After barking at two others to accompany the boy, he dragged a low stool through the nearly empty room and sat heavily at the open end of the triclinium table, where Barra sat with Leucas. Graegduz, who'd been napping, comfortably snuggled against Barra's feet under the table, opened one eye, and sniffed lazily. Recognizing Lidios, he went back to sleep.

"Folk had best come out tonight," Lidios said. "It's the tenday, and I owe two large weights to the bottomless purse of Jephunah. Though what I'm paying for, I can't say. Haven't had a single Jephunahi tough in here since Othniel was killed and you folk came, three days now—they can't get mud on their precious feet—and he can't even protect his own bloody captain!"

Barra nodded sympathetically and sipped the rich Egyptian beer that filled her mug. Leucas grunted, chewing on the last mouthful of his stew, then he lifted the big wooden trencher and tipped the last of the broth into his mouth. He belched and set it down. "One more, Lidios."

"One *more*?" Lidios said incredulously. "That's your third and it's only midday! You'll eat me right out of business!"

Leucas wiped his lips with the back of his hand. "I'll pay double," he offered with a ghost of a smile.

"Oh, very good! Very funny! If it wasn't for Kheperu—may the blessings of Astarte follow him all of his days—I'd make no money from you folk at all. And even he cost me my second-best whore!"

"If you'd prefer," Barra said icily, setting down her mug with a thump that slopped beer onto the scarred tabletop, "we can take our custom elsewhere."

"What's the matter with you people? Can't a man even *gripe*? Please! Eat up! Drink up! Let the bloody storm god destroy my livelihood! I'll breathe not a word of complaint!" He heaved himself to his feet and collected the trencher, heading toward the back door and the cauldron of stew that sat on the hearth built over flagstones behind the inn. "No, let the bloody sorcerer's curse fall upon my house as it did upon Nicoras and Xuros! Will I complain? Not a word!" Without even pausing for breath, he disappeared through the door.

Leucas grinned. "I like him."

"Ay," Barra said glumly, "me, too."

For three days, they had waited here for some offer of employment from Idonosteus. Barra had grown afraid she might have miscalculated. If she had pressed for a reward for the bear, at least they'd have something to show for their efforts, something to pay for Leucas' wounds. The huge Akhaian, stolid as ever, had said nothing on the subject, but the only relief she got from Kheperu's needling came when, as now, he'd paid a shekel or two for a couple of Lidios' whores and was amusing himself with some unnatural acts in a private room.

So far, their only reward for the bear was free food and lodging with Lidios.

Lidios had recognized Kheperu and had greeted him by name when they arrived, in the afternoon shortly after Othniel's death, just ahead of the first thunderstorm. The common room was nearly empty then, only four or five men and three whores; at the sound of Lidios' bellowed "Master Kheperu!" one of the whores had started to her feet, her face suddenly pale and twisted under its paint. "Hello, Belthe," Kheperu had said pleasantly. "It's flattering to be remembered. And this time, I've brought friends." The whore had shaken her head wordlessly, then uttered a piercing screech and bolted for the

back door. The only sign of her thereafter came the next
morning, when one of the whores, a Kena'ani named Lenka,
smilingly claimed that she'd glimpsed Belthe at the edge of
town, heading north at a dead run. Everyone played along
with the joke; Barra loudly calculated that if her wind were
strong, she could reach the outskirts of Sidon sometime this
afternoon.

Lidios had seemed confident she'd return eventually, and
he'd welcomed the three companions warmly, if somewhat
nervously. Rumor of their heroic capture of Idonosteus' bear
was by that time all over Tyre, and there was no mistaking the
combination of gigantic Akhaian, red-haired axe-woman and
reeking Egyptian. He offered them the free hospitality of his
public house, asking in return only that they make themselves
visible in the common room, so that word of their presence in
the inn would get around and perhaps bring in folk who'd be
curious to get a look at the subjects of the hottest rumors in
months. Then the first of the winter storms had come; three
solid days of rain had kept Lidios' common room as empty as
a plague house, but Lidios had not recanted on his deal. Even
on their first night there, Barra had figured out why.

All businesses in Tyre are affiliated with a Great House;
they pay taxes to this House or that, and in exchange they
receive the House's protection, and other considerations. A
merchant who is in dispute with another can go to his patron
for justice; an innkeeper nervous about lodging a rough crew
of sailors can go to his patron for armed and armored toughs
to help him keep the peace. Transactions between affiliates of
the same House take place at reduced prices, and in dealing
with foreign traders or affiliates of another House, a merchant
has the might of a Great House behind him to ensure that contracts are honored.

Lidios paid his taxes to the Jephunahi. Othniel had been the
right hand of old Jephunah himself. Othniel, so the rumor
went, had been torn to pieces in broad daylight on a crowded
street, with no man's hand raised against him. Barra and her
companions had considerately refrained from revealing their
personal knowledge of the truth of that rumor.

Any freelance robbers, or thugs from other Houses, might
think twice about causing trouble for the inn of Lidios—no
matter how weak and threatened the Jephunahi might be
rumored to be, now that they seemed the target of some sor-

cerer's vendetta—while three budding heroes took their ease in the common room.

Lidios kept up a fair pretense of good cheer, but in unguarded moments his face would go slack and sag, revealing the dark purple rings of his tension beneath his bloodshot eyes. Lidios was frightened; many of the slaves were outright terrified. Barra wondered if perhaps all that kept them going was their talismanic faith in her, Leucas and Kheperu.

That was fine with Barra; she was perfectly comfortable playing scarecrow in exchange for free room and board—her purse still held six shekels—and it bought them time for Leucas' shoulder to heal, which it was doing with the Akhaian's usual swiftness. It also bought time for her to recover from some minor illness. She and Leucas both had been troubled in stomach since they'd come to the public house, sweating and hot of face, and the occasional shafts of sunlight that had showed through the rain clouds had spiked her head like a sword through the eye. Kheperu had seemed immune, happily whoring away whole days, and now she and Leucas seemed to be recovering. The day before she'd felt well enough to drag herself across town in the rain, to share a quiet meal with Peliarchus and Tayniz, and listen to their complaints about the trials and tribulations of hosting King Demetor and company. As for Leucas, even intermittent vomiting hadn't dulled his appetite, and now he was joyously making up for lost food; Barra felt clearheaded for the first time in three days. She only wished that she'd played things differently with Idonosteus.

Lidios returned, the trencher heaped with steaming stew. He set it before Leucas and said, "You'll excuse me if I don't stay and watch you eat me out of house and home. If I don't start sanding the mud outside my door I'll get no trade, sunshine or not."

Leucas nodded, already shoveling stew into his mouth, and gestured for him to be on his way. Barra sipped her beer as she watched him waddle to the sand barrel that stood by the front door and fill a pair of pails.

Idonosteus, you worthless jiggle-prick bastard, she thought, *why don't you send for us?*

* * *

Kheperu rejoined them as twilight began to close down the day, a whore leaning upon each of his arms, exhaustion counterfeiting affection. As he approached, winding between the posts that supported the ceiling and the now-crowded tables, it became apparent that he was all but carrying them. When he finally released them, the whores—a boy of perhaps seventeen and a woman a few years older—staggered stiffly away to collapse onto the couches with the other whores in the business corner of the common room. Kheperu watched them go, shaking his head sadly, then came to the table and slid onto the bench beside Leucas. "It's a sad commentary on the state of the world," he said. "Even the whores no longer take pride in their trade. No stamina. Lidios should make them run along the beach in the mornings, build up their wind. When I was young, a small silver weight would buy you a woman who could bounce you on her lap two nights and a day together and stop only for a mug of wine and hunk of cheese. Now they start whining about being tired after only a single afternoon. Hardly worth the money. That bloody boy's arm began to wear out after less than thirty lashes—"

"Kheperu." Barra cut him off firmly. "No details. I just ate."

"Oh, relax, it wasn't even a real whip, just a length of cane no thicker than my—"

"I'm warning you."

"—finger," Kheperu finished innocently.

Barra looked at Leucas, who was smiling behind his beer mug. "What's so damned funny?"

"Don't snap at me, Barra," Leucas said mildly. "I'm not the one you're mad at."

"What difference has that ever made?"

Kheperu lifted an eyebrow. "No word yet from our great and lordly bear-master, I take it?"

Barra shook her head disgustedly. Kheperu murmured something in a mincing, effeminate tone, that sounded to Barra very much like "Our price goes up . . ."

"One more word out of you," she hissed, "and I'll slam your face on this table so hard you'll have to pry that beak of yours out with a knife!"

Kheperu made his customary hand-to-heart *Who, me?* gesture of injured innocence, and Barra subsided, scowling. A moment later, she nudged Graegduz with her foot and told him to go to the room; the common room was filling rapidly and the last thing she needed was for the grey wolf to get playful with some unassuming trader. Graegduz gave her one long, reproachful look, then padded toward the dormitory corridor with his head hanging low. He didn't even look at the people he passed—he was accustomed to humans stepping aside to make way for him, and these were no exceptions.

The bright afternoon sun had worked its magic on Lidios' trade; now, with night falling, the common room of the public house was becoming crowded with sailors of all nations and tradesmen with their women, even two youngish women Barra had tagged as freelance whores. Lidios, if he spotted the pair, would toss them bodily into the street, so Barra didn't point them out; she begrudged no one the opportunity to earn an honest living.

A pipe-and-lyre duo performed on stools set up on a table in one corner, earning meat and beer with an evening's entertainment. They weren't very good, the lyrist chanting Phoenikian sailing lays in a rusty bellow; most of the folk ignored them, some even singing songs of their own in a variety of languages. The crowd was well lubricated already; for a single silver shekel—about a tenth the size of an Athenian weight—a man can eat and drink to his heart's content. Another shekel buys him a space on the floor if he can't walk home, as well as breakfast in the morning. As darkness wrapped the inn, Lidios hung oil lamps from pegs on the ceiling posts, their steady yellow light blending with the orange flicker from the hearthshrine, and soon the light attracted the swirling clouds of moths and mosquitoes that were an ever-present part of night in Tyre.

A group of five bearded men in belted chitons occupied a corner table; when they bellowed at the lyrist in Greek for a song of Akhilleus on Skamander's banks, Leucas rose and excused himself. "One of them looks familiar," he explained. "I may have fought beside him at Troy. It's proper for me to greet a brother-in-arms, and to share in a libation to the gods." He moved off with slightly sodden dignity.

"Sentimental mope," Kheperu muttered at his retreating back. "Troy this, Troy that, if the Akhaians were so bloody heroic, why'd it take ten years to sack one city?"

"Shut up," Barra said wearily.

"Ramses the Great sacked Qadesh in three days," Kheperu

went on. "Even the Habiru—a pack of thieving savages—took Jericho in a week. But every time you mention Troy, every Akhaian in the damned room gets all misty-eyed over their great heroes who spent ten years playing with themselves on the coast of Thrace."

"Troy was on the coast of Lydia," Barra said, "and if you don't shut up about it, I'll break your jaw."

"Aren't we testy?"

"Shut up."

When Barra had first arrived in Tyre on Peliarchus' ship the Siege of Troy had been already in its second year; no one in Tyre knew of it—or, if they did, thought much about it. But later, as the Akhaian ships raided for supplies and slaves up and down the coast to support their troops, some even reached as far south as Tyre. They came not to raid—the swift response of Phoenikian charioteers ensured that—but to trade their loot for food and wine. Stories the Akhaians told began to filter through the Market, of the epic battles of sons and grandsons of gods on both sides, of the Aiantes, of Diomedes and Odysseus, of Agamemnon and Menelaos the Red King, of Hektor and Aeneas, of Sarpedon and Penthesileia the Amazon Queen. Once, in the half-light of early dawn, Barra had glimpsed an Akhaian captain on board his mighty hundred-sweep warship as it pulled out to sea with the tide. Tall and straight he had stood, his hair the shining, impossible white-gold of spring sunlight on the crest of waves. The armor he wore was curiously worked, of some metal that did not shine with the warm glow of polished bronze, but was a dull, matte grey-black; it was not until years later that Barra would again see arms of iron, the sky-stone metal the secret of whose forging was closely held by the royal house of the Hittite Empire.

Even now, after ten years, she nursed and cherished in her heart the notion that the man she had glimpsed once, briefly in the dawn, was Akhilleus the Godlike. Less than a year later, at the age of seventeen, she ran away from the house of Peliarchus, all her thoughts fixed on reaching Troy.

Events had intervened, painfully; she'd never reached the city. Among the many regrets with which she regarded her past, missing her chance to see the great heroes, Akhaian and Trojan both, fight before the god-built walls of Troy was one of the sharpest.

She strained to her the lyric of the lyrist's song, but it was hopeless through the babble of competing languages. She sighed and sipped her beer. Kheperu surveyed the room with eyes bright and beady as a drunken squirrel's, muttering to himself; she kicked him under the table.

"*Ow!* Hey!" Kheperu said, rubbing his shin. "What was that for?"

"For being an asshole," Barra told him moodily. "Just on principle."

She felt a presence at the triclinium's chest-high wall behind her; even before he spoke she smelled the sour wine on his breath, underlain with juniper and cinnamon and the faint organic decay that comes of too much meat in the diet.

"Hey, little fella," the man said. "What say I dance with your girl?"

An evil grin began to spread across Kheperu's face, until he noticed Barra's expression. He coughed into his hand. "She's not my girl. You'd better ask her yourself."

"Not your girl? Oh, I get it. What's your price, honey?"

Barra carefully set down her beer mug.

"That hair of yours, it's really something," the man went on. "I'll take you, even if you are skinny as a boy."

Barra slid out from the bench, stood and faced him. The man grinned and took her arm. "Come on, then! I'm horny as a goat."

"You like that hand?"

"What?"

"You'd better take it off me before I feed it to you."

"Hey, hey," the man said, looking down at her with an expression puzzled and hurt. "I didn't mean anything by that skinny crack. That's just *negotiation,* you get it? I got money to spend, and plenty of it."

Barra stepped forward, bending her neck to look up into his face, inches from hers. "If you only knew," she began quietly, "how tired I am of every cockeyed Phoenikian son of a bitch I meet assuming I must be a whore because I've got breasts and I'm not married."

"Hey—hey, now . . ."

"You see this axe?" She held her hand level with the broadaxe's head. "I said, *do you see this axe, you worthless goatfucker?*" The shrill power of her shout quieted the common room; even the musicians stopped to watch.

The man nodded and swallowed, taking a step back. Barra took a step forward, staying right in his face.

"How would you like to have this axe planted so far up your ass you'll be shitting flint till Midsummer's? Hey? How would you *like* that? *Answer me!*"

The man's backward pace accelerated. "I, uh, come on now—"

"If your ugly ass is still in this building by the time I count three, I'm going to kill you. You understand? I'm going to fucking *kill you right here and right now*! *Understand?*"

"Hey, but, I didn't mean anything—"

"One!"

The man bolted for the door.

Barra watched him go, smiling with a little sigh. Nothing could cheer her mood faster than shouting down a jackass; she hadn't had to lay a finger on him, hadn't even drawn her axe. The common room rocked with laughter and applause, which she turned and graciously acknowledged with a sweeping bow.

A familiar voice spoke from behind her, in Corinthian-accented Greek. "Hey, it's the axe-girl."

She looked back. "Chrysios?"

He still wore the long-sleeved overrobe of a Phoenikian merchant, although below it he wore only a belted chiton. He flashed those perfect teeth of his and said, "I caught the end of your little scene, Axe-girl. Were you really going to kill him? Over that?"

His legs, Barra noted, were fully as beautiful as the rest of him.

She shrugged. "Maybe. Uh, listen, is that job still open?"

"Something fall through for you?"

"No, no, I was only wondering. My friends and I might have a day or two free."

Chrysios nodded, still showing his arrogant smile. "And I heard about your dance with the bear. We should be able to work something out."

"Why don't you join us at our table," she said, unconsciously smoothing her tunic. It took a conscious effort for her not to check her hair. His, she decided on second look, was closer to golden than to straw-colored. "We can talk it over."

"What, sit with Stinky? Hey, Axe-girl, I came here to eat

and relax. I might sit down after supper, if my stomach's up to it."

"All right. And, Chrysios? My name's Barra."

His smile spread. "Yeah, I know." He moved off toward a long table that had a seat open. Barra watched him go, measuring his breadth of shoulder against the loose way the robe moved around his hips. She shook her head and went back to her table.

"Wasn't that the Greek boy you chased off the beach the other day?" Kheperu said as she sat down. "I never forget a pretty face."

"Forget his—you're not his type."

He shrugged. "With Greeks, you can never tell. He *is* pretty, though, isn't he?"

Barra drained her remaining beer and waved the empty mug at Lidios, who nodded at her from across the room. She said, "He's an asshole."

"Is that so? I notice you didn't kick him."

"Shut up."

Lidios arrived at the table with another brimming mug. "Master Kheperu, Miss Barra," he said with a short bow, "there's a tradesman, name of Murso, he'd like to meet you without putting his life and health at risk. You think he could come over here without you chasing him off? Like you did that other paying customer?"

"Sorry about that," Barra offered, not too sincerely.

Lidios shrugged. "Oh, I don't really mind, you know—I'd already collected his coin. Once I get the money, the faster they leave, the less they eat and drink, the better my profit. Just please don't run off anyone who still owes, all right?"

Barra leaned back to be able to see around Lidios' bulk. "Which one is he?"

Lidios was far too old a hand at public-house assignations to turn and point. "Skinny and tall, against the wall to your left of the hearthshrine. Brown cloak with the hood up."

The man Lidios described sat on a crowded bench, spooning stew from a trencher that rested across his knees. He seemed to be watching the musicians between bites, eating with such concentration that he seemed quite alone, despite the shoulders that pressed against his to either side.

"Shy, is he?"

"He said it's the three of you he wanted to speak with. Want I should get rid of him?"

"Loving Mother, no! It might be a job."

Lidios looked pained. "You *have* a job. You have any idea what it costs me just to feed you?"

"Yes, in fact, I do," Barra told him. "Send him over."

Lidios sighed, nodded, and waddled off.

Kheperu eyed the trader lazily. "This won't be much. Look at the way he's dressed—if that's a rich man I'm a camel."

"You smell like one."

"That, dear girl," he said haughtily, "is a disservice to camels everywhere." His face brightened as he caught sight of something behind her. "Now him, *he* looks like a rich man!"

Barra twisted on the bench to look over her shoulder. Through the street door came a tall man who was nearly as fat as Lidios, dark of skin and hair, carrying a lamp of polished brass. He was flanked to either side by surly, competent-looking men in halfcoats of layered bronze; each of the pair had a short broadsword belted to his waist and carried a heavy, wide-bladed spear half again his own height. Gems glittered from rings the tall fat man wore; on the thumb of the hand that held the lamp gleamed a heavy gold seal ring. He strode into the common room with the effortless authority of a man born to power.

"He looks," Barra corrected her companion, "like a Jephunahi tax collector. Poor Lidios—it must burn him like a hot coal up his butt to pay this guy."

Kheperu coughed significantly. Barra turned back around to find the tall trader in the brown cloak standing at the open end of the table. He gave the two a minimally correct bow.

"Kheperu. Barra. May I sit?"

Barra inhaled deeply through her nose, but any scent of the man that might have carried in the thick air of the common room was masked by the heavy perfume of crushed amber. His face was skeletal, cheekbones standing like knife blades, his skin fair—and his eyes were blue. "Murso," Barra mused. "Your name's Phoenikian, and so is your accent, but your face isn't."

The man's thin lips stretched into a humorless smile. "Murso is not my name," he explained softly. "I represent House Meneides."

"You have," Barra said, "my complete attention. What should I call you?"

"Murso will do, for now. May I sit?"

"Please," Kheperu said expansively, "make yourself at home. My table is your table. Lidios! More beer!" He winked broadly at Barra and mouthed: *Finally!*

Murso slid onto the bench next to Kheperu. "Will you summon the Athenian? I have business to discuss."

Barra squinted at Leucas. He was on his feet now, drunkenly pantomiming a jab-jab-hook combination to a chorus of admiring laughter from the Akhaians: she guessed he was telling the bear story. She shook her head. "Make your offer. He'll stand by whatever deal I strike."

She watched him closely as she said this. The man calling himself Murso had a good trade-face, but she could see the slightest widening of his eyes as he took this in. "Really?" he said slowly. He turned to Kheperu. "And you, as well?"

Kheperu shrugged. "Of course."

"It doesn't bother you to have a woman do your speaking?"

Barra smiled thinly. Kheperu edged away from Murso, drawing himself out of the line Barra might swing an axe through.

She said calmly, "In my homeland, men and women are judged more by their abilities than by their genitals. Does this bother you, to deal with a woman?"

Murso lifted an eyebrow consideringly. "I suppose . . . a deal is a deal, isn't it? Regardless of whom it is made by."

Kheperu breathed a sigh and visibly relaxed. "Where's that beer?" He called, "Lidios! Beer!"

"All right, Murso, let's deal. What do you want us to do?"

He leaned toward her and spoke rapidly in a low tone, barely moving his lips. "In Tyre, lately, there have been any number of mysterious . . . difficulties. Unexplained fires, mysterious deaths, caravans delayed or diverted, murders without motive. Idonosteus believes that one of the Great Houses is fomenting war; he believes, specifically, that the House responsible has employed a sorcerer or group of sorcerers to weaken its intended victims and turn them against one another. There are no reliable indications which House is behind it; one act will point to one House, the next to another, the following to a third. The situation is volcanic; open war may erupt at any time. Idonosteus believes that if the sorcerer can be found and his affiliation uncovered, the worst effects of war can be averted. The other Houses will join together to destroy the offender with minimum disruption of trade."

"Do you want him only found? Or do you want him dead?"

"Barra?" Kheperu said, looking off across the room.

"Don't bother me, I'm doing business. Well, Murso?"

The man smiled appreciatively. "You're correct; Idonosteus wishes to hire you to find this sorcerer. But only to find him; his death may alert the Great House at his back, and precipitate the war we're attempting to avoid."

Barra thought of Othniel. "Dangerous work," she said.

"You are mercenaries, aren't you? You'll be well paid."

"Barra," Kheperu said more urgently, "you might want to watch this."

She ignored him. "How well paid?"

"How much do you want?"

"A round hundred."

Murso shrugged. "Shekels," he offered.

Barra snorted, "Egyptian debens. Do I look cheap?"

"Athenian large."

Barra pretended to think it over, then smiled. "Done."

Kheperu put his hand on Barra's arm. "Listen, your boyfriend Chrysios is about to get a new arsehole carved across his belly. Don't you want to watch?"

"What?" She looked up, finally.

The common room had gone very quiet without her taking notice. Chrysios was standing, swaying drunkenly, facing the Jephunahi tax collector. He had one hand on Lidios' chest, holding a handful of the publican's greasy apron, and he seemed to be making a speech, slurring his words and spraying spit. ". . . Just don't think y'should pay this goatfucker, thass all! Whadder y'paying him for? Huh? What work does he do? Howz he earn it? Suck your cock in the alley?"

Lidios was sweating profusely. "Your pardon, Melchazar," he said hastily. "He's drunk, and you know what Akhaians are like with too much wine in their bellies. Please don't hurt him—I haven't had a killing here in weeks."

"Hurt me?" Chrysios wheeled unsteadily on Lidios. "Hurt me? Who's gonna hurt me?"

Men were drifting toward the scene from around the room. Barra thought: *He didn't seem this drunk when he came in . . .*

She stood up on her bench. She called, "Hey, Chrysios! Add a little water, huh? Come on over here!"

"Here?" Murso said dubiously.

"Shh," Barra hissed. "I'm trying to save his life."

Chrysios peered around the room until he finally located her. "I'll deal with you later, woman!"

"I strongly suggest," the tax collector said silkily, "that you take the lady's suggestion. Or I may be forced to have my two companions here"—indicating the pair of armed and armored guards—"quiet you down."

"Oh yeah? Oh yeah?" Chrysios held his belly as though he were either about to burst into laughter or be violently ill. "Well, try it, then. Go on, try it! *Now!*"

The onlookers that had been drifting toward the scene suddenly sprang on the guards. One man pinned each guard's arm from behind, while others produced gleaming bronze daggers and, with very professional speed and economy of movement, cut the guards' throats. Chrysios straightened up; when his hands left his belly one of them had a knife in it, and he didn't look drunk at all. He drove the knife into the belly of the tax collector, sawing upward with a sound like the tearing of wet cloth. The tax collector made a high, confused squealing noise as he looked down at his intestines uncoiling onto the floor. The two guards spun in staggering circles, air whistling through the red-lipped lunatic's grins that opened beneath their chins, spraying blood. Chrysios stepped back neatly as the tax collector collapsed slowly to his knees, still trying to gather up his entrails with both hands.

There came a moment of stunned, motionless quiet in the common room while everyone watched the three Jephunahi die. Barra's eyes drifted closed as she shook her head disgustedly. "God damn shit," she said heavily, her words carrying clearly in the silence. She opened her eyes and spoke softly to Murso. "Excuse me."

She stepped up onto the tabletop. She counted six of them, all told, two for each of the guards and another who'd been coming up behind the tax collector. "Chrysios!" she shouted. He turned toward her, his arm drenched crimson to the elbow, the hem of his overrobe dripping blood. She said, "Nice moves, you son of a *whore!*"

With the last word she smoothly drew the throwing axe at her right side and hurled it overhand; he saw it coming and dodged, but he couldn't avoid the second axe, coming side-arm with a left-handed throw, that whirled toward him while the first was still in the air. It struck him just below the breastbone and he folded around it with an agonized outrush of breath.

The common room exploded into action.

Whores and patrons dove for the floor or jumped up, screaming, running for the street door. Lidios clutched at Chrysios, who drove him back with a slash of his knife that opened a long diagonal gash across the publican's chest; Lidios fell back, squealing and holding himself to stem the streaming blood. Murso slid beneath the table as Kheperu struggled to get clear, staff in hand. "Barra, damn your eyes!" Kheperu shouted. "Warn me before you start something!"

Every year, when springtime brought Barra to Knossos for the Cretan Trade Fair, she'd arrive several weeks early to practice and train with the bulldancers, the sacred acrobats who tumbled about the horns of bulls in celebration of the heritage of Minos. She was, compared to them, a bit old and a bit slow—she'd never quite had the courage to perform the bulldance with them—but she kept up her practice, and incorporated some of those skills into her fighting style; by the standards of the wider world, she could do some spectacular things.

Barra leaped from the table and somersaulted over the triclinium wall to the next booth. She landed on the table there, which tipped and dumped her to the floor, but she was ready for that: she landed catlike on her feet and sprang back over the downed table, drawing her broadaxe, leaving the table on its side before her as a wall to hold off the two assassins who now charged toward her.

Unlike Kheperu, Leucas needed no warning. When Barra had thrown her axes, he'd leaped to his feet and picked up the huge oaken table he'd shared with the Akhaians. Now he roared *"Athene!"* and thundered across the common room like an oncoming avalanche, the table held before him as a battering ram, crashing through the struggling mass of patrons to slam into the three assassins between him and Chrysios. Two of them went spinning to the ground on either side; the third, less fortunate, was borne backward into the hearth-shrine and fell across it, screaming as the coals set fire to his clothes and seared his flesh. Leucas held him pinned there for a moment, his drunken battle lust making him laugh like a demented god.

Chrysios yanked the throwing axe out of his belly; some blood flowed through the rent in his chiton, but not much: he must have worn light armor beneath his clothing, perhaps a girdle of boiled leather. His gaze fixed on Barra and rage twisted his face beyond recognition. As he charged, screaming like a mandrill, Kheperu skipped toward him, unexpectedly nimble for such a short fat man. His staff whickered down to rap Chrysios sharply on the shin and send him sprawling. The Corinthian turned the sprawl into a clumsy shoulder roll and came up swinging. Kheperu retreated, parrying the slash with the middle of his staff, between his hands; his counterstrike thumped Chrysios on the hip without apparent effect. The Corinthian advanced on him, long knife reversed in his left hand so that the blade lay flat along his forearm, held high to defend his head and chest, the axe in his right swirling and slashing. Once Kheperu blocked the axe and committed to a head strike, hoping to drive through Chrysios' guard; the Corinthian ducked the blow and slashed with the knife, slicing through Kheperu's layered robes and deeply scoring the thick leather beneath. Without that armor Kheperu might well have joined the tax collector on the floor—he swore silently that if this bastard killed him, his shade would haunt Barra to an early grave.

Barra had trouble of her own: the two assassins weren't fools enough to clamber over the downed table too close to her—wide two-handed strokes of her broadaxe assured that—but now they split to either side to come at her over the walls of the neighboring booths. If she turned to strike at one of them, the other would be over the wall to stab her from behind in an instant; if she left her improvised fort, the two of them with their knives—lighter weapons, much faster than her axe—could cut her to ribbons on the open floor. She backed toward the wall, trying to watch both of them, and someone on the floor behind her wrapped arms around her knees. She shouted wordlessly as she swayed and almost fell. Instinctively, she glanced down: a trader who had hidden beneath the table she had toppled now crouched low, clutching her knees in supplication. *"Leave off, y'bastard!"* she shrilled, her sudden panic returning her to her native tongue. *"Let me go!"* The trader, likely hearing Pictish for the first time, only held her tighter.

Even that swift glance nearly cost her life. Only a flicker of motion in her peripheral vision warned her in time to sway back from the assassin's knife that came stabbing at her throat over the wall. She cut at his arm but only grazed it, not even drawing blood; she caught a glimpse of cross-hatched leather strips that wrapped his forearms. She entertained an instant's notion to simply kill the whoreson who held her, but even that second's work could be fatal. Her desperation left her only one option: she drew her lips back from her teeth and gave a piercing whistle. She wrenched around in the trader's grip to face the assassin nearest to the street door, still whistling sharply. The assassin at her back never saw what hit him.

As he leaned over the wall to stab at her, Graegduz slammed into his back like a grey thunderbolt. The impact of the wolf's leap drove both of them over the wall, tumbling into a scrabbling tangle at Barra's feet. The wolf rolled away, scrambling to get upright; the assassin had time only to look up and see the edge of Barra's broadaxe an instant before it was buried in his skull. A twisting wrench splintered bone and freed the axe; the assassin's mangled brain gleamed wetly through the wound.

The other assassin stared wide-eyed at his companion's shuddering corpse, and made a gagging sound.

Barra hefted her bloodstained axe, a few shards of bone still clinging to the smooth basalt. She tasted blood when she smiled at him. "That's one," she said in Phoenikian. "Now it's just you and me."

He leaped off the bench and broke for the door.

Graegduz started after him. Barra commanded him sharply in Pictish to guard the door; she didn't want the wolf to get sliced up bringing down the fleeing man—better to have him in a position to give warning if the assassin summoned reinforcements.

The merchant who clung to her legs sobbed and shook. Barra clubbed a fist and pounded at the back of his neck until his grip began to loosen. She looked for her companions as she struggled free. Kheperu seemed to be holding his own, his staff blurring in defense against Chrysios' knife-and-axe combination.

Leucas was in trouble.

The table he'd used as a ram lay atop the booth walls on the far side of the room, below a wide splintered dent on the wall; she guessed he'd been trying to swing it as a weapon and had lost his grip. Now, unarmed he was caught between two assassins, while a third, clothes still smoldering, clambered to his feet. His battle-rage enhanced by the huge amount of wine he'd drunk, he seemed blind to the third man joining his opponents. His left hand, extended for defense, caught at the tunic of one of the assassins; the assassin made the mistake of cutting at the Athenian's forearm instead of raising his guard, and Leucas' huge fist blurred into a right cross that snapped the assassin's head back with an audible *crack!*

Someday, Barra thought as she overtopped the downed table with a smooth dive roll, came to her feet and sprinted toward him, *charging into the midst of his enemies is going to get him killed.*

Leucas spun like an athlete throwing the discus, whirling the limp body of the assassin in a wide arc to crash into his companion; they both went down in a skidding heap. But the third assassin, the smoldering one, lunged at the Athenian's unprotected back with both knives. Barra screamed, *"Behind you!"*

Leucas turned: right onto the blades.

She skidded to a stop as he took both knives low in the belly. Leucas roared his berserk joy and seized the assassin by the shoulders, lifting him off the ground and shaking him like a dog killing a rat. Sharp dismay drove the breath from Barra's chest and sudden hot tears started in her eyes: men don't survive deep belly wounds. Leucas might breathe a few more days, but he was already dead.

It didn't seem possible.

She swept the tears from her eyes with a quick hard shake of her head, then turned and ran toward Kheperu. He, at least, might still be saved.

Fat beads of sweat rolled down Kheperu's face as he blocked and parried furiously. Chrysios was no mere barroom thug: he was a highly skilled professional killer who attacked with lightning speed that rivaled Barra's, and greater strength. Chips flew from Kheperu's staff every time he blocked a slash of the axe; the staff itself was weakening, flexing dangerously against every blow. His counterstrikes were limited to occasional raps at Chrysios' knuckles and forearms, trying to disarm him. He'd gotten in a poke or two at Chrysios' ribs, stabbing the staff like a spear, but now he was backed against a wall and had no clearance as Chrysios pressed him. To extend for a swing at the Corinthian's body or head would buy Kheperu a split skull or a span of bronze between his ribs. He glimpsed the vivid red of Barra's hair as she came up behind Chrysios, and his face suddenly split into a broad grin.

"What's so funny, dead man?" Chrysios rasped.

Barra said, "I am."

Chrysios whirled instantly, the axe whistling through a downward cut at the joining of Barra's neck and shoulder. Kheperu poked the end of his staff into the weapon's arc from behind, catching the axe's haft below the flint head, for an instant holding the Corinthian wide open.

More than an instant, Barra would never need.

Her broadaxe whirled up through that same vicious underhand she'd used on the bear and hacked into Chrysios' groin. The boiled leather beneath his chiton slowed it no more than did his pelvic bone; the axe chopped up into his belly and emptied his guts onto the floor. His eyes bulged, and he swung the knife in his other hand in a last desperate attempt to take her with him into the Grey Lands, but behind him Kheperu had reversed his staff and struck the blade away to clatter against a wall.

Barra braced one foot against his chest and yanked her axe free. Chrysios swayed, his face drained of blood.

"To answer your question?" she said. "Ay, I can swing it, too."

Chrysios crumpled, slowly, his face showing uncomprehending disbelief.

She turned, seeking other opponents. Leucas still held the man who had stabbed him: one hand tangled in the man's hair, the Athenian held the assassin's head facedown in the hearthshrine, still laughing that demented roar, oblivious of the blood from his belly that painted his thighs.

He caught her eye. "One of mine got away!"

"I'm on it," she answered. She turned to Kheperu and said more softly, "See if there's anything you can do for Leucas." Then she sprinted out the door, calling for her wolf.

Kheperu spent a moment leaning on his staff—which

bowed under his weight, he'd have to cut a new one—
breathing heavily in the sudden silence. People began to tentatively move out from their shelter under tables, looking
about cautiously to reassure themselves that the killing was
over. Lidios sat on the floor, his back against a wall, holding
his bleeding chest and cursing steadily in a low monotone.
Leucas lifted the assassin he held out of the hearthshrine, grinning; the man's face was half burned away. "You can carve
this roast," he said laughingly. "He's done." He dropped the
corpse at his feet.

Kheperu made a quick survey of the bodies. Chrysios was
unconscious and dying; the man whose skull Barra had split
was well dead; another lay on the floor a few feet from the
hearthshrine, his neck broken by Leucas' punch.

"Leucas," Kheperu said gently, moving toward him,
"you're hurt."

"Nonsense," Leucas said heartily. He lifted the hand with
which he'd held the assassin's head in the fire. The skin was
reddening, but not charred or even scorched. "See? Just a
little broiled, that's all."

Eerie, resonant laughter came from behind him. Kheperu whirled, bringing up his staff, but a moment later he
realized that the laughter came from Chrysios, still lying on
the floor. The Corinthian writhed in pain, his back arching as
he convulsed, blood pouring from his mouth, yet still he
laughed; the sound raised prickling hairs on the back of
Kheperu's neck.

"You think you've killed me." The voice that came from
Chrysios then was thick and choked, but still somehow chill-
ingly potent. Kheperu scowled and plodded over to him.

His eyes were open, but they rolled blindly at the ceiling.
"I can never die!" His neck twisted with more gurgling
laughter.

"Really?" Kheperu said tiredly. He reached within his robe
and brought out one of the black, tarry balls. He murmured
the charm under his breath as his thumbnail scraped away a
strip of the tar. The ball began to smoke.

"Never! Never! Nev—"

Kheperu crouched and tucked the ball into Chrysios' open
mouth. "Shut up," he said. He turned and walked back toward
Leucas; a moment later there came a muffled, wet *whumpf*
and a burst of flame as the ball exploded, then a scattering of

clicks as fragments of Chrysios' jaw and teeth hit the floor around the common room.

Leucas looked slightly green. "Why'd you do that?"

Kheperu shrugged, looking numbly at the sluggish crimson that flowed from Leucas' belly. "I didn't like him. Now, come on, you'd better sit down over here," he said, taking the big man's arm. "I'll see what I can do for your wounds."

"I told you, I'm all right!"

Kheperu looked down. "No. You're not."

Leucas followed his gaze. "Oh," he said softly. "Oh, my. I barely felt it. Oh, damn."

CHAPTER FIVE

Secrets

The moon, still three-quarters full, cast an oyster-shell glow on the streets and limned shadows black as holes into nothingness. Barra walked slowly, head down, sick at heart. The splattered wash of blood drying on her face and arms, and across her thighs—none of it hers—itched and flaked away as she rubbed at it. Graegduz kept pace at her side, looking up at her occasionally, crooning low-voiced whimpers of concern. Ahead of her, the assassin she had captured also whimpered, tears rolling down his face as he dragged the corpse of his companion by the heels, the dead man's head bumping along the street.

The two who had run away had gotten only a few heartbeats' head start: they'd had no chance to escape. Barra had loped along the moonlit streets, Graegduz ranging slightly ahead. When she'd caught sight of the trailing assassin, a simple Pictish command to the wolf, "Ankle," had sent Graegduz streaking toward him. The wolf's grip on the assassin's ankle brought the man crashing to the street; Barra killed the man with a single stroke of her axe, hardly breaking stride. She'd spared the second for no reason other than that she didn't want to drag both corpses back to Lidios' inn by herself; she'd kill him once they got there. Why work harder than she absolutely must? It wasn't like she was being paid for this.

It was my duty, she told herself. *What else could I have done?* Arawn, Lord of the Grey Lands, required of his children that they suffer no murderer to live to slay again, or so the druids taught. But she could have waited, she could have hunted them as she'd done to others in the past, caught them one at a time.

No matter how she might twist or turn to evade it, the

simple truth was that she'd lost her temper, and now Leucas must pay for that with his life.

Damn you, Chrysios, you bastard! May the Ravens of Arawn tear at your soul for a thousand years! If only he hadn't been so damned beautiful! She well knew that she'd lost her temper like that because she'd been attracted to him; she didn't often meet men who caused her pulse to quicken, and now when she did, he turned out to be a damned bloody-handed murderer.

Now she could see the lamplight spilling out from the door of Lidios' inn. The stew she'd eaten tried to rise back up her throat; she had to swallow hard before she could speak.

"Take him inside," she told the assassin. "And remember, I'm right behind you."

"Don't kill me," he whimpered. "Don't kill me."

"Move."

Murso stood anxiously by the door, peering out from beneath his hood. His eyes widened when she entered behind the crying assassin. He touched her arm and hissed urgently, "We must leave here. We should go immediately."

She ignored him, saying to the assassin, "That's far enough. Lie on the floor, facedown, hands behind your neck."

The corpse's feet thumped to the floor; the assassin looked at her with tearful eyes. "I didn't hurt anybody . . ."

"Get down and live a few minutes. Stand and die now."

He got down.

Murso's grip on her arm tightened. "Barra, it is essential that—"

"You don't want to touch me right now."

His hand dropped, but he persisted. "If you're going to work for me, you must learn to follow my orders!"

"Teach me later."

She moved away, leaving him standing by the door clenching his fists in frustration.

The common room was littered with corpses, and the air was thick with the slaughterhouse stink of blood and shit. All the patrons had left. A slave dabbed at the blood that still flowed sluggishly down Lidios' chest. Kheperu bent over the body of Chrysios; he'd removed the chiton and light under-armor and was examining the corpse with great attention. Leucas sat on a stool, his back against the wall. His face was grey and drawn, as he bound his own wounds with ragged strips of linen. The pink tip of his tongue showed at the corner of his mouth as he tied off the bandage with drunken concentration. She had to step over two bodies to make her way to Kheperu. Graegduz nosed at one, and dipped his head to lap at the blood. When she told him sharply to get out of that, Kheperu raised his head at the sound of her voice.

"Barra." His voice held crisp excitement, and he beckoned to her. "Here, come here, I have something to show you."

She crouched next to him, looking at Leucas, and said softly, "How bad is he?"

"Leucas? Forget him, he's fine. The knives didn't penetrate his abdominal wall," Kheperu said impatiently. "Look at this." He lifted Chrysios' lifeless left arm, but she ignored it. She rocked back on her heels.

"How do you *know*? How do you know he's all right?"

Kheperu gave her an exasperated look. "Plenty of onions in that stew he's been packing away all day long, aren't there? Sniff the wounds for yourself." He shook his head and muttered something about "ignorant savages."

"Leucas?" she said wonderingly. "You're all right?"

Leucas' bloodshot eyes gradually focused on her. "I'll live."

In an eye blink she was at his side, her arms thrown around his chest. He felt solid, warm, and very alive. "Loving Mother, I thought you were dead for sure! You must be the luckiest bastard who ever lived!"

Leucas blinked slowly and said with sodden dignity, "Weapons often do not bite me as deeply as they do other men." He smiled weakly. "Although I do think I owe a bull to Athene for this one."

Barra laughed, a small chuckle that swelled to a shout of joy. "I can't believe it!" She shook her head sharply, and her gaze fell on two knives that lay on the floor near the hearthshrine, and her laughter trailed off to awed silence.

One of them was *bent*.

She let go of him and walked toward the knives slowly, with great care, as though she expected the floor to give way beneath her at any step.

"Barra?" Leucas asked. "Is something wrong?"

She bent down and brushed her fingers along the bent knife, its blade stained with blood. *Someone stepped on it,* she thought. *That's it; that must be it. It bent in the middle— this had to be the result of being stepped on. . . . And the*

point—the point of the other knife as well—was rounded, and
blunted, as though it had been driven into stone. *These
probably aren't even the same knives,* she told herself. These
probably belonged to one of the other assassins. But when
she looked from the blunted and bent blades to the puzzled
expression on Leucas' face, she was powerfully struck by the
realization of how little she actually knew of her companions.

Since their meeting and their decision to travel together,
two months before, Barra had been constantly aware of
keeping her own secrets from Leucas, and later from Kheperu. She had told them little of her family and her life in the
Isle of the Mighty; when she had, she'd always carefully
made sure they thought she was playing her game of Tall
Tale. She'd told them nothing of her sons, or her share in the
ships, nor of the merchant fleet she dreamed of building;
she'd barely told them three words of her whole life. With so
many secrets to keep, it had never occurred to her that her
companions might have secrets of their own.

Now they both stared at her as she crouched there by the
hearthshrine. She felt a dizzying alteration of perception, as
though she'd been hit by one of her grandmother's spells. This
new awareness was so potent that it verged on pain; for the
first time, regarding them, she became aware of them as
people, as human beings with lives and histories of their own,
completely separate from hers. Up to now, she realized,
Leucas and Kheperu had inhabited her life only as surface figures, as a collection of characteristics like painted heroes in a
Cretan fresco. In her mind, this man had been Leucas the Warrior, strong and slow of speech, faithful and none too bright.
The other had been Kheperu the Pervert, greedy and clever, an
adventurer who fought only to finance his disgusting tastes.
She had made of them archetypes, familiar characters from a
campfire legend. This sudden shift felt like awakening from a
long dream; now she saw, stretching behind them, the vague
ghosts of their experiences, the choices and turns of chance
that had brought them here, that had made them what they are.
This seeing was not visual; their appearance had not changed.
The change was somewhere within her, in how she looked at
them: she saw them with new eyes.

Sceon tiof, she thought. *Loving Mother, it's the sceon tiof!*
Barra's heart pounded, and she dug her knuckles fiercely into
her eyes. Coll, her mother, was well-known for it, this power to

see into the makings of a man, but it was no skill for a warrior. Among the Old Tribes in the Isle of the Mighty, the *sceon tiof* was revered, a gift from the Mother that could mold a blood-mad tyrant into a wise and gentle king; for one who makes her living as a warrior, it could cripple as surely as an axe to the hamstring. She pressed her hands against her head, the hafts of the knives she held digging into her temples. The dizzying spin of perception faded, and her breath began to ease.

She opened her eyes and glared blankly at the floor. An offering . . . she'd best make some offering to the Mother, and soon; the gods take it ill when their gifts are refused.

She shook her head again, as though throwing off a dream, and stood up.

Kheperu asked, "Is something wrong? Are you hurt?"

"No," she said. "I just got a little dizzy for a moment. What was it you wanted to show me?"

He beckoned her over once again; she casually dropped the pair of knives into the hearthshrine. The hearthshrine of a Tyrian household is never extinguished—by the time someone fished those knives out again, this fight would be old news, and there'd be no way to connect those bent and blunted blades to Leucas.

She knew how to keep others' secrets, as well as her own.

Now as she stood over Kheperu she saw the mangled ruin that had been Chrysios' face. She winced and looked away. *So much for being handsome,* she thought. "What did you do to him?"

"I blew his face off," Kheperu said briskly. "It's not important now. Look at this!"

He lifted Chrysios' left arm. On its pale underside near thearmpit, half hidden by the silken gold of his underarm hair, was a figure designed in careful tattoo:

"Another Egyptian glyph," Barra said.

"Just like Othniel," Kheperu agreed. He lowered his voice and gestured for Barra to crouch beside him. "Well, not just like: the location, of course, is different, as is the method. Othniel was branded; this is a tattoo, a much more tedious, and ultimately more painful, process. Furthermore, it's not difficult to brand a man against his will, but if you notice how clean and precise the line of this glyph is, you must conclude it was done either while Chrysios was unconscious, or with his willing cooperation."

"And it's a different glyph. What's this one mean?"

"Oh yes, well, there is that. It means: Destroy."

Barra rubbed her face with both hands. "So," she said slowly, "you're thinking that Chrysios is—was—a henchman of whoever it was that did that to Othniel."

"To you, Barra," Kheperu said solemnly, "my mind must be as an open book."

"An Egyptian sorcerer."

Kheperu raised a pedantic finger. "A sorcerer using Egyptian magic. Whether or not he, himself, is of my race, is an open—"

"You know what I'm thinking?" she interrupted.

Her tone warned him. "No . . ." he said warily.

"I'm thinking that we've just been hired to locate a sorcerer who's been stirring up trouble in Tyre. I'm thinking that we could have questioned Chrysios—he would have lived long enough that we'd've probably found out who this guy is and where he lives . . . if some *idiot* hadn't *blown his face off!*" She punctuated her statement with a hard shove that sent Kheperu sprawling across the gore-smeared floor.

He levered himself up onto his elbows. "Perhaps I was a little impulsive. . . . You, on the other hand, have always been the very model of self-restraint."

She stood and looked around the room. "Just count yourself lucky there's nothing within arm's reach that I can throw at you," she muttered. It was difficult to fight down a creeping grin, though; against her will, she found herself in the grip of a cheerful mood. Forget the bloody carnage around them; she and her partners were alive, they'd won, and—most important—they had a job.

Murso came toward her, fastidiously skirting the corpses,

robes gathered in his hands to keep their hems above the blood. "I insist that we leave this place," he said urgently.

She raised a hand to acknowledge him, and turned her face toward Leucas. "Are you mobile?"

He nodded solemnly. "I should go to our room," he said, patting the bandage around his midsection. "I'll need to sew these cuts."

"Later. Lidios? Are we square?"

"Square? You're asking me if we're square?" The fat publican's voice was a pale shadow of its usual outraged bellow. He tried to push himself to his feet, there against the wall, but his hands were occupied in pressing his wadded apron against the long slash that divided his chest, and he sagged down once again. "Oh, bloody fuck," he said weakly. "I suppose we are. I'm too bloodyfucking tired to scream at you for tearing up my house and trying to get me killed."

"You better have somebody stitch up that wound," she said.

He shrugged. "Lenka—one of my girls—she was a camp follower with the League of Five Cities; she picked up a bit of surgery."

"All right, good. Listen, we're going to clear out of here. Anyone who comes asking for us, or asking about the fight, you don't know where we've gone. Have a couple of your girls pack up our gear—we'll be back tomorrow or the next day to collect it. And to drop a shekel or two into your hand for your trouble."

"A shekel or two? That's what a mugful of my blood is worth? A *shekel*?"

"Anyone who does ask about us? If you get names and where to find them, that'll be worth a few shekels, too."

She turned her back on his grumbling and helped Kheperu to his feet. He indicated her hand and suggested she should wash it; she rubbed her palm on her chiton. A bit of searching located her throwing axes. She wiped them, and her broadaxe, clean on the tax collector's clothing, then returned them to her belt.

"Well, Murso? We're ready."

"Ready for what?" Leucas asked, using the chair to push himself upright.

Barra waved him off. "I'll explain on the way."

Murso pursed his lips, and twitched half a nod toward the surviving assassin. "What about him?"

The man was still facedown on the floor, fingers laced behind his head. His back trembled with an occasional sob. Barra spat on the floor and moved toward him, drawing her broadaxe. "I'll take care of it."

Leucas said, "Barra, wait."

"What?"

"You can't just kill him. Not while he's helpless."

"Why not?"

"At least give him a chance to defend himself."

"He's a murderer," Barra explained patiently. "Those Jephunahi had no chance—there was no challenge, no warning. They might as well have been poisoned. The Grey Lord demands his life."

At this, the assassin cried out, "But I didn't kill *anyone*! I didn't even draw blood!" To Barra's surprise, he spoke in Greek—he must have understood the whole conversation.

Leucas came toward her, his palms up and faced toward her. He patted the air with a *Be calm, now* gesture. "If you kill him while he's helpless, what does that make you?"

"An executioner."

"I swear I hurt no one!" the assassin said, still in Greek. "May Zeus Skyfather, keeper of men's oaths, strike me dead with his thunderbolt if I so much as bloodied my knife!"

Leucas reached down and took the man's wrist, hauling him easily up to his knees. He peered into the assassin's tear-streaked face. "Are you Akhaian, son?"

He nodded, wiping snot from his upper lip with his sleeve. "My name's Mykos, lord—I was born in Thebes."

Barra said, "He's lying. He would have been, what, three? Thebes was sacked sixteen years ago." Thebes had been put to the torch, its men slaughtered, women and children slaved, by the combined armies of Athens and the Epigoni, the sons of the seven great heroes who had fallen before those walls in a war some five years earlier. The victorious Thebans had dishonored the corpses of their enemies, and for that crime had paid with all they had: their city, their lives, and the lives of their sons.

"I know that, Barra." Some haunting memory hovered behind the Athenian's eyes. "I was there," he said softly. "My mother's brother and his four sons fought for Kreon, against us."

He paused, and Barra wondered if he saw within his mind

the leaping flames and greasy, pork-scented smoke of the funeral pyres that must have ringed the city when all its men were put to the sword. Finally he continued, "If he escaped the sack, that would explain why his accent's not Theban, as he grew up in a foreign land, away from all his kin."

Barra scowled. "That doesn't change what he is, or what he's done."

"No, I suppose it doesn't," Leucas said heavily. He turned away. "Do what you must, but I'll not watch."

"Please," Mykos whimpered. "Please . . ."

Barra looked into his face, saw the youth there, saw the terror of death. Now he was no longer simply an assassin; the *sceon tiof* drew aside that veil. Against her will, she looked on him as hardly more than a boy, facing death in a foreign land. And she realized that he'd spoken the truth—he was the man who'd been coming up behind the tax collector when Chrysios stabbed him: he himself had harmed no one.

It makes no difference, she snarled mentally, drawing back her broadaxe. Mykos closed his eyes, tears leaking from beneath their lids. She remembered having seen him in the common room over the last three nights, eating and happily swilling beer; she remembered thinking that he wasn't much older than Chryl, her own son.

She spat a curse and threw the broadaxe to the ground before him. "Pick it up," she said, drawing the pair of smaller axes. "Go on, pick it up. *Fight* me, you bastard!"

He only pressed his eyes more tightly shut and continued to whimper.

"Shit." She placed her fists against her hips, and looked at Kheperu.

He spread his hands. "Your Grey Lord is your god, not mine."

Barra sighed and shook her head. "All right, you little limp-prick bastard, listen. In my land we sometimes allow a killer to pay wergild—to buy off his guilt. If you can tell me who was behind Chrysios, who he was working for and where to find him, I'll let you go."

"I don't know!" Mykos cried. "He hired me and my friends at the beach. I didn't see anyone else!"

Barra nodded disgustedly; she'd suspected that Chrysios had been too smart to trust any secrets to a third-rate street thug. "What am I going to do with you?"

Lidios called from behind her, "You could make him clean up this bloodyfucking mess! Little rat bastard—"

"That's an idea . . ." Barra said. "Ay, all right. Mykos, you're going to clean up all this, and . . . and serve Lidios here as a house slave for a . . . for *one year.* You will perform any task he gives you, no matter what it is, but you will never leave this house. If I ever see you on the street, or if I ever learn you've run off, I'll hunt you. And I'll find you. And when I do, I'll kill you. No begging, no tears—you won't have time for them. You won't even see me coming. One moment you'll be alive, the next you'll be dying. Painfully. You understand?"

"I understand." Mykos pitched forward and clutched her knees, his tearstained face slimy against her legs. "Thank you, mistress! Thank you!"

She kicked him off her, sending him sprawling. "Don't ever touch me, you pile of shit." She put away her axes and turned to Murso. "Let's get out of here before I throw up."

The *sceon tiof* showed her the boy's hurt and humiliation, and she felt their shadows on her spirit; she clutched her determination with both hands and said a silent prayer to the Mother, that she be relieved of this gift.

The tenement that loomed into the night sky before them might once have been the home of a wealthy landed family, a century or more ago. Successive generations of owners and tenants had built on to it haphazardly, connecting rooms to neighboring buildings; what once had been public thoroughfares around it had become mazy passageways, roofed by rickety floors of rooms above. The passageways were choked with piles of food scraps and the contents of chamber pots, as well as the pallets of men and women: many of the folk who lived here could not afford the price of a room of their own. The light onshore breeze that had followed the storm drew a stench from these passages as it would draw smoke from a chimney, a stench that could bring a retch to anyone's throat, saving only, perhaps, Kheperu; for Barra, it was nearly unendurable.

Murso moved across the street. He said, "Observe. You must do this whenever you return to this place after dark."

"Or?"

"Or the men who guard the place where you will be staying will try to kill you. They've had some trouble with thieves, and bandits; they care little for either."

He lifted his lamp high enough to illuminate his face and held it there for a long breath.

"How do you know they've seen it?"

"They have. Come."

He headed toward the dark mouth of a passage. Barra looked at her companions. Leucas shrugged; Kheperu gestured her onward with a slight, mocking bow.

On their long walk through the night-shrouded streets of Tyre, Barra had stuck closely to Murso, maneuvering herself to stay downwind. Soon she'd been able to get the man's scent, even through the perfume he wore. There was no immediate reason for this, beyond general principle; like the wolf who walked by her side, she could identify many of the people she met by smell alone, and she firmly believed that talents exist to be used. She noted that he favored food heavily spiced with tarragon. To give herself an excuse for walking so close to him, she'd kept up a conversation, pretending to seek information about the job. She found that he knew little he hadn't already revealed.

She changed the subject. "When do we get our front half?"

"I beg your pardon?"

"Half our pay. Up front, before we begin the job. That way, if something should happen—say, you're taken suddenly ill—we haven't done all our work, risked our lives, for nothing."

Murso looked offended. "You have the promise of House Meneides guaranteeing your pay."

"That's why I'm willing to trust you for the other half."

He sighed. "I will personally deliver silver equivalent to fifty Athenian weights into your hand tomorrow morning. Satisfied?"

Barra squinted at the sky as they walked along. "There seems to have been some misunderstanding about our deal. The hundred weights—that's *apiece*."

Murso stopped in his tracks and stared at her. He made a gargling noise, as though something was caught in his throat. "That's three hundred weights!"

Barra nodded. "That's the deal."

"That's *outrageous*!"

Behind him, Leucas and Kheperu looked at each other and grinned. Barra said, "Shh, people are trying to sleep."

"What service could possibly be worth three hundred weights?" Murso hissed.

"Well," Barra said slowly, "you saw our little scuffle at Lidios' house. You can take that as a guarantee that money paid us is a sound investment—we'll definitely survive to complete the job. The job itself, well"—she shrugged and puffed out her cheeks—"that's probably worth only, say, fifty apiece. The other half, you should think of as being the price of our silence. You said you didn't want the other Great Houses to learn of this; the extra fifty apiece assures that we won't be so strapped for cash that we have to sell some information to cover expenses."

"This is extortion."

"This is negotiation."

Murso scowled. "I will convey your ... offer ... to Idonosteus."

"You do that."

Now, as he led them along the mazy, evil-smelling passages, climbing stairs and turning corners, lamp held high to illuminate their progress, he said, "The men with whom you'll be staying are mercenaries like yourselves. They are trustworthy, and can be depended upon to conceal your presence here. Nonetheless, they are not to know of your mission."

"What should we tell them, if they ask?" Barra said.

"They will not," Murso said positively. "Only their captain has the Phoenikian tongue, and little enough of that. Have you three a common tongue beyond Phoenikian and Greek?"

Barra glanced at Leucas, and shook her head.

"Then I suggest that you limit your conversation to trivia."

Barra said, "Dozens of people saw you at our table. Someone may see us come and go here. How are we supposed to keep secret our connection?"

Murso smiled thinly. "My face is not generally known, nor is my association with Lord Idonosteus. I serve him in confidential matters only. These mercenaries have contact with him only through me, and they are neither sociable nor talkative. They, also, have been explicitly instructed to conceal their employment. Is that sufficient?" There was just enough extra emphasis there to betray impatience, nothing more.

"That'll do," Barra said.

As they rounded a corner into a short hall, a door ten paces ahead swung slowly open, spilling yellow lamplight that silhouetted a tall, broad-shouldered man, one hand holding a shortsword low and casual by his side. "Lysandros?"

"Yes," Murso said in Greek. "I've brought the guests you were told to expect."

The broad-shouldered man swung his body aside to clear the doorway. "They, and you, are welcome."

"Lysandros?" Barra whispered. "Is that your real name?"

Murso only smiled.

"Barra," Kheperu said softly, "we are being watched from both ends of this hall." Barra looked ahead and behind; ahead, through a crumbled hole in the far wall, she saw a glint that might have been eyes picking up lamplight.

"Do not worry," Murso told him. "They are archers who guard this hall. Now that they've seen you with me, you are in no danger."

Inside, the room was softly lit with a pair of large lamps. A number of straw-stuffed pallets—Barra counted twelve—covered the floor. Makeshift armor stands of rope-lashed pine lined the walls, most of them full. A few bits and pieces of bronze plating lay here and there about the room, near to pouches of fine sand and moistened rags. There was only one small table, set with a pelike and cups of fired clay. Seven men came to their feet when the companions entered; they, and the man who had opened the door, looked enough alike to be close cousins, if not brothers. They were all stocky, broadly built through the chest and shoulders, dark of hair, and wore close-trimmed beards over the heavy bones of their faces. The man who had opened the door was missing one ear, and had a long diagonal scar across his cheek that connected a white streak in his hair to one in his beard. "I am Kamades of Phthia," he said in formal Greek. "I invite you to share our food and wine."

Phthia? Barra's heart suddenly pounded, and she found herself short of breath. Was it possible? With great self-control, she introduced herself in equally formal fashion, and accepted.

Leucas said, "I am Leucas Deodakaides, of Athens. I am honored to accept."

Kheperu said nothing for a moment; Barra kicked him none too subtly in the shin. Akhaians hold the guest-host relationship to be nearly as sacred as the bonds of blood; even to hesitate could be taken as a deadly insult. He jumped at her kick, and said in his badly accented Greek, "I am Kheperu of Thebes."

Kamades' eyes widened in astonishment. "Thebes?"

"The *real* Thebes. Er, Thebes of Egypt," Kheperu amended hastily, then offered a small bow. "I am honored to accept."

Kamades gestured to one of the other men, who tore chunks from a loaf of hard bread and poured wine into four cups, handing one to Kamades and the other three to Barra and her friends. Together they poured a libation to the gods, wine splashing into little sawdust clots on the floor, then ate and drank.

Kamades set down his cup. "Lysandros. Is there word from Lord Idonosteus?"

"Only that your service is valued, and to hold yourself in readiness. Now, duty calls me to the side of my lord." Murso's response had the flavor of ritual formula.

Kamades held the door for him when he left.

These Phthian mercenaries were a strange and silent group; they passed their time as do any soldiers who must wait for action, telling stories, drinking, dicing, yet all their activities took place within a shell of hushed tranquillity. No voice was ever raised, in anger or in song, and even their laughter was muted. The only voice ever louder than a murmur was Kheperu's; he'd immediately joined a game of dice with three of them, near the window, and occasionally loudly exclaimed over his "unusual luck." Barra scowled; he was cheating, of course. He had a small pot of incense burning near his ankles—even though nearly all the smoke was drawn out the window, Barra knew its smell, and knew that the three men who were breathing it would see whatever number on the dice that Kheperu told them to see. She hoped he'd have the good sense not to win too much.

Kamades directed one of them, an older man with a grizzled beard and thinning hair, whose left forearm ended in a leather-bound stump, to tend Leucas' wounds. His name was Peroön, and he cleaned and stitched Leucas' wounds swiftly and neatly, packing them with cobwebs he carried in a pouch at his belt before bandaging them with fresh linen.

He pulled the last knot tight with his teeth and sat back on his haunches. "What god is it that stands at your side in battle, Leucas?" he said with a slim smile.

"God?" Leucas said, frowning.

"Come on, boy. Those were no ladylike little slices; they're stab wounds from somebody trying to empty your guts. Without a god to turn the blade, we wouldn't be having this talk, you follow?"

Leucas shrugged and shook his head. "I don't precisely know, unless it's Athene. I was born in her city."

Kamades spoke musingly from his seat at the table. "Leucas of Athens . . . I know you, I think. Weren't you charioteer to Pylaimenos?"

"I was, sir. Until Alexandros took his life with his cowardly arrow from the wall."

Kamades nodded. "I remember you from the funeral games for Patroklos. You boxed with Diomedes Tydeides." He smiled broadly. "He beat the snot out of you."

"Yes he did," Leucas said, returning his smile. He touched his nose and cheekbone. "He gave me my first two fractures. I didn't mind—it was honor enough even to step into the ring with the lord of Tiryns. Epeios revenged me, though, and took the prize. But I'm afraid, sir, that I don't recall you."

Kamades lifted his hands. "No surprise, Leucas. I was in the company of the Prince of Phthia and, well . . . wherever Lord Akhilleus stood, all eyes fixed on him."

"I well recall."

"You're *Myrmidons*!" Barra breathed. She'd suspected, even hoped, but still found it difficult to believe.

"Some name us so. We take it as a name of honor."

Kheperu looked up from his dice. "Ants?" he said in Egyptian. "What do you mean, they're ants?"

"It's just an expression," Barra snapped in the same language. "Shut up."

His fingers waggled an obscene gesture behind his back as he returned to his game. Barra once again barely managed to restrain the urge to throw something at him.

She could have sat all night and listened to them trade stories of the war. Leucas was in an unusually expansive mood—no doubt he was still a little drunk—and Kamades and Peroön and two or three of the other Myrmidons vied with each other in their storytelling, as men will do when they find a fresh and attentive audience. Barra wondered if it would always be this way, if Akhaians would define themselves by what they'd done at Troy—Akhaian men of a certain age, from their late twenties to their late fifties, all seemed to know with a simple look at one another, a silent *You were there, weren't you?* As if the Siege of Troy was the center of their lives; as if most of their lives had been spent there fighting on Skamander's banks. No matter that the siege lasted ten years, and most of these Myrmidons were near forty; Leucas had been twenty when he left for Troy, and thirty at the end, but the twenty years before the war were irrelevant, and the five years since were a slow slipping-down anticlimax.

Barra drank in every word of these tales; even ones she'd heard before brought a knife-edged pain to her breast and a glimmer of tears to her eyes. She'd seen her share of wars, and knew the truth of them, the dirty, bloody business, unheroic and terrifying—still, she wished with all her heart she could have seen this one. It was a childish longing, for something she couldn't have, but somehow, deep within her, there lived a hope that she'd never outgrow it.

Strangely, though, the Myrmidons' stories only rarely concerned foes they themselves had faced, or feats they had accomplished; they were always of the great heroes, usually of Akhilleus himself, some of Patroklos, or Aias, Diomedes, Agamemnon, Odysseus—as narrators they were self-effacing to the point of invisibility: ". . . and when Patroklos' spear drove into the joining of the shoulder and neck of Sarpedon the blood sprayed even across my legs, and as he fell the skies were torn with thunder and we all turned our faces up to taste the sudden tears of Zeus' grief for his son . . ."

Leucas, on the other hand, soon drifted into tales of his wanderings since the war, displaying surprising skill and lyricism. When he told the story of the Kyprian Boar Hunt, the Myrmidons began to give Barra curious sidelong glances. By the time he finished his rather embellished version of the fight at Lidios' house, their looks were of open puzzlement.

Finally, Kamades had to ask. "Is Barra your captain, then?"

Leucas blinked. "I never really thought about it," he said slowly. "In a way, I suppose, yes."

"Well," Kamades said, frowning, "is it her orders you follow? You take orders from a woman?"

Barra sighed. She'd really wanted to like this guy . . .

"No, not exactly . . ."

"Then, whose orders do you follow?"

"We don't exactly work that way," Leucas told him. "We never actually decided who's in charge."

The Myrmidons exchanged doubtful looks. "Then, how do you organize?" Kamades asked. "I don't understand."

Leucas turned his head to one side and thought for a moment. Then he said, "We each have our particular talents, you see. I'm very strong, and good with the spear or sword, or without weapon. I'm the best fighter, though we all give potent account of ourselves in battle. Kheperu is very clever, and he is skilled with powders and potions, at figuring things out, and making plans. Barra is, well . . ."—Leucas looked at her and shrugged—"well, she's Barra. She doesn't give us orders, but somehow we end up doing what she wants anyway. I fight. Kheperu calculates. Barra, well, leads."

Kamades scowled. "It's not natural."

Barra sat up, forcing an easy smile. "In what way, Kamades?" Her friendly tone and appearance of nonchalance would have been more convincing if Graegduz hadn't come to his feet, staring at Kamades and growling low in his throat. She put her arm around his shoulders and murmured in Pictish, "Be calm, Graeg, I'm not that angry yet."

"A man needs to know his place," Kamades said firmly. "My men, they take orders from me. I take mine from Lysandros. Lysandros serves Lord Idonosteus. It's the natural order of things."

Barra blinked. This wasn't about her sex? She squinted at him. "You're not really Akhaian, are you?"

"What do you mean? Are you trying to insult me?"

"No, no, Great Mother, no," Barra said hastily. "I'm just surprised, that's all. Tell me something, Kamades—what are you doing in Tyre?"

"Serving House Meneides," he answered simply.

"No, no, I know that. I mean, why did you come to Phoenikia? What made you leave Phthia?"

Kamades' voice went flat. "Lord Akhilleus led us to Troy." He held her eyes for a moment, then deliberately shifted his gaze to Graegduz. "This is a fine dog. What's his name?"

"He's not a dog, he's a wolf," Barra said dismissively. "What I meant was, why didn't you go back to Phthia after the war?"

Kamades nodded. "I have heard of wolves. How do you call him?"

"Look, forget the wolf, all right? I'm wondering—"

"Barra," Leucas interrupted.

"What?"

His answer was a long, significant look, a tilt of the head and lift of the brows.

"Oh, all right," she said disgustedly. She sighed. "His name's Graegduz."

"Grigdoozh," Kamades repeated. He looked politely interested. "Does that have a meaning?"

"Well, sort of. It's two Pictish words, kind of mashed together. *Graeg* means grey, and *greduz* means, like, hunger."

"Does he bite?"

Kamades himself and two of his men gave up their pallets to their guests. Most of the Myrmidons had settled in for the night, including four who came from outside in full armor. Peroön and the three men Kheperu had been dicing with armed themselves and went out. Kamades had extinguished one of the lamps and tucked the other's wick down within it, so that the room was only dimly lit. Barra lay on her stomach, absently ruffling Graegduz's fur. Her axes were carefully arranged under the pallet, so that she wouldn't cut her hand reaching for one in the dark. Leucas snored steadily but more softly than usual, a constant rumble that faded into the background of her consciousness. The sleeping Myrmidons made no noise at all.

Beside her, Kheperu rolled over and she saw that his eyes were open. He grinned at her.

"How much did you win?" she whispered in Egyptian.

He dug out a pouch and opened it, revealing a handful of the small, irregular coins. "Eighteen," he responded softly. "These poor shits are paid only a shekel a day; if I win too much, none of them will game with me."

"Lose it back."

"What?"

"Shh. I know how you were cheating; you've used that incense before. If you don't lose it back, I'll tell them. They won't just beat you bloody and take back the money. These are Myrmidons. They'll kill you."

"That's kind of harsh . . ."

She nodded. "You're a guest. Cheating your host is just as bad as murdering him in his sleep, as far as they're concerned. In fact, I think you'd better lose a few shekels of your own."

"You can be a real bitch sometimes, you know that?"

"You'd best believe it."

Kheperu thought about this in sullen silence for a while, then whispered, "Doesn't it worry you, to sleep in a room with a band of bronze-chewing mercenaries?"

"Not really," Barra said. "They won't try anything. And if one did, Graeg'd have his hand off before he could touch me. How do you think I survived on the road before I met you guys?"

Kheperu levered himself up onto his elbows and looked around at the sleeping Myrmidons, lips pursed musingly. "Still, there are twelve of them . . ."

Barra chuckled softly. "From what I've heard about Phthians—Myrmidons especially—you have more to worry about than I do."

Kheperu sighed, smiling wistfully. "I should be so lucky."

"Get some sleep," she told him, rolling onto her back. "Tomorrow morning, we're going to work."

Barra was up with the dawn. She looked at the Myrmidons, who were awakening about her, and she gingerly squinted and otherwise felt around in her head, searching apprehensively for any sign of the *sceon tiof;* she found none. Perhaps the Mother had retrieved her gift—she breathed a little easier and again resolved to make an offering.

The watch had changed during the night: Kamades wasn't there. Peroön, who seemed to be his lieutenant, insisted on checking the status of Leucas' belly before he'd let them go out. He found no sign of suppuration, and Leucas maintained that he felt just fine, other than a massive headache from Lidios' wine.

Peroön shook his head, smiling. "You're healing well. No fighting though, or even heavy lifting, for at least a week; you'll tear the stitches. Give the flesh time to knit."

Leucas rumbled, "I'll try to avoid it. Sometimes, it's not up to me."

Peroön grinned broadly, and spread his hands. "You can always run away . . ."

There was an instant's shocked silence, then Leucas burst into roaring laughter and slapped Peroön on the back. "And folk say that Myrmidons have no sense of humor!"

The other Myrmidons joined his laughter, in their quietly restrained way, and Peroön said, "Truly, though, be careful. I did a fine job on those stitches, and like any craftsman I hate to see good work go to waste."

Barra told Graegduz to stay here and behave himself, and she promised to bring him some scraps from breakfast. He hunkered down sullenly, head on his front paws, but whined only a little as they left.

One of the Myrmidons led the three companions through a different winding way out from the building. The alleyway they came out in was empty, save only for the morning fog that swirled pearl-grey in the slanting sunlight.

They'd decided to breakfast at Lidios' house, and pick up their gear now, in the early morning, before the mist burned off and the streets became crowded. The mist would help them return with their possessions to the tenement without being seen; Barra didn't want anyone seeking revenge for the fight at Lidios' house to be led to the Myrmidons.

Only a few slaves moved about on the street before Lidios' inn; as the companions approached, they saw a pair of water-carriers pause to look at something over the door, then exchange a glance and hurry away with their heads down, making the horned-god gesture with their hands.

Barra muttered, "Oh, no," and broke into a run.

When Leucas and Kheperu caught up with her, she was standing in the street, looking up at a design that seemed to be burned into the very stone of the huge lintel. Barra recognized the twined-snakes sign of *Forever*, the upraised arms of *Soul*; the whole glyph was boxed within the representation of *House,* and her heart began to boil within her chest.

She didn't look around as Kheperu approached, only continued to stare at the design and said, "Does that shitcake thing mean what I think it means?"

Kheperu translated in a low voice: " 'This door is the threshold of the death eternal.' Oh, it's definitely a curse—that death being not only the death of your body, you understand, but a sort of infinite rotting of the *ka*—"

"Bastard," she interrupted harshly. "Fucking son of a whore."

Now she turned to look at them. Leucas gazed up at the design thoughtfully; Kheperu looked a little sick, sweat standing out on his forehead and cheeks.

She spat in the street. "Well, what are we waiting for? Let's go in."

CHAPTER SIX

The Prince

Haral Mesti paused before the gaily painted door to his prince's bedchamber to catch his breath and gather his courage. The bright paint of the door was shaded into silvery grey in the moonlight. The only sounds in the broad moonlit antechamber were his own harsh breathing and the high, thin sobs that came from beyond the door. In a way, those child-like sobs came as a relief; that meant the prince had one of the slave children in his bed this night. When there was no slave child within the prince's chamber, one always ran the risk of encountering Simi-Ascalon—even when a child was there, the risk was only lessened, not eliminated. Haral well knew that Simi-Ascalon was in town this night, supervising the laying of the curse upon that Jephunahi inn, but the nervous tightness in his guts did not abate; who knew what powers that man might have? If any man alive could be in two places at once, it would be Simi-Ascalon. Haral was as brave as most men, he thought, but no man could meet the dead-crocodile eyes of the prince's steward without a coil of fear twisting into his belly—especially if he encountered Simi-Ascalon after dark.

Haral moved on tiptoe to a nearby couch and lowered himself gingerly onto it; his heart froze as one of its joints creaked piercingly in the silence, but the sobbing within the bedchamber continued without pause, and now was joined by the low grunts of a man's voice in passion. Haral looked down at his hands; a shaft of pale moonlight fell across them, and they trembled like the wings of a moth in the wind. He clasped them together and pressed them between his knees.

Only four days ago, Haral had been followed by that Jephunahi fellow. He'd redeemed himself by sapping the man in an alley and delivering him to Simi-Ascalon, but he knew that he'd come close to disaster, that it was only by a whim of the prince that he himself had not ended his life on Simi-Ascalon's table. Now he arrived with more bad news; this is why his hands trembled so. But his faith in the prince's affection drove him to bring the news himself—it was this faith that passed for courage in Haral's character. And the prince's inspiration had turned the Othniel incident to his advantage. Perhaps he could do the same with this.

The grunting crested in a child's shriek of pain, then both faded to silence. Haral stood, taking a deep breath and coughing once to clear his throat. He knocked lightly upon the bedchamber door.

"My prince? It is Haral, with news."

The prince's voice came back thick and languid. "Go away, Haral. No news can be so important that it cannot wait for dawn."

"My prince, it is the Greek, Chrysios. He is dead."

"Dead?" The prince's shout came like a thunderclap. An instant later the bedchamber door was yanked open. The prince stood naked, his broad chest heaving, sweat glistening across his heavy muscles. Haral could not meet the lightning of his eyes, and so looked down; the prince's groin and trim flanks were painted black with blood.

"Tell me," he commanded.

Haral coughed. "He is dead; killed at the Jephunahi public house."

"That fool! What, did he attack the tax collector alone?"

Haral shook his head vigorously; when the prince was in a mood like this, Haral knew that he himself might pay a heavy price for Chrysios' mistake. "No, no, lord. He hired men, at least six; some tales say as many as fifteen."

"Some *tales*?" the prince repeated in a low and deadly tone. "You had best explain."

"It's the p-pub-talk tonight all over Tyre," Haral stammered. "Chrysios followed your command, and attacked the tax collector in a crowded public house, so that all could see. The tax collector is dead, and so are his guards, but those three mercenaries—you know, the ones you were interested in . . ." His voice trailed off.

Dark clouds gathered along the prince's brow. "The three foreigners? The ones who caught the bear?"

Haral took a step back; his legs trembled until his kneecaps jumped like a drop of water on a hot skillet. "Y-yes, my prince. The story is told that these three alone—and their dog, the girl is said to have a huge dog—killed Chrysios and all his men."

"So," the prince growled, "you say that instead of spreading a tale of madmen who do not blink at slaughtering Jephunahi tax collectors in a crowded pub, they are speaking of these mercenaries?"

"I, ah . . . well, yes, lord . . ." Haral fought desperately against the urge to flinch and cringe away from him, but the prince did not strike him.

Instead the prince's brow began to clear, and now a smile quirked at the corners of his lips. "Extraordinary. Three against seven—at the very least. Quite extraordinary. Do you know what this is?"

"N-no, lord."

"It is a sign," the prince said. "I see now—it is their fate to be entwined with my own destiny. The gods themselves tell me to reach forth my hand and take them. Summon my captains. I will have these three; they will serve me." The prince turned back into the bedchamber and strode toward his wardrobe. Through the open door Haral could see the bed, and the small body trembling and bleeding upon it; the prince spared it not a glance as he selected a kilt from his rack. Haral backed away until he was out of the prince's presence, then turned to run.

"We meet now, because at dawn I must ride for Sidon," said the prince. He reclined on a couch in his antechamber, while Haral and the other five captains stood in attitudes of respectful attention before him. Watching him, Haral was powerfully reminded of a glimpse he'd gotten once of the Pharaoh's pet lion, a great dusky beast named Akhu, sunning itself near the corpse of a cow it had fed on, there in the Pharaoh's park in Per-Ramses. The prince had that same blend of power and boneless relaxation—but he was much more frightening than any lion.

A pair of lamps supplemented the moonlight, and gave the prince enough illumination to read the scroll in his hands. "The Governor will be there soon, and I must deliver an invitation to guest with me. Persip, it will be your responsibility to have the estate prepared to receive him, since Sim shall be riding to accompany me."

The captain named Persip inclined his head. "It will be done."

Haral thought that it would be a relief to have Simi-Ascalon out of town for a few days; as he looked at the faces of the other captains, he saw expressions that could be read as private agreement.

"Illush and Tekt," the prince went on, brandishing another scroll, "the two of you will begin preparations to curse these inns; also, if you see any opportunities to burn a building here and there, or a ship, you will do so. Very shortly, we should be able to quit with these things, as the Houses turn on each other and do them for us. Bezai, you will take over for Chrysios. I want as many public murders as you can manage; and, I think, you should start with a Tomitiri tax collector—we have a Tomitiri public house that is just about ripe. Any high-ranking Great House officers that you can identify, you will abduct and bring to Simi-Ascalon—especially any of Nephrol Tomit's—that would have a certain symmetry that will please me a great deal. And, all of you, think about who would make a suitable replacement for my unfortunate Greek."

He sat up suddenly, and gripped his knees; the captains stood like statues, barely breathing, as they watched color drain from his knuckles and veins stand out along his forearms. "And Silam, this you will do. These mercenaries, the ones that killed Chrysios. I want them. You will find them, and bring them to me."

"But—but my prince, if I cannot find them—? If they will not come?"

"It will be bad," the prince said, in a tone more chilling for its matter-of-fact bluntness, "for you to fail. But you will not. They are fate's gift to me—all three of them. They will come." He clapped his hands together twice, loud enough to make every other man in the room twitch. "That is all for the five of you. Go. Haral, remain."

The five captains exchanged glances, and all five of them gave a look of apprehensive pity to Haral. Haral was acutely aware of the cold sweat that trickled down his spine. The five captains left. Haral didn't move.

The prince slowly rolled the scroll that he'd consulted and returned it to its case. "For you, Haral, I have a special task."

"M-my lord?" Haral fought to control his trembling.

"Yes, yes indeed." The prince suddenly stood, and stretched

with a deep yawn. "Take two men—two of our men, not hirelings—and bring Chrysios' body to Sim's cavern."

Haral blanched. "But, but my prince—"

"No excuses, Haral. Oh, you don't have to do it tonight; but he'd best be there by, say, midnight tomorrow. Sim can wait that long, I think, and catch up with me in Sidon in time to meet the Governor—it's only a few hours' ride."

"B-but, but what if I can't . . . or what if, well—"

"There are no what ifs, Haral. Deliver his body to the cavern by midnight tomorrow." The prince sighed, yawned again, and headed back toward his bedchamber. "I made a promise to him, Haral, the same promise I made to you. In exchange for his service, I promised eternal life." The prince disappeared within his bedchamber, but his voice carried hollowly out to Haral. "You would regret making me a liar."

Haral never doubted this; he was still shaking when he left.

CHAPTER SEVEN

The Curse

Barra rattled the door; finding it locked, she pounded on it with the heel of her hand. "Lidios! Lidios, open up!"

"Have you lost your senses?" Kheperu said, staring at her.

She shook her head. "The story on the curse is that folk who were living in the cursed inns already don't die. We were living here; we should be safe." She pounded again. "Lidios! Shake your ass!"

Kheperu caught her arm. "*Were* living here," he said. "But we weren't here when the curse was laid. How do you know it will not kill us?"

"How do you know it will?"

"I do not . . . For all I know, we could die from *not* going in—that is what's supposed to happen to people who try to leave, is it not?"

She shook her arm free and faced him, hands on hips. "For a sorcerer, you don't know bloody much about magic, do you?"

Kheperu scowled up at the glyph on the lintel. "Not this kind," he said grimly. "I have never seen anything like it. What about that precious grandmother of yours? Could she do something like this?"

"Probably," Barra said with a shrug. "I don't know."

Leucas reached up, toward the design. Kheperu barked, "Don't touch that!"

Leucas snatched his hand away and looked with mild inquiry at the Egyptian. "Why not?"

"Because I don't know what will happen when you do," Kheperu said. He laced his stubby fingers together and popped his knuckles one by one. "This worries me. Curses on inns and public houses are usually economic, you see. Curdled milk, spoiled beer, mold on the cheese, wine goes to vinegar, that sort of thing. You cost the publican so much money that he is forced to close his doors. About the worst you can do is make the men impotent or cause the occasional miscarriage. But this, this business of wholesale death . . ." He shook his head.

"I've heard stories like this, though," Barra said doubtfully.

"Superstition. Campfire tales to chill the ignorant. Trust that I know more of magic than most, and I can tell you that magic is *orderly*. It operates by rules that are very clear, at least to the initiated. This, though, this is outside the bounds, so far as I know. This is more like some work of a god: a disease or somesuch."

"I was curious," Leucas said, "about the design itself. Looks like it's burned into the stone. Even that must have been done by magic, mustn't it?"

"Hmpf," Kheperu grunted. "That's hardly a mystery. It's easy, I could do it myself. This sandstone, it's very soft, and porous. All that's required is some of this—" His hand dipped within his robes and came out with one of the black, tar-covered balls; he spun it between his fingers, making it disappear and appear again. "Worked into rope, it could be applied directly to the stone—or, better yet, to a thin plank, you could lay out the design beforehand, reversed, and carry the plank with you, then press it against the lintel and fire it. But the glyph itself has no power, you see, except perhaps as a deterrent to the superstitious. You'll find these sorts of designs somewhere on nearly every tomb in Egypt. If the glyphs themselves had any effect, there would be many, many dead tomb robbers, and looting graves would never have become the popular pastime it is today."

"Then why put it there?" Barra said, frowning.

"As I said before, as a deterrent to the superstitious," Kheperu explained. "The vast majority of the populace is uneducated to the point of bestiality—"

"Not on the tombs, idiot!" Barra snapped. "Why here? Why put it on the lintel? Why set a killing trap and then *announce* it?"

"Well," Kheperu said thoughtfully, "if I was laying curses, I'd probably be going around to the publicans—or even to the heads of the Great Houses—pretending to be a white sorcerer, and get paid for lifting it again."

Barra lifted an eyebrow, then shook her head. "No. It's too much trouble for a simple protection racket." She looked at the door and hissed impatiently through her teeth. "Where is that fat bastard?" She drew one of her throwing axes and hammered at the door.

Lidios' voice came faintly from within. "Go away! Can't you see I'm under the curse? Do you want to die? Go away!"

"Open this goddamned door!"

"Barra?"

"If this door isn't open by the time I count five, Leucas will break it down!"

"I will?"

"Shh."

She heard the heavy scrape of the bar being lifted and set aside, and the door creaked open a bare handbreadth. Lidios peered out, squinting and shading his black-ringed bloodshot eyes against the sunlight. "What do you want?"

"Our gear. You've got all our armor and spare clothing."

"Oh, your gear, is it?" He threw open the door and stood aside. "Well, come right bloodyfucking *in,* then! Come on! Come on and die, you worthless bitch! Do you know you've *ruined* me? I've run this house for twenty-three years, and it took you one night to destroy it forever! *One night!* Never mind me, who cares about poor Lidios? *Come in and get your bloodyfucking gear!*"

Foam flecked the corners of his lips; he stared at them, panting, his head twitching to one side, his hands trembling. He seemed to have lost weight overnight—his jowls sagged, and purple-black shadows streaked beneath his eyes. The bandage that wrapped his chest like a ceremonial sash was already brushed brown with dirt, and he smelled strongly of vomit. Behind him in the darkness of the shadowed common room, his slaves and whores sat clustered in frightened groups, some of them crying, some only staring at the door.

"Hey, cheer up," Kheperu said. "If you have any luck, it'll kill us, too." Barra's foot came down on his instep, but he only shrugged at her.

Leucas said, "Do you think you were cursed because we fought those men last night?"

Lidios only stared at him, still twitching; his brown eyes looked almost black.

Barra stepped toward him, to the threshold of the door. Now that she'd come up against it, she couldn't quite bring herself to go in. She said, "Lidios. Lidios, listen."

Slowly, very slowly, he turned his head to look at her.

"Lidios, has anyone died?"

His brows drew together, and again his head jerked to one side. "No. No, not yet. Everyone knows the curse only slays guests—all my guests left. You chased them off with your brawl. None will return, either. None will ever return. I wish that knife had struck deep," he said, slapping the bandage on his chest. "I wish Zeus had loved me enough to strike me dead before I ever saw this day."

"Hush," Leucas said severely. "Do not wish worse luck upon yourself; the gods hear such prayers."

"Worse? Worse than *this*?" As he got excited, working himself up to another explosion, his twitching increased and expanded from hands and head to his whole thick body.

"Lidios," Barra cut him off. "What about that boy, Mykos, your new slave? He became part of your household only last night—does he live, or did the curse kill him?"

Lidios blinked at her like a day-blinded owl. "He's gone."

"But . . ." Her tongue felt suddenly thick and clumsy, and she had to force her words through her tightening throat. "But you said no one had died . . ."

"I didn't say he died, I said he's gone! Ran off in the middle of the night! I hope he's lying dead in the street! I hope he's choking on his own blood!" Once again, his trembling and twitching increased; this time, though, as he stepped through the doorway to shake his fist in her face, he came into full sunlight. His tirade twisted into a cry of pain; he clapped a hand to his eyes and pitched forward to the ground, flopping spastically like a game fish in the bottom of a boat. Barra and Kheperu stepped back instinctively; equally instinctively, Leucas stepped forward and knelt beside him. He took Lidios' head firmly in one tremendous hand, and with the other he drew a knife.

"Help me hold him," he said.

Kheperu flinched. "What, *touch* him? Are you mad?"

"Help me!"

Barra forced herself forward and knelt. "What do you want me to do?"

"Sit on his back and hold his head," Leucas said. "Keep him still for just a moment."

Her flesh crawled at the thought of his twitching body

against hers, but she complied. He bucked under her like an unbroken horse. Leucas pried Lidios' jaws apart and inserted the hilt of the knife between his teeth.

"We must get him inside," Leucas said. "He's been seized, and he can die of it; I've seen it happen."

Kheperu went to the doorway and shouted, "Hey! Hey, you lazy shits! Get over here and drag him in!"

A couple of the slaves started tentatively to rise; Barra shouted, "No! Stay where you are!" She snapped at Kheperu: "Stepping out here did this to him. You want to kill them, too?"

"Then what are we supposed to do? Carry him ourselves? In *there*?"

Grimly pinning Lidios' jerking body to the ground, Barra looked at Leucas. He returned her gaze steadily and said, "If he isn't put somewhere warm and soft—like his bed—he'll probably die."

"Better him than us," Kheperu insisted.

"We guested in his home," Leucas replied simply.

Both of them looked at Barra.

Lidios made a choking, gurgling noise around the knife hilt. His breath reeked of vomit, with a bitter, nutlike underlay, like acorn tea.

Barra looked down at him. Why should she risk her life for him? She owed him nothing—the lodging he had given was in return for the business they'd bring in. Her attack on Chrysios had probably saved his life. She wasn't Greek, to be bound by their obsession with guest-friendship. There was no reason why she shouldn't come down on Kheperu's side, and the three of them could turn their backs and walk away, especially after the way this stinking prick-bastard had cursed at her only moments ago.

No reason except one: the *sceon tiof* flared up behind her eyes. She saw how years of hard work had carved his face, the warm and generous heart that supported his slaves in their declining years, the ready laugh, the stout resistance to adversity . . .

Dammit, she thought, *why can't I unlearn this trick?*

She gathered in a flailing arm that had escaped her grasp and pressed it tight against his side. She turned her head and spat in the street.

"We're taking him in."

*   *   *

The slaves stared in open astonishment when Barra and
Leucas carried Lidios into the inn. Kheperu remained outside on the street, on the dubious premise that if his friends
were struck by the curse, he, as a seshperankh, was the only
one of them who'd have a chance to save the others' lives.
They carried Lidios to his darkened bedchamber and wrapped
him in blankets, where his convulsions quickly quieted, and
he passed directly into a fitful sleep. Leucas carefully wiped
Lidios' mouth foam off his knife hilt onto the bedcovers
before returning the knife to its sheath. While Leucas gathered their possessions, Barra questioned the slaves. None of
them had seen Mykos make his escape, not even the pair
who'd slept on the floor at the thresholds of the two doors,
front and back. One of the slaves pointed out the blankets Mykos had used as a bedroll, and Barra, muttering dire
curses through clenched teeth, folded one and tucked it under
her arm.

When Barra and Leucas returned unharmed to the street,
Kheperu looked mildly surprised, then deeply thoughtful.
"Very curious indeed."

"So," Barra asked, "what do you make of it?"

Kheperu shook his head, frowning. "Obviously, we haven't
been hit with the curse ourselves, or being outside the inn
would have the same effect on us that it had on Lidios, don't
you think? So, we escaped that part of the curse, the way it
affects the resident. But, on the other hand, if we weren't
affected by the resident's portion, you and Leucas should
have been struck by the guest's portion. But apparently you
weren't."

"Perhaps that's because we didn't go in as guests," Leucas
mused.

"Nonsense. You think the curse determines your intentions
before deciding whether or not to kill you? That's ridiculous!"

Leucas shrugged. "You explain it, then."

"I cannot, yet," he said, fuming. "But I will. There is something shit-rank peculiar about this magic, and I'm going to
figure out what it is."

"While you calculate," Barra said dryly, "why don't we
work on a question we know we can answer?" She waggled
Mykos' blanket significantly. "Come on."

They quickly made their way back to the apartments of the

Myrmidons, Barra and Kheperu toting the gear to preserve Leucas' stitches. Murso/Lysandros had come and gone again in their absence; they found, when the Myrmidons escorted them inside, a large leather purse bulging with silver. Barra favored Kheperu with a predatory smile. "Weren't you mocking me, yesterday afternoon?"

The Egyptian hefted the purse, weighing it in his hands. He whistled appreciatively. "Mocking you, Barra?" he said warmly. "Never! I wouldn't do such a thing."

"I seem to recall, over the last couple of days, hearing you saying 'Our price goes up' in that mincing, effeminate tone—"

"Really, Barra, I can't be responsible for how you interpret my tone. I've never had any but the greatest faith in your abilities and judgment. Why, only yesterday, I was telling Leucas how I thought you were being far too hard on yourself; I was telling him that our unemployment wasn't your fault, and that if you only had patience, I was quite sure something would come through. Wasn't I, Leucas?"

Leucas lifted an eyebrow. "When was this?"

"Oh, you were drunk, of course you don't remember—"

"Never mind," Barra sighed. She went over and crouched beside Peroön. The one-armed physician sat cross-legged on the floor, a plate of thick barley gruel balanced on his ankles. He grunted a hello, and said, "Did you breakfast?"

Barra shook her head. "No time. Listen—"

"You should breakfast early, you know," he said, mopping at the gruel with the chewed heel of a loaf of bread. "Wait till too late in the day, it'll make you sleepy; that's a medical fact."

"Ay, thanks. Listen, Peroön, you're Kamades' second, right?"

"By his authority, yes."

"We have to go out again. All our gear and our"—she couldn't say *money,* that would have been too bald—"other possessions will be safe here with you guys, won't it?"

Peroön stopped chewing and fixed her with a long flat stare. He said softly, "You're a foreigner, and likely know no better, so I'll let that pass. We are not thieves."

"Oh, no no no," Barra said hastily. "I'd never even think it."

"See that you don't."

"I only wanted to make sure that you fellows wouldn't,

like, all go off to the Market, or something, and leave the place unguarded."

"We won't. Your possessions will be as safe as our own."

"Thanks," she said, with her best friendly smile. "I just wanted to hear you say it."

She whistled up Graegduz out of his corner, tucked the blanket under her arm again, and looked at her companions. "Let's go."

After they hit the streets and the Myrmidon who had led them there returned to his post inside the building, Kheperu murmured, "You think that's wise? There's more silver in that purse than any of these fellows see in a year."

Barra nodded, smiling dryly with half her face. "They're a bit underpaid, don't you think?"

"They are stinking peculiar, is what I think. And I think you are mad to trust them with our money."

"The money is safe," Leucas rumbled.

"How do you know that, though?"

"Peroön said so."

"Oh, fine. Oh, lovely. And you'll simply trust his word."

"Yes, I will," the Athenian replied stolidly. "You, Kheperu, shouldn't judge men's characters by your own."

"Well, I like that!"

"What Leucas means, I think," Barra said, "is that these men are Myrmidons—in Akhaia, their name is a byword for faithful service. Their honor is tied to how well they follow orders, and how well they keep their word; and their honor is everything. It's all they have."

"Too right!" Kheperu murmured. "At a bloody shekel a day, they cannot afford anything else."

"Tell me again why we're doing this."

Barra ruffled Graegduz's heavy fur as she held the blanket for his inspection. The young wolf shook his head and snuffled at the blanket's folds, ears flicking. "There's a good boy," she murmured in Pictish. "This is the fella we need to find." She looked up at Kheperu and switched to Greek. "I think I've made that clear."

"Of course you have," he replied. "And if I did not know you so well, I would likely believe you."

"I'm telling you, something spooked him," she said with flat assurance. "I had that boy so scared he should've been

still shaking this time next year. The only reason he'd have
bolted is the curse. One, he knew about it in advance. Two, he
saw our sorcerer lay it in. Three, he learned of it somehow
after the fact. In the first two cases, we need to have a little
talk with him. In the third, just finding out if he's still alive
will tell us more about the nature of the magic involved. All
right?"

"If you say so," Kheperu said with a shrug. "But, for some
reason, I suspect that we are tracking him simply because
he did not do what you told him to, and you want to kill him
for it."

"Really?" Barra's smile stopped well short of her eyes. "In
that case, I'm telling you: shut up and follow along. Think
you can do that?"

Kheperu sniffed. "Empty threats."

"You think so?" she said, standing up.

"Now, Barra," Leucas said, his hands up in that *be calm
now* gesture. "Much as I'd enjoy seeing you knock him down,
we ought to get on with this. If he's heading for the beach . . ."

She nodded. "You're right. Graegduz," she said in Pictish,
"let's go find this little bastard."

The trail was short: it ended at a dung heap less than two
hundred steps away.

Barra stood before it, her nose wrinkled and her hands on
her hips, and said grimly, "Or, on the other hand, maybe he
wanted to take a nap on a big pile of shit."

The dung heap was nearly as tall as Kheperu, and it occupied the central two thirds of a cul-de-sac formed by the rears
of three buildings. Huge glossy flies lumbered in clouds
around it, and its lower edges gleamed with busy scarabs.
Graegduz nosed all the way around it, but in the end he
sat down and eyed the dung heap mournfully. Barra rubbed
the loose skin behind his ears. "It's not your fault, Graeg.
Good job."

Leucas said, "In there, eh?" He untied his belt and pulled
his chiton off over his head. "I suppose this is my job," he
said, touching his battered, useless nose.

"I think not," Kheperu told him, rolling back the long
sleeves of his overrobe. "Shit—especially human shit—has
certain magical properties, carrying away as it does all
residues of the failed magical and evil influences to which a
man is subjected each day. One must deal with it cautiously, if

at all. If, for example, the smallest amount came in contact with your wounds, Leucas, it could put you down with a raging fever. Insidious stuff, shit is. Best to leave it to an expert."

"You don't have to persuade me," Leucas said, stepping aside with a slight bow.

"Humpf," Barra grunted. "This is all only an excuse for you to dig your hands into a dung heap."

"Oh, please," Kheperu said haughtily. "As though I need an excuse . . ."

Barra crouched on her haunches, Graegduz at her side, her back against the chilly al-tobe rear of a building on the upwind side of the cul-de-sac, watching Kheperu probe the dung heap with his staff. He didn't seem to mind that the countless flies found him nearly as appetizing as the heap; he didn't bother to brush them away unless they landed on his face.

Not far from Barra's feet, an industrious scarab toiled along, rolling a ball of dung twice its own size. Two others approached it, as though to help, but shortly they had stolen the ball and were fighting over it between themselves. They shone in the sunlight like burnished brass. Barra scowled at them; they reminded her of her life. You work hard and apply yourself, and just when you're starting to make headway, to get somewhere, somebody steals everything you've worked for, and then somebody steals it from them, until nobody can figure out whose it was in the first place—and through it all, nobody seems to realize that in the end it's just a big ball of shit. Barra suddenly gritted her teeth and brought her foot down on all three scarabs and the shitball, smashing them to crackling paste.

She settled back against the wall, her face frozen with cold anger. She'd tried, she'd really tried to save this little bastard Mykos' worthless life—she'd played fast and loose with her own principle, risked a stinging slap from her gods—and here he was, dead as dead and stuffed into a pile of shit. And he'd been only a few years older than Chryl, her own son.

Leucas crouched beside her and draped her shoulder with his hand. "He might not be here, you know." She looked into his grave grey eyes, and saw there his all-too-clear understanding of what she felt. "He knows you hunt with the wolf;

it's how you caught him last night. He could have rolled in the dung heap to confuse his scent. He could be on a boat to Egypt even now."

Barra turned away to squint along her shoulder at the mid-morning sun, now a fist above the building across the alley. It was only the sunlight that brought the quick sting of tears to her eyes. "Thanks, Leucas," she said softly.

"For what?"

"For reminding me that if he wasn't dead, I'd have to hunt him down and kill him. Sweet Mother, sometimes I don't understand myself at all."

A smile tugged gently at Leucas' lips. "Aren't you a little old to be noticing that for the first time?"

"Found him," Kheperu said cheerfully. He pulled his staff free of the dung heap, wiped it with his hands, and set it to one side. He bent at the waist, to reach into the dung heap at about knee height; his face lit with a smile when his probing fingers found an arm, warm as life from the dungheap's internal heat. It was the work of a breath or two to pull the body free—it hadn't been buried deeply, and the outer levels of the heap were still loose. "Well, my my my." Kheperu straightened up and beckoned to his companions. "This is interesting. Look here. And I thought we'd have to wash him off before we'd be able to tell what killed him—to look for a brand, or a tattoo."

Barra nodded, looking down at Mykos' body. There was a deep dent in his forehead, above his left eye, and his throat was cut raggedly, as though the killer had sawed through it with a small knife. "Damn," she said tightly. "God damn."

Leucas sighed. "Well, it probably wasn't a bandit—a robber would have settled for the crushed skull."

"Oh, no, that is, yes," Kheperu agreed. "Oh, absolutely. No, my guess would be that he came out Lidios' window just as our sorcerer and his friends were laying in the curse. He saw them, and they killed him for it."

"Friends?" Barra said.

"Well, friend, at least. There must have been two of them—you do not stop in mid-murder to change weapons, do you?"

Barra shrugged. "All right, two of them." She shook her head, swallowing past the sick constriction in her throat. Graeg leaned against her thigh, crooning consolation. She ruffled his fur absently, fighting to keep her mind on business. "This is too peculiar. It's too strange. I mean, if this boy was killed by a sorcerer, why would they cut his throat? Why didn't the sorcerer blast him, or strike him dead with a glance, or change him into a lizard or something?"

Kheperu cleared his throat importantly. "There are a number of possible explanations—"

"But the most likely one is that he didn't because he couldn't, right? I mean, I've seen you fight—you never use that staff unless you don't have a spell that'll do the job."

"Perhaps he was otherwise engaged." Kheperu began scraping his hands clean on the flagstones. "Perhaps laying a curse of this type is a lengthy process, and his confederates killed our young friend to prevent interruption."

"They could have chased him away," Leucas rumbled.

"Yes they could have, easily enough, if all they cared about was protecting the sorcerer," Barra agreed. "But they killed him, suddenly and without warning. I mean, if I saw somebody burning glyphs into solid stone, I'd head the other direction as fast as my feet could carry me—but the club hit him from in front, and hit him before he could cry out, or he would have been heard by Lidios or the slaves inside. And then they hid the body. That's strange, isn't it? Why not just leave him there in the street, the way bandits do?"

Kheperu picked up his staff and regarded his smeared hands with distaste. "Fascinating, Barra. Now, if you please, I must find a place to wash."

Leucas stared at him in wonder. "Wash? You?"

"Only my hands," Kheperu said stiffly. "Because of its magical properties, shit can interfere with my—"

"Be quiet, both of you," Barra snapped. She spread her hands, slowly, frowning her concentration. She raised a forefinger. "Think about this. Why did they hide the body?"

Kheperu blinked and looked at Leucas, who responded only with a shrug. "Well . . . I suppose . . ." he began, then suddenly grinned. "Well, it would look bad, would it not? A guest of Lidios found on the street with his throat cut. Might make people think the curse is not all that potent—sorcerers can be touchy that way, you know."

"You say that as a joke," Barra said, her eyes gleaming with inspiration, "but you know what? I think you are dead-center right. You understand? You're right as the bloody rain. Plumb line straight on the bloody target."

"Oh, come now, Barra," Kheperu scoffed in his most avuncular, patronizing manner, "a curse works precisely the same way whether people believe in it or not. Why would our sorcerer worry about people thinking it did not work? That would, if anything, only increase the number of deaths. I mean, the only reason he would care is if . . ." His voice trailed away, and his eyes widened in astonishment. "Well, bless my bloody balls."

"Exactly. Oh yes, indeed," Barra said, a grin lighting her face like the sunrise.

Leucas' frown deepened. "Are you saying that—"

"We need to get a look at the other cursed inns," Kheperu murmured.

"Yes we do," Barra said. "Right now."

"What I want to know now," Kheperu said with hushed determination, as though he could drive his words through the hard oak of the door by sheer force of will, "is how many of your slaves have tried to leave—and what happened to them." He pressed his ear against the door to hear the soft, despairing voice of Xuros the innkeeper.

Xuros' establishment was not so grand as Lidios' place, but it was part of an overbuilt block that fronted on a broad right-of-way just south of the Market and only a few steps from the beach. The curse had been on this place the longest—more than a month—and it was only by long and persistent cajoling that they persuaded Xuros to speak with them at all. Money was useless to him, when he couldn't come out to spend it, and threats were equally useless, when his only activity was to sit at his door and wait to die.

On the other side of the right-of-way, Barra leaned against a brick pillar that was warm in the sun and rough against her back, Graegduz drowsing at her side. The pillar was one of a series that supported a broad, gently sloping roof over an open expanse of flagstones; this roof served as a rain shed for the disordered clutter of tradesmen beneath, mostly vendors of roasted pork and spiced mutton, of smoked flatfish and boiled shrimp. At Barra's side, Leucas kept stealing longing glances over his shoulder into the grill court, his sighs reminding Barra that none of them had eaten more than a crust of bread and a mouthful of cheese snatched on the run, with the sun bending now from afternoon toward evening. Though he couldn't smell the food, he didn't need to—the sizzle and crack of fat dripping onto the coals was all the encouragement his appetite required.

The cursed inns had been easy to find; there was always a slave about who'd make the horned-god sign and whisper hasty directions. The inn of Xuros was the last—they'd already spoken with Nicoras, at his large house not far from the Penthedes compound, and they'd dealt through a closed door with the wife of the late Sutuliumas, who had died two weeks ago from a seizure not unlike that of Lidios.

The various inns themselves had little in common save their general design. All were two-story affairs built around a central court—roofed over in the case of Lidios and Xuros, open to the sky for Nicoras and Sutuwallas. In the open-court inns, the kitchens were under rain sheds in the main yard; in the other two, the kitchens were behind, below the rain barrels that squatted on the roofs.

It seemed clear to Barra that their sorcerer was trying to implicate the Tomitiri. Three of the Great Houses deigned to dabble in local inns; Nicoras, Xuros, and Sutuwallas were all Mursuwallites, and Lidios was a Jephunahi; none of the inns loyal to the House headed by the Egyptian Nephrol Tomit had been cursed, and the sorcerer was certainly taking pains to present his curse as Egyptian magic. This, of course, had nothing to do with the sorcerer's actual affiliation. If, for example, it was the Hittite House of Mursuwalli that was trying to spark the war, cursing three of their own inns would be an inexpensive bit of misdirection—inexpensive for the Mursuwallites, less so for Nicoras, Xuros, and Sutuwallas.

Shortly, Kheperu left off his questioning and joined them. "Not much to be learned," he said, leaning heavily upon his staff. "No affray with his tax collector here. He had nine guests the night of the curse; all dead by noon. Two slaves and one of his daughters made it as far as the Market before they went into convulsions and died."

"I told you the business with Chrysios was coincidence," Barra said. "It wouldn't surprise me if the curse was an afterthought—the House behind our sorcerer was trying a new tactic, and when we got in the way they went back to their old one. Or, if the curse had already been planned, the killing of the tax collector was just a new way of stoking the fire, you know? The next step in the plan. Chrysios was Akhaian—if he'd gotten away with it, the murders might have looked like they were ordered by the Penthedes." She shook her head sharply. "Forget why. I'm wondering how. In the food, you think?"

Kheperu nodded, fingernails scratching thoughtfully on the knob of his staff. "The question is, what food? All of it? You'd need to dose everybody, or the illusion collapses. Seems difficult. More likely, some spice or something that would be commonly used . . ." He brightened suddenly. "In the salt!"

Barra shrugged, unconvinced. "I don't know. You'd still have to get into and out of the kitchen—or the storeroom— and I don't know about these other three, but Lidios kept a bloody peeled eye on his stores."

"Do you think we could eat now?" Leucas murmured, still gazing wistfully into the grill court.

"In a moment," Barra told him. "We need to work this out."

Leucas sighed. "What about the water?"

"If you had your mind on any business more urgent than the cry of your belly," Kheperu sneered, "it would be obvious. Water comes from the public wells, fresh every morning or two. There'd be no way to renew the poison, as the inn would be already closed under the curse. Is it *clear* now? Do you *understand*?"

Leucas nodded slow acceptance. "I was confused. You're right, of course. I guess I was thinking that these four inns wouldn't use the public wells till their rain barrels ran dry."

Barra frowned at Kheperu. He grimaced back. They both looked up at the rain barrel on the roof of Xuros' house. Lidios had a similar one, and Barra remembered rain barrels on the roofs of Nicoras' and Sutuwallas' houses, as well.

Kheperu said softly, just above a whisper, "Do you suppose he does this on purpose, to make me feel like a fool?"

Barra glanced over her shoulder at the huge Athenian, who was once again staring at a mutton shank the size of his thigh. There just might have been the tiniest twitch of a smile at the corner of his mouth, but she couldn't be sure.

"I don't know," she said, "but I hope so. Come on, let's take a closer look."

The companions put a corner of the block between them

and the crowded food court, and not far along the side of the block found an alleyway narrow enough to force them to walk it single file. The lowest point within it where they could reach the roof was two stories high, slightly more than three times Leucas' height. Barra squinted critically at the wall. "I'm not sure I can climb it," she said. "It's pretty smooth."

Leucas made a basket with his fingers. "If you jump as I toss, I'd imagine you won't need to climb at all."

Kheperu snorted. "You're mad. You're a strong lad, Leucas, but be serious!"

Leucas replied with a shrug. Barra said, "It's worth a try." She looked at the wolf. "Stay here and watch," she said in Pictish. "Howl if anyone comes, and don't bite Kheperu." Graeg whined, but sat obediently.

"Ready?"

Leucas nodded, took a deep breath, and bent his legs. She stepped into his hands, crouched, and sprang upward as he heaved. She was still rising as her hands passed the rim of the roof; she latched on and had enough momentum left to swing smoothly onto it. She lay there for a moment, then shook herself and poked her head back over the rim. "I'm impressed."

Leucas shrugged. "At the Olympian games we tossed a bronze ingot that weighs not much less than you do."

"Oh, sure," she said, "but someday you'll have to come up to the Isle of the Mighty, and try hurling the caber—that's a *real* test. It's a great log the size of a mainmast, not some teeny bit of bronze—"

"I'm sure of it," Kheperu interrupted. "Very interesting, Barra, I'm sure we'd both love to hear all about it. Later."

"Oh, fine," she sighed irritably. Then her eyes went wide. "Leucas—what about your *stitches*?"

Leucas looked momentarily puzzled, then put his hand to his belly and winced. "I forgot." He pulled his chiton out away from his chest and peered down through the neck hole. "Don't seem to be bleeding, though. Peroön is a fine surgeon."

"He'd have to be," Kheperu muttered, "if he's sewing up you scatterbrained Akhaians all the time."

Leucas looked at him consideringly, as though calculating

precisely how hard Kheperu could be hit without killing him outright. Barra said, "Don't even start. Either of you."

She rolled to her feet and ran lightly along the rim of the roof toward Xuros' rain barrel, avoiding stepping out onto the probably more fragile—and certainly more noisy—open roof. Leucas and Kheperu followed her from the ground, picking their way around the piles of trash that nearly blocked the passage. Graegduz stayed on guard at the alley's mouth.

The barrel rested at a back corner, slightly overhanging the walls that supported its weight. It was deeper than Barra was tall, and wide enough that she could have lain full length within it and never touched the sides. She leaped upward over the narrow alley that separated the inn from the rest of the block, as the inn's roof was slightly higher, and swung herself to safety. Nearby, a small door was set flat into the roof, and up one side of the barrel were nailed a set of rungs. The hinged lid of the rain barrel was closed for fair weather, to keep out bird droppings. She lifted it briefly, and took a deep sniff. The water's dominant scent was simply the musty smell of being closed up and stale, but underneath that, she detected a familiar bitter, nutlike aroma. A moment's thought told her where she knew it from: she'd smelled the same scent on Lidios' breath. Another moment of searching the roof discovered all the confirmation she required: she brushed her fingers across a roughened scuff mark on the rim of the roof.

She called down, not loudly, "Leucas—you were right. There's a mark here, probably from something like a siege ladder."

"That explains why your little friend was killed," Kheperu said, nodding. He and Leucas stood in Xuros' back-alley kitchen, unused now that no slave dared leave the building. "Our pretend-sorcerer wouldn't want anyone talking about seeing a couple of men running around in the dead of night carrying a ladder. Get a sample of the water."

"Why?"

He leaned casually on the cold brick of the hearth and examined his fingernails. "Because, with the right equipment, I should be able to isolate the poison. That sort of thing is rather my specialty, you know. There are several poisons that might have this effect; they are all expensive, and none come from anywhere close by. All we'll need to do is talk to the alchemists, to find out who's been buying it and . . ." He snapped his fingers insouciantly.

Barra blinked in astonishment. "You're brilliant, do you know that?"

"I've been waiting for you to notice."

CHAPTER EIGHT

Chrysios

Barra sat on the street, her back against the pine door frame of the shop of Tekrop-nekt. The interior of the shop smelled worse than Kheperu, so she had left him and Leucas to deal with the alchemist while she sat out here feeding strips of smoked fish to Graegduz as the lopsided moon rose over the black mass of the mountains.

Before the moon had come up, she'd amused herself by watching the dancing glow of a shop—she was pretty sure it had sold carpets—that had burned merrily in another part of the Market. A few of the rugs themselves had been lifted into the night sky, writhing as they burned within the thunderhead of smoke, salamanders blindly seeking wood or cloth on which to spawn. She'd listened to the distant, desperate shouts of merchants as they'd pursued the salamanders, guessing at the next move of the shifting wind. By the time the brow of the moon had peered over the mountains, the Market was once again dark, and quiet.

Occasionally, she heard Kheperu and Tekrop-nekt speaking in low-voiced Egyptian together, of temperatures of volatility and rates of distillation; the alchemist's shop was one of the merely semipermanent structures in the Market, framed in pine but walled only with heavy striped cloth.

Leucas pulled aside the door curtain over her head. "You'll want to hear this."

"I would've anyway," she sighed, but nonetheless rose, told Graeg to guard the door, and followed Leucas inside.

Within, the shelves and racks that divided the floor were empty, the alchemist's wares already packed away for the evening—the day had been fading from the sky when the three companions had arrived. Another curtain led to an inner chamber; beside that door stood Met, Tekrop-nekt's massively rotund guard, arms like hams folded over his bare chest, one hand close to the hilt of his long, broad-bladed scimitar. Barra noticed Leucas gazing at the sword with something akin to lust; its blade had the dull grey-black sheen of Hittite iron. Tekrop-nekt himself was a thin, languid man who looked at the world through eyes kept half lidded by mandrake root.

"Fascinating stuff," Kheperu told her, in Egyptian. His color was high and his eyes danced with excitement. He waved a small glass bottle at her, within which was some milky, viscous liquid. "This is an extract of the pukenut, which grows far and away on the other side of the Cape of Comorin. It does all kinds of things, really, useful and otherwise, you know."

"Hm-hm," Tekrop-nekt murmured. "In its undistilled form, it is a powerful emetic, used for cattle, and occasionally men. In small doses, the distilled form is a potent stimulant, increasing alertness and strength. In slightly larger doses, it produces convulsions, and death by choking of the lungs."

"You see? You see?" Kheperu said gleefully. "It produces a *tolerance*, you see. A dedicated user can safely take dosages that would kill an inexperienced horse. And, the convulsions can be triggered by excitement, a loud noise, even a bright light—do you get it?"

"So," Barra said, "they would take a few days, even a month, putting tiny doses—"

"Oh yes, yes indeed absolutely," Kheperu interrupted her forcefully. He stepped grandly in front of Barra and swung himself to face Tekrop-nekt. She restrained an impulse to punch him in the kidney; not even Kheperu would be foolish enough to interrupt her without a bloody good reason. "Our only other question regarding this is: who would be importing pukenut extract?"

"Well, the only place one would find pukenuts commercially available would be the isle of Dilmun, through the overland route south of Babylon . . ." Tekrop-nekt said consideringly. "Where, mm, where did you come across this sample?"

"That's our business, I believe."

Tekrop-nekt shrugged. "As is the name of the importer mine."

Kheperu hissed through his teeth and stepped forward. Behind Tekrop-nekt, Met unfolded his arms and smiled.

Kheperu stopped, his face contracted into a pout. "Very well, then. Another shekel."

"Five."

"Fine! Five! Who is it, then?"

"In advance."

Muttering vile curses under his breath, Kheperu dug five shekels from his purse of dice winnings. Tekrop-nekt accepted them graciously, and said, "The House of Jephunah holds the sole contract to bring pukenuts to Tyre."

Kheperu's eyes went wide, and he slowly turned toward Barra, until Tekrop-nekt added, "Of course, many alchemists maintain a substantial supply, buying them from the Jephunahi. I do, myself."

Kheperu deflated. "Ah, well," he sighed. "I suppose that would have been too easy."

Barra asked, "Has anyone come around buying up unusual amounts of your pukenuts, or the extract?"

Tekrop-nekt's eyelids drooped as he considered holding out for more money, but apparently he decided to be merciful. "Why, yes, in fact. A man bought every scrap I had, six weeks ago. A tall, fair-skinned fellow with golden hair. Had an Akhaian name, as I recall."

"Chrysios," Barra said.

"Why, yes, I believe that was it."

This time, she did punch Kheperu in the kidney, a short right hook hard enough to buckle his knees.

Barra recounted the conversation for Leucas, who had no Egyptian, while they walked slowly through the moonlit streets toward the apartments of the Myrmidons.

He nodded and sighed when Barra told him who the sorcerer's agent had been in purchasing the poison. He looked over Barra's head at Kheperu, who walked sullenly behind. "Is it too late for me to hit him, too?"

Kheperu made a complicated, two-handed gesture that was unquestionably obscene. Leucas shrugged. "Perhaps we should go to Idonosteus with what we've learned so far."

"Oh, please!" Kheperu sputtered. "Why are you both so eager to cast aside our commercial advantage? I give thanks to the watchful Uraeus that I thought quickly enough to stop Barra's babbling—"

"Which reminds me," Barra cut in through clenched teeth, "I don't like to be interrupted. Don't do it again."

"Piffle. You should bless me. Do you not understand the *opportunity* we have here? We are not being paid to determine the nature of the curse, but rather to discover its author. Once that is done, and we have been paid, *we are the only people in Tyre who know how to lift the curse!*"

"What, all this is about making a few shekels off the poor bastards that run these inns? So you can lift the curse, big deal—they can't afford to pay much, no matter what."

"My dear lady! I would not waste your time with squeezing shekels. Why 'lift the curse' . . . until *after* we have bought the inns?"

Barra stopped in the street and stared at him.

"Do you appreciate how little we would have to pay?" Kheperu continued. "Practically nothing! These men would pay *us* to take these establishments off their hands!"

"Kheperu." Leucas looked down at the little Egyptian with pity. "You are the most thoroughly venal and disgusting man I have ever met."

"Brilliant, though," Barra said thoughtfully. "No one could accuse you of thinking small."

Leucas frowned at her. "Please say you're not considering this!"

Barra squeezed her eyes shut, then shrugged and shook her head sharply. "No, I won't go for it."

"Barra—"

"Think about it, Kheperu. If we bought four inns in Tyre, we'd have to stay here and run them. Do you really want to be an innkeeper? It's a shitty life. And it's boring."

Kheperu pursed his lips, then nodded surrender. "It was a pretty idea, though, wasn't it?"

Barra started walking again, thumbs hooked behind her belt and Graegduz at her heel. Leucas and Kheperu fell in behind them. "On the other hand," she said, "if we were to buy them, lift the curse with some sort of spectacular public ceremony—Kheperu could put something together—and then *sell* them again . . ."

Kheperu's head jerked up when he realized he was alone. He rubbed his eyes, cursing his absentmindedness under his breath. He'd been walking along, thinking hard, watching the creeping tendrils of mist swirl before his feet, and somehow had continued straight at some point where Barra and Leucas had turned. Now as he looked about himself, the mist rose up more thickly from the moist earth of the street and the black-shadowed faces of unfamiliar buildings pressed close around.

"Lost." His voice rasped loudly in his ears, and he tightened his grip on his staff. He repeated, this time only a whisper, "I'm bloody lost."

His friends couldn't be far away—and when they noticed he was gone, they'd search for him. He'd simply retrace his steps and probably find them around the first corner.

But as he turned to go, he found that he was no longer sure from what direction he had come. He'd gotten turned around somehow. North, he told himself. They'd been walking north, so if he turned and put the moon on his left, he'd be heading back south toward the missed corner. But the mist had extended a milk-pale shroud above his head, and hid the moon behind a shifting veil that glowed faintly silver.

He drew breath to shout for them, but held it and listened, instead. He heard only the whisper of a breeze and the unsteady thump of his own heart. Why weren't they calling for him? Had they ditched him on purpose, as a joke?

Had something happened to them?

The sorcerer—could he have sent some otherworldly servant, one of the beast-headed demons of whom the other apprentices had whispered dark tales during the endless nights of Kheperu's childhood? If Kheperu called out, would he draw down upon himself the same hideous death that had taken his friends?

Nonsense, he insisted, but silently. He shook the knots out of his shoulders, firmly grasped his staff, and set out toward his best guess of south. The street narrowed as he walked, becoming little more than an alley that he could span with his arms, the buildings leaning together high above his head to shut out the sky. Obviously, this wasn't the way he'd come—he snorted and turned resolutely, then stopped. Footsteps—that sound was clearly footsteps, approaching through the mist. He started toward them—this must be Leucas or Barra, looking for him—but the stride was wrong, neither the sharp staccato of Barra's step nor the measured beat of Leucas; this step shuffled more than it strode, and it was *moist,* scraping through the alley's dirt with a wet sucking sound that lifted the hairs on Kheperu's arms and made his heart stutter.

His nerve broke; he turned and fled, deeper into the alley.

The buildings that made up the walls closed overhead, blotting out the light. Kheperu pressed on, stumbling through trash and slipping on unnameable slime; he couldn't get enough traction to gain ground on his pursuer. The walls squeezed against him in the darkness, the colored eyelights of utter night were all he saw, but he felt the moisture on the walls. They were sweating in the unbearable heat, and he forced himself between them, onward, turned sideways, half trapped, unable to breathe, and still the footsteps came behind, closer.

With panicked strength he burst free of the alley, and found himself in a small cul-de-sac that was thick with mist and bounded by high blind walls. He turned, panting, to face his pursuer, visible now as a vague man-shape. He whirled his staff whistling through the air before him and snapped it into a guard position.

"Come on, then!" he shouted. "Come on, you bastard! I'm ready!"

"Kheperu . . ." The voice was as thick and wet as its step, guttural and moaning. *"Kheperu, I want my face . . ."*

The figure shuffled forward, and now Kheperu felt his staff softening under his hands, flowing limply like supple rope that wrapped around his wrists and tied itself into unbreakable knots, pinning his hands helpless before him.

The mist parted around his pursuer and a shaft of silver moonlight lit its face, glossing the dead fish-belly white of its skin, turning the bloody shreds that dangled in place of its lower jaw to gleaming black. The fine corn-silk hair glistened; the shredded lump that had been its tongue pulsed. Slowly and deliberately it came, pushing Kheperu back against the sweating wall, its hands clutching his face, forcing its fingers into his mouth. He tried to scream, but the fingers choked him; he bit down and their flesh burst with squirming foulness that filled his mouth, but their strength was irresistible as they took hold of his tongue, his teeth, his jaw, ripping bone and tendon, tearing it free . . .

"I want my face!"

Then, from the back of Kheperu's head, came a burst of white light.

* * *

". . . A burst of white light, not unlike one of these," he said, producing one of his tarry flame balls. "And then, of course, I woke up, because the boot whatsisbugger threw hit me in the head. That could have been what produced the burst of light, I suppose."

Barra nodded thoughtfully, keeping her eyes on the sleeping Myrmidons from where she crouched beside Kheperu. It had taken a long time to settle them down again after they were awakened by Kheperu's moaning and his eventual scream, but now they lay dreaming on their pallets, scattered across the apartment's floor, except for those on guard, who were once again outside, and Kamades. She couldn't tell if Kamades was awake, or if he was dozing there in his chair with his chin on his breast. The scar-faced captain might well be cagy enough to pretend to sleep while he listened.

"There's gratitude:" Kheperu went on in his deeply offended whisper, "a boot to the head. One would think he might have been a little solicitous, a little concerned for my welfare, even friendly, after all the *money I lost* to him this evening." Under Barra's watchful glare earlier that evening, with the aid of the persuasive incense he'd used the night before, Kheperu had cheated himself out of twenty-one shekels during the nightly dice game.

Barra shrugged. "If you're trying to make me feel sorry for you, Kheperu, you're shopping at the wrong store."

Leucas sat cross-legged on the bare plank floor, his back to the Myrmidons. He scratched gently at his bandages and said, "What significance do you give this dream?"

"I am not sure that it *is* significant."

Leucas regarded him with lifted brows. "That's why you told us every detail, because you don't think it's—"

"Oh, all right," Kheperu surrendered disgustedly. He leaned forward, glancing past Leucas at Kamades, and lowered his voice even further. "I am wondering if it might be a threat."

Without perceptibly altering his expression, Leucas managed to look deeply skeptical.

"It's not as silly as it sounds, Leucas," Barra whispered. "My grandmother can send dreams, and folk she's mad at might ride the nightmare for weeks at a time."

"And Chrysios was saying something about how he can

never die," Kheperu said, licking his lips as though his mouth was suddenly dry. "Right before I killed him."

"When I was a little boy," Leucas said, "my father told me about the dreams sent by the gods, false ones through the gates of ivory, true through the gates of honest horn. He never spoke of dreams being sent by a mortal."

"Yes, yes," Kheperu said impatiently, "I've heard the same story. That doesn't mean it's true."

Leucas regarded him steadily. "My father wouldn't lie."

"Aren't you a little old to still hold that opinion?"

"Aren't you a little small to be calling my father a liar?"

"Stop it, both of you," Barra cut in. She took a deep breath and released it slowly. "The sorcerer couldn't have sent you this dream—he doesn't really have any magic, remember?"

"We have not established that," Kheperu said primly, forefinger lifted to make his point. "We know that he didn't use magic to curse the inns, not that he has no magic at all." He coughed into his hand, and gave a nervous little laugh. "Remember Othniel?"

The shadows cast by the steady flames of the lamp on Kamades' table seemed to lengthen, and to deepen to a darker black. Skin tightened across the back of Barra's neck, and she found herself glancing behind—just to be sure the wall of bare planks at her back was still there, still bare and empty.

"Well," she said heavily, turning back to her friends, "in my homeland, they say that many dreams come from deep within the mind of the dreamer, to remind him of something he's forgotten. The way I see it, whether this dream comes from the gods, from our boy the sorcerer, or out of your own twisted little mind, Kheperu, there's one thing we should do, first thing tomorrow." Barra cracked her knuckles, and took a deep breath; she rubbed her arms to smooth away the gooseflesh, and when she spoke, she had to whisper to keep her voice level. "We need to find out what happened to Chrysios' body."

Barra lay in the semidarkness for a long time, thinking about Chrysios, about Lidios and Nicoras and Xuros, about Peliarchus and Tayniz living in the same city with the man who'd branded Othniel and dropped poison in rain barrels. Thinking about finding a brand like that on her own palm, about drinking that water. Thinking about the seizure of Lidios, about how it would feel to have her muscles betray her and flop her like a landed fish. Thinking about how it would feel to have her flesh torn by demons that only she can see, as people press away from her on a noonday street. Fingers laced behind her head, she stared up at the ragged glow of lamplight on the ceiling, and decided to think about something else.

She lay for a while wondering about Kamades. The solemn Myrmidon captain had sat with her for more than an hour earlier that evening, filling her eager ears with stories of the Siege of Troy. She gathered that he'd been well respected, and had held a very responsible position in the Phthian force that had followed Akhilleus, although—in the self-effacing way that seemed common to him and his men—he never came right out and said so. She was helplessly, irresistibly fascinated by any story that had to do with the Akhaian heroes, especially Akhilleus, and she'd slowly become interested in just how in the names of a thousand gods a man like Kamades had come to be a mercenary captain in Tyre. After all, he wasn't a greedy money-grubber—as Barra occasionally saw herself—nor was he, apparently, ambitious or bloodthirsty. He seemed to see soldiering as a trade, like carpentry; a trade where he would routinely risk his life for a salary a bit smaller than what a decent cooper would make in the Market. But no matter how she tried to steer his stories, he would never refer to why he and his men didn't simply go home; the best she could gather was that there had been some sort of difficulty with Akhilleus' son and heir, Neoptolemos; Kamades' face would gently flush whenever the young man's name was mentioned. On the other hand, Kamades didn't seem to mind her probing. If he hadn't had to take his turn standing watch, they might still be sitting at that table, speaking softly across a lamp flame that wavered with each word.

It was that central mystery of him that drew her; Barra couldn't bear a mystery—the knowledge that someone was keeping a secret from her would buzz in her ears like a persistent mosquito. In fact, if she let herself think about it, she could very well lie awake here all night. Once again, she resolutely determined to think about something else.

She thought about Leucas. The *sceon tiof* was showing her much, letting her see a man who was intelligent and thoughtful, but only when he stopped to think; a man who lost all caution—all *reason*—whenever weapons were drawn and blood began to flow; a man who didn't need caution, because he had luck. Barrels of luck. He'd been a charioteer at Troy; if the songs Barra had heard were true, it was always the charioteers who were killed by the first spear casts between opposing heroes. *Weapons,* he'd said, *do not bite me as deeply as they do other men.* Nor do the tusks of boars, nor the claws of bears ... It was probably one of his gods, watching over him; the Akhaians had a shipload of gods, starting with a ruling council of twelve, along with all their attendants and servants and children, then they had more minor deities than she had hairs on her head, gods of this mountain and that stream and such-and-such wind and on and on and on till it made her head spin to think about them. It was easy to see how one of them might have taken a liking to him; there was charm in his grave equanimity, in his sly humor so dry that sometimes you couldn't tell whether he was really joking; he was generous, and openhearted, and his rare flashes of anger were always the swelling fires of an open furnace, never constricted into bitterness, never twisted to petty treachery; he was as honorable as a Myrmidon. He could, she thought, have the blood of gods running through his veins—some immortal ancestor would explain much. And really, she mused, squirming down deeper beneath her blanket, if it wasn't for that busted face of his, she'd probably be in love with him. Actually, busted face or not, Leucas was an enormously attractive man . . .

During her years on the road as a mercenary, Barra had developed a mental discipline, a rule that she used to govern her thinking; there were some things that she did not allow herself to do, or even think about. She had a list, in her mind, of topics that she wouldn't address, even in daydreams, topics like "What if Chryl's father hadn't left me?" and "What would my son be like if I'd stayed at home to raise him?" She called this list, privately, the Suicide Table; thinking too much about any entry on it could lead her into doing the kind of foolish things that tend to buy people in her line of work a short trip to a shallow grave. Very high on the Suicide Table was "I'd like to bed one of my partners"; it fell right between "I'd like to bed my employer" and "I'd like to bed my target."

This semiconscious state, drowsing half asleep on her pallet, had always been a dangerous time for her; still awake enough to spin fantasies, she was too close to sleep to keep them tightly reined. But now, as the lean battle-scarred figure of Leucas drifted across the inside of her eyelids, she found that he brought no heat to her loins; she felt affection, but no lust. She wondered, in her vague and aimless state, if he felt the same for her, if he felt this same serene *philios*. She realized that she did love him already: the same way she loved her brother Llem, and, perhaps, trusted Leucas a little more. After twenty-five years as High King, Llem was now an accomplished diplomat; Leucas wouldn't be as smooth a liar if he lived a thousand years.

Kheperu, now, he could drive the flow of words through his mouth as the gods drive water down the Nile, and whether they're true or false had as little effect on whether you'd believe him as the color of your hair has on the path of a thunderstorm. Even knowing that he prided himself on the quality of his lying didn't help; you could catch him in five lies and fall for the sixth. A shift of the shoulders, an inclination of the head, a softening of his tone, all to imply, "All right, I was only joking before, but now, *this* is the truth," and you're swept helplessly along. Drifting, she wondered if even Kheperu knew how *angry* he was, if he still felt the rage that fueled his contempt for the social mores; the *sceon tiof* could not show her what injustice the world had inflicted upon his life, but the lingering scars were all too clear. Perhaps he entertained fantasies of returning one day to his home city, wealthy as a monarch, to live in luxury and lord it over those who'd scorned him; perhaps he intended to waste his life as some obscure revenge against a half-forgotten parent, or lover. Or perhaps some terrible despair had taught him that he deserved no better than what he sought. In her lands, a man with even half of Kheperu's habits would be regarded as a *silba'itan*, an eater of self, to be pitied and avoided. Here in the decadent south, his behavior must be even more extreme—or else he'd blend right in with the crowds, which is the equivalent of death to a *silba'itan*.

Kheperu, blending into the crowds . . . the very thought was ridiculous. Sorcerers don't blend, it's contrary to their nature; they irrevocably set themselves apart from the balance of humanity when they begin to study magic . . .

This led her to consider sorcerers, and soon she found those thoughts of the brand on Othniel's palm sneaking past her guard. Before she could drive them away once more, the shutter slats on the window began to glow crimson with the first bloody rays of dawn.

The grey-faced, groaning innkeeper still lay twisted among the blankets on the bed where Barra and Leucas had placed him. When the three companions were led in by a pallidly silent slave, Lidios' clouded eyes rolled toward them within an otherwise slack and motionless face. The room was heavily shuttered against the morning sun, gloom so deep that Barra wasn't sure he recognized them. The slave bowed, a pained look on her face, and discreetly stepped back out into the passageway.

Leucas and Kheperu both favored Barra with an expectant stare, as though to say *this was your idea*. . . . She pressed her lips together, sighed through her nose, then stepped forward to crouch beside Lidios' bed.

"Lidios?" She gently touched his shoulder. "Lidios, can you hear me?"

" 'Course I can hear you!" he snapped so loudly it made Barra flinch. "I'm dying, not deaf! What do you want now?"

Barra straightened up. "That Akhaian I killed in the fight the other night—Chrysios. Lenka, out in front, she told us that some men came and took his body away late that night. Do you remember?"

His brows drew slowly together. "Yes . . . yes, surely. Korab and Yeshu—a couple Jephunahi toughs, they came with a few hirelings to clear the bodies."

"Do you know what they were going to do with them?"

"Why, bury them, of course. I mean . . ." He lifted a trembling hand to smooth his hair. "I mean, they would bury them, wouldn't they? They wouldn't . . . wouldn't do anything to the bodies, would they?"

"I don't know."

"I'm, well, I'm not, I suppose, the most pious man who ever lived, but I know what Zeus promises to those who dishonor the dead. I mean, you remember what happened to King Kreon, and his city Thebes . . ."

Leucas rumbled, "I remember." Barra could hear his knuckles pop as he unconsciously knotted his fists.

"I don't want to be mixed up with anybody who'd do anything like that," Lidios murmured, rubbing anxiously at his face. "The vengeance of the God spills over sometimes—you don't want to be standing next to the man who catches a thunderbolt. You don't, you don't suppose that . . . oh, they wouldn't! You don't think they might have left the bodies out to rot into flies and be picked at by buzzards—that could be why I've been cursed! It's the vengeance of Zeus!"

He sank back into the bed, his eyes drifting closed as though this outburst had exhausted him. Barra looked down at him, at this mound of sagging flesh that only two days ago had been a fat and jolly man, and at the large stoneware pitcher that rested on a table at his bedside. The pitcher drew her eyes, and the mug that sat beside it; the scent of the pukenuts was strong in the room, probably strong enough for even Kheperu to smell it. She looked over her shoulder at him. He must have somehow seen her thought, for his eyes widened and he began to gesture frantic negatives. She shrugged a half-rueful apology and turned back to Lidios.

"You're not cursed, Lidios."

His eyes fluttered open. Kheperu said warningly, "Barra . . ."

She leaned down to speak softly and clearly, directly into his face. "Tell no one of this, do you understand? No one. There is no curse. There's poison in your rain barrel. Drink only wine and beer, or take all your water from the public wells, and you'll be fine."

"But . . . but . . ."

"Listen to me. No one must know of this for a few days yet. If word gets out that you've broken the curse, the men who poisoned your water will be back; they will kill you and everyone else in this house. Do you understand?"

"I don't understand why . . . you're telling me this. I cursed you, and you saved my life—now you give me this gift as well. Why?"

Barra shrugged and shifted like there were ants inside her tunic. "You were our host."

"We're a long way from Akhaia, and you're not even Greek."

"Ay, well . . . whatever." She turned and pushed Leucas and Kheperu ahead of her. "Let's get out of here."

Once out on the street, Kheperu wheeled on her. "I'd like to know just what you thought you were doing, telling him that?"

Leucas said with hefty finality, "The right thing."

Barra shook her head, and scratched at her scalp, and said, "No, I don't know. I was afraid he'd die, that's all."

"So? Since when do you care?"

Since the sceon tiof *showed me he was a person.* She shut her lips against that thought; the *sceon tiof* was an embarrassing secret that was none of their business. "I don't know. I just do."

"You're changing, Barra," Kheperu said severely, "and I am not sure it's for the better."

She shrugged and whistled to Graegduz, who nosed at a rat hole down the street. "Let's go talk to Jephunah."

The House of Jephunah was of a different style than the walled compound of the Meneides or the sprawling palatial home of the Penthedes. It resembled the mazy block where the Myrmidons kept their apartment: a huge mass of interconnected buildings, three stories and more tall. The original street doors and outer windows of all these buildings had been bricked in over the last twenty years, patches of rich bloodstain-red set sporadically within the sun-bleached walls. The only remaining entrance faced east, a low-ceilinged passageway wide enough for two carts, closed at each end with a heavy bronze gate instead of a door so that the *potameus*—the east wind—could blow freely through it into the courtyard within. That front wall, facing the mountains and the rising sun, was also pegged with bronze hooks the size of Barra's bent arm, all of them crusted and stained black-brown. Below one hook close to the gate, still in shadow as the companions approached, was a blackened patch in the sand from which Barra could smell rotting blood. Kheperu nudged Leucas and nodded toward the hooks. "An unlikely spot to hang meat, don't you think?"

"I was," Leucas rumbled, "thinking just that."

The sleep-ragged voice of a sentry answered their banging on the gate. Barra's demand for a meeting with Jephunah was greeted with blank refusal until she identified herself and her friends as the warriors who had avenged the death of the tax collector.

"Old Melchazar?" the sentry said, a sharper edge coming into his tone. "You're the ones who killed the Greek? Wait there; I'll ask Jephunah if he will see you."

Moments later, a pair of older men came to swing open the gates. They wore only belted robes of striped linen, their faces appeared as weathered and cracked as mountain stone; their invitation to follow them within was grimly polite, but held no hint of deference. *Not slaves,* Barra decided, *likely they're family. Nephews, perhaps even sons.* The low passageway through which they were led had numerous vents in the ceiling. Barra could smell the armed men who watched them from above—she knew they were armed by the pungent scent of the oiled cedar of their spear shafts, distinct from the oiled-bronze smell of the gates. Obviously, the Jephunahi took the events of the last few days very seriously indeed.

Graegduz growled, low in his throat, and pressed close to Barra's leg as they came out of the passage. The courtyard looked deserted; even the balconies that ringed it one atop the other were empty, but it still carried the strong scents of people and dogs. Likely the courtyard had been cleared just now, so that the companions could get no hint of the numbers and capabilities of the inhabitants: here, it seemed, precaution piled upon precaution to the point of absurdity.

Kheperu touched Barra on the shoulder, and murmured, "They certainly know how to welcome guests, do they not?" This earned him a hard look over the shoulder of one of the guides, a look that stopped just short of open hostility.

Leucas barely moved his lips as he whispered, "Be polite."

Barra nodded fervent agreement. She had a feeling that if old Jephunah took a dislike to them, or decided that they were any kind of a threat, they'd be buried here in this very courtyard.

Jephunah himself greeted them in a ground-floor room just off the courtyard. A large chair was this room's only furnishing; he leaned against its back. He was tall, perhaps only a hand shorter than Leucas, and gaunt as a shipwrecked sailor. His close-set eyes held the glossy, inhuman stare of an eagle below brows the color of salt, and his braided beard was dyed ebony-black. His dress was similar to the two guides, a simple shift of striped linen over pants of the same, and his hands, neck, ears, were all bare of jewelry. He took a single step toward them without any hint of a smile of welcome. He said, in fluid Phoenikian that still held a trace of his native Canaanite, "Please excuse my poor hospitality. These are difficult times, and this is an exotic hour to be entertaining mercenaries. What is your desire?"

The chill in his tone gave all the warning Barra needed. She ducked her head and carefully thickened her accent. "Please, sir, I'm sorry t'be botherin' you at this hour in the morning, but I must get a look at that Greek boy, the dead one." It galled her like bee stings to pretend to be stupid and harmless, but she didn't need the *sceon tiof* to show her that Jephunah was the sort to see plots against himself in every heart; the state of siege in his household made that all too clear.

Jephunah's brows drew together. He looked up at Leucas, and snapped, "Why is this woman speaking to me?" Leucas looked back at him, gravely puzzled.

"Your pardon, my lord," Kheperu interjected smoothly. "My friend here has but little of your language, and his woman is from a far foreign land, with strange customs and no knowledge of the proper way of things."

"See that she is instructed."

"I will, oh yes, I certainly will, my lord. Please, though, sir, if it is not too much trouble, we must know what was done with the body of Chrysios, the man who killed, er, Melchazar."

"Why?" he snapped.

"Well, my lord, that's the real question, is it not? I mean, you might well wonder why we should be asking for such a boon . . ." He looked at Barra, and she could see the dawn burst over his brain. He turned easily back to Jephunah and spread his hands, wearing a self-deprecating smile. "It's a religious rite, my lord, to the gods of far-off Albion. She needs a piece of him—a lock of hair, a finger, nothing large or difficult—to be burned in a ritual to honor his shade and to thank her gods for bringing her through the fight."

Jephunah snorted. "I have no interest in barbarian ritual. I meant, why did you not see what you must see and do what you must do without disturbing me? Have the buzzards made him unrecognizable already?"

"I'm sorry?" Kheperu said carefully.

"His is the body that hangs from the hook by the east gate; it is the one that wears the sign 'I Killed a Jephunahi' in three languages."

Barra and Kheperu looked at each other. It was clear that the hook he spoke of was the empty one above the clotted blood that they'd passed on the way in. Barra bared her teeth, and one of her hands curled into a fist at her side. Kheperu sighed and shrugged.

"What is it?" Jephunah barked. "What? Tell me what you know."

"Well, mm, my lord," Kheperu said, "perhaps you—or some others of your household—would like to come outside with us. I wouldn't have you think that we stole the body ourselves."

"The body's gone? Someone *stole* it?"

"I'd assume so, unless you think it got up and walked a—" He suddenly looked acutely uncomfortable. "I apologize, my lord, please forget I said that." He shivered, once, like a man shaking off goose bumps.

"Why would someone steal his corpse?"

"I am quite sure, my lord," Kheperu said, "that I do not want to know."

"I still believe we should have accepted the job," Kheperu said.

"Be quiet," Barra told him. "I think we're getting close."

Graegduz snuffled among the scrub grass and over the rocks and sand. He trotted a ways farther east, and put his head down again. Leucas squinted against the sun—the near faces of the hills, and the caves that opened within them, were still deep in morning shadow with the sun above, shining full on the companions.

"One of those caves," Leucas said. "Any odds you'd care to make, I'll bet. Isn't that the way you Tyrians bury your dead? Block them into a cave?"

"Some do," Barra allowed. "The poor folk burn their dead, or put them in the ground, in passage-graves rather like the ones we have back in the Isle, only smaller and poorer, with no stonework. The wealthier buy a spot in the caves, here. If you're bloody rich, you can buy a cave all your own, sweep out the old bones and have it blocked up with just you inside, and maybe your family and a few choice slaves. But what makes you think they'd bury Chrysios?"

"Because he's *dead*," Kheperu insisted, too loudly. "That's what you do with dead people. You *bury* them."

"Relax, will you?"

Kheperu huffed a sigh through his nose. "Well, I still

cannot see why we could not have taken Jephunah's money. Whom would it hurt, if we tell the Jephunahi where to find his body? We're looking for it already; why shouldn't we be paid for finding it?"

"Because, for the tenth time"—an edge crept into Barra's voice—"finding the body might lead us to the sorcerer. Idonosteus is paying us a hundred and fifty large weights of silver to keep our mouths shut about who this sorcerer is. If we give up the location of the body, we might be giving away the identity of the sorcerer at the same time—and I guarantee that we do not want Idonosteus to think that we're cheating him."

Kheperu sniffed. "What can he do, spank us?"

"He can sic the bloody Myrmidons on us, at the very least."

"Oh, piffle" was his response, but he let the subject drop.

Whoever it was who'd stolen Chrysios' body had done a sloppy job of it. It had still been leaking some various fluids when they carried it off—not enough to leave an obvious trail, but an intermittent splat here and there was enough for Graegduz to follow, even through the city. It had shortly become clear that the corpse and its carriers were headed north and east, into the cave-riddled hills where the dead of Tyre were interred. The swirl of the wind as it twisted between the hills and whistled through the wadis made it impossible for Barra to smell anything beyond sunbaked rock and pine resin, but Graegduz still had the trail, and the companions followed in his wake.

The trail led up through wadi after tangled wadi; these dried watercourses left the hills looking as though they'd been carved by jagged knives. It led through and beyond the funerary ground, ending at a deep cave whose mouth was too wide to be easily sealed. Barra called to Graeg to sit there at the mouth while the companions approached, and he obeyed, shifting his weight impatiently. She stood at the entrance and peered into the deep blackness inside, hands on her hips. "Did anybody think to bring a lamp?"

"Fear not," Kheperu said warmly, digging within his robe to the many pockets inside. "I can do better than a lamp." His hands came out with several small pots of hard-baked white clay. After apparently examining them for markings that neither Barra nor Leucas could discern, he selected four of them, pulled the corks, and began measuring out various portions of

their contents with a small wooden spoon no larger than
Barra's little finger. He placed these powders in the palm of
his left hand, spat into them twice, and rubbed his hands
together to work the compound into a paste. The smell that
came from this made Graegduz whine and Barra gag: it was a
scent rich in decay, a foulness like that which comes from the
corpse of a tortoise baking in the sun; but soon the paste on
his hands took on a pale, greenish-yellow glow that was
faintly visible even in the sunlight. "It's called *tekat-neha,*"
he said. He smeared a broad stripe of it across his forehead,
and then held out his hands. "Come on—a bit of this on your
face, and you'll have light enough wherever you happen to
look."

Barra said, "A bit of that on my face and I'll vomit every
meal I've ever had, back to my mother's milk."

"You're so particular," Khepreu sneered. "Leucas?"

Leucas shrugged and allowed Khepreu to paint his face
with the light-paste. "It tingles."

"That's how you know it is working."

"Can't you simply *see* it—?"

"That is a joke, Leucas; you know, humor? I'm sure you've
heard of it."

"That's enough," Barra said. "Let's do this."

Khepreu wiped the rest of the *tekat-neha* from his hands
onto one end of his staff, and led the way. Once within the
darkness, the glow of the paste was vivid, and cast considerable light. Khepreu held his staff high up over his head like a
torch. The jagged rock of the roof of the cave was faintly
stained a flat matte black. Khepreu smiled and said, "This is
it. See that? Lampblack on the ceiling."

Barra drew her broadaxe and held it across her chest, at the
ready. Leucas watched thoughtfully as she did this, then
nodded silently and drew his sword. As they moved farther
into the depths of the hill, the cave began to narrow and close
in above, the floor rising from hard-packed earth to bare and
jumbled rock. Though the light from his and Leucas' faces
stayed bright, the light from his staff would gradually dim;
Khepreu would renew it from time to time by rubbing his
hands together briskly and using them to warm the paste.
After a while, a thought struck Barra and she whispered to
Khepreu, "Maybe Graeg and I should go a little ahead. In

case someone's still here—they might see our light before we see them."

His reply was also a whisper. "Piffle. No man will stay down here in darkness—it is against nature. Anyone here will have light of their own, which we will see. If they can see ours, we can see theirs. Relax. I think you only want to get away from the smell."

"If I was that worried about getting away from bad smells—"

"All right, all right, *shh*. All this whispering is making me nervous."

A few steps farther on, the cave itself settled the question: it made a gradual bend to the left, and ended in a blank chamber perhaps three paces across.

The walls of the chamber were even more ragged and crumbling than the preceding parts of the cave, and its floor was paved with gravel ranging from the size of sand to the size of Leucas' head. Graegduz nosed around its perimeter, and seemed to find something: he stopped at one point, stared at the wall, and whined.

Kheperu came over and stared at that part of the wall, pointing with his staff to supplement the light from the stripe on his forehead. "Curious. Curious indeed."

Barra and Leucas followed, to peer over his shoulders. "What is?"

"Well," Kheperu sighed, "either they've found a way to pass through solid stone, or we must assume that your mutt here has made a mistake."

"Graeg doesn't make that kind of mistake. And call him a mutt again and I'll let him eat you."

Kheperu sniffed and folded his arms, leaning back against the wall. "Then, perhaps you can explain how the men we are tracking managed to walk through this rock?"

"You're the bloody seshperankh—that's your job, isn't it? We know they came in here—the lampblack, remember?"

"I have been a scholar of the magic arts for more than thirty years. I can state definitely that there is no way. It cannot be done."

"Yes, it can," Leucas said slowly; he'd been staring thoughtfully at the wall.

"Oh? Well then, O Master of Mighty Magics," Kheperu sneered, "perhaps you'd care to enlighten us poor mortals?"

Leucas shrugged. "All right." He too leaned against the wall, near Kheperu, but sideways, his breast against it as though he would press his ear to the stone and listen. He braced his feet, and suddenly cords sprang out in his neck and the long muscles of his thighs bulged in sharp relief; a low scraping grind filled the little chamber. The greenish-yellow light of his face-paint flared bright, he grunted once, and a small jagged section of the wall gave way before him, falling inward with a dull thud that Barra could feel through the soles of her sandals. The opening it left was at about waist-height for Barra, like a window, and just wide enough for one man to pass through comfortably. Leucas picked himself up and dusted off his hands, wearing a small satisfied smile.

Kheperu shook his head disgustedly. "May the gods witness how I despise you."

Leucas' smile widened to a grin. He reached out and patted the stubby Egyptian on the top of the head. "Don't take it hard, Kheperu," he said. "You should just remember that sometimes things are simple." The paste on Kheperu's face brightened considerably, but then he frowned and looked behind into the opening.

"What's that smell?"

The stench that rolled out from the opening was beyond description—worse than a slaughterhouse, worse than a battlefield of unburied dead. Barra backed away, gagging, holding her tunic up over her mouth and nose, Graegduz whimpering and sneezing and pressing against her thigh. Kheperu's eyes filled with tears, he shook his head sharply, coughing, and hurriedly began digging within his pockets. Even Leucas, shattered sinuses notwithstanding, made a face and spat—he could *taste* this foulness. For Barra, with her preternatural sense of smell, it was overwhelming; she staggered away into the darkness of the cave, fell to her knees, and spasmed into throat-racking vomiting.

Then she felt strong hands take her head, and something moist and greasy was smeared across her upper lip; its scent stabbed into her nose at once, sharp and unrecognizable—and then she smelled nothing at all. She opened her eyes to the glowing faces of Leucas and Kheperu—the Egyptian also had something shiny smeared below his nose, and he was in the act of returning a small corked pot to an interior pocket. She took a deep breath, but the stench did not return. She spat and wiped her mouth on her sleeve.

"Again and again I'm impressed with how useful you can be, Kheperu," she said unsteadily. "I don't suppose you'd have anything to *drink* inside that robe, would you?"

Kheperu smiled and offered his hand to help her up. "Nothing that you'd want to put in your mouth, I'm sure. By the way, don't lick your lips—that nose-killer on your upper lip is a bit poisonous."

"Right," she said, nodding, leaning on him as she regained her strength. "Don't put any on Graeg."

"Oh? Can't you simply *tell* him not to lick his nose? In *Pictish*—all animals speak Pictish, do they not?" Kheperu's voice held no hint of sarcasm, but his slight superior smile made up for it.

"Shut up. Let's see what's in there."

Back at the opening, Kheperu looked over the stone plug. "More and more I believe the Tomitiri must be involved in this. See here? From the looks of it, the opening was natural. This was cut and shaped to fit perfectly—this is Egyptian stonework, or I'm a camel."

Beyond, the opening led to a passage only a span or two long, just tall enough for Barra to slip through in a low crouch; both Leucas and Kheperu came through on their hands and knees. It soon opened out into a wide, roughly circular chamber. There were a number of wooden tables in the chamber, five of them that would be chest-high on Barra in a ring around a sixth, somewhat lower, that was slightly slanted, with channels dug into its top, like the drains on a carving board. The five outer tables were crudely constructed, simply boards hammered together with bronze spikes; the one in the middle appeared, by contrast, very sturdy. The table itself was stained and crusted with some substance that looked black in the light from Kheperu's paste; Barra guessed it was old blood, although without being able to smell it, she couldn't be sure. Graegduz whined from the other side of the passage. He didn't want to come in, and Barra didn't blame him.

Various cutting implements rested haphazardly on the outer ring of tables, curved knives and small saws and hammers with long picks on their backs, as well as long-handled spoons and ladles, a selection of bronze tubes of various lengths and diameters, and a few spatulas, some studded on one side with nails. Mounds of unidentifiable detritus littered the floor around the central table; from their appearance Barra guessed them to be discarded bits of internal organs blackened by decay and caked with a paste of blood, dirt, and gravel.

Leucas examined the central table with interest, running his fingers through designs crudely carved into the wood. "Does any of this mean anything to you?"

Barra looked at the designs, clear in the light from Leucas' face-paint. Some of them resembled Egyptian glyphs, but most seemed to be writing of some sort, in an alphabet that Barra didn't recognize, all short strokes, vertical and horizontal, sometimes connected, sometimes apparently modified by a dot above or below. "Kheperu. What do you make of this?"

"I don't know," Kheperu said hoarsely. He stood very still near the opening through which they'd entered, both hands clutching his staff as though it were a blanket protecting him from a bitter wind. "I, ah . . ." he coughed to steady his voice, then continued, "I simply cannot be sure . . ."

"You haven't even really looked."

"Barra," he began, and paused, turning his head as though to swallow with some difficulty. He wiped his mouth and continued. "There are some branches of magic with which I am acquainted only by rumor. My alchemical researches necessarily restrict my field of view within the—"

"What're you so afraid of?" Barra snapped. "Come on, out with it."

Leucas looked around, rubbing his hands together to dust off the crusted granules of whatever caked the central table. "This is necromancy, isn't it," he said heavily. "I have heard of such practices."

"Oh, *necromancy*," Kheperu said dismissively. "Well, in a way, I suppose, but you must understand that necromancy is a perfectly honest way to make a living, with a long and honorable tradition; raising the shades of the dead to divine the future or discover hidden treasure, that sort of thing, along with preparing the bodies of the dead properly for their journey after their interment . . ."

Barra cocked her head and squinted at him. He wasn't only afraid—he wasn't even *mostly* afraid; it was anger that drove this babble. Kheperu trembled with anger, veins pulsing at his temples, his breath coming in short choppy gasps; it was as though he spoke to distract himself, as though he feared that if he acknowledged his anger, it would swell beyond control and burst his very chest. "So this is no mere necromancy," Barra said carefully. "Can you tell me what it is?"

"Among the implements on the tables," Kheperu said, his voice thin with effort, "are there any of iron? Or even of silver?"

Leucas shook his head, and Barra answered, "No."

Kheperu seemed to become smaller, to press in upon himself like a boar gathering itself for the charge. "You see, necromancers are scrupulously clean. A necromantic workshop is customarily open to the night sky, well lit, and washed with water every day. A necromancer's implements are polished like mirrors, and made of the most expensive materials available, usually silver, sometimes even Hittite iron if he can afford it. All this is to avoid mixing the tissue—the organs, the blood, fecal matter, even hair—of one client with that of another, and thus confusing the influences and possibly canceling the efficacy of the magic in use. But this . . . this *slaughterhouse*"—his suppressed rage infused the word with acid contempt—"this is no work of any necromancer."

He drew himself up and spoke through clenched teeth. "This man, whoever he may be, traffics with demons."

Leucas' brows drew together. "Half-godling children?"

Barra shook her head. "The same word for different things," she told him. "Demons in Egypt are spirits that thrive on pain and suffering, and rend the souls of the dead for their amusement."

"It is forbidden," Kheperu said, "to even speak the name of a demon, for it may come when called, and thus break through into the world of light. This, this *demonist,* summons them deliberately. That is why there are no tools of silver or of iron; these metals are anathema to the Children of Apep. In Egypt, we would be rewarded for putting such a man to death without mercy."

Leucas appeared skeptical. "How is it that you have so much of this 'forbidden knowledge'?"

Kheperu regarded Leucas steadily and silently, without moving, for a long and measured breath. The paste on his brow grew brighter and brighter. Finally he said, in a low and controlled tone, "I was once accused of being such. I learned much from my questioners during the weeks of their inquisition."

"You—?" Barra breathed.

He nodded with stiff dignity. "It is why I cannot return to Egypt. The order for my execution still stands."

"But how . . . why . . ."

"I do not wish to speak of it. We have other more pressing business." He gestured toward another cleft in the stone walls of the chamber, that seemed to lead to perhaps another passage beyond. "Perhaps they have left a trail that can still be followed by your . . . by Graegduz."

Barra nodded agreement, but said, "Someday, you'll have to tell me the whole story."

"Someday. Perhaps."

The three companions lay flat among the rocks and tufts of grass at the summit of a low, gentle hill, mid-afternoon sun hot on their backs.

"How is it," Leucas muttered, "that we always manage to skip our noon meal?"

"Don't remind me," Kheperu replied. Shortly after they'd left the cave, he'd cast aside that strange and unaccustomed dignity like an ill-fitting tunic and slowly, as though awakening from a dream, he'd become once again his familiar whining, petty self. "Next time we go tracking someone, we should remember to bring a few waterskins, as well."

"Whine, whine, whine," Barra said, her hand on Graegduz's back. "All this city living has made you soft. Now shut up and look—riders."

Perhaps fifteen or twenty horsemen filed into view between rolling hills. They were obviously heading for the wide estate, olive groves and placidly grazing goats and sheep surrounding an enormous, palatial house, that centered on the top of the highest hill in view. Barra could see now a small party of riders—three of them—come from a smaller structure near the main house, that must serve as a stable, and ride out to meet the approaching column.

The cleft on the far side of the chamber had indeed led to another cave that opened on the opposite side of the hill. That cave was littered with horse dung and patches of drying urine; Barra was able to determine that seven horses had ridden out from there. The combination of her ability to read tracks and

Graegduz's keen nose had led them into view of this massive estate, an hour's ride to the southeast of Tyre. Leucas had been all for assaulting the place themselves: "We could attack them—we wait until nightfall, then sneak in and grab the son of a whore, just like Odysseus and Diomedes went into Troy to steal the Palladion." Barra reminded him that they didn't know who, among the estate's inhabitants, the demonist was. "And, anyway, we're not being paid to kill him. We're being paid to tell Idonosteus who he is."

Kheperu had looked thoughtful. "Do you remember," he'd said slowly, "what I told you about some rich Egyptian coming in to buy up all the slaves under twenty? It's said that the traffick with demons ages a man unnaturally; it's also said that demons can renew a man's youth—provided they have blood of youths with which to work."

Barra's eyes had drifted closed against this thought. "Maybe we should sneak in there and kill him. Just kill him, forget the money."

"Forget the *money*?" Kheperu had said, appalled. "I think not! We can collect from Idonosteus, and let the Meneides kill this man—much safer, and more profitable."

"I think we should steal him," Leucas insisted stubbornly. "Imagine the kind of ransom such a man could pay."

"Forget it," Barra said firmly. "Kheperu's right."

"I am?"

"Ay. Let's collect from Idonosteus, then, maybe if we're lucky, he'll hire us to kill the guy."

But now, as they lay on the hilltop watching the riders, a banner unfurled from the pole of a standard-bearer who rode at the head of the column; it was bloodred and purple, and a matching banner ran up the pole on the estate house's roof, and when Kheperu saw the design on it, he gasped.

"Oh, Great Ra and the Living-bloody-*Horus*! Do you know who that *is*?"

"You're turning pale," Leucas observed with a smile.

Barra said, "Shut up. Who is it?"

Kheperu wiped his mouth with a trembling hand. "What was that you said about being lucky if we're hired to kill him? Perhaps you should rethink that idea, Barra. Perhaps we should think about collecting our fee and taking a nice long trip to Crete."

"Why?" Barra said, barely resisting an urge to throttle him.

"Because when the Meneides kill him—or someone in his household—there will descend upon this pisswater port a storm of war like none of us have ever seen. That fellow down there—who, I'd guess, owns this place—that's a fellow named Meremptah-Sifti."

"Never heard of him," said Leucas, and Barra shrugged.

"Perhaps not. But you've heard of his grandfather. Meremptah-Sifti is a grandson of Ramses the Great."

Barra felt a shock go through her, and her stomach suddenly clenched like a knotted fist. Leucas still looked blank.

"The Living Horus," Kheperu explained. Leucas shook his head.

Barra said, "Ramses is the *Pharaoh,* Leucas. Ramses the Great, this guy's grandfather, is the god that rules Egypt—and, for that matter, Phoenikia as well."

Leucas said, "Oh. Oh, my."

CHAPTER NINE

Meremptah-Sifti

Meremptah-Sifti dismounted with acrobatic smoothness, swinging his off-leg forward, over the horse's head, to pivot in the saddle, and slide gracefully to the ground. His horse took this motionlessly. Lesser creatures never defied Meremptah-Sifti's will; if this horse had had the audacity, the bad judgment to shy at such treatment, Meremptah-Sifti would have killed it on the spot, as he had the last two horses he had ridden. This was a whim he was more than wealthy enough to indulge.

He strode away from the horse, leaving it to wander. Now that the prince had touched the earth, the men-at-arms who accompanied him could also dismount; one of them would catch and tend to Meremptah-Sifti's horse. It was of no concern to the prince who cared for his beasts, so long as they were always at his disposal when he wanted them. If they were not, someone would suffer.

He struck a thoughtful pose as he looked down upon his lands; they spread below this hilltop in all directions, groves of olive and fig and citrus trees, and open meadows where goats placidly grazed. He knew that he cut an impressive figure, the heavy muscles of his bare chest and arms bronzed, setting off the broad arc of black iron and shining gold of the pectoral that covered his shoulders, his unbound hair flowing, streaks within it bleached red by the sun.

Meremptah-Sifti was always keenly aware of how he appeared to others; movement for him consisted of flowing from one pose to another with pantherish grace. He stood there, well satisfied with what he saw, and with what he knew his men saw of him, while the sun sank into the sea. On the hill below him, they fell into twilight first, leaving him shining in the scarlet sunset before the high walls of his manor.

The nervous cough behind him was unmistakably Haral Mesti's. "Welcome home, my prince. How went your business in Sidon?"

Meremptah-Sifti moved only his head to glance at Haral, and he showed his gleaming teeth in a broad and predatory grin. "Perfectly. The Governor was pleased to accept my offer. Thank you for asking, Haral."

"And Simi-Ascalon? Did he not return with you?"

Meremptah-Sifti waved a languid hand in the direction of the funerary caves. "He stopped at his workshop to retrieve some tool or other. He was a bit rushed when he left—dealing with not only the Greek but that Tomitiri fellow, that Bezai managed to lure to the caves . . . what was his name? Peth . . . something. Not important; he's certainly dead by now. Sim should be here shortly."

Alongside the nervous captain was a pair of slaves, one bearing a small stamnos of wine and a cup, the other with a tray of toasted breads and slices of cheese. Meremptah-Sifti accepted the wine, and waved away the slave with the food. He drank deeply, calmly, meditatively, and presented the empty cup to be refilled. When he had sipped again, he said, "And where is Silam? Where are my mercenaries?"

"Silam is within, my prince. He—he asked me to tell you, that the mercenaries are, are not to be found . . ."

Meremptah-Sifti turned fully to face Haral, the scarlet remnants of the sunset gleaming in his eyes. He said only a very soft: "Oh?"

Haral swallowed. "The Jephunahi innkeeper told him that they went off with some trader named Murso. But no one seems to know who this Murso is, or where to find him. The mercenaries were seen, though, yesterday, in several different parts of the city. They seemed, uh, Silam said they seemed to be"—Haral visibly steeled himself—"they might have been asking about the cursed inns."

Meremptah-Sifti looked beyond his sweating captain, far to the west, where storm clouds gathered over the thin grey sliver of the sea. Jagged thunderbolts flickered beneath them, and the prince of Egypt fought to keep his rising excitement out of his voice. "Indeed. And why, Haral, is it that Silam does not make this report himself?"

"He, well, he asked me to tell you."

Meremptah-Sifti only gazed into Haral's watery eyes. He

knew full well the reason Silam asked Haral to give this message; it is a burden of leadership, that no one wishes to bring bad news in person. He dismissed this; his blood sang to him a more interesting melody: *There is more than chance in this, perhaps more than simple fate,* he thought. *Now they mix in my affairs not by chance, but by intention. I must meet them. I must have them.*

And he would; there was no doubt of this. Meremptah-Sifti had built a lifetime on getting precisely what he wanted.

Meremptah-Sifti's earliest memories were of his aunties, an ever-changing flux of young women that passed through the cool, curtained bedchambers of Kallela's, an expensive and exclusive brothel on the outskirts of Ascalon. Ascalon was a main way station on the Coast Road from the Nile Delta to the Hittite capital of Hattusas on the bluffs overlooking the river Halys; the whores at Kallela's often chanced to bed nobility of one or the other of the allied empires, when these passing men espied their exceptional beauty and compared them with the now-familiar faces and figures of the women they'd brought along from home.

His aunties came and went with baffling regularity, sometimes leaving to join the wives of a wealthy man, more often being turned out as their looks began to fail; occasionally they died of the fevers that seemed to strike Ascalon so regularly. Meremptah-Sifti was a beautiful child, who swiftly learned how to wheedle a sweetmeat or a sip of wine out of any woman, whether they were already friends or not, with a combination of sly smiles and quivering pouts. He was a great favorite among the whores, and a joy to his mother. With best guess, she raised him to have the courtly manners of the Egyptian nobility, and the whores would often gather around to hear him sing or recite a legend, and pay him with hugs and kisses and strokes on his silky hair.

Kallela's had another side, as well, a duplicate courtyard and chambers, on the other side of a high, unclimbable wall. It was well-stocked with young men and boys, but Meremptah-Sifti never saw it; his mother had in mind a more special occupation for him. Despite her sheltering, he knew all about the other side, of course—his brother Simi, four years older, already worked there. Meremptah-Sifti, aged five, knew bitter envy for the first time, when Simi would sometimes brag of gifts given him by wealthy men, in exchange for the simple use of his young body; sometimes, Simi said, it didn't even hurt. Meremptah-Sifti prayed to the immortal Ra every day to give him gifts that would surpass Simi's, and to give him the size and strength he'd need to beat his brother, to grind his face into the ground and make him eat the dirt, as Simi had sometimes done to him. Meremptah-Sifti had his initial glimmering intimations of his special destiny when the first of these prayers was answered.

In the spring of his sixth year, Meremptah-Sifti met his father for the first time.

He still remembered this clearly, even now. In fact, when some minor reversal of fate would threaten his ambitions, he'd call it deliberately to mind, dwell upon it, ease his worries with the warm and glowing memory of being presented to that fat and sweating man to whom everyone bowed. He remembered the terror of walking alone, away from his mother's side, along a carpet lined with grim, threatening-faced men. He remembered the rotten-barley scent of the beer that leaked out through the fat man's pores and impregnated the rich clothing the man had worn, he remembered being taken in the man's arms, onto his minuscule lap and receiving a sloppy kiss that smelled of bad teeth and old meat. He hadn't flinched, though, had given no sign how repulsive he found this man; his mother had schooled him well—it is an essential skill of a successful whore. And then had come the moment, the single instant that defined his life: the fat man had set him back upon his feet and gently turned him to face the gathered assemblage . . . and everyone had bowed to him!

To Meremptah-Sifti, the little whoreson, all these distant, frightening men had lowered their frowning faces to the floor; they had prostrated themselves to honor him. He'd been shaken with some emotion for which, at six, he had no name. All he knew was that this rapture answered some need within him that he'd never known he had.

The fat man was Namisallu, a younger son of Ramses the Great; he was still, in those days, a vigorous man despite the increasing tolls of age and drink, still believing that little Meremptah-Sifti was only one among what would be great hordes of children. He'd given his little by-blow gifts of gold and robes and spices, and prepared to leave; he was only passing through Ascalon on the Pharaoh's business, after all.

Meremptah-Sifti had clung to his kilt, weeping the sort of tears he'd learned were most effective, and had touched his father's beery heart. Namisallu promised to call again, to visit his son whenever his business took him through town.

Meremptah-Sifti's rapture lasted only until his father's departure. His mother took his fine gifts away and sold them, and his brother Simi—half brother only, child of some anonymous sailor, or soldier, or beggar, as he now knew—beat him ever harder each time Meremptah-Sifti mentioned his father's wealth, or position. Namisallu was never to return to Ascalon, although a steady stream of gifts came up the Coast Road— gifts that Meremptah-Sifti rarely had a chance to so much as see, let alone touch or play with, before they were sold by his mother.

It was about this time that Simi became interested in death. He'd talk about it, sometimes at great length, to his little brother. He'd spin theories, and try to show Meremptah-Sifti why they were true by slowly killing beetles and spiders, observing them minutely as he pulled off their limbs. Once, when Meremptah-Sifti was seven, a gull had fallen into the courtyard, and Meremptah-Sifti had swiftly gathered it up inside a blanket and carried it to his brother, a reverential offering. The gull was sick, too ill to fly; its black-opal eyes were filmed and crusted with yellowish scurf, and a pinkish froth leaked from its beak. Simi was delighted. He secreted the gull away in a back corner of the wine cellar and spent three happy days sticking it with bronze needles. When it finally died, he lovingly plucked it and gently cut it to pieces with a small knife he'd stolen from the kitchen, and during this whole three days he'd completely forgotten to torment his little brother. Meremptah-Sifti had finally discovered how to handle him.

After this time, Meremptah-Sifti became Simi's enthusiastic accomplice. Pets began to disappear around Kallela's; first birds, then cats, and even small dogs. It was not unusual for a wealthy client to try to please his favorite whore with a well-bred puppy or kitten, and it was hard for any whore to resist Meremptah-Sifti's tearful pleas to be allowed to play with this one or that one. And when he'd return, without the animal, he'd be crying even harder—the bird had slipped from his hands and flown away, the kitten had scampered over the wall, the puppy had bolted through a door left carelessly ajar—and the whore would take little Meremptah-Sifti onto her lap and rock him and comfort him until he could dry his eyes. It was here that he truly began to comprehend his power over women; at the age of nine, he gave his virginity to an achingly beautiful little whore, only five years older than he, whose favorite puppy he had helped Simi to skin alive less than an hour before.

It was not long after this that he overheard a conversation between his mother and the brothel's scribe. It seemed that Namisallu had written a letter asking that Meremptah-Sifti be sent to him, to Egypt, to be raised properly, as an Egyptian prince of the royal house. It seemed that Namisallu's loins had not been as fertile as he'd wished; the other two sons he'd fathered had both died without issue, and Meremptah-Sifti was his only living heir. Meremptah-Sifti's heart had surged with joy, until he heard his mother's dictated reply. No, she'd said, her health wouldn't stand the journey, and she couldn't allow her son to leave her. Meremptah-Sifti knew that what she really wanted was to simply stay here in Ascalon and continue to receive the sumptuous gifts that his father sent for him; it had been four years since his mother had needed to have sex with a client. She was perfectly comfortable here, lording it over the other whores, and had no desire to ever leave. Her letter in response said that she could never give up her little Meremptah-Sifti, not while she lived; and so it was at this time that Meremptah-Sifti began to plan her death.

He never considered simply running away, and if he had he would have dismissed the idea instantly. Egypt was unimaginably far away, and besides, as he'd told himself thousands of times, he was a prince. Princes do not sneak, nor do they hide, and they certainly do not run away from home.

That summer, swamp fever raged in Ascalon. Half the town was sick with it, a fever that would keep a strong man in bed for eight or nine days, trembling in a pool of his own sweat— many of the weak and sickly did not survive it. Meremptah-Sifti's mother was stricken, but she was strong and not yet old, or so the other whores said, and she had lived through a fever like this one only six years before. Meremptah-Sifti was never slow to seize an opportunity, nor afraid to recognize his own limitations; only ten years old, he didn't yet have the strength to battle his mother, even in her fever-weakened state . . . but Simi, he was fourteen, and already showing signs of the breadth of shoulder he'd acquire with manhood.

Recruiting his older brother was simple. After all, Meremptah-Sifti was leaving Ascalon to be a prince of Egypt, and he could offer his brother a simple choice: Help me, and I will take you with me, and I will be your friend and protector, you will always be by the side of a prince of Egypt, even unto the day of your death. With all my wealth and power, I will support you. Help me not, and stay here, poking little birds with needles and taking grown men up your ass until you are too old or your looks fail, and you are turned out into the street.

Simi had readily agreed; he'd been dreaming of studying the necromantic arts of Egypt for years—and this would be his first opportunity to kill a human being.

The murder was also simple. They came to her room while their mother tossed in the grip of a fever dream. Meremptah-Sifti's talent for getting his own way served him well here, as he soulfully requested that the pair of whores who attended her leave him and his brother alone with their mother for a moment; there are things a boy can say to his mother only while they are alone together, and he was afraid she might die before he could tell her . . . and that was all it took. The whores left the room, and Meremptah-Sifti watched while Simi held a pillow over their mother's face, pressing her down into the bed as she started to struggle. Her legs kicked and twitched, he thought, very much like they used to when a grunting man lay atop her, and she was pretending pleasure. Eventually, she stopped moving, and the boys spent a moment working up their tears before rushing out to cry her death.

Within a week, they were on their way to the Nile Delta, to Namisallu's estate on the outskirts of Per-Ramses, the capital. It was on this journey, on the road, that Simi the whoreson became Simi-Ascalon, the prince's manservant; it was also on this journey that Simi first showed his younger brother some of the tricks of pleasure that he'd learned on the other side of Kallela's, as a way to pass the time on the long trip. Their blood bond was never spoken of again, but once in Egypt Meremptah-Sifti proved to be a man of his word, even at ten. After all, princes are supposed to be men of honor, to keep their word, and Meremptah-Sifti saw to it that his father sponsored Simi-Ascalon into the priesthood of the House of Life.

Through the years that followed, it seemed that nothing could ever be denied to him, and so his ambitions grew with his body. As he grew, he learned—as befits a prince of Egypt—to command more, and wheedle less. He joined the army, as was expected of him, and rose swiftly through the ranks by a combination of his native ability with politicking and the occasional convenient deaths, covertly accomplished by Simi-Ascalon, of men who could not be moved from his path by any other means.

Simi-Ascalon, meanwhile, showed talent of his own. He threw himself into his studies in the House of Life with passionate abandon. In a few short years he was confirmed as a seshperankh; a few short years after that he had surpassed his teachers and followed his own path of study and experiment into ever-darker realms. His health began to fail, and he became more and more withdrawn and isolated, even among the priesthood; the other priests would whisper to each other and sidle away when they saw his hollow-eyed form approach or heard his rasping cough, but Meremptah-Sifti always had time and warmth to spare for him, always attended to his interests, listened to his complaints and his enthusiasms, hugged and held him with more-than-brotherly love.

Meremptah-Sifti might have been in Egypt still, were it not for his Uncle Merneptah, eldest surviving son of Ramses the Great and heir apparent to the throne. Merneptah was a gruff, stolid, unimaginative man who'd made his home in the Pharaoh's army for more than forty years. From their first meeting—when Meremptah-Sifti realized that his late mother had given him the first half of his name in a transparent attempt to flatter the next Pharaoh and, in her ignorance, *hadn't even gotten it right*—this seemed to be a doomed relationship. Merneptah seemed immune to every conceivable combination of flattery, bribery, and comradely backslapping; in fact, it seemed that the harder Meremptah-Sifti tried to gain his confidence, the warier and more distant his uncle became. The man seemed to have no vices or shameful secrets, or anything else Meremptah-Sifti could use against him. Worse, the soldiers he commanded were so loyal as to report Meremptah-Sifti's discreet inquiries back to their commander, and late one night Meremptah-Sifti was hauled shivering from his bed, arrested, and brought before his uncle at the army's camp outside of Thebes.

"I do not like you, boy," Merneptah had said. "I do not like you, I do not trust you, and if you were not my drunken brother's only son, if you did not have my father's blood in your veins, I would have you killed. Stay away from me. Stay away from my men. In fact, get out of Egypt for a few years; I do not want to be worrying about what you're up to back here while I'm off on campaign in Kush. Don't think I will tolerate disobedience; I can hurt you in ways that will spill no sacred blood."

Meremptah-Sifti had gathered his scattered dignity and said, "I bow to your will, Uncle. I do not know with what I am accused, and it does not matter; any claim against my honor can only be a lie. There is no man living who loves and honors you more than I. I pray that you will come to know this, and when you do, send for me."

After that, his only hope of remaining in Egypt was a swift and secret poisoning, but Merneptah remained in camp, preparing for his campaign among his loyal men; there was no opportunity.

His uncle's enmity proved to be a blessing in the end, though, as Meremptah-Sifti moved his household north and east into the District of Canaan, where he was born. Here, away from the prying eyes of crowded Egypt, he could do things he'd never dare attempt at home. In Egypt, it seemed that there were endless ranks of royal grandchildren, most of them having precedence of some sort or another over him, and there were countless high priests, and military generals, and friends of the court of this and that variety, all men that he must treat with respect, and deference. But here, here near the frontier with Hattiland, ah, everything was different. Here the politics of Egypt were meaningless.

Here there was no one who could tell him no.

In taking Egypt from him, his uncle had given him the world.

Meremptah-Sifti was dining when Simi-Ascalon rushed in, breathless and sweating. The prince reclined on a couch-length pillow of vermilion hexamitos; a pair of young slaves, brother and sister, knelt to either side of his head and gently fed him steaming bites of lamb and sips of imported Egyptian beer.

Simi-Ascalon, in his wide-eyed panic, did not await permission to speak. "Remmie!" he gasped, "Remmie, someone's been in my sanctum! *Someone's been to the caves!*" He would have gone on, but a fit of coughing overtook him, doubling him over and driving him red-faced to his knees.

Meremptah-Sifti came off the pillow to his brother's side in an instant; he'd done this many times, and he knew what was required. He laid his powerful arm across Simi-Ascalon's shoulders and hugged him tightly, gathered his head to his breast. "It is all right, Sim. Calm down, it will be all right," he murmured softly, over and over again. Simi-Ascalon's coughing began to quiet, to become little more than a shuddering of his shoulders like a child's sobbing that slowly trails to silence. Meremptah-Sifti glared at the boy-slave. "My napkin," he snapped. The boy flinched, and stared back with wide, uncomprehending eyes.

The prince pantomimed wiping his face, and pointed at the napkin. The boy swiftly gathered it up and brought it to him, and received in return a backhanded blow across the face that sent him sprawling, for not understanding Egyptian.

Meremptah-Sifti held the napkin to his brother's mouth, and pounded Simi-Ascalon's back. Simi-Ascalon coughed again, gagged, and finally spat forth a mouthful of bloody goo. Meremptah-Sifti wadded the napkin around it and tossed it aside. "All right now?"

Simi-Ascalon nodded mutely as he regained his breath, then added, "Yes—yes, Remmie, thank you. But the cave— the *cave*, Remmie—"

"Now, do not excite yourself again. Are you certain that someone has been there?"

"Yes—yes, he found the hidden mouth, he—*hrakhakh*—he threw up there. And I think there must have been more than one; one man alone cannot shift the slab."

Meremptah-Sifti shrugged dismissively. "How many of the hyaenae did we lose, in destroying that Jephunahi caravan? Three? Four? Take the rest to the cave and put them on the scent; have them kill everyone they find. Better yet: have them kill everyone they meet along the way. This will make another lovely rumor to spread terror through the city."

"Mmn, all right, Remmie." Simi-Ascalon breathed more

easily now, and the apoplectic scarlet began to drain from his face. "I'm sorry—I'm sorry I got so . . . . well, you know. I just keep thinking of them in there, walking around in there, touching all my stuff—"

Meremptah-Sifti gave his brother's shoulders a comforting squeeze, and gently stroked his face. "But they'll be dead soon, Sim. All of them will be dead before sunrise." Sim nodded silently, and the prince returned to his pillow and accepted another sip of wine from the flinching girl.

"How do you think they found it?" he said. "How could they possibly have found that cave?"

Simi-Ascalon shook his head; he came over and lowered himself into a sitting position near Meremptah-Sifti's feet. "Perhaps someone saw Bezai's men capture Peth An'khefi, and followed them?"

"No, Bezai is hardly that great a fool. Besides, you had that Peth fellow there for hours; I should think Nephrol Tomit would have mounted a rescue, if he'd had any scrap of information. And Haral, with the Greek's corpse . . . could he have disgraced himself again? Could he be followed through a moonless night?" Meremptah-Sifti swirled the wine within his golden goblet; the reflections on its surface, echoes of the lamp flames above him, were as darkly red as a dead man's blood. "But the girl . . ."

His voice trailed off. Simi-Ascalon waited a properly respectful interval—to make sure he was not interrupting—before prompting: "Yes, Remmie? The girl?"

"My mercenaries," said the prince slowly. "My three mercenaries—*the girl has a dog!*" He jerked himself up straight, his face alive with delight; the motion slopped wine from his cup across Simi-Ascalon's leg, but he didn't notice and Simi-Ascalon wouldn't dare to protest. "My mercenaries killed my Greek . . . what if they tracked his corpse?" He threw back his head in gusty, joyous laughter. "Of course it's them! Who else would it be?" He held up a fist, to display the thick gooseflesh that wrapped his forearm. "Look at my skin!" he said. "It's them! Listen, Sim, I don't want them killed—how can we bring them here alive?"

"Alive? But, but, Remmie, you promised—"

"Oh, don't trouble yourself." Meremptah-Sifti patted him on the knee with a fatherly hand. "I would not force you to forgo your proper revenge for their violations; only think how

IRON DAWN *179*

much greater that revenge can be, if they still live when they
are dragged to your sanctum?"

Simi-Ascalon looked considerably mollified.

"Still," the prince said, frowning. "I like the idea of the
hyaenae running through the streets of Tyre, killing all they
meet . . ." He brightened. "I have it—send the Greek with
them! He knows my mercenaries, does he not? When the
hyaenae come across my mercenaries, he can point them out
to be captured, rather than killed."

Simi-Ascalon now looked doubtful. He said, "But, but he's
not ready. He's not ready yet, Remmie."

Meremptah-Sifti turned his palms down upon his knees and
leaned forward, and his voice took on a dangerous silkiness.
"How long before he can walk and talk?"

"Well, for that, only a few hours, but—"

"Do we have another man who knows my mercenaries by
sight?"

"I, I, ah, I don't—*hrakhakh*—I don't know . . ."

"Then make him ready, Simi. Before I get angry."

Simi-Ascalon scrambled to his feet, but remained at the
foot of the pillow, wringing his hands. "But, but, but Remmie,
my control, my control won't be very good—and Chrysios,
you know, he was a little crazy anyway, what if he doesn't
want to—"

"Do whatever it takes," Meremptah-Sifti told him. "Bar-
gain with him, if necessary. Promise him whatever you like.
Only remember: kill *everyone*. Except my mercenaries—I
want at least one or two of the three alive and in shape for
interrogation. Everyone else, *everyone*—no mistakes—dies.
Do you understand?"

Simi-Ascalon bowed to his younger brother. "It will be
done, my prince."

CHAPTER TEN

The Report

The servants' quarters of the house of Peliarchus were quiet again, now that Leucas had rolled over on his bunk and his snoring had trailed off. On the bunk above, Kheperu smiled and murmured something in his sleep, then he, too, quieted and the only sound was the scritch-scratch of Barra's reed pen. Graegduz snoozed silently against her ankles, warming her feet in the late-evening chill. The tiny fish-oil lamp on the table before her cast a ring of light just bright enough to illuminate the long strip of sun-bleached parchment scroll on which she wrote. The smoky grey-black taste of the burning oil nearly covered the inevitable reek of sharing a room with Kheperu, and buried completely the scent of the ink and the lamb fat that had been rubbed into the parchment to keep it supple.

Dear Antiphos and Chryl,

You must be surprised to get this letter. When I sent the last one, I thought that the Skye Swift *would be my last chance to send you a packet, but your Uncle Peliarchus is leaving for the Isle of the Mighty in a few days, as soon as he clears away some obligations here in Tyre. This time, he'll be bringing his wife, Tayniz. You'll love her as much as I do, I know; she reared me well here in Tyre—she's practically as much your grandmother as Coll is.*

The three of us—that's Leucas, Kheperu, and myself, you remember—are staying with Peliarchus again. We had to spend a few days guesting elsewhere, because he's been hosting King Demetor of Kypros, who's a relative of Agapenthes, who is Peliarchus' liege lord (in a sense), and well, it's really rather complicated. This is the obligation I was writing about earlier.

I can't tell you much of what I've been doing here. I've

*been paid a great deal of silver to keep it secret, and
despite the fact that your Uncle Peliarchus can't read
Greek, I'll be sending this with him, and you know how
nosy he is. He'd probably go to the Market and hire a
scribe to translate it for him.*

I'm planning to take the Langdale's Pride *north after
the Knossian Trade Fair in the spring. Business is going
very well; Tyre has proven as profitable as I'd hoped, and
we may perhaps even be able to afford to add a third ship
to our tiny fleet this year.*

*There are a few things I can tell you about, though. On
our very first day here, some sailors brought a bear
through the Market . . .*

She wrote on for some time, dodging details, pausing occasionally to trim her pen against the keen edge of her broadaxe; soon one corner of her mouth was blue-black from chewing the reed tip into a suitable brush. During one of those pauses, she tapped her teeth with the pen, thinking of the day's events, then shrugged and continued to write.

*. . . in your education. Tell Abdi—as I will in a separate
letter—not to neglect the study of politics, especially the
dynastic politics of Egypt. If you boys plan to travel suc-
cessfully here in the East, you'd best be aware of some of
the civic realities . . .*

The sun had dipped toward the west and extinguished itself in the sea by the time the three companions had walked back into Tyre from the estate of the Pharaoh's grandson. They'd walked in silence, mostly, each in their own way daunted by what they'd learned. Meremptah-Sifti was, by Kheperu's account, one of sixty-three legitimate grandchildren of the Living Horus; he was descended through the eldest of Ramses' three living wives, Isinofre. His father was the younger of Isinofre's two sons; there was a rumor that his mother was an Ascalonian whore, but this was not confirmed. Kheperu guessed his age to be somewhere within a few years either way of Leucas' thirty-five, and said that while Meremptah-Sifti had distinguished himself as a very young man during a campaign in Kush—in the Pharaoh's own Ra Division—and kept a home in Per-Ramses, the capital, he'd lately been living in Upper Egypt, in the former capital of Thebes, to ingratiate himself with his powerful grandmother Isinofre, who maintained her household there. "Lately," in this case, meant a few years before Kheperu's exile—he had no information more recent than the past decade—but even so, he recalled tales of scandalous libertinage and suggestions of two or three hushed-over deaths.

"And Ramses, as you may know, is an old-fashioned sort— his father, Seti, came up through the military, and raised his son the very same way—and so I'd guess that our young Meremptah is none too popular with the court. It could explain what he's up to here. He can set the Great Houses against each other, embarrass the Governor, perhaps get himself the rule of Phoenikia, which, as the main conduit between the two greatest empires of the world—Egypt and Hattiland—it would serve as an admirable base from which to contend for the throne, should Ramses die without naming a successor. This, of course, is possible, even likely, because after all, Ramses is the oldest man in the world, nearly ninety years of age, and even his deific vitality cannot hold out forever. He could die at any time, and the consequences would be staggering. As a matter of fact, I can recall a time when—"

"So," Leucas had interrupted, to forestall another lengthy disquisition of the labyrinthine politics of Egypt, "if the Pharaoh doesn't like him, why can't we simply kill the man?"

Kheperu sighed. "I despair of ever bringing you to any sort of political awareness. Put simply: it is not only the royal blood of Egypt that flows through his veins, it is the very seed of Horus the Avenger. Any spill of the blood of gods must be revenged a thousandfold. It's traditional. You see? In practical terms, if Ramses does not exact a horrific punishment for this sort of crime, then none of his blood will be safe. He could despise his grandson with a searing hatred beyond your understanding, and it would matter not a whit."

"Only cowards count the cost of doing right," Leucas rumbled.

"A fine philosophy, that led to half a million funeral pyres on the plains of Troy," Kheperu countered.

Barra had been too consumed with her own worries to step in; she let them bicker continuously until they reached the apartments of the Myrmidons. They had no lamp to go through the face-lighting business that Murso had shown them, but Kheperu swiftly mixed together a handful of his light-paste to use instead. Within minutes of their arrival, a Myrmidon runner had departed for the Meneides compound with news that they'd completed their mission and a request for a meeting with Idonosteus so that they might give their report.

> *I suppose I should also tell you that I've something of a gentleman admirer. He's a mercenary captain, very brave and very smart—he's a veteran of the Siege of Troy, in the company of Golden Akhilleus, whom you might remember from stories I've recounted—he's a fine warrior, taken all for all. It came as a bit of a surprise, though, I must tell you . . .*

All three of them were glad enough to get off their feet. Leucas and Kheperu had reclined on their pallets, while Barra sat with her back against the wall, knees drawn up and wrapped by her arms. Graeg lay beside her, head on his paws. They'd missed the evening meal, and so snacked on cheese and hard bread. Barra drank water instead of wine; she wanted her head to be perfectly clear for the meeting with the Head of House Meneides.

While the companions waited, Barra watched Kamades pace the length of the room back and forth; he occasionally flicked a glance toward her and her friends, a deepening scowl furrowing his brow, or made a conspicuous show of examining some piece of armor hanging on a rack. She didn't need the *sceon tiof* to show her that the Myrmidon captain was worried about something. Finally he stopped, huffed a sharp sigh, and strode toward her. "You'll be leaving soon, then," he said gruffly.

Barra nodded. "Within the next few days, I'd imagine. We've completed our mission—I'd guess we'll be here for a couple of days just to see what shakes out when Idonosteus beats the rug."

Kamades nodded stiffly in return. "It's been . . . well, it's an honor to have hosted you, Barra."

"Thank you." She squinted up at his open, craggy face, at the long scar that joined the streaks of white in his hair and his beard. He colored and looked away, looked back, looked at his hands, rubbed them together and hooked his thumbs behind his belt, and finally found something interesting about the straps of his sandals. Barra grinned at him. "You're just dying to know what we've been up to, aren't you?"

"I am not," Kamades replied, drawing himself up. "Not at all."

"Oh, come. Tell the truth."

Kamades' gnarled hands pulled his tunic straight. He cleared his throat. "It would be dishonorable to inquire."

"It would?"

"Yes. You are employed by my lord. If Idonosteus wishes me to know of your mission, he will tell me."

"No offense, Kamades, but that attitude is going to dunk you in a barrel of grief someday."

"It serves me well enough."

"It serves to keep any thoughts out of your bloody head except the ones your precious lord puts there."

Blood rose through Kamades' face all the way to his hairline. A vein bulged in his neck as he pressed his lips together against some hot reply. Finally, he said quietly, "There are some thoughts, in my head, that my lord did not put there. Good evening, Barra. Leucas. Kheperu." With that, he turned and stalked out into the corridor, his ear flaming.

Kheperu thoughtfully chewed his upper lip as he watched Kamades go, then turned to Barra. "I think he likes you."

"Of course he does," Barra said, frowning dangerously. "What's not to like?"

"No no no, you misunderstand," Kheperu told her with a naked leer. "I mean he *likes* you."

Barra suddenly felt very tired; she sagged back against the wall, painfully aware of her extremely long day. "But . . ." She looked at Leucas, who managed to suggest a shrug with only a twitch of his eyebrows. "But he's a Myrmidon," she protested wearily.

Leucas said, "So?"

Kheperu smirked. "If they were *all* like that, from where would come little Myrmidons?"

Barra pressed her eyes closed and rubbed her forehead with her fingertips. "Y'know, that's one thing I never expected, to have a Myrmidon lust for me."

Leucas rumbled, "Perhaps you should talk to him."

"Oh, no, I don't think so," she said. "I know better. He'll think I like *him*. He'll think I'm playing hard to get."

"You mean you don't?" Leucas said.

"Why should I? I mean, well, I don't know . . ." She frowned and shook her head. "It's not that I dislike him, really—I guess I hadn't really thought about it."

"*He* has," said Kheperu.

Barra took a deep breath and let it hiss out slowly between her teeth. Now that she thought about it, Kamades was a handsome man, scar or no; he was respected, perhaps even revered, by his men; he was almost certainly competent, reliable, probably a fine warrior—what her brother Llem would call *steady*. "Well, Mother's Blood," she said, now more thoughtful than tired. "A Myrmidon captain. Who'd have guessed it?"

"Anyone would, but you," Leucas murmured, a summer's smile warming his broken face. "You always forget how beautiful you are."

"Oh, stop it, you'll make me blush. Beautiful, my eye." She shifted her weight and pulled back the hem of her chiton to expose the rippling muscle of her upper thigh. "See? Look how skinny I am."

Kheperu peered clinically at her exposed flesh. "Skinny? I should say instead rather: sleek." He coughed into his hand, and stroked his long beak of a nose to hide a smile. "Hmm, well, and remember that in these lands, most wealthy men keep their wives exclusively to produce children and to run the household—for fun, they prefer teenage boys. Some men might look at you as"—he coughed again, delicately—"an ideal compromise."

"Oh?" She dropped the hem, and her voice took on that dangerous hectoring tone. "Are you trying to tell me I look like a boy? Is that it?"

Leucas hugged his knees and smiled at the ceiling.

Kheperu spread his hands, revealing his grin. "That is, my dear lady, only an expression of my, mmm, admiration for your lovely"—his gaze shifted downward—"physique."

Barra leaned her head back against the wall and closed her eyes. If only she could catch a few minutes' sleep. . . . "I don't want to know about it, all right? I just don't want to know."

Soon the runner returned with word that Idonosteus wished

to meet with them immediately. The three companions followed him out of the apartment and away from the building without encountering Kamades, for which Barra breathed a sigh of relief—and also felt a bare twinge of disappointment. She found herself vaguely hoping Kheperu was right about Kamades; the attention was flattering, whether anything came of it or not.

Tell Coll that I seem to have inherited the scéon tíof *from her,* she began, and then scratched it out. She hadn't yet given up on the hope that it would be only a passing thing, that the Mother would take back this gift that Barra so fervently did not want. She tapped her teeth with the pen, and went on:

> *I wish I could think of a way to teach you two how to deal with the sorts of powerful men you'll find down here around the Inner Sea. I'm only just now learning how, myself . . . and my business here in Tyre has brought me into arm's reach of several of these powerful men. They're different down here, neither quiet and grim-honest like Llem nor a cheerful braying liar like your grandda. I like ours better, I'd say—these pretend princes can't be trusted out of sight, is what I think. The trouble with these Tyrians is that they have no noble tradition; their nobility is a pack of weaklings that nobody pays any attention to anymore. The real power is with the "princes" of the merchant Houses, who are no more than average Phoenikian traders writ large. Even a bloody New Tribes king—like your grandda Ouendail—has a century or more of tradition to guide his hand, to keep him mindful of his people's needs and his own responsibilities toward them. These merchant princes here do no more than keep both eyes fixed on their profit, one hand holding their own purse and the other reaching toward yours . . .*

The *scéon tíof* hit Barra like a thunderbolt, stopping her voice and widening her eyes.

The companions had been making their report, with Barra as their speaker, here in the same room where they had first met Idonosteus, and all had seemed well, until Barra's voice caught like a blade in her throat.

Her *scéon tíof* vision of Idonosteus shook her like a

freezing wind. She saw Idonosteus not as a mercenary sees her employer, nor as an ordinary Tyrian sees the head of a Great House; the *sceon tiof* stripped away any lingering aura of wealth and avuncular dignity—rather than a Power of Tyre, what sat before her was an aging fat man with grease in his beard, sweating even in the evening cool, harboring desires and appetites within that quivering flesh that would make even Kheperu blanch and turn away.

We are in danger here.

Her hands clutched the silken pillows beneath her, and her mouth worked open and closed; she faked a convulsive sneeze, to cover her sudden incapacity.

Kheperu, ever vigilant, managed to pick up the thread of the story with hardly a break, as though he'd interrupted her on purpose. "It is painful to recount the contents of that chamber in the hills," he said smoothly, "for one is then forced to recall the smell." He glanced sidelong at Barra, as if daring her to comment. When she didn't, he continued. "Put simply, we believe that the man who cursed these inns and murdered Othniel traffics with Children of Apep. With demons, that is, my lord."

Idonosteus' thin-plucked brows drew together, and his piggy eyes narrowed until they nearly vanished within the rolls of his cheeks. In gloom broken only by the light of a single lamp, flame so still that it might have been carved of glass, his face seemed to float above his robes like the harvest moon. The porpoises and octopi of the room's frescoes seemed quietly asleep, and painted Meneus on the ceiling paused in his heroic labors to watch over the meeting like an indulgent Zeus. Idonosteus pursed his rubbery lips and waved distractedly to Murso for more wine. "Troubling, indeed," he said, while watching Murso refill his goblet from a tall amphora that stood at the head of the couch on which he reclined. "Thank you, Lysandros." He took a long draft, smacked his lips, and wiped them on his brocade sleeve. "Very troubling."

Murso/Lysandros returned to his stiff stance in back of the couch, his hands clasped behind his back, his high and narrow forehead bisected by the upward shadow of his long nose. Kheperu sat beside Barra on a similar couch, his hands waving as he described the demonist's workshop and their tracking of the riders. Leucas stood behind with folded arms, looming over them, his face disappearing into the gloom; he had only a few words of the Phoenikian that was being spoken here, and so he settled for looking grim and threatening.

". . . And so it is, unfortunately, almost certain that the demonist who has been troubling Tyre is a member of the household of Meremptah-Sifti."

Idonosteus sagged like a sun-heated wine bladder that's been moved into the shade. "Not Meremptah-Sifti himself, you don't think?"

Kheperu shook his head. "Quite unlikely, if I may make so bold a statement, lord. Magics of this sort require years of careful study; from what I recall of his early reputation, he showed no indication of developing the level of discipline this would require. Wealth, on the other hand, he would have in abundance—our demonist is almost certainly a hireling."

"Even so . . ." Idonosteus murmured, "even so." He sucked on his lower lip for a brief moment, and took another long swallow of wine. "In a way, this is worse. His protection would extend to every member of his household . . . hmmpf. This would be simpler if Meremptah *were* the magician; if that were proved, Ramses himself would order his execution . . ." He shook his head and sighed, lips stretched in a rueful smile. "An outsider—small wonder we were all helpless to detect him. Our eyes remain locked to each other's, we heads of the Great Houses, by the custom and ritual of our ceaseless dance. It took outsiders like yourselves to even consider that the culprit might not be one of us . . . hmmpf." He heaved himself upright into a sitting position and clasped his hands together. "You have done all I asked of you. The balance of your payments will be delivered to you at the apartment of the Myrmidons by noon tomorrow."

Each individual hair along Barra's arms lifted from its place with a tingling like that which heralds a cloudburst thunderstorm. She took a deep breath, forced a smile, and said with as light a voice as she could manage, "If you don't mind, lord, I think we'd just as soon take our silver with us. I'm not sure we'll be going back to the apartment now."

Kheperu gave her another swift sidelong glance, but covered his surprise with a sudden feigned sneeze of his own; he wiped his hand on his robe and frowned at her with the half of his face that was turned away from the Meneides.

Idonosteus cocked his head at her, and she continued hurriedly, "With our mission completed and all, and with everything in your capable hands, I don't think we need a safe bolt-hole to sleep in anymore. I should think the whole affair will be over before anyone seeking revenge for that little business at Lidios' house could find us, and so I think I'd like to go back and stay, mm, with my *family,* you know?"

Murso/Lysandros murmured, "Peliarchus the shipmaster." Idonosteus nodded to indicate he remembered, and Barra felt a cold hand clutch her belly.

"So," she went on, "I think it'd be more convenient for all of us if we could just take the other hundred fifty with us when we leave tonight, if it's all the same to you, lord."

"It's somewhat *in*convenient," Idonosteus began. Kheperu murmured in Egyptian, "What are you doing?"

Barra replied in the same tongue, "Shut up and let me handle this." She switched to Phoenikian and said, "The longer we stay with the Myrmidons, the more chance there is of our connection being discovered. After all, we fought Chrysios' men, questioned Jephunah about his body, were seen all over town at the cursed inns, and were no doubt seen moving out toward the funerary caves. It wouldn't be that hard for someone to figure out what we've been doing, if anyone thinks to ask. And, I've had no contact with my family since the day before you hired us—if they begin inquiries through the Penthedes, well, I thought you wanted our association to remain a secret . . ."

Idonosteus' piggy eyes narrowed until again they almost disappeared, and for a moment the naked calculation she saw there chilled Barra's blood. Then he sighed, and pressed himself to his feet, and his smile was warm, almost fatherly, as he said, "You're good at this, Barra—but then, you were reared by a Tyrian trader, weren't you? And I never heard that Peliarchus the shipmaster was anyone's fool." He waved a hand over his shoulder, and Murso/Lysandros expressionlessly backed into the shadows and slipped from the room.

This seemed to call for no reply, and so Barra bit her lip to hold one back; if it pleased Idonosteus to believe that she'd have grown up stupid and gullible if she'd been reared by her own people, well, that was fine. She was getting what she'd come for—there'd be no profit in cursing him for a bigot.

Before the silence could become awkward, Lysandros returned with a large purse. He stepped around the couch to hand it personally to Barra. She weighed it in her hand, and felt her face slowly growing hot: he couldn't have counted out this much silver in the tiny interval of his absence. The purse must have been waiting in the corridor since before they'd arrived. Idonosteus smiled into his goblet, wiped his lips, and said, "This is a free reminder: sometimes *your* maneuvers can be anticipated, too. You may go now."

Lysandros showed them to the door. On their way out, as on their way in, they encountered no one. Barra retrieved her lamp from the stand by the door, and lit it from the one Lysandros carried. "Pleasure doing business with you," she said.

"It would be as well," Lysandros said softly, "if we do not meet again." He closed the door in her face. Barra shrugged and gestured for her companions to precede her.

As they walked away, Kheperu said, "Now will you please tell me what that was all about?"

"Actually," Leucas murmured thoughtfully, "I'd appreciate it if someone would tell me what any of it was about."

"Just keep walking until we're out of sight." Barra held the lamp high to illuminate their way, even though the three-quarters' moon above was plenty bright for walking.

Kheperu summarized the conversation for Leucas, who listened in his usual gravely attentive manner. He said, "Someday I should learn this language. It's tiresome to watch and listen when I have no idea what's being said."

When they'd turned a corner from the Meneides compound, Barra snuffed the lamp, said, "Come on," and started to jog swiftly through the streets. Kheperu, puffing after only a few steps on his plump stubby legs, gasped, "Why are we running?"

"Because if we hurry, we might beat Lysandros to the Myrmidons. I only hope Idonosteus didn't send his orders back with the runner who led us here tonight. Just in case, one of us will have to stay outside, so they can't make it clean. That'll be you, Kheperu. I'll need Leucas to carry all the gear, and Graeg won't follow anyone but me."

Leucas' long legs carried him smoothly and effortlessly alongside her. "What orders? What are you talking about?"

"Idonosteus wanted to send us our money at the apartment.
That's why I reminded him that I have family here who'd be
making inquiries if they didn't hear from me. If he thought he
could get away with it, he'd have had the Myrmidons kill us
all. Better there than in his home, where we'd have made a
terrific mess, and might have drawn a cup or two of *his* blood,
as well."

"Kill us?" Leucas' voice rose at this suggestion of dishonor. "Why? To save a few bits of silver?"

Barra grinned at him. "More than a few: three hundred
Athenian large. That's my guess, anyway. Maybe he'd have a
different reason, but the result would be the same. He's a
treacherous bastard who'd sell his mother for a fistful of
pepper and a blowjob."

Kheperu gasped, "If you've known him . . . all along . . . as
a cheat and a murderer . . . why did we . . . ever take his
employment . . . in the first place?"

"It's too complicated to explain. Now, shut up. Save your
breath for running."

> And here's another thing: never be ashamed to plan for
> the worst. Sometimes it can seem a bit cowardly, and
> insultingly distrustful, but as a rule of thumb, I'd tell you
> to keep one hand on your axe and a sharp ear cocked for
> the soft step behind. You'll be wrong three times for every
> time you're right, but don't fear that; just consider that if
> you're brave and open and trusting, you'll pay for it with
> your life the first time you're wrong. Though, I must say,
> when you get older and you know a bit more of what drives
> some men, you can use a certain pretense of trust to bring
> out the better side of a man who might otherwise be your
> enemy . . .

They loped through the streets under the swelling moon.
There was little enough night traffic in Tyre at any time, but
tonight they seemed to be entirely alone. Early though it
was, the only glimpses of lamplight they got was what little
leaked through chinks and gaps in windows tightly shuttered
against the night, as though the townsmen believed that these
slats of wood could block out the creeping uneasiness, the
deepening uncertainty and mouth-drying apprehension of *something about to happen*: even those dull souls who missed all

hints of trouble gathering like thunderheads on the horizon, even they couldn't help but register the tension in their neighbor's voice, in the quick shift of the eyes, the tendency to startle at any sudden noise, and they too locked their doors and windows and huddled around the warmth of their hearthshrines.

Three blocks from the apartment, Kheperu made a flame to relight the lamp, and then found himself a comfortable doorway in which to relax. He pointed up at the declining moon. "You have until the moon goes behind that rooftop. Then I go straight to Peliarchus and tell him you've been taken by the Meneides, yes?"

"Yes. Don't even think about trying to come in after us."

"Fear not," Kheperu said, sighing gratefully as he leaned his butt against the wall and slid to the ground. "I have little interest in heroic gestures, and I'm quite comfortable here. It has been a tiring day."

"Don't remind me," Barra said, fighting back a yawn. She gave him the purse and he plumped it into his lap. She looked up at Leucas. "Are you ready for this?"

His cracked face smiled down at her. "Always."

"Ay, I know, stupid question."

They left Kheperu behind; on the street outside the apartment block, they went through the face-lighting business and then went inside. Without a word to the Myrmidons, who lounged about the apartment polishing armor or casually dicing, Leucas set about bundling up their gear, his and Barra's armor, his weapons, their bedrolls, and the like. After she reassured an anxious Graegduz that indeed she did love him by letting him lick her face, Barra made small talk while she collected the purse and tied it over her shoulder.

One of the Myrmidons, on watch in the darkened room adjoining, called, "Rider," and an instant later Barra heard hoofbeats approaching at a canter. "It's Lysandros," the watcher said, appearing at the connecting door, a light of sudden hope illuminating his youthful features. "Perhaps he brings orders to action!" The other Myrmidons sat up straighter, a couple of them rising and flexing their arms and legs to work out the kinks of long inactivity, some grumbling murmurs of support, some expressing cynical disbelief. Leucas looked around the room at them, exchanged a meaningful glance with Barra, then very deliberately finished securing the knots that held his bundle of armor and weapons.

He slung it over his shoulder, then drew himself up to his full height—this alone was enough to quiet the room—and he said, in a soft but penetrating voice, "Bring Kamades here to me." When no one moved, storm clouds gathered on his brow and a tone of command that Barra had never heard from him before gave his voice an edge of authority like the clash of bronze blades. "You," he said, pointing to the youthful watchman. "Bring Kamades here. *Now.*"

Suddenly the door was empty, the only sound the clatter of his sandals on the wooden floor.

Barra said softly from the side of her mouth, "I hope you know what you're doing."

He frowned down from high above her, then through his frown cracked an instant's fleeting wink. "Me, too."

Kamades appeared in the doorway and strode into the room. "Leucas Deodakaides. You sent and I have come." He came forward and stopped only an arm's length from Leucas. Barra admired his nerve: the huge glowering Athenian looked as threatening as a mortal can, and Kamades was well aware, from recounting of the fight in Lidios' inn, that Leucas had killed men with a single blow of the fist. The top of the Myrmidon's head came barely to Leucas' lower lip, yet Kamades looked up into those cold grey eyes with perfect calm.

"Let me pose for you this question, Kamades of Phthia," Leucas growled. "Your obedience is legendary. Does your obedience to your lord overwhelm the laws of the God?"

Kamades' brows drew together. "They are the same," he said simply, as though unable to conceive of a conflict between them.

"What if your lord orders you to violate the commands of Zeus? To leave dead foes unburied"—Barra could hear the undertone of loathing left over from the Theban Campaign—"or, worse even yet, to *murder those who are your guests*?"

Movement from the outer doorway caught Barra's eye: Lysandros, lantern in hand, had gained the corridor in time to hear Leucas' question. Now he paused, long face pinched with some unnameable emotion, as Leucas shifted his gaze to look at him over the head of Kamades, and the Myrmidon captain turned to see his proximate superior standing at the door, mouth open as though he wished to speak but was unable to find words that could express his thought.

At once, everyone in the room understood precisely what it

was Leucas had asked; there came a pause, a suspension as though everyone collectively held a single breath. Kamades looked at Lysandros for a long time, his mouth grinding shut, muscles bunching at the corners of his jaw. Kamades' eyes slitted, and he released a long, slow breath, and Barra's sight was flooded with the *sceon tiof*.

Kamades stood before her, shining as though cloaked in woven sunlight. The purity of his devotion to the principles by which he lived caught at her heart, and made her ashamed that she'd ever doubted him. No wonder he could stand chest to chest with an angry Leucas: he feared nothing save dishonor.

With serene deliberation, fully aware of the import of what he said, he turned back to Leucas. "My lord would not order such things."

Leucas raised his head to stare directly at Lysandros. "And if he did?"

"He would not," Kamades pronounced with perfect assurance. "Such an order in itself is an offense to God; such an order would be proof that my lord had been forsaken by the gods and taken leave of his senses; thus the order would not have come from my lord, but from the madness which had seized him. I would not obey an order that came from a fit of madness, and I could not remain in service to a madman."

Leucas nodded, once. Kamades allowed himself a slow, grim smile, then turned to Lysandros. "Lysandros," Kamades said with the barest fraction of a bow. "Is there word from Lord Idonosteus?"

Lysandros, nothing if not resilient, stepped briskly into the room and said, "Yes: he wishes that you see to it that your guests get their gear well in order. They are leaving tonight; I had understood that they did not intend to return here, and came to arrange the delivery of their goods."

"It's well, then," Kamades replied gravely, a hint of a sardonic twinkle sneaking into his serious eyes. "We obey—sometimes, before the order is ever given."

Barra smothered a chuckle as a rosy tint crept up Lysandros' neck, and she came to a sudden decision. As she made to follow Leucas out, she stopped beside Kamades and placed her hand on his arm, and the warmth of his skin kicked her heartbeat into a gallop. He looked down at her hand, then his gaze swept upward to meet hers.

"Kamades," she said, just above a whisper, "I may be leaving town in only a few days. Would you like to visit me for dinner before then?" Her face felt hot; she hoped it wasn't too visible.

His eyes widened, and his face kindled an answering blush like a Babylon sunset. He took a deep breath, blinked, and then said in a voice thin with strain, "Yes, Barra, I'd like that very much. Where may I call on you?"

"At the home of Peliarchus the shipmaster—my foster-father. Lysandros knows where it is; I should be there any evening for the next few days, at least."

Kamades bent his head toward hers. "Unless my lord calls me to action, I'll be there. Mm, Barra . . . ?"

"No," she said quickly. "No questions, no talking, no nothing. Just show up, and we'll take everything from there. See you." She was painfully aware of the stares from the Myrmidons and Lysandros as she headed for the door.

Graegduz clicking along at her side, she joined Leucas in the corridor beyond, and together they left the building.

When they arrived back at the doorway where they'd left Kheperu, the stubby Egyptian was happily blowing spit bubbles in his sleep, a line of drool cleaning a path through the dust that caked his face and pooling in a fold of his robe. His hands were folded protectively around the purse on his lap, and he looked supremely comfortable.

Barra and Leucas exchanged another glance, one that spoke volumes, and they together shook their heads and sighed.

Barra shrugged and said, "You know, I'm thinking I could really use a bath myself."

Leucas nodded, lifting one of his hands to smear a cleaner patch through the grime on his chest. He examined his palm thoughtfully. "You think Peliarchus might have enough water left, tonight?"

"Maybe. If he does, though, I get it first."

In the meantime, Graegduz had taken it upon himself to wake Kheperu by licking the Egyptian's face. He smiled and squirmed happily in his sleep—which brought a host of revolting images unbidden into Barra's cringing imagination—and she ordered him sharply in Pictish to back off. Kheperu's eyes popped open and he wiped at his face. "Gyahh—get that beast away from me!"

"He likes you."

"It's disgusting, what you let that dog do."

"Tell me about it," Barra said feelingly. "Just imagine what this'll do to his breath."

Kheperu pushed himself to his feet, grumbling, "Now I must re-grime that whole cheek."

Together the companions walked toward the home of Peliarchus. Leucas filled Kheperu's ear with the scene in the apartment; when he reached their leave-taking, Kheperu's eyes lit up. "An assignation with Kamades?" he burbled delightedly. "Why, Barra! Let me be the very first to taunt you about this! Hmm, let's see, he's over forty, no money, no lands, no education, and no ear—he's perfect for you! When's the wedding?"

By way of answer, Barra wheeled and swung a fist that landed hard enough on the side of Kheperu's head to knock him sprawling. He blinked and rubbed his face, and grinned happily up at her. "Sensitive subject, mm?"

"Don't get ideas. That," she said through her teeth, "was for falling asleep on watch."

Kheperu said to Leucas, as the Athenian helped him to his feet, "Do you know, that's the first time she's ever hit me? I'm relieved—I'd begun to worry that this vaunted temper of hers was all an act. Do you think if I make another joke about Kamades, she'll kick me in the crotch?"

Leucas said, "I hope so."

A pair of lanterns that hung from bronze hooks cast pools of light to either side of Peliarchus' door, even though the time neared midnight. A sleepy Milo, the porter, opened a spy gate at Barra's knock, recognized them, and let them in, then went to wake Peliarchus. The old trader came stumbling out, rubbing sleep from his eyes, and spent the obligatory few minutes grumbling at Barra for dropping out of sight. Barra, for her part, spun an outrageous story about being kidnapped by pirates and waiting and pining for three days for the sight of her foster-father's ships rowing out to rescue her—she said that after three days had passed, she'd figured that Peliarchus had forgotten all about her, so she went ahead and escaped on her own, no thanks to him!

"Oh, sure," Peliarchus grumped. "More likely you got so pissy that they threw you overboard to shut you up. What've you really been doing?"

"Can't tell you," she said with a careless shrug. "You know how it is."

"No, I don't. And I heard about your brawl over to beachside."

"Keep your voice down, you'll wake Tayniz. I gave my word, Peliarchus. I really can't tell you. Listen, I need a favor. We can't go back to the place where we've been sleeping, and it's too late to find an inn. Can you put us up for a night?"

Peliarchus squinted at her and rubbed his palms across his scalp. "Who's after you?"

"No one, honest. We just need a place to sleep tonight—and to stash our gear and some silver."

"Ahh, shit. All right," he said, scowling. "Bloody Demetor and his whiners have the whole ground floor—each of the whiners had to have his own room—but the servants can sleep out here, I guess. It's a nice night, doesn't look like rain."

"Aw, don't push them out, Peliarchus. Just double them up—I don't need a room to myself."

His eyebrows arched, and he looked from her to Leucas, then at Kheperu, and back at her with an unspoken question.

"Oh, no, sir," Kheperu said, with just a hint of his usual leer. "Nothing like that—in fact, she's courting a Myrmidon!" He smoothly shifted his foot out from under Barra's stomp.

Peliarchus grinned at him. "From that fresh knot on your head, I'd guess you've been teasing Barra about something already tonight. Don't push your luck."

He led them up the rail-less inner stairs to the new second floor, still fresh enough to smell of the polished cedar of which it was built. A couple minutes of rousting servants got the arrangements made, and the three companions settled into the room for the night. Peliarchus stood at the door, leaning wearily against the frame. "You maybe don't want to go to sleep right away," he said, yawning. "King Demetor and the whiners are still out on the town; if they decide to come home tonight, they'll raise enough noise to wake Ba'al-Marqod. G'night."

As Peliarchus moved off toward his own temporary room, Leucas turned to Barra. "Did you ask him about the bath?"

Barra shook her head and nodded toward the large pitcher of water and the towels that were folded on the table beside it. "You can wipe down now, I guess. We'll get our baths tomorrow." She began to untie the knots on the bundle of their gear and dig through it.

Kheperu had already flopped, fully dressed, onto the lower bunk. "What are you doing?"

Barra held up the pencase and the roll of parchment. "I'm not sleepy right now. I'm going to write a letter."

"Oh, really?" He levered himself up onto one elbow. "To whom, might I ask?"

"You might. I won't tell you."

"All right," he said easily, and lay back down again.

Barra shook her head and chuckled. "And I'm writing it in Pictish," she lied. There was no need to tell Kheperu that Pictish had no written form.

"Barra!" he said, sounding shocked and deeply offended. "That's not fair!"

"Go to sleep."

Leucas slowly wiped himself off and climbed into the upper bunk. He closed his eyes and within seconds began to snore. Kheperu sighed, rolled over, and began his own wheezing counterpoint. Barra made herself comfortable on the stool, Graegduz settling in around her feet. She rested her elbows on the table, dreaming of home, of the late autumn storms cracking branches from the sky-topping oaks, of the frost that rimes the heather and the pale northern sun that can barely melt it by midday. She yawned deeply, stretched, and then slowly bent her head over the parchment and began to write.

PART TWO

Eirish
Stand Down

CHAPTER ELEVEN

The Favor

> *And, while I'm thinking about it, I want to tell you one more time to not be afraid to do favors for people, because you never know when you'll need a favor in return. You have to not be too shy about pressing for a return, too; don't be afraid to push hard. And don't leave a favor uncollected for too long—you'll get the reputation of being softhearted, which is dangerous, especially so if it's a bit true. Also, a favor becomes more meaningful—a bit more special to the person you're doing it for—if you present yourself as the sort of person who doesn't ordinarily d—*

The thunder of fists against a door and the clamor of shouting men made Barra jump and drop her pen. These were no playful hammerings and prankish shouts: they had the tempo of panic and an edge of desperation. She found herself on her feet reaching for her axes before she really registered what was going on—that the pounding and the shouting all came from outside, on the street, that her axe belt was draped over the chair across from her, that she was barely half-dressed. Graegduz scrambled to his feet shaking off sleep, his ruff fully expanded and a low snarl in his throat. On the bunks across the room, Kheperu tossed himself into bleary-eyed semi-alertness. "What . . . ? Mmm, what?" Leucas snored on, undisturbed.

"Get your butt out of bed and kick Leucas," Barra snapped as she tied off her breechclout and reached for her belt. "Something's wrong."

" 'S just King Dinky and the, the whiners—"

"*Listen,* shit-in-the-head! Does that sound like some happy drunks back from a night on the town?"

Kheperu frowned and cocked his head; his face cleared as

recognition triggered his pulse and sleep washed away. He rolled out of the bunk, popped energetically to his feet, and began to shake the snoring Athenian.

"No time for that shit!" Barra barked. She sprang over to the bunk and smacked a stinging slap across Leucas' face.

His eyes popped open. "Hey—"

"On your feet and arm yourself!"

Though he slept like a stone, Leucas had the ability to come fully awake in a single surge. In the space of two breaths, he had his round shield of layered bronze and ox-hide on his arm and his man-length spear in hand. Barra spun away from him and kicked open the door to the balcony. In the courtyard below, Milo was unbolting the door. Quicker than thought, she drew a throwing axe and whipped it singing through the air to thud deeply into the door a foot away from his face. The porter jumped back with a cry, the bolt dropped back into place, and Barra shouted, "Touch that door and the next one goes into your skull!"

"Shit, Barra," Leucas murmured behind her. "Isn't that a bit harsh?"

She wheeled and jabbed him in the solar plexus with her stiffened fingers. "We have no *fucking clue* who's out there, and this is my *family*! Any more *stupid fucking questions*?" She punctuated this with a shove sharp enough to make the boxer grunt and step back. She turned away without waiting for a response, snapped, "Now get your butts down there!" and threw herself over the rail. She dropped into a roll on the flagstones and was at the door peering through the spy gate in the blink of an eye.

Kheperu said, "She seems a bit tense."

Leucas nodded tightly. "I'm a bit tense, myself."

Peliarchus and Tayniz both appeared at the door to their room, making inquiring noises and rubbing their eyes; Leucas and Kheperu brushed past them without a word. By the time her two partners made it to Barra's side, the whole house was in an uproar, the seven servants streaming down the stairs jabbering to each other, Peliarchus in the middle of them shouting about the damage Barra's axe had done to his cedar door. Tayniz stopped two steps above the yard, drew her shawl tighter around her shoulders, white-knuckled hand holding her robe closed over her ample breasts, and shouted, "Everyone, *be quiet!*"

Years of haggling in the din of the Market of Tyre had given Tayniz a voice that could pierce a bronze cuirass front and back. Her tone made it clear that she was mistress of this house and by God every single soul who lived here would do as she says or suffer for it. The babble abated as everyone turned to look at her, except for Graegduz, who stood expectantly at Barra's side, and Barra herself, who was already fumbling with the bolt. Outside the clamor had turned to recognizable words, begging for entrance.

Tayniz said, her voice overcontrolled and leaning toward shrill, "Barra. What is happening? Tell me what's happening!" Tough and loud as she might be, an explosion of shouts and hammering in the middle of the night takes some getting used to; even Peliarchus, more accustomed to sudden awakenings due to his travels on the trade routes, was clearly unnerved.

Barra began to swing the doors back. "Leucas—Kheperu. Stand ready." She spoke in Greek—she had always been the lone member of the household who could get away with ignoring her foster-mother. "It's Demetor and his men, and he looks sick. Just be ready until we know for sure there's nobody else out there."

Two of his men carried in the Kypriot king, supporting him by holding his strengthless arms about their shoulders. Demetor was only semiconscious, and Barra knew instantly what had happened to him, even before the light of a lamp held too close to his face made him begin to thrash against the grip of his friends. His flowing white beard dripped vomit, and the rich embroidery of his overrobe and stole were both soaking, and the roast-acorn smell of the pukenut extract was, to her nose, unmistakable even through the overpowering reeks of beer, wine, half-digested meat, and stomach juice. Three of his eight companions were similarly affected, and Barra waited for no explanations and would allow no one to question them until all four men were gently laid on fresh linens in the master bedroom and the windows were safely shuttered against even the light of the waxing moon.

She shooed everyone out, and stood a moment alone in the middle of the room, to look at the stricken men around her and think. They'd have to be cleaned up, have the vomit swabbed off their skin and combed out of their beards, but gently; any sudden movement, noise, or bright light could seize them and kill them. She thought that they just might

live—the vomiting must have ejected a substantial amount of
the poison, and they wouldn't be drinking any more of it. On
the other hand, these were none of them young men, and
Demetor himself had seen more than sixty winters, possibly
nearly seventy. She looked down at him, at his flowing spray
of surf-white hair across the pillow, his eyes rolling behind
closed lids, and thought of the cheerful, befuddled old king
she'd seen in his hall at Paphos, eyes wide as he'd hemmed
and hawed at Kheperu's Wandering Seer act, willing to try or
pay almost anything to protect his people from the manslaughtering boar. She'd despised him then, for his pompous
foolishness, and laughed at him in memory many times since,
but now as he lay before her, that scorn and laughter lay bitter
in her throat. How many years would it be before her own
father Ouendail would lie as helpless as this? How long before
Peliarchus would? In some depth of her spirit, chains of kinship were being forged, how or where she neither knew nor
cared; wherever the connection she felt with this fallen king
came from, it was undeniably real. She felt the slow, rising
surge of her temper coiling upward to aim at Meremptah-Sifti
and his demonist, and clamped mental hands around it to hold
it in check. The Meneides, she told herself, would handle that
problem for her. Her efforts would be better spent right here.

The Kypriots clustered like nervous sheep around the
courtyard door. Barra had to force her way between them as
she strode out from the bedroom, back into the crisp night air
of the courtyard, and took a deep breath to clear her nose.
She ignored the questions they pressed on her and grabbed
the arm of one of the Kypriots. "You, and maybe one other
guy, can stay in there with them. Clean them up, gently, and
keep them quiet—nothing loud, keep your voices down, no
lamps, no nothing. If any of them get seized, try and hold
them so they can't hurt themselves. Understand?"

The Kypriot, a tall man with a bloated face behind his
beard, glared blearily down at her. "Who th'fuck are you?"

Barra was a past master at handling drunks; she grabbed a
handful of his beard and hauled his face down even with hers,
ignoring the watering of his eyes and his yelp of pain. "I'm
the woman who'll split your thick bloody skull if you don't
do as I say. If you don't, and King Demetor dies tonight, so do
you. You understand?"

He nodded mutely, and she released him. The other

Kypriots wisely refrained from questioning her orders. She left them behind; she went to where Kheperu and Leucas stood at the street gate, side by side, peering out into the darkness beyond. "There's no one else outside," Kheperu said. "King Dimwit and the whiners—it's the curse, isn't it?" A pair of servants, inching close to eavesdrop, gasped and skittered away to pass along this tidbit.

Barra sighed tiredly. "Oh, well done. Very nice. You're a fine one to be calling someone else a dimwit. Now they'll all be in a panic."

In seconds Barra was at the center of a crowd. All the Kypriots unaffected by the curse yammered questions at her, since she seemed to know things they didn't; the servants clutched at her and begged to be told if the king had brought the curse down upon this house as well. Barra howled at them to shut up, but even Graegduz's snarled support was lost in the noise. Peliarchus gave no help—the shipmaster sat on one of the yard couches, his head in his hands. Finally, Barra raised her head and caught Tayniz's eye; the pleading expression on her face spoke clearly. Tayniz took a deep breath and blared, *"Quiet!"*

Once again, it worked.

With Tayniz's support to lend authority to her orders, Barra swiftly got the courtyard under control: the Kypriots calmly seated, with mugs of wine at hand, and the servants—except for the porter—packed off to their room. It took a bit of work to get the near-incoherent story.

Demetor's party had split into two groups, when the king had wanted to move on from the brothel where five of his men—these five in the courtyard now—had cheerfully passed out. They'd heard a story earlier about a Tomitiri tax collector and his bodyguards being murdered on the street, and in their alcohol-dazed state, they'd decided it would be fun to see where the killings had taken place. Massacres and brutal murders, after all, are subjects of the most enduring interest—especially when they're so recent. They'd ended up at a nearby inn, one nearly deserted, where they more or less took over the place and drank themselves stupid. This place had been, Barra surmised with some assurance, a Tomitiri inn; the pattern seemed identical to what had happened to Lidios. Meanwhile the men they'd left behind had regained consciousness, though not sobriety, and these had decided to venture forth into the night in search of their friends. It was the bowl of water that Demetor and his friends had downed to clear their heads for the walk home that had struck them with the curse, Barra knew, though she said nothing; the curse and all knowledge surrounding it was covered by the contract with House Meneides. She had given her word, and been paid, and even Idonosteus' presumed treachery didn't release her from the obligation to keep her mouth shut.

Peliarchus was near shock; the devastating image of Demetor dying while under his hospitality drew haunted shadows under his eyes. Though Agapenthes himself was as Tyrian as any sharp-eyed trader in the Market, the House Penthedes traditions traced proudly back to Mykenai. By the sacred laws of hospitality as practiced in Akhaia, Peliarchus—as host—was personally responsible for any untoward fate that befalls his guest, even one hosted unwillingly. Add to that bonds of blood—Agapenthes may despise his cousin, but blood is blood, after all—and the future Peliarchus saw before him was bleak indeed.

Barra crouched before him and gripped both his shoulders. "Hey, cheer up, Peliarchus," she said softly. "I think we can save him. Save them all."

Leucas and Kheperu frowned at each other. Peliarchus said, "You think so?"

"Kheperu can . . . lift this curse. Can't you, Kheperu?"

The Egyptian looked doubtful. Barra said leadingly, "If we can find the right components . . . if we go out for a little while . . . and talk to a friend of his . . ." She nodded and smiled at him, but the knot of muscle at the corner of her jaw and the tight-clenched teeth said, *Back me up or I'll smack you one.*

The realization that Barra was, for once, *asking* him to lie brought a bright manic gleam to Kheperu's beady squirrel's eyes. He rubbed his hands together briskly. "Oh yes, well, actually, she's being a bit overly delicate. Yes, in fact . . . I must go out into the darkness and summon a spirit, yes, well really a sort of minor god, if you must know—yes, that's indeed what must be done. The only question is, *when* will it come?" He stretched his thick neck to ostentatiously scan the sky. "All portents appear to be good, and, of course, I can make it clear in my summoning how urgent the matter is; this is done by the melody of the chant which accompanies—"

"Save the details," Barra interrupted firmly, "there may not be time. Leucas and I will go with you—to . . . er, guard against dangerous influences." She looked up, and chanced to meet the eyes of Tayniz. Her foster-mother stood behind Peliarchus, arms folded and her lips pressed together. Tayniz had a way of looking at you that reminded Barra of Coll, her real mother. They both had a manner of silently gazing into your heart, like they know you better than you know yourself, and they're mildly disappointed in you but love you in spite of it, like there's something that you would know you should be doing right now, if you were any kind of proper daughter. It always gave Barra a mild case of the creeps. Tayniz lifted her eyebrows by a hairsbreadth, and suggestively swung her gaze down to where the porter stood sulking by the foot of the stairs. "All right, all right!" Barra muttered through her teeth. She grabbed Kheperu's sleeve and slapped Leucas on the shoulder. "Come on, get a couple lanterns, we're going out."

Leucas said, "Out?"

"I'll explain later." With an exasperated glance back over her shoulder at Tayniz, she marched over to the porter. Milo pretended to be examining his folded hands, while flicking fearful glances toward Barra from beneath his lowered brows. "Look," she said, "I'm sorry I frightened you."

At this, the porter's head came up, while Barra cast around in her mind for something else she could say, to make the poor man feel as though she valued him and his service. "My friends and I are going to go out now, for a while. While we're gone, don't let anybody in, all right? It's very important, and we're all counting on you for this. Don't let in anybody at all, not even me, unless Peliarchus or Tayniz personally tells you to. All right?"

"I weren't frightened," Milo mumbled. "You was always excitable. I knew it weren't personal. I'll take care of it, Miss Barra, you know I will."

"You're a good man," she said. Tayniz, above and behind the porter's shoulder, gave Barra an infinitesimal nod. Barra sighed—that was her foster-mother all over, to be worried about proper handling of the servants while the world burned down around her.

Milo held the door for her while she retrieved her throwing axe, and the companions went out.

Once the door was closed behind them and they were

moving away in Barra's wake, Kheperu said, "Let me see if I have this wrapped and tied. We're going to the Market to see Tekrop-nekt, are we not? We shall haul his ass out of bed and pay his exorbitant price for whatever useless herb he claims will cure pukenut poisoning, and for what? For King Demetor, whom you despise?"

Leucas said softly, "It is our obligation. He was our host on Kypros; we are guest-friends."

Barra nodded. "That's right. You're both right. We're guest-friends and I despise him. So what?" She smiled thinly to herself as she thought of the words she had just written in her letter to her sons. "First, though, we're going to go down to that Tomitiri inn and knock a hole in their rain barrel."

"But why?" Kheperu insisted.

Leucas looked down at him. "Because we might be able to save several lives."

"So? What good does that do for us? It will stir up Meremptah-Sifti—he'll know someone is on to his pukenut curse."

"He already knows somebody's on to him," Barra said grimly. "I yarked my breakfast at the demonist's chamber this morning, remember? The next time he shows up to do a little magic, he'll bloody well know someone's been there. As for the inn, I don't expect you to understand." How could she explain? She didn't know what the *sceon tiof* might show her on a corpse, especially one whose death she could have prevented; she didn't know what it would feel like to see deeply into the life of someone she'd chosen not to save. She never wanted to find out.

"What about our *rest*?" Kheperu went on. "Have you lived through the same day I have? Do you remember what *sleep* is?"

Barra nodded and fought back a yawn. The last thing in the world she needed right now was to be reminded how tired she was. "Let's say only that I feel a little responsible. I live here—these are my people, I guess. Nobody chooses where they're born, but you can choose where to live your life, and—ah, forget it. I don't need a reason. We're going to do it because I want to, that's all."

"Oh?" Kheperu replied haughtily. "And what if I do not?"

Barra grinned at him. "Nobody asked you."

*   *   *

Even the moon was slanting toward the sea as the companions threaded through the silent maze of the Market toward the shop of Tekrop-nekt. They moved cautiously, carrying no lamp, through strips of silver moonlight separated by shadows so deep that to step into one was to wink out of existence. When Kheperu stumbled against some carelessly left rake, with a sharp clatter and a sharper curse, Graegduz whirled snarling to face him, and Barra found her axe had come to her hand and her heart seemed to choke her throat. Even stolid Leucas jumped, and after that, walked with his shield in place on one fist and his naked sword in the other.

Ever since they'd left the Tomitiri inn, its rain barrel draining through the hole chopped by three swift strokes of Barra's axe, Graegduz had walked pressed against Barra's thigh, and she'd felt his long, low growl rumbling warmly through his deep chest. It was then that she'd had Leucas and Kheperu douse their lamps, and follow a path that wound through alleys and along rights-of-way between houses with barred doors and locked shutters; the prickling at the nape of her neck persisted, though, and had grown to a skin-crawling conviction that they were no longer alone on the starlit streets of Tyre. A shifting breeze hushed in her ears, and the occasional scrape of stone or wood might have been as much a natural sound of settling buildings as a sign of pursuit; twice, though, her nose had caught a whiff of animal musk, underlain with meat rich in black decay and the faint greenish reek of an egg left for days in the sun. On the first of these, the wind had been from the west, and the second had come from the south. Dark masses of clouds roiled there, in the south, flickering tongues of thunderbolts between them, and the scent of rain was also in the air. Barra nursed a prayer in her heart that whatever was out here had nothing to do with them, and that they wouldn't attract its attention.

All three of the companions were exhausted; a day of relentless activity from before dawn to well after midnight had left Barra's legs heavy and stiff as stone. Even Leucas walked with his head down, his shield and bared sword swinging limply beside his thighs, and Kheperu was so tired he'd barely said a word since they'd left the inn.

From ahead, now, came definite sounds of activity, low voices snapping irritably just below the threshold of comprehensibility, the clap and clatter of boards being stacked and the fresh rip of tearing cloth, and one voice raised in a fulminating Egyptian curse.

"That sounds like Tekrop-nekt himself," Kheperu murmured. "Perhaps we should hurry."

Leucas frowned. "It might not be a good idea to rush up on them."

"Oh, ay," Barra said. "On these streets in the middle of the night? They're likely as nervous as I am."

"True enough, I suppose," Kheperu said with a sniff. "There's no honest business that would take a man to the Market at this hour."

When they came in sight of Tekrop-nekt's shop house, Tekrop-nekt and his huge bodyguard Met were busily stacking the pine slats that had formed the frame of Tekrop-nekt's shop onto the back of a mule cart. There was no mule in sight; Barra suspected that those empty traces would end up going around Met's meaty shoulders. Nor were there lamps; like the companions, these two Egyptians relied on the moon's intermittent illumination. Barra cautiously hallooed from well down the street. They both startled like spooky horses: Tekrop-nekt clutched his chest, gasping, and Met leaped wild-eyed in front of him, that grey-black scimitar finding his hand with impressive speed.

"An odd hour to be out of bed, Tekrop-nekt," Kheperu called softly. "It is I, Kheperu, with the northern girl and the Greek."

Met shifted his weight forward into a more assured fighting stance, both hands on his sword. Tekrop-nekt came up behind his shoulder, squinting suspiciously through the moonlight. "I know you, Kheperu. What do you want?"

"Only a few moments of your time," Kheperu said soothingly. He spread his hands, showing his empty palms, and began walking toward the nervous pair. Barra beckoned to Leucas, and followed. "I take it that you have suddenly discovered urgent business in some less troubled city?"

Tekrop-nekt's answering laugh was thin to the verge of being shrill. "Urgent business? Oh yes, it *became* urgent when Peth An'khefi was slaughtered by invisible demons in bright Ra's afternoon glory this day in Nephrol Tomit's very courtyard!" His mouth twisted, and his hand speared out over Met's shoulder. "And that is *close enough!*"

Kheperu slowed, but kept approaching, speaking in his best

wheedling undertone. "You won't turn us away, will you? On a night like this, I suppose our next destination must be that very home of Nephrol Tomit, to carry the tale of his oath-bound alchemist taking his powders elsewhere in the middle of this dark night . . ."

This brought a clear tic to Tekrop-nekt's thin and lipless mouth. "No, no please—what do you want, I can help you . . ."

Without taking her eyes off Met's glowering face, Barra put her hand on Leucas' arm, and said softly in Greek, "He's leaving because one of the Tomitiri men was killed the same way as Othniel."

"Hmm, I don't blame him," Leucas said, nodding with a thoughtful frown. "Ask the fat one if he wants to sell that sword." Barra rolled her eyes at him, and he said defensively, "I haven't seen an iron blade since the Sack of Troy—a sword like that should be in the hands of a man who can use it."

In the meantime, Kheperu had explained what they were after. Tekrop-nekt scratched at his topknot and chewed his lower lip; like many men who love their work, Tekrop-nekt could be put almost entirely at ease by calling upon his expertise. "Well, there is no cure for pukenut poisoning; that is, no antidote," he said slowly. "The best one can do is offer an infusion of poppy oil and nightshade in straight wine—it's commonly the convulsions that kill, not the pukenut itself. Of course, the cure can be deadly, as well, if too much is taken."

"Yes, yes, of course," Kheperu said irritably. "Am I a bloody novice? I'll take the poppy oil and nightshade straight—I can prepare the infusion myself."

"Oh, no, no," Tekrop-nekt said, his eyes going wide once again. "I was not proposing to *sell* these things to you. All of my wares are packed away; I cannot spare the time to unpack them." Met, who still held his scimitar before him, emphasized his agreement with a twitch of the blade.

Kheperu's hand dipped within his robe and came out with a fist-sized leather purse that jingled suggestively. "How much is your time worth?"

Tekrop-nekt's feathery brows drew together as he considered the question, and the wind shifted, blowing now full on Barra's back. The fine hairs on the nape of her neck lifted, and Graegduz began to growl: that musky reek of decay and rotting eggs forced its way into her head, strong enough now to wrinkle the noses of the Egyptians, even Kheperu. Barra said in Greek, "This negotiation? Kheperu, I tell you, make it fast. I want to get out of here."

Kheperu nodded and turned back to the other Egyptians, but before he could speak, Met lifted his head to peer beyond Leucas' shoulder and said in a high, fluting eunuch's voice, "We are not alone, here."

A thick bank of cloud blotted out the moon; suddenly the Market vanished into darkness so complete they might as well have been struck blind. Barra cursed under her breath and reached out to touch Leucas. When her hand found his massive oak-hard arm, she drew one of her small axes and slid around to put her back against his; his back was as reassuringly solid as a wall of stone, but through it Barra could feel the pounding of his heart. The smell was thick enough to taste on her tongue.

As she moved into place, she murmured in Greek, "Kheperu—ready some light."

His reply was low but crisp. "Two steps ahead of you, my dear."

The voice that grumbled in the darkness spoke Greek, but nothing else about it suggested that it came from a human throat. Lisping, with a halting stammer that chopped at its vowels, it spiraled between a moan and a shriek and back again without any recognizable inflection, or aspect of reason, as though it were a first attempt at speech by a creature who had read of the concept, but had never had anyone with which to converse.

It said, *"My Master . . . has instructed . . . me to extend his hospitality . . . in this invitation . . . to you, Leucas, Barra, and Khe . . . and Khe . . . Khe . . . Kheperu! Khehhperrruu!"* This drawn-out shriek became a scream of inhuman rage, a bubbling roar of berserk fury that battered Barra's ears and leeched strength from her knees—she could feel even Leucas flinch. The scream cut off cleanly, as though chopped through with an axe, and in the ringing silence she heard Kheperu's wordless moan of terror and a sudden patter of fluids on the street—from the sound, his bladder had let go.

The scream returned, louder than before: *"Kheperuu! Kheperu! I want my faaace! I want my face Kheperrrrruuuu!"* It was joined by Kheperu's rising howl of mortal fear, and then by other voices, yipping laughter from a dozen throats, from lunatic giggles to high-pitched screaming guffaws, staccato bursts of mindless hilarity from every direction.

She felt, rather than heard, the rumble of Leucas' low chuckle against her spine. "What's so funny?" she snapped, and in his reply the warm beginnings of his berserk battle joy heated up each word.

"After all this time in this godsforsaken hole," he said with a laugh, "how pleasant it is to finally meet someone who speaks Greek!"

An instant later, all voices were blasted away by the explosion of a brilliant thunderbolt directly overhead. The vivid flash stilled forms already in motion, capturing a single instant of the arc of the leaps that brought the creatures forward to attack. Only one man hung screaming in the blaze of after-image that filled Barra's eyes—an unarmed man, who wore only a girdle and Egyptian kilt—but at his side bounded night-mare dogs, powerful forequarters leading to long, flexible necks thicker than their fox-like heads, foam trailing from their jagged needle teeth, tails that seemed to hang loose and limp between their short and spindly hind legs.

It was the *dogs* that laughed.

Another thunderbolt opened the sky, and rain drove down upon them. Barra reached down and grabbed a handful of Graeg's ruff, with a sharp command in Pictish to stay at her side. She felt Leucas tense at her back, and knew that these nightmare dogs must be racing in from his direction as well. She couldn't tell what had happened to Met and Tekrop-nekt, though she could hear Kheperu's shriek still rising. The rush of the rain covered the footsteps of the dogs, and they'd stopped their insane laughing, so she waited, blind and deaf, trying to breathe past her hammering heart. The moment stretched out agonizingly, endlessly, an eternity passed between each heartbeat; when they hit her it was almost a relief.

They hit her low, going for her legs—needle teeth sank into her calf, and she swept her axe downward. It struck something that gave a hollow thump, not like flesh at all, but the teeth released her. She heard Leucas shout, and the sure support of his back left her, and scrabbling claws were all around her, and the dogs crashed into her and took her facedown to the street that was rapidly turning to mud. She tried to scream past a mouthful of water and earth as strong jaws gripped her wrists. She felt power in these jaws that could bite through her bones like dry pastry, but she also felt the restraint that stopped them; they pulled at her arms so she couldn't turn over, trying to hold, not to maim. And then one stepped onto her back, and its jaws took her neck.

In her mind, the words spun crazily: *My Master has instructed me to extend his hospitality in this invitation to you.* Maybe in some insane way, he'd meant it. Maybe if she didn't struggle, they wouldn't hurt her. Maybe resisting would only make it worse. Maybe—

Then light came, some kind of flickering orange glow like torchlight. And something from behind her hit the one whose teeth gripped her neck—the teeth raked free, and the dog rolled into the mud before her, locked in a snarling maelstrom of fur and fangs with Graegduz. Barra yelled and twisted desperately, swinging her legs up to kick at one of the dogs holding her arms. They giggled high in their throats, and stared at her with malevolent yellow eyes, and held on.

It was the limberness of her bulldancing training that finally freed her. She managed to get her left foot locked against the jaw of the one that held her left wrist—she shoved with her foot and yanked her arm, her flesh ripped through its teeth and her arm came free. Its drool burned like fire in the wounds, and it scrabbled to regain its hold, but Barra had already freed her broadaxe. She struck it a glancing blow that set it back on its haunches, then swung the axe in a whistling arc at the forelegs of the one that held her right wrist. It connected with a thud, and the dog barely seemed to notice. She twisted and got her legs under her, came to her feet to get a real swing, and this time the axe bit into the dog-thing's spine just behind its skull, a decapitating blow that didn't decapitate. No blood spurted; the axe didn't penetrate more than a finger's length. The dog-thing released her, though, and Barra watched it for an instant of frozen disbelief.

It stood, unsteadily, its head dangling from the thick muscles at the front of its neck, nose twisting an inch above the mud, the ends of its severed spine clearly visible in the dry, bloodless wound, then it turned uncertainly and trotted off into the darkness, moving half-crabwise so that one eye of its dangling head could be kept pointed in the direction in which it moved.

The thought, when it came, made her hair lift and her hands

tingle like a near miss by a thunderbolt: *Graeg is fighting one of these monsters.*

She sprang up and over the snapping jaws of another one, an aerial somersault that brought the blade of her broadaxe into its skull with crushing force—again, the sound it made through the shouts and hideous laughter of the battle was a hollow, bloodless thump, as though she'd struck a leather-wrapped barrel—and when she landed skidding in the mud, the dog-thing jumped at her belly as though it had felt nothing, as though the gaping wound showing splinters of bone was no more than a scratch. She batted its slashing jaws aside with the haft of her axe, and on the backswing she buckled her knees and swept the axe in a flat arc only a span off the ground: it still wouldn't cut deeply, but the dog-thing's foreleg snapped with a satisfying crack. She turned away from it instantly, in search of the young wolf.

Graeg still struggled, held down in the mud by a pair of them: one's jaws chewed a hind leg and another's teeth sank deep into his shoulder. Barra shrieked and leaped among them, straddling Graeg's body and swinging wildly before and behind. Her axe struck them again and again, doing no very serious damage but driving them snarling back long enough for Graeg to gain his feet. Barra risked a quick look around, hoping to find some help on the way or an inviting piece of wall that she could get her back to.

The light by which she saw came from flame that sprang out of the mud, as though it was the street itself that burned, the rush of rain hissing into steam above it. It flamed in a broad ring around the place where Kheperu struggled with the dogs' master. The man's clothing was on fire as well, and his smoking hair was blackened and sparked here and there with glowing coals. As she watched, Kheperu tripped the man up with a very neat sweep of the staff, sending him falling back into the flames once again.

Understanding came to her in a single instant flash: that piddling sound, when Kheperu had first moaned in terror—that hadn't been Kheperu's bladder emptying onto the street, it had been one of his potions, some distillation he must have carried within his robe. Clever man—no matter how fright-ened he got, it never stopped him thinking of ways to shave the odds in his favor. And he needed it: the dog-master—even now, Barra couldn't think of him as Chrysios—climbed back to his feet, out of the flames.

Kheperu struck him a wicked blow across the temple that split skin back from bone, and the dog-master didn't seem to notice. Kheperu followed with a whistling overhand, and the dog-master caught his staff with one hand, twisted, yanked it away, and threw it aside. His howl, "*I want my face!*" was matched by Kheperu's scream, and Barra could hear the difference now, the raw ragged edge of true terror. The dog-master clubbed a fist and, almost casually, battered Kheperu to the ground with a single blow. Kheperu's shrieks never stopped; he covered his face with his arms and tried to roll away, but the dog-things closed in laughing upon him.

Barra drew her remaining throwing axe and hurled it through the flames; it struck the dog-master in the back, and bounced off his bare flesh. He did not trouble to so much as turn and look.

"All right, I admit it," she muttered. "We're in trouble." As always, when in desperate circumstances, there was one thing she could do. She shouted, "Leucas!"

The giant Athenian danced among a giggling, snapping mass of the dog-things, weaving a whickering net of bronze with his shortsword. The small shield he used also became a weapon, hammering left and right with crushing force. The dog-things kept a respectful distance around him, not willing to press too closely, always trying to dart in to snap at his heels. Any that came close enough to bite paid for it with a dry cut or a broken skull. He matched their lunatic laughter with some of his own, and his eyes danced with manic joy. At his feet lay the massive mound of Met, scimitar lying carelessly alongside—two dog-things still tore at his unmoving body, their heads disappearing within the yawning wound, lipped with yellow globs of fat, that opened across his belly. Barra thought, *I guess he wasn't invited.*

"*Leucas!* Quit fucking around, Kheperu's in trouble!"

Leucas lifted his head at her shout like a chariot horse hearing distant battle horns. She had no chance to see what he did about it because she had to turn and cut at another one of the dog-things that tried to take advantage of Graeg's unsteadiness. Graeg limped badly, struggling on three legs—his left rear leg, the one the dog-thing had latched on to, could bear no weight. He still snarled and half-lunged at the snapping dog-thing, but Barra could tell his heart wasn't in it, it was only a show, a pretense. He was seriously hurt.

The pelting rain had pulled Barra's hair free of the pins that held it, and now she had to slap it out of her eyes as she searched desperately for some place of safety. Leucas waded slashing through the pack of dog-things that harried him, heading toward the fire and Kheperu. Most of the dog-things now circled the ring of flames, panting and chuckling as they drooled at the sight of their braver companions tearing at Kheperu, while the dog-master judiciously applied an occasional vicious kick to the ribs or crotch—but they *circled*, they didn't cross the flames, and that made up Barra's mind. It was the only place where the dog-things wouldn't come at Graeg.

"Graegduz!" she said in Pictish as she slid the haft of her broadaxe back into its scabbard. "Gimme a hug!"

The young wolf reared unsteadily on his one hind leg, and Barra wrapped her arms around his chest. She grunted as she lifted him up off the ground—it'd been a year since she'd picked him up, and now he was better than two thirds her weight. "You eat too bloody much!" she wheezed as she turned and ran as hard as she could toward the flames, screaming a Pict war howl that startled the dog-things into scattering momentarily, clearing a path. She put her head down and held her breath as she burst through the wall of flame. The heat blazed for only an instant, and then she was through.

Within, the ring was more confined than it had looked from outside; the heat was intense and now the center, the coolest place, was crowded with the dog-things that chewed at Kheperu, and the dog-master, who grappled with Leucas. Leucas' shield lay in the mud nearby, not far from the hilt of his sword—the blade had snapped off a handbreadth above the guard. Barra released Graeg and drew her broadaxe. She leaped over the whimpering wolf to attack.

The dog-master had Leucas in a bear hug around the short ribs, lifting the Athenian off the ground. Leucas' knotted fists, manslaughtering weapons, hammered at the dog-master's head and shoulders without effect. Barra skidded across the mud behind it, took a solid stance, and swung from her heels. Her broadaxe bit deep into the small of the dog-master's back: the razor-sharp flint sheared through the base of its

spine, and the blade sank in to the very haft. She braced one
foot against its butt to yank the axe free—but even as the axe
tore loose, the dog-master tossed Leucas carelessly aside.
Leucas tumbled bonelessly through the flames like a broken
doll, and the dog-master turned to Barra and smiled.

"Hey, it's the axe-girl." The words were familiar, but its
voice shrieked and howled like a damned thing. *"Remember
meeeee?"*

Firelight gleamed in its eyes, but there was no other
suggestion of life there. The blackened flesh of its face still
smoldered—smoke drifted from the glowing charcoal of its
upper lip, and its jaw—its jaw didn't look human, some kind
of piece of some animal's mouth, jagged tusks on bone that
had been sewn to its face with leather thongs. Some milky
fluid oozed like cold oil from the holes where the thongs
entered the bone. Similar thongs strapped across a huge cut
from its crotch to its breastbone, exposed now that its
clothing had burned away, and when it stepped toward her, its
walk was liquid and ungainly at the same time, a swaying,
dipping unhuman stagger—for a numbing, nauseous instant,
Barra thought she could hear the ragged ends of his pelvis
scrape together with each step, grinding where her axe had
split them days before.

When it said: *"Let's tryyyy that one again, shall weeeee?"*
she knew exactly what it meant.

Her throwing axe had bounced off its back—its skin must
be like leather boiled in brine. She hoped that, like the dog-
things, its bones would be as fragile as a mortal man's. The
bite wounds on her wrists bled along her hands to slicken the
haft of her broadaxe with her blood. She stepped back as it
lurched at her, axe up in both hands before her; it came with
arms spread wide like a favorite uncle. She'd picked her
target to attack—maybe she could break its knee, get it off its
feet—but somehow she couldn't step up to swing. The heat at
her back increased painfully, and the scent of scorching linen
and hair told her she'd run out of room. Her axe became suddenly heavy in her hands, weighing on her arms like bronze
shackles. The simple *unfairness* of this stung the most bitterly: she and her friends could beat any *human* foe—and
they wouldn't even be *out* here if she hadn't come to the aid
of a man she despised.

She summoned up her will and whipped her broadaxe into

a singing arc around her head. Remembering how bloody fast he'd been when he was alive, she eye-faked to its neck and continued the arc of the axe into a circling slice at the side of its left knee.

It was faster now; and stronger.

One hand met the arc of her swing, *one hand* to take the haft of her axe and stop a flint blade weighing more than half a stone that moved with every ounce of force Barra could muster. It disarmed her with a casual flick of the wrist and caught her elbow with its free hand. It lifted her into the air; she kicked like a thief in a hangman's noose. Its eyes blazed, and its blackened tongue snaked out to lick at the milky fluid that leaked like tears down its face.

"I'll bring your corrrrpse to my Masterrr. You'll live as I do. And He'll giiiivve you to meeee!"

Its skin was like armor of boiled leather; its muscles were like plates of bronze. But neither leather nor bronze can stop a heavy, curved blade of cold-forged iron swung by an enraged Athenian giant; no more so did the arm that held Barra.

She found herself staggering to her feet, Chrysios' severed arm dangling from the grip it still held upon her elbow. The thing that had been Chrysios roared an ear-ripping shriek and wheeled on its attacker.

Leucas towered over it like a god from the songs of Troy, outlined in rain and fire, his down-plastered hair and beard trailing smoke, glowing cinders climbing the hems of his chiton. The thing reached for him, the scimitar flashed, and its other arm tumbled away from its shoulder and splashed to the mud. Its legs buckled, pitching it forward as though to clutch at Leucas' knees to beg for mercy, but it had no arms with which to grab, and the scimitar's merciless downstroke clove its skull and split its mutilated face like a length of firewood, one eye to either side of a gaping slash that drove down to open its whistling throat and notch its collarbone.

It swayed there on its knees while Leucas regarded it with a breathless snarl. He gasped in air, his shoulders heaving, then wrenched the scimitar with a sideways twist that freed the blade and flopped the halves of the thing's head apart from each other like petals of some flower of flesh and bone.

Leucas thoughtfully wiped the blade on the thing's blackened chest, and said, "I like this sword."

Barra caught at the severed arm above the elbow with both
hands; then she had to pry the fingers loose one at a time to
break its bruising grip on her arm. Two dog-things still tore at
Kheperu, whose struggles seemed weaker. There was nothing
Barra could do for him, unarmed as she was with her weapons beyond the wall of flames, out with the circling pack.
"Leucas! Help Kheperu!"

"All right."

"Oh, don't bother!" Kheperu snapped. Suddenly, one of the
dog-things reared back gibbering away from him, its entire
body engulfed in flames. An instant later, the head of the
second exploded with a muffled *whump!* and Kheperu sat up.

"Do you think you could have taken a bit *longer* to deal
with him?" the Egyptian groused.

Barra threw the severed arm disgustedly down into the
mud. Leucas merely stared.

Kheperu turned up his palms. "These creatures couldn't do
much harm to me through the armor under my robes. It was
simply a matter of keeping them off my face and hands until
the two of you could handle Chrysios. He was certainly too
much for me." He offered a winning smile. "I knew I could
count on you."

The rain had ended, and the ring of fire around them was
dying away. The hyaenae—the name Kheperu had for the
dog-things—had slunk away into the night; even the one with
no head had dragged itself blindly off. Obviously, they had
come of the same sort of magic that continued to animate
Chrysios. Its body still twitched aimlessly; even the severed
arms flexed, clenching and unclenching their fists. Leucas
kept one foot on its chest, holding it pinned to the ground.

Met, the guard, was thoroughly dead, his massive form
sprawled near the mulecart of his master's goods, his guts
spilled in the mud around him. Tekrop-nekt had fared no
better; the lanky alchemist's body lay in an alley nearby.
Apparently, he'd either tried to run, or a couple of the
hyaenae had dragged him there to chew on undisturbed; he
was barely recognizable.

"What I don't understand," Leucas murmured, surveying
the scene, "is why no one came to *help* us. We must have
woken every soul in the Market."

"Think about it," Kheperu advised sarcastically. "You're

awakened in the middle of a thunderstorm by bloodcurdling screams and lunatic laughter, and when you peek out you see, well, this." His gesture took in the whole scene. "Who in their right mind would get out of their warm, comfortable, safe bed to fight for someone they don't even know?"

Leucas frowned. "I would."

"Well, all right," Kheperu conceded. "But, remember, I said 'in their right mind.' "

Neither Leucas nor Kheperu was badly injured. Kheperu had another swelling knot on his face to match the one Barra'd given him earlier; Leucas was mildly scorched—both he and Barra would need to trim their hair—and his ribs were tender, but that was all. Both of Barra's wrists were torn, and she had a nasty-looking bite wound on her calf, but she wouldn't let her friends bandage her until she'd seen to Graegduz.

The wounds in his shoulder still oozed blood, thinned by the rainwater held in his fur; all she could do there was wrap some wet cloth around it—nothing more could be done until she had the time and a dry spot to shave the fur away. Nor was there much to be done for his hind leg: it was broken.

Barra's eyes filled with tears when Graeg licked her hand, tears that dropped one by one across the jagged ends of bone that showed within the wound. Kheperu rested a surprisingly gentle hand upon her shoulder. "We can set that bone, once we get him somewhere out of the rain," he said softly. "We'll hold him; Leucas can set and splint it. It'll be all right, Barra. Really it will."

Barra angrily knuckled away her tears and stood up. Without a word she went to where Chrysios lay writhing. The scorched linen of her chiton tore easily; when she had three long strips, she took them in her teeth. She reached down and took the halves of Chrysios' head in her hands, the charred muscles crusty and jumping against her skin. She pressed them together, the two halves roughly aligned, and the eyes rolled and focused on her. She looked up at Leucas and said through her teeth, muffled by the strip of linen, "Hold him like this."

Leucas looked extremely dubious, but complied nonetheless.

Barra swiftly tied Chrysios' head in place with the linen strips. One went around his throat to stifle the whistling of his breath, another across his mouth, and the third just above his eyes. All three were instantly soaked through with the viscous, milky fluid that leaked from every wound. Barra said grimly, "I know you can still hear. Blink twice if you understand me."

The fierce blaze in his scalded eyes never wavered, but he did blink slowly: once, twice.

She said, "You go back and tell your master that we know who he is. Understand? We *know*. And you tell him that, as far as his invitation goes, we have a previous engagement for the rest of our lives."

Kheperu snorted. Barra shot him a *shut up or I'll pound you* look.

"Tell him we're leaving town tomorrow," she went on. "If he wants us, he'd better move fast. On the other hand, if he's smart, he'll just let us go. His business is none of ours, you understand? We don't care what he does in this shitcake town. We're already gone, you understand?"

Chrysios blinked, twice.

"All right. Leucas, let him up."

Leucas frowned. "Are you sure?"

She shrugged. "What's he gonna do, bleed on me? Let him go."

The Chrysios-thing slowly climbed to its feet. It looked at the three of them as though its gaze could kill them where they stood, then it wove off into the night, its dipping stagger fading beyond sight.

The three companions watched it go, and then Kheperu turned to Barra. "What now?"

She could barely hold up her head. "Now we're going home. It'll take him at least till dawn to make it out to the caves or the estate, whichever. We'll take care of Graeg and then catch a few hours' sleep."

"No, I mean, what is your plan? What shall we do about"—he gestured around them—"this?"

"Exactly what I said. We're leaving."

Leucas looked stunned. "You're joking!"

"I'm not."

"I was sure," Leucas said, "that this was strategy, that you didn't really mean to . . . run *away*."

She stepped up to face him, and sudden anger shrilled strength into her limbs. "Look around you, you shit-eating idiot! Those . . . things . . . could have found us at home! Go over to that shitcake alley and take a long look at what's left of Tekrop-nekt. That could just as well have been my *family*!" She paused, gasping in her rage. "That asshole-biter Idonosteus wants us out of the way—not even the gods know why—and the goddamned demonist knows who we are, and there is no one in this town that will lift one shitcake finger to save our lives. You had best believe that we are leaving. Tomorrow."

Kheperu nodded silent, grim agreement, but Leucas still looked hurt. "I never thought you'd let someone run you out of town, Barra."

She looked over to where Graegduz lay in the mud, panting out his pain, then looked down at the earth at her feet. "That's the thing about me," she said grimly. "I'm just full of fucking surprises."

CHAPTER TWELVE

Scent

The Governor was coming.

It was all the buzz under the harsh morning glare in the Market of Tyre. Forward outriders had arrived at dusk last night, and the contingent of the Canaan Division that accompanied the Governor's Household would reach Tyre by noon. Opinions were mixed as to the significance of this occurrence. For some, the storm that had blown through the night before represented the current unrest and troubles in the city, and the Governor himself was the sky-cleansing wind. Others spent the morning locking up their best wares along with their daughters, and hunkered down to wait out this visit with the same stolid patience with which they'd greet a cloud of locusts or a long drought. Still, overall, the mood among the smaller merchants and innkeepers seemed to be one of cautious optimism. There was a certain sense of being rescued, just in the nick of time—the mangled corpses of Tekrop-nekt and his bodyguard Met had been found in the Market this morning, and the rumor went that they were only two of more than ten corpses strewn in streets and alleyways across Tyre. Someone had seen a pack of ghostly dogs jittering with unearthly laughter as they pursued a screaming man in the Egyptian quarter, and it was generally assumed that the rogue magician was responsible for these murders, as well; everyone hoped that the Governor could bring it all back under control, and in the meantime, here was an opportunity that was literally golden. The streets were packed today, filled with slaves and shoppers streaming into the Market, stockpiling food and horse feed and spice and beer, in anticipation of a local economic surge as 5,000 Egyptian regulars poured into the city.

Barra listened to an Assyrian horse dealer chatter about this in Egyptian, to Kheperu, while she examined the spavined joints of the pair of mules he was trying to sell them. Apparently, the Assyrian owned a part interest in a medium-size brothel, and was most excited by the army's arrival. She palpated the poor mule's swollen hock one last time, then stood, shaking her head disgustedly and crossing her arms to scratch at the bandages wrapping both of her wrists: they'd already begun to itch. "They'll do," she said in Greek, "but don't pay more than ten shekels for the pair." Kheperu nodded his understanding, and she left him to handle the haggling. She went over by Leucas, who sat on the al-tobe wall that surrounded the horse yard and thoughtfully watched the passing crowds.

"I see lots of folks going around dressed like that," he murmured, nodding toward three boys wearing very clean, new-looking kilts and stoles of bloodred and purple: the colors of Meremptah-Sifti's banner. One held the leads of a pair of oxen, and the other two walked behind, occasionally encouraging the oxen with slender switches. "You think those belong to our buddy outside of town?"

Barra said, "I'd imagine so."

"Why so many, you think? Why today?"

Barra shrugged. "I'd guess Meremptah-Sifti is throwing a party. The Governor's supposed to be an old friend of the Pharaoh; he was a standard-bearer or drummer or something in the Ra Division when Ramses took Qadesh—like, fifty years ago. Maybe sixty. Anyway, I'd make a bet that Meremptah-Sifti is having some kind of feast to welcome him. To show respect, get in on his good side. It's what I'd do. And the Governor can't turn him down—when the Pharaoh's grandson invites you, you come. Period. He might even invite the Governor to stay at the estate while he's dealing with Tyre. I'd do that, too. Easier to keep an eye on him, make sure he doesn't get any wrong ideas."

Leucas' eyebrows pulled together, and a low grumbling grunt resonated through his chest. "That'll cause a problem for Idonosteus, getting at the demonist, won't it?" he said softly.

"Doesn't matter," Barra told him. She touched the gold ring on her first finger, twisting and turning it—not yet comfortable with it, nor with what it represented. "It's not our problem anymore. We're leaving."

* * *

Barra had been literally staggering with fatigue by the time
the companions had made their way back home the night
before. They'd found an overhanging roof with a dry spot
beneath where they could set Graegduz's leg with a piece cut
from one of the pine slats off Tekrop-nekt's dismantled shop.
He took it like a champion, panting mostly, only one little
yelp when Leucas pulled the leg straight and the bones
ground together. She'd carried the young wolf in her arms, all
the way home.

Once there, she'd passed off their wounds and Kheperu's
shredded robes as coming from the "deadly influences
and supernatural creatures" attendant to "Kheperu's summoning"—explaining the truth to the cluster of anxious, red-
eyed Kypriots would have taken too much time and effort.
One of Demetor's men had convulsed and died in his bed
while the companions were away; his body, wrapped in a
winding sheet, lay on one of the couches where the servants
eyed it fearfully. The Kypriots were grieving for their friend
and terrified for their king; Barra wisely kept her explanation
brief and reassuring. Explaining the large bronze-bound
wooden chest they brought back with them was less easy.

The chest had been Tekrop-nekt's, and it contained all of
his alchemical wares, hundreds—perhaps thousands—of
shekels' worth of rare powders and poisons, bits of this bark
and that shell, everything from old toenail parings to gold-
filigreed shark's teeth. In the words Kheperu had used, his
beady squirrel's eyes gleaming with avarice: "Little point in
leaving it here—I'd venture Tekrop-nekt has no use for it any
longer." To Peliarchus, he'd airily described it as a "gift
of Thoth, God of All Knowledge—for I am his most faithful
servant," as Leucas carried it up the stairs on his back. At her
foster-father's sidelong glance, Barra wearily promised
to explain everything in the morning. Leucas, returning,
appeared acutely uncomfortable at the flow of Phoenikian
around him; Barra translated the conversations, and Leucas
shook his head sadly and murmured in her ear, "I suppose
this means I won't be able to brag about the fight."

"No, you won't. Not for a while yet, anyway."

He laid himself sprawling along the length of one of the
courtyard couches and laced his fingers together behind his
head. "Hardly seems worth winning in the first place, if you
can't brag about it."

Kheperu had vanished into the second-floor bedroom and swiftly prepared the infusion. Barra administered the potion; she half feared the effect Kheperu's smell might have on men in their sensitive condition, and by the time the potion was ready, Leucas was sound asleep, snoring thunderously on the couch.

Demetor and his two surviving friends lay wide-eyed, staring and terrified in the dark. Barra shooed out the Kypriot that sat with them, gave them each one of the three wine-bowls Kheperu had prepared, and sat with them while they drifted off into a drugged sleep. In the darkness Demetor did not know her, but he clutched her hand and swore his grati-tude in words increasingly slurred as the potion took effect, and held her hand in his strengthless fingers until he fell asleep.

After that, it was all Barra could do to drag herself up the stairs to their room. Even Graegduz's occasional whimpering—he shared her bed this night—couldn't keep her awake. All of them overslept; the sun was well up, streaming through the window while Barra freshly re-bandaged her wrists and Leucas' belly and shoulder, and then tied a patch around her calf. Kheperu spent the time sewing shut the bite tears that riddled his overrobe. She chipped a new edge on one of her throwing axes, and used it to gently shave the fur around Graeg's wounds. Leucas held him still while she cleaned them with fresh water and re-bandaged those, as well. She'd shaken her head grimly at the array of wounds and observed that Tyre was chipping away at them, little by little, and it was a good thing they were leaving.

There was much consternation in the household when their imminent departure was revealed. Especially among the Kypriots—Demetor seemed to have passed the crisis during the night and was well enough to sit up and take broth for his breakfast. The old king was dazzled that it was the three boar-slayers who had saved his life; in the full light of day, he recalled them from their meeting in Paphos—where he claimed they'd saved his kingdom just as even now they'd saved his life—and he pressed three gold rings into Barra's hands; not as payment, for it would be impious to offer a fee to ones who were so obviously servants of the gods, but as tokens of the gratitude he owed to them for saving him. He invited them to guest with him whenever they passed Kypros,

and asked them to join him at the funeral feast and games for
his slain friend, and then passed into a long and windy expo-
sition of how well Kheperu's ointment had served him at the
brothels here in Tyre until Barra began to feel a guilty regret
for saving his life and thus inflicting him upon her family
once again. Whatever chains of kinship had been forged the
night before may only have been the result of exhaustion and
the warm letdown that comes after one has escaped danger;
by morning's light she found him absurd and more than a bit
repellent.

Tayniz had saved a breakfast of barley toast and lamb
gravy for them, and she and Peliarchus sat with them while
they ate. Tayniz was not the sort to give sighing, sidelong
glances or make oblique comments; she leaned toward Barra
and said, clearly enough that the servants had no need to inch
closer to eavesdrop, "It's *shocking* that you'd leave again so
soon. We've barely had a chance to say hello, and now you
tell us you're off again. And look at you. You're a mass of
bandages, your clothes are barely more than filthy rags, and
I'll bet you can't even remember the last time you washed
your hair."

Rather than rise hotly to the challenge—she bloody well
could remember, it was at Lidios' house, only four or five
days ago—she had held on to her temper and beckoned
Tayniz close, gesturing for Peliarchus to lean in as well.
"Please don't be angry with me," she'd said, low. "We did a
little job this past week, and it's turned out to be—well, we're
in a certain amount of danger. It's not too serious, really, but
I don't want to bring down any more trouble here than you
already have, with Demetor and all. There are a few people
who are a little upset with us; we're going to head overland to
Sidon and stay there until they calm down a bit here—
shouldn't be more than four or five days, maybe a week, then
we can come back."

"I've never liked the whole idea of you traveling like this,"
Tayniz said. "I don't understand it, I don't like it, I don't
know why you refuse to simply settle on some good Tyrian
boy. I know you're getting a bit old for a first marriage, but
you still look like a girl, he wouldn't have to know . . ."

Barra examined her hands, callused and powerful for all
their small size, spent half a moment picking at the bandages
on her wrists. Every time this particular conversation had

begun in the past, it had ended in shouting or tears, commonly both. She resolved to make it different, this time, so she clamped her teeth against the reminder that if she were a simple Tyrian housewife, Demetor and his friends would be dead right now and this whole household would be swimming in Agapenthes' shitpot. All she would say was, "Maybe I'm just stubborn."

The companions swiftly packed up their belongings, under the watchful eye of Tayniz. Barra had to explain twice that no, she didn't need any money for new clothes or food or lodging or pack animals or anything else, thanks anyway, she'd made plenty off this job. She gave careful instructions as to the care of Graegduz, and recommended that the Kypriots handle it; "He got hurt saving their bloody king, let *them* look after him." She spent a few minutes alone with the young wolf, feeding him hunks of gravy-soaked bread and fresh cheese, trying to make him understand that she would only be away for a few days. He licked her hands, and her heart hurt in her chest as she left.

Kamades wasn't home when the partners arrived at the apartment block with their new mules in tow. Barra had decided—reluctantly—to tell Kamades that she was leaving town. She didn't want him to think she was ducking him; he was the best man in years who'd shown a spark of interest in her. She didn't want to think about how many years it'd been, and she didn't want to slam the door against any future chance.

The lone Myrmidon present was Peroön, the one-handed physician, who wouldn't tell them anything about the others until he'd had a chance to re-bandage Leucas and tsk-tsk Barra for the sloppy way she tied bandages. He also insisted on rubbing some salve into her bite wounds—"What in the name of the Moonbitch did these? That hairy beast of yours finally go feral?" Barra assured him that it was none of his business, and pressed him about Kamades.

"Oh, they're out," he said, scratching his stump absently. "Shopping. Probably be in the Market till mid-afternoon. Lysandros came by with a stack of new clothes, to dress 'em up like servants, and a list of stuff they're supposed to buy and cart out to the Egyptian's place."

Barra winced. "The Egyptian's?"

"Oh yeah. Throwin' a big do for the Governor, all the Great House folks're invited. I'd suppose," he said with a wise squint, "that Lord Idonosteus is having them dress up to keep an eye on things, like he doesn't exactly trust this Egyptian fella. That's why they left me here; with the arm gone and all it's pretty clear I'm either a veteran or a thief, and somebody has to watch the armor. Don't know why all the fuss, but then, we never do."

"Yeah," Barra said heavily. "Listen, can you give him a message—ah, forget it. I'll find him and tell him myself." She left, muttering darkly, "This whole having-a-suitor business is complicating my bloody life before I even have a suitor."

Amber and tarragon.

Barra's head came up like a hound's, and she scanned the upwind crush of the Market. The gentlest of breezes came off the sea, and on its salt wings rode a thousand scents. There— there it was again, tarragon and crushed amber, over the clean-sweat smell of a freshly bathed man, and beneath that a rich, corrupt trace of a diet heavy in veal and lamb. Barra's nose was not as sensitive as her wolf's, but it was nearly as accurate, and she recognized that scent as one might recognize a familiar voice within a crowd's babble.

Murso. Lysandros. Whatever his name might be today.

She stopped, still looking for him, some unexplainable apprehension trickling into her belly. He couldn't be far away, if his scent was readable in the midst of this press. Leucas and Kheperu, walking alongside with the leads of their pack-laden mules, also halted and scanned the crowd, an instinctive reaction to Barra's peering.

"Uhm, Barra?" Leucas said after a moment. "What are we looking for?"

For an instant a corridor opened within the moving crowds, a channel straight toward the sea, and there he was, his back to her, skeletal shoulders obvious beneath a gaily dyed robe and a square cap in the Hittite style, not even a stone's throw away. He moved with deliberate speed toward a large oxcart that was being loaded with barrels and sacks by sweating slaves, and the two men who sat on the driver's bench wore livery of bloodred and purple.

A cold hand clutched her guts. Without any knowledge of

how she knew, she murmured in Pictish, "This is a problem," and knew the words were true.

The channel within the human sea surged closed once again, but now she saw the men on the oxcart conversing, and one of them pointed toward a nearby warehouse.

Murso's words came back to her: *I serve him in confidential matters only.*

"Barra?" Leucas repeated. "Are you all right?"

She turned back to them, and her expression was as bleak as her flattened voice. "You two stay here. Better yet, stay over there." She pointed to a narrow walkway between a farrier's and a shop that sold wine. "You're too damned conspicuous, both of you," she said, tying her hair up in a twist. She pulled a robe from one of the mulepacks and slipped it on over her clothes and weapons, then plucked out the long strip of cloth that had been bought as a new breechclout, and wound it around her head, tying it off like a Tyrian sun bonnet. "I'll be back soon."

Kheperu and Leucas had watched this whole process with identical bemused frowns. Kheperu said, "Are you going to tell us what this is all about?"

"I'll know more when I get back," she told them over her shoulder as she vanished into the crowd.

The man that Murso met coming out of the warehouse was clearly not himself the Pharaoh's grandson: he looked more Phoenikian than Egyptian, for all his sumptuous southern attire. The bloodred and purple colors of his dress were blazingly vivid and his torc gleamed with gold and lapis lazuli, matching the bracelets that clasped his upper arms. He was of medium height and stocky build, perhaps could have been very strong if he'd gone for a laborer or a warrior, but now gone mostly to fat. His beard was bound into a stiff rod down to the middle of his smooth chest, and though his head was shaven like a priest's—and his skin was fair—his head was pale, showing no sign of exposure to the sun.

The man began issuing orders before he'd even cleared the doorway. White-kilted slaves and liveried servants scampered around him, heading inside. In the midst of this flow, Murso stepped up to him, head bent respectfully. The man jumped visibly at Murso's words and looked around nervously, and Barra—watching from the corner of her eye while pretending to consider the wares of a fabric merchant at whose stall she stood—carefully lifted the cloth she held as though to examine its weave in the sun. The two men conversed briefly, then the man took Murso's arm and led him around the corner of the warehouse. Barra dropped the cloth to the ground and walked through a wide arc to get a view around the corner, ignoring the curses of the merchant that faded into the crowd's babble behind her.

Idonosteus, you cocksucker, she thought, blood freezing in her veins. *You worthless jiggleprick bastard.*

Alongside the warehouse stood a line of wagons, all draped in Meremptah-Sifti's colors. One of them, actually painted thus, was also hung with roof and curtains of heavy brocade. The man respectfully held the curtains aside and allowed Murso to precede him into the wagon, and Barra—as if from a distance—felt her knees buckle and breath drive out from her lungs as the *sceon tiof* took her.

This came not as it had before, a deep sense of the forces that drove the man she looked at; this came like a sudden storm wind that pushed her toward a precipice.

The sun faded in her eyes. The breath that left her was pulled out, torn from her by the whirling winds that were sucked down into the maelstrom of darkness within this man's spirit. She put out a hand to steady herself, and found nothing there to clutch. A dizzying vertigo, like that which may come of leaning out too far over an abyss bottomed only with mist, nearly overcame her.

It's him, she thought. *No person inside, only a gulf, an emptiness—that's the bloody demonist. An ordinary little man standing in broad daylight— Oh, Loving Mother!*

And he paused there, hand on the curtain and one foot lifted to climb into the wagon, and now his head cocked to one side as though he'd heard a familiar voice behind him or some unseen hand had politely tapped his shoulder, and he turned—

And from far across the Market, a swirling crowd of hundreds between them, he looked directly into her eyes.

"I don't know what might have happened if I hadn't pulled away and run like a bloody deer," she said grimly. "I don't know if he could've done something to me out in the open, in broad daylight and all, or not. I don't know if he's got some sense of me, like I've got a sense of him, or if it might be worse than that. But I do know what I've got to do now."

Kheperu stared morosely into his mug. Leucas drained his and set it down. He rested his forearms on the table before him and said, "You know I'm with you, no matter what. I never liked this idea of letting them run us out of town."

Barra looked around the smallish common room of this smallish public house, at the benches that were beginning to fill with hungry shoppers as noon approached. The big bowl of straight wine she'd drained had stopped her shaking by the time she'd gotten halfway through her story, but her arms and legs were still pimpled with gooseflesh.

"There's a chance," Kheperu said slowly, fingers pressed against his eyes as though he tried to massage away a headache, "that you misjudge the situation. It's possible that this is some maneuver preliminary to destroying them."

"A chance," Barra allowed. "That's all. Believe me when I tell you that I know things about Idonosteus"—she had *seen* them—"that make this all too convincing. That's why we were isolated from the beginning, why no one was to know of our job. That's why Idonosteus tried to get the Myrmidons to kill us—it had nothing to do with the money, it was because we're the only people in Tyre that know he knows who's behind all this. Mother's Blood—that's probably why he hired us in the first place! We're foreigners, all of us. If we're killed, he'd only have to pay a blood price to Peliarchus, maybe, and a blood price doesn't come to much for a twenty-nine-year-old spinster. For you two, nobody cares. A couple of anonymous bodies in an alley somewhere. And if he misses, so what? Who can we tell? Who'd believe three foreign mercenaries against the word of a Head of a Great House?"

"So. Where does this leave us?" Kheperu said, examining his fingernails. "On our way out of town, purses heavy with silver, as I recall."

She shook her head stubbornly. "We're the only ones left who know what's going on. House Meneides has joined the bad guys. If we leave now, we're handing Tyre to them on a platter."

"So?"

"Bloody Idonosteus is selling us out!"

"I say again"—Kheperu shrugged—"so?"

Barra gripped the edge of the table and lowered her head like a bull, struggling to keep her voice down regardless of her temper. She understood Kheperu's point all too well. They were foreigners here, even she—how much of her life was really invested in this city, after all? Three years? Four? She'd arrived on Peliarchus' ship at fourteen, and at eighteen she'd run away to see the Siege of Troy. In the years between then and now—more than ten, now, incredible as that was— Tyre had been only a stopping place in her mercenary travels around the Inner Sea, a place to come and rest, sometimes to heal. Tyre was small, and the world was large.

She hardened herself against a certain twinge at her own ruthlessness; she knew how much what she was about to say would hurt. She growled slowly, grinding the words out between her teeth, "This man—this demonist—practices the very art that you were accused of. You were taken, and tortured, and exiled on threat of death. You were innocent. He is guilty. He lives in comfort and honor, and his art will bring him wealth beyond your dreams."

Kheperu had gone ashen when she began; now his fingers whitened around the fired-clay mug and his voice rasped with real pain. "That's low, Barra. You shouldn't say that to me. That's not fair."

She didn't press him further, for she knew she didn't have to; the insight about him that the *sceon tiof* had given her told her well that his own mind would push the idea harder than she could.

She laid her palms flat on the table and looked around the common room, filling now more and more with townsfolk patiently waiting to be served the noon stew, chattering at each other in five different languages, talking of the army, of the weather, the prospects for trade; in her mind, each of them became a staggering, lurching Chrysios leaking milky ooze from its eye sockets. She said, "I never expected us to get this deep into something this dangerous. If I'd known, really known, what we were getting into, I'd never have taken this job—"

Leucas interrupted her with a gentle smile. "I don't think that's true, Barra. I saw it in your eyes when you looked at that fellow who died in the Market, that Othniel."

Barra shrugged irritably. "It doesn't matter. The point is that the Great Houses could have banded together against an outsider like Meremptah-Sifti, and probably beaten him, Pharaoh's grandson or not. But Idonosteus got a bright idea. He said to himself, 'Let's hire me some mercs who're smart—but not too smart. Let them find me that sorcerer so I can go to him and form a new partnership. Between the two of us, inside and outside, we can take over Tyre in no time, and leave me in the chair beside the new tyrant, whispering in his ear.' And, you know what? I think he's right." Muscles bunched at the corners of her jaw, and pulsed at her temples. "Don't you see? If it hadn't been for us—for me—Tyre might have had a chance. This is *my fault*, and I've got to fix it."

Her hands unconsciously sought the hafts of her axes and stroked them lovingly. "And Idonosteus used me in a way I don't like to be used. You'd best believe I'm not going to let him get away with it."

"Even . . . assuming," Kheperu said, his voice still harshly rasping, "that you are not completely full of shit, what can you do? What could we do? You said it yourself: we're outsiders here, we have no status that puts our words on a plane with those of the Head of a Great House or an Egyptian prince. Who would even listen to you, let alone believe you?"

Barra tried to drive the butterflies from her belly with a deep breath. She heard the distant thunder of her heart's blood in her ears. "Well, see, I've an idea about that. I don't need all of them to believe me, just one or two who can convince the others. Or maybe just one man: Tal Akhu-shabb—the Governor."

"What makes you think the Governor of the Canaan District would spare one minute for a bedraggled Pictish mercenary?"

"Well . . ." Her stomach knotted around the wine she'd drunk. "He wouldn't. However, he might be willing to spend a few precious moments with a nice-looking redhead who approaches him at a party . . ."

Kheperu looked thunderstruck. "You cannot!"

"I think I can," Barra said. "I'm sure Peliarchus was invited, or will be, as the Penthedes shipmaster. He can get me in."

"But, but," Kheperu sputtered, "the party's on his estate, on the bloodyfucking *home ground* of Meremptah-Sifti!"

"That," Barra said, "is what makes it, well, challenging."

Leucas leaned forward, his brows drawing together. "I

don't like it. You'd have to be alone. I'd be recognized instantly, and Kheperu—"

Barra shrugged. "I'm not helpless. And if things go bad, there wouldn't be much you could do except die at my side."

"That is not such a little thing," Leucas said.

"Well, forget it," she told him. "I'll be perfectly safe; that feast is the last place on earth Idonosteus would expect me to be—and, believe me, I won't be looking like I do right now. Meremptah-Sifti has never seen me. I can do this. I'm going to do this. This is my home, my problem. My job."

"But you're working for free, Barra," Kheperu said, shaking his head grimly, "and that is a dangerous way of doing business."

CHAPTER THIRTEEN

Idonosteus

"So, my prince," Idonosteus said, smacking his lips wetly as he inhaled, "though I know your plans as I know my own name, and could certainly interfere if I chose, I do not intend to. Quite the opposite, in fact." He shifted in his sedan chair; the noonday sun had snuck around the edge of his embroidered linen shade. The day was, in fact, growing uncomfortably warm, out here near the reflecting pool behind Meremptah-Sifti's manor house; sweat began to prickle on the backs of his hands. "Do you think you could invite me inside, my prince?"

Meremptah-Sifti stood staring down at the Head of House Meneides with undisguised loathing, as his steward translated this request. Idonosteus could well imagine what this extremely fit, extraordinarily handsome and youthful prince of Egypt thought of him; Idonosteus had dealt with several of Egypt's military-raised minor royals in the past. He knew how he appeared, with his pale flesh smooth over its rolling hills of fat, with the perfumed oil in his braided beard and the kohl shaded beneath his brows to make his piggish eyes look larger. Meremptah-Sifti would be thinking, more likely than not, that he resembled some plump, bejeweled maggot feeding on the corpse of an honest man. *Well, fair enough,* Idonosteus thought. *So long as he thinks I have the intellect of a maggot as well—it's always useful to be underestimated.*

The prince said something in Egyptian, in that tone both languid and peremptory which Idonosteus admired so much— one must be an aristocrat born to command with such a tone. The steward, Simi-Ascalon—a strange, pale man who never seemed to blink—didn't bother to translate this, as he had their earlier conversation, but then a translation was not required. The action of the two Egyptian men-at-arms, as they

strode forward and pulled their axes from their belts, made
the prince's meaning perfectly clear.

The Myrmidons, standing around Idonosteus' sedan chair
in their servants' guise, made no move to intercept; they
played their parts very well. They only watched Kamades,
and Kamades watched Idonosteus, waiting for his signal.
Idonosteus, instead of giving this signal, only examined his
polished fingernails.

Kamades and his men could certainly handle the approaching soldiers, as well as the other two armed and armored men
who stood stiffly nearby, even though the Myrmidons wore
no armor, only their white servant's chitons, and carried as
weapons only daggers concealed in sheaths strapped to their
thighs. Handling the prince's men was not the issue; Indonosteus wanted the Myrmidons to still be available, still be
regarded as mere servants, in case the time came when they'd
have to handle the prince himself. Idonosteus turned back to
face Meremptah-Sifti, and offered him an oily smile. "If those
men touch me, you'll lose Tyre, and most likely return to
Egypt in shackles."

He'd already seen that Meremptah-Sifti understood Phoenikian, by watching the play of expressions across the prince's
face while Idonosteus had spoken earlier; he didn't know why
the prince refused to speak it in return, and he cared not a
whit. Meremptah-Sifti held up a hand to halt the approaching
men-at-arms, and murmured a few words in Egyptian, to his
steward.

Simi-Ascalon cleared his throat explosively, and said, "My
prince instructs me to inform you that he is not susceptible to
extortion. I, ah,—*hrakhakh*—assume that you have committed your knowledge to paper, or confided in someone who
will go to the Governor or the other Great Houses in the event
of your untimely . . . whatever." He shook his head irritably,
and wiped his mouth with a linen handkerchief. "Now you
want my prince to cease and desist, or to pay you not to interfere. He will do neither, and now your life is forfeit for the
insult of making such a presumptuous demand."

So much for the packets of letters I left with Lysandros.
Idonosteus spread his plump, moist hands. "Not at all. You
mistake me, entirely. I come, not to demand, but to offer. My
services, and those of House Meneides."

At this, the prince's eyebrows lifted, and he fixed Idonosteus with a penetrating stare. "Have your warriors withdraw," Meremptah-Sifti said distinctly, in perfectly accentless Phoenikian.

"My warriors?" Idonosteus struggled to conceal a sudden surge of panic. "I don't know what you mean." *How had he known?*

"You are a fool, Idonosteus Meneides, to think that I could mistake the discipline of warriors for the obedience of servants. To persist in your failed deception would be a deliberate insult; you might as well call me a fool to my face. If you do so, I will have you killed." Meremptah-Sifti folded his arms. "Have them withdraw."

Idonosteus' hand fluttered a slightly shaky gesture, and Kamades looked silently at the prince of Egypt while he waved his men toward the reflecting pool. Meremptah-Sifti returned this impassive look with a smile and a mocking lift of the brow. Kamades dropped his eyes in a minimally correct bow, and he too stepped back to join the others near the fountain.

Meremptah-Sifti watched him go, then swung his contemptuous gaze deliberately back to Idonosteus. "So, Idonosteus. What can you do for me, that I should let you live?"

Idonosteus licked his lips. The steward, standing at the prince's side, stared at him with a lizard's unblinking fixity. Rolling sweat the size of teardrops painted Idonosteus' cheeks. "I, well, I . . ." Idonosteus coughed and leaned out around his sedan chair's canopy to squint up at the blazing sun. "Do you think we could get out of this heat?"

Meremptah-Sifti's lips stretched into a broad, mocking smile. "Ra blesses our meeting with the passion of his kiss," he drawled. "We shall stay here."

And he and his steward stood with folded arms and watched him sweat, waiting for him to continue.

"Hm, well," Idonosteus said, mostly to fill the uncomfortable silence. "As a guest of House Meneides, the prince would have access to each of the Great Houses; I could arrange an invitation for the prince with any Head—"

"My grandfather is the Living Horus. I have no need for such as you to be my pimp. No Great House would dare refuse me."

Again silence extended like the sudden yawning drop of an unexpected cliff. The rings on his fingers clicked loudly as

Idonosteus rubbed his hands together. "I have extensive resources on the streets of Tyre, men whose only job is to bring me news of the city—"

"So do I."

It seemed now to Idonosteus that the blankness in the steward's eyes had taken on a new expression: no longer a lizard's bored stare, it was now more the gaze of a cobra coiled at the mouth of a rat hole.

It went against Idonosteus' nature to come right out and say what he wanted. There was a cherished dream, an idle fantasy in which he had indulged on the ride out from Tyre, a dream that he'd intended to work his way toward gently, and subtly, making his services indispensable, slowly gathering power until his fantasy became truth. He'd look at this building, and that shop, and this stable and that inn and imagined what he would do there, with them and to them. He'd looked at young men on the street, and little girls playing in the sun, and he imagined what he would do there, too. Now he realized that he had little else to offer . . .

"Perhaps," he said, "my services can be of only little value in the taking of Tyre. I would not presume to imagine that I can do anything for the prince that he cannot do for himself. I would, however, venture that once the prince has taken Tyre, after the conquest, as it were, perhaps it would be the prince's desire to rest and enjoy the fruits of his labors, rather than taking on the onerous duties of actually administrating the city's business. This is where I can be of service. I have a thousand loyal men to do my bidding, men whose whole lives have been spent in learning the intricacies of the Tyrian trade. With House Meneides administrating Tyre, as a, well, satrap, as it were, Tyre would become an ever-increasing source of revenue, pouring gold in endless streams directly into the prince's coffers . . ."

"Money?" Meremptah-Sifti barked a laugh. "You think this is about *greed*? You poor, shortsighted, bumbling fool. I *have* money! When I am done with Tyre, you can turn the city into your own personal bordello, for all I care."

Idonosteus' heart leaped within his chest. "Your word on it?"

The prince waved a hand dismissively. "I have said so."

"I am, ah, only curious," Idonosteus said, "about how you plan to take Tyre. My agents didn't seem to know—"

"I am not planning to take Tyre," Meremptah-Sifti said smugly. "I am planning to accept it, when it is given to me."

"Your agents?" Simi-Ascalon the steward seemed to suddenly come to life again, as though he were a statue that had been animated by a passing god. His voice became disagreeably sharp, and he stepped forward and grasped the chair's canopy-poles in white-knuckled fists. "Did you have someone following me in the Market this morning, someone other than the Lysandros that I spoke to?"

Idonosteus flinched back from the fine spray of spittle that flew from his lips. "I, ah, well—" Really, this man had appalling manners, for the steward of a prince!

Meremptah-Sifti said warningly, "Sim, don't become excited—"

The steward whirled upon his master so quickly that for a terrifying instant Idonosteus thought he would strike him. "I told you—about that boy in the Market today, the one who . . . did that, who looked and, and *did that to me*! It felt like, like . . . I didn't like it! I told you! Someone was, was, I don't know what!" He spun back to Idonosteus, and the Head of House Meneides looked into eyes that were utterly deranged. "A boy, fifteen perhaps, no beard yet. Hair red as sunset. Is he your agent? I want him. I want him here, where I can *hurt* him."

Idonosteus' mouth went dry as desert sand. He shook his head hastily and spoke in a rapid stammer. "No, no, no, my agents were, they were foreign mercenaries, two men, Greek and Egyptian, and a woman from the north, she claims to be some sort of Barbarian princess—"

Now Meremptah-Sifti suddenly appeared at his steward's shoulder, looming over him with blazing eyes. "They were your agents? My mercenaries?"

Idonosteus cringed helplessly. What sort of madmen had he involved himself with? "Y-yes, my prince, those three were— did you say, *your* mercenaries?"

The prince brought his hands together in an explosive clap loud enough to make Idonosteus jump. *"I knew it!"* His eyes burned, not with anger but with some sort of mysterious exhilaration. "The woman, her hair is red, isn't it?"

"Y-yes, my prince . . ."

The prince pounded his steward on the back, and grabbed his shoulders, their eyes locked together. "You see? What

have I been telling you, all these days! Now they have
brought me another gift—a viceroy for my city!"

Simi-Ascalon said, "The boy, it could have been a
woman ... a slender one, in man's clothing. I want her.
Remmie, I want her here where I can hurt her."

"Hush, Sim, it's all right. You'll have her." Idonosteus
watched in disbelief as the prince kissed his steward gently on
the cheek. He slid his arm about the steward's shoulders, and
turned back to Idonosteus.

"Now, Idonosteus," Meremptah-Sifti said, his face alight
with anticipation, "you will tell me all you know about these
three foreign mercenaries."

CHAPTER FOURTEEN

The Feast

The sweep of hill below and around the manor house of Meremptah-Sifti's estate blazed with countless constellations of torchlamps, as though the rippling Phoenikian countryside were in fact the sea, and the hill a cresting wave reflecting the glory of a midnight sky. Ba'al-Marqod looked kindly on the gathering this night, and sent his servant Karbas, the dry desert wind, to sweep the sky clean of storm clouds. Even Karbas trod gently here, as he was out of his accustomed season, and flames of the torchlamps flickered only pleasingly. Sweating slaves in livery surrounded the fire pits, faces red-lit from below by pulsing coals that hissed with fat dripping from the slaughtered lambs which turned slowly on spits above them.

The manorial house itself was three majestic stories, surmounted by a flat roof that was itself torch-lit and scattered with guests, surrounded by a sprawling complex of wine vats and olive presses, stables and storehouses and barracks, pools and even one cunningly constructed fountain, all connected by roofed colonnades that shone with whitewash. Around and through and over it all wove the party, hundreds upon hundreds of guests and dozens of servants hustling throughout carrying huge two-handed trays of winebowls, or baskets piled with fruit from as far away as Kush or Doria, loaves of bread still steaming from the ovens, or golden plates piled with spiced lamb and roasted apples, smoked oysters and broiled shrimp. Strolling musicians offered songs sweet and tuneful or cheerful and openly bawdy, per the request of those nearest, or played accompaniment for the dancers, jugglers, acrobats, and minor conjurers that entertained here and there throughout the grounds.

The feast had begun at noon, and now, long after dusk, it showed no sign of abating. All the most important men of

Tyre were there, even the hapless, somewhat nervous commander of the Egyptian garrison, who stood around licking his lips and looking like he very much hoped that his garrison troops wouldn't start something foolish with the Governor's Canaan Division personal guard. The heads of the Great Houses had arrived in early afternoon, accompanied by their retinues of servants and hangers-on.

Regal, silver-haired Agapenthes, tall and still trim with a hunter's athleticism, walked in a cloud of Penthedes retainers, his gait having acquired a stately weave. He was rarely found these days without a winebowl in his hands, and today had been no exception. Nephrol Tomit held court not far from one of the fire pits, his vast bulk comfortably ensconced within an even vaster mound of cushions, his booming laugh ringing out infectiously, bringing chuckles out of men and women even on the far side of the feast. Five maidens reclined on the lower slopes of his silken mountain, sampling bites of this and that before offering them to their master; he'd eat nothing unless it came from the supple brown fingers of his slaves.

Xuxusimilli, grandson of Mursuwalli, who had founded his House, was the single Great House Head who had arrived openly armed, a straight broad-bladed sword thrust behind his wide leather girdle, and five of his thirty-odd companions were armed and armored with a king's ransom of grey Hittite iron. He took no chances anymore, not since his mother—the former Head—was poisoned a few weeks ago. But no one at the party so much as looked twice at these weapons, and soon Xuxusimilli had begun to look a bit shamefaced and defensive at the implied melodrama of bringing armed guards to a feast of welcome. Even grim Jephunah seemed to unbend a bit, fleeting ghosts of smiles skittering across his skeletal face, but he kept his sons close around him—eighteen sons total, from his five wives—and his glinting eyes never paused in their suspicious scan.

It was Idonosteus, of course, that Barra watched most closely. Now in the evening, the sweating Head of House Meneides still worked the crowd tirelessly, shaking hands, introducing himself to anyone he didn't already know, doing quite the opposite of the other lords, who held themselves apart and relied on their companions to sift out any unwelcome petitioners, or even the merely boring. Barra herself had been put off by several; she'd given up on the lords of the

Great Houses. The Myrmidons came and went around him, in their servant's guise, playing their parts convincingly enough; it was actually only Kamades among them who looked acutely uncomfortable. Close observation enabled Barra to spot the weapons they carried strapped to their thighs, by their occasional brief outlines through their chitons. She had been looking for them, reminded by the continuing friendly discomfort of the two bronze daggers she wore beneath her skirts.

She wondered how many servants of the other Great Houses here tonight were actually disguised warriors—there were undisguised ones enough, here and there, Egyptian regulars and men of various races in armor painted with the colors of the prince of Egypt, eyeing each other with friendly mutual contempt. The Myrmidons scrupulously stayed entirely away from the masculine chest-bumping that the other guards indulged in.

None of them had seen her; or if they had, they didn't recognize her.

Tayniz's lead clay had paled Barra's sunburned face and throat to a fashionable white, kohl enlarged her eyes, and crimson wax had been gently spread to emphasize the delicate bow of her lips. Her hair, freshly washed and lightly brushed with scented oil, piled up above her head in a gleaming mass of sorrel curls, set off by the ribbons of Tyrian purple that held them in place. A flowing dress of the same color, heavily draped in the Athenian style, softened the hard lines of her muscular figure; Tayniz, frowning, had added an extra drape across the shoulders that such a dress normally leaves bare. She had forgone jewelry—she didn't have the resources to compete with wealthy Tyrian wives and courtesans, and so had decided on a daring simplicity. Tayniz had swiftly sewn together elbow-length gloves, more in the Cretan style, out of fabric to match the dress. These hid not only the wounds on her wrists, but also her callused, grimy, nail-bitten warrior's hands. As they left their home in the late afternoon, Tayniz had declared herself satisfied, and had promised that if Barra didn't receive at least five proposals of marriage tonight, she'd eat that dress.

For her part, Barra felt clumsy and ridiculous, and vaguely helpless. She'd become convinced that the custom of wearing long dresses was invented by men, and intended precisely to make women helpless—you can barely fight, and you sure as bloody death can't run. If something went wrong, the daggers strapped to her thighs would be of little use beyond making sure she was not captured alive. She was completely out of her element; her skills as a warrior and as a sharp-eyed trader were useless here. To catch the eye of the Governor, and convince him of her truth, required the sorts of skills Tayniz had developed in her youth, or Barra's sisters, back home in Langdale, or Barra's mother Coll, who even now in her fifties could catch a man with a sly look and a tilt of the hips. She'd never had time nor interest to devote to such things; now she swore silently that she would study this, and practice it, as she would some new weapon.

She'd arrived with Peliarchus and Tayniz just at twilight— she had no intention of letting Idonosteus or the demonist get a look at her in broad daylight. She'd played for time all day, with changes to dress and hairstyle and such, to make sure that the feast would be in full swing and the day fading, so that no one would take too much notice of their arrival. This worked quite well—rather too well for Tayniz's taste—except for the seven or eight young men who always seemed to be drifting close to wherever Barra would stand, trying to draw her into conversation; not even her most pointed sarcasms seemed to dampen their enthusiasm at all. Finally, she let one of them lure her into a small yard behind the barracks, screened from the torchlight by a well-kept hedgerow. As he tried to pull her close, she delivered an efficient knee to the groin that lifted him off his feet and dropped him crumpled and gasping against a wall. Before he could so much as open his eyes again, he felt the edge of a dagger against his throat. "If you and your boys don't lose interest in me right now," he heard, "I'll make bloody sure you'll never be interested in a woman again, y'hear?"

The barracks itself had interested her somewhat; the strong scents of oiled bronze and leather clung heavily to it, worked into the wood itself. While the estate clearly required a small army of gardeners and other laborers to maintain, gardeners don't sleep with their tools—they would put their tools in the locked sheds that dotted the grounds. There's only one kind of professional workman who routinely sleeps with his tools: a soldier.

She worked her way back to a line of sight on the Gov-

ernor. He'd been perambulating throughout the crowd, con-
genially accepting greetings and courteously laughing at stories. His topknot and braided beard were the color of a wave
crest whipped by the wind, and the creases in his weathered
face were visible even by torchlight from a bowshot away.
She'd dared not approach him, for wherever he went,
Meremptah-Sifti and his demonist were not far away.

The Pharaoh's grandson was tall and very fit; he wore the
embroidered kilt and wide pectoral of the royal house, and his
bare chest was broad and heavy with muscle. Looking at him,
she doubted Kheperu's stories of drunkenness and dissipa-
tion; nothing about him bespoke anything other than strength
and capability. His features were sharp, not blurred with
drink, and when he laughed, his teeth shone very white. Barra
had considered the idea that he might be duped, or even a
helpless pawn under the demonist's control—but now, seeing
him, it was hard to believe he wasn't in complete command.

She didn't even want to *look* at them too long; should the
sceon tiof take her, she felt sure the demonist—whose name,
she'd learned, was Simi-Ascalon; he posed as the estate's
steward—would feel it and point her out, which could be very
bad indeed. She needed some sort of distraction, something to
draw the pair away. She wished desperately that she hadn't
had to leave Leucas and Kheperu behind.

Kheperu had begged off: "I am sorry, Barra, but as you
may recall these are Egyptian lands and I'm still under sentence of death. One of the many advantages of my particular
personal hygiene is that no one looks too closely at me; if I'm
clean and well dressed enough to mingle at this feast, I may
be recognized. Meremptah-Sifti and his household are from
Thebes, you know—it's not impossible that one or more of
them may know me. One word to the Governor and *snick-
snack*, there goes my head." Barra could hardly argue with
that, and she'd been forced to agree with what Leucas had
said; he was just too conspicuous, with his great height and
broken face; little could be done to conceal either.

After circling back by the home of her foster-parents to
inform them of the change in plans the day before, the companions had indeed headed out—conspicuously—into the
desert. This required nothing in the way of further planning—
after all, the mules were already loaded with supplies for a
journey. They'd spent the night in rotating watches against

the chance of being found by those hyaenae or other creatures of the demonist, sleeping in shifts, wearing full armor,
tucked into a highly defensible crack in a hillside not far
beyond the funerary caves. It was an utterly miserable night
of rainsqualls and biting flies, made only worse by its
uneventfulness. By morning Barra found herself wishing for
an attack; it would have made the torturous semi-sleep that
she'd suffered through seem almost worthwhile.

Now—presuming nothing had changed since she'd left
them—Leucas and Kheperu lay patiently on or near the hill
from which they'd originally observed the estate, taking turns
watching the feast. They would have retied the packs onto the
mules sometime around sundown. Barra had told them to pick
an inn in town, but Leucas insisted, "We'll watch from the
hills. So we might know if something has gone wrong."

Both Barra and Kheperu pointed out that there would be
little to be done, and less yet that *could* be done by a lone
warrior and an Egyptian alchemist from half-an-hour's march
away, but their pair of cranky mules had nothing on Leucas
for stubbornness. "You don't know," he stated calmly, again
and again. "I might be able to help. You don't know." In the
end, he got his way through sheer persistence.

Now Simi-Ascalon the steward/demonist had vanished
somewhere among the guests and servants. Meremptah-Sifti
still hung near the Governor's elbow, but Barra had no better
ideas and had run out of patience. She threaded among the
knots of guests, keeping a weather eye out for Simi-Ascalon.

Watching the Governor as she closed on him, Barra caught
herself wishing for the *sceon tiof*. For once, it would be
useful, perhaps even essential, to get a glimpse inside a man.
He looked genial enough, with laugh lines deep as knife
wounds across his temples, and he had a reputation for being
both kindly and tough, if perhaps less than ideally smart.
Barra was acutely aware of how far reputation could diverge
from reality. Could he be swayed by argument, or would tears
work better? If he didn't believe the story, was he cautious
enough to quietly investigate it anyway? If he did believe her,
was he strong enough to stand up to a prince of Egypt? How
close was he to Ramses? Had the Pharaoh sent him here as a
reward for past service, or as a politically safe exile to the
Hittite frontier? Was Akhu-shabb really a capable adminis-
trator whose strength was needed, or was he an annoying

weaselly back-stabber that Ramses had shoveled off here where he could do little damage? Once she opened her story, there would be no going back—and she just didn't know. This bitter twist did not escape her, how this gift that she'd earnestly wished the gods would take back would serve her perfectly now, when it wasn't working, but she was too worried to fully appreciate the irony.

Then she was among his personal guard; they lounged at their ease not far from the Governor, and several eyed her appreciatively. None made any comment, however, lewd or otherwise—not even a whisper—and they smelled clean and healthy, even the greying ones who were obviously longtime veterans. This made Barra feel a bit better; you can judge a commander by his men, and these were clearly disciplined, respectful, high-morale troops. But anyone with half a brain will choose his best men for his personal guard, she reminded herself. Still, it was a good sign.

Then she was before them, the wrinkled old warrior and the prince of Egypt. They broke off their conversation and turned to look at her. Her breath caught in her throat as her eyes were helplessly drawn to those of Meremptah-Sifti.

Oh, Loving Mother! she thought desperately, her heart pounding. *That's the most beautiful man I've ever seen.*

Nut-brown skin, smooth and creamy as butter; high, broad forehead above liquid brown eyes; straight blade of a nose and a full, sensual mouth above a sculpted jaw; skin stretched rippling over smooth muscles, powerful shoulders beneath the arc of the pectoral tapering to a trim waist; just a trace of fine black hair climbing the furrow of his belly above his girdle. Then he smiled, his eyes lit from within by a flame of aristocratic assurance, and she wondered how she'd ever get enough breath to actually speak. *Tale of my life,* she thought.

He said, "Why, greetings, child. How is it that the sun has come back from his bed to light your face?"

"I, ah, well . . ." *Can he really see me blush even through this bloody paint?* Even as she stammered, she had the presence of mind to accent her Egyptian with Greek vowels. Meremptah-Sifti only smiled tolerantly; he was clearly accustomed to stopping the speech of women with his grin and a word or two. He reached out and gently laid his hand upon her arm. His touch burned.

"Tell me your name, that the pleasure of introducing you to our Governor may be mine."

"I am Briseis of Argos, Most High—of House Penthedes now," she said, dipping her knees in her best imitation of a courtesan's courtesy; her face heated up even more. *I hope that didn't look as clumsy as it felt.*

Meremptah-Sifti turned indulgently to the smiling man beside him. "Tal Akhu-shabb, it is very much my honor to present to you Briseis of House Penthedes."

The Governor looked her up and down, a frown both critical and avuncular furrowing his brow. He cleared his throat wetly, and held his winebowl out to one side, where it was instantly refilled by a slave bearing a large pelike. His eyes glistened, and his critical frown was replaced by the first twinge of a smile. "You're a lovely young thing, my dear. Are you a slave?"

Barra dipped her head, casting her gaze down at his sandals, trying to look demure. *Everybody likes demure, don't they?* "Yes, lord. Taken at Troy, gifted to Leokalkes, nephew of Agapenthes." This particular nephew she'd lately seen snoring behind a hedgerow. "I am offered again, for this night, as a gift to my lord."

Meremptah-Sifti's eyes danced, and he clapped the old man on the shoulder. "A princely token! I've half a mind to take her myself." He stepped close to her and took her shoulders, looking down into her face. He smelled of fresh bread and open space, of olive groves and wild figs. "How would that be, child? Would you like to grace the bed of a prince?" Barra met his gaze again, melting helplessly at his staggering beauty. She hoped she wouldn't have to kill him.

"I am only a slave, Most High," she mumbled. "I can only go where I am sent."

"Well, then, let us find your master and let him change his direction." He squeezed her shoulders, a frown stealing over his perfect features. "Why, you must be near as strong as a man! What sort of work did those Argive beasts force you to do?"

Barra thought quickly. This wasn't going at all well. "I, I'm a dancer, Most High, and a tumbler and acrobat."

"Hmm. Indeed. Well, then, you shall dance for me, eh? In my chamber. You don't mind, do you, Tal?"

The Governor gestured expansively. "It seems some small

repayment for your glorious hospitality. I'm an old man, you know, age and drink have taken their tolls. A gem like this should be polished by a man who yet has some zest for the task, eh?" Meremptah-Sifti agreed with an appreciative chuckle.

"But, my lord Governor—" Barra began, alarmed.

"Yes, child?"

She needed a lie, quick and good. What would Kheperu say? "I, ah, well, lord, I have some small experience in kindling fires from the faintest of smoldering embers. . . . Do you not think . . . ?"

The Governor's spray of snowy eyebrows lifted, and a broader smile twitched at his lips, but then he shook his head sadly. "No, I think not, sorry to say. What trick could you play that I've not seen or done?"

"Well, I, mmm . . ." Barra clasped her hands behind her back and looked shyly at her feet. "I don't like to say."

The two men exchanged a look that burst into shared laughter. "A bashful whore!" the Governor chortled. "This may be an evening's entertainment better than any I've had for many a year."

Barra said, still with her head down, "Perhaps I could whisper in my lord's ear?"

"Oh, well," he replied, "I suppose I can go that far, with no strain on my poor old heart." He spread his arms. "Come here, child."

She folded herself into his arms and pressed her lips to his ear, cupping her hand around to hide them. She whispered, "I am neither slave nor whore. Your life and your command are in deadly danger. There is enemy magic in the air, and the gods do not protect us. If you would learn more, come with me to some place where we may speak in private." The Governor clutched her more tightly while these unexpected words registered in his mind. Around them, Meremptah-Sifti and the Governor's personal guard watched this charade with open amusement.

"By Ishtar and Astarte!" the Pharaoh's grandson said. "I think she's raised the Governor's banner!"

The Governor held her a moment longer, and Barra could feel the quickening of his heart against her chest. Then he released her, stepped back, and offered his arm gravely. "This endeavor may be worth the trying," he said gamely, but

Barra's heart sank to see the concern clearly written on his face. Perhaps it wasn't as clear to the others, or perhaps they mistook its source. She had no better hope. As they walked away, she felt the gaze of Meremptah-Sifti blazing against her back.

They strolled arm in arm toward the house, and when they got to the doorway Barra cast a last glance over her shoulder. Across the party, far from his master, stood Simi-Ascalon, apparently deep in conversation with Idonosteus, but:

He was looking at her.

Barra leaned out the broad window, pressing back the shutters of polished cedar. The colonnade that led to the stable was empty, as was the small stretch of open yard between. She turned back to the Governor. "I think we can get to the stable without being seen. Come on."

He folded his arms across what once must have been a most impressive chest. "I think I have come far enough, on only your word."

"We may be interrupted here, lord." In fact, if that chilly bastard had recognized her, she could guarantee it. "I only want a bit more privacy." *And to have a horse at hand in case I need to bolt.*

"Not even Remmie would dare to disturb me. Speak on," the Governor said sternly, with a strength in his voice that lifted Barra's spirits.

But: "Remmie?"

The Governor grunted. "Meremptah-Sifti. I've known him since he was a boy. Ramses is like a brother to me."

Oh, Loving Mother. Still, he was her best hope. She looked at the dozens of figures painted on the walls that surrounded this expanse of floor; not scenes of battle, or of the daily life of an estate such as this one, but endless erotic variations of men and boys and women and animals and above it all the smiling Osiris, a gaping hole between his legs, giving his loving approval. The room was big enough to double as a dance ring, and was spread with cushions after the Tyrian fashion. She said, "Can we at least move to a smaller room?"

The Governor shook his snowy topknot stubbornly. "I have trusted you thus far, but no further. Begin your tale."

She gripped her nerves with both hands and clenched down on them. After a deep breath, she began. "I know you're here to keep a lid on the trouble in Tyre. I'd guess you already know that someone's been stirring this pot with dark magic."

His brows drew together. "I do know, yes. And I have taken steps to protect myself and my men against it."

"Good, good," Barra said, nodding. "I know who the sorcerer is, and I know why he's doing it."

The Governor's eyes lit up, and a certain thickening of his voice betrayed a rising excitement. "Oh, really? Sit with me here, and tell me this story. I would very much like to get my hands on this black magician, and my sword at his belly."

They lowered themselves onto a pile of cushions. Barra said, "You won't like this story, all right? Just hear it out, no matter how much it surprises or hurts you. All right?"

The old gentleman nodded gravely. "Speak on."

Barra told her story rapidly, leaving out only incidentals. She told of Chrysios, and the fight at Lidios' inn, of Mykos and the curse, of Tekrop-nekt, of Lysandros and Idonosteus, and the theft of Chrysios' corpse. The Governor's face showed his excitement mingling with mounting horror as she approached the end of her tale.

". . . And his banner unfurled, bloodred and purple, and it was this very estate," she finished breathlessly.

The Governor looked stunned. After a moment of dazed silence, he jerked himself to his feet. "Remmie's steward, Simi-Ascalon, was once of the priesthood; he has considerable knowledge of magic. . . . I've, I've already consulted with him on this matter . . . I always wondered how it was that a skilled priest would leave to take service under a minor member of the royal house—but this is madness! Am I to accuse Remmie of leaguing with a demonist on the word of this . . ." He caught himself, and shrugged at her apologetically. "I cannot believe this would be so."

Barra rose beside him. "You don't have to take my word for it. Investigate for yourself, look into it, have Meremptah-Sifti and Simi-Ascalon questioned, do whatever you think needs to be done to be sure, but for the Love of the bloody Mother don't do it here. *You're not safe here,* do you understand? I don't know what the limits are of Simi-Ascalon's power, but I wouldn't put it past either of them to drop a vial of pukenut extract into your soup, or simply slip a knife into you."

"But, but I don't understand," the Governor said, shaking

his head as if to clear it after a blow. "Remmie is a grandson of Ramses himself! The blood of God flows through his veins! He has wealth, women, anything a man can want—why in the name of the Living Horus would he want Tyre? Why would he do this?"

Barra stopped, and thought about it. Why, indeed? "I don't know," she said after a moment. "I can't even guess what drives him."

The Governor met her gaze, but then his eyes flicked over her shoulder and widened in surprise.

"Perhaps it is because," came the rich and resonant voice with undertones of mocking laughter, "I simply cannot bear the thought of having anyone around me that doesn't have to do exactly what I tell them to."

Leaning against the post of the door behind her was Meremptah-Sifti, and at his side stood the cold void of Simi-Ascalon.

Barra thought, *Oh, bloody fuck.*

"Barra. Coll. Eigg. Rhum." Meremptah-Sifti pronounced each syllable with distinct pleasure, as though savoring some unusual sweet. "Do I have that right? Idonosteus is a bit drunk." He flowed into the room, a loose-skinned predatory stalking like the cheetahs in his grandfather's menagerie. "You are very bold, Barra Coll Eigg Rhum, princess of Great Langdale—though Idonosteus tells me that this means only that your family has the largest mud hut—ship owner, tin trader, sometime scribe, mercenary. Whore. I admire you. Why did you not simply introduce yourself? We have a friend in common, after all. He sends his regards, as he is regrettably indisposed."

"Well, I . . ." The pounding of blood in Barra's ears made it difficult to think. She said, "If you don't even have the courtesy to learn how to properly pronounce my name, I'm leaving."

As she whirled toward the open window, Meremptah-Sifti said, "I think not."

It wasn't open anymore.

An instant's vivid image of crashing through the splintering shutters crossed Barra's mind, but now, for the first time, she became aware of their construction: diagonal slats of springy cedar on the inside—and she'd bet the slats on the outside crossed them at the opposite diagonal. No one crashes through shutters like those, and she had a sneaking suspicion that they were being held shut by men outside.

She turned back. "You're a shitty host, you know that?"

The Governor drew himself up to his full height. "Remmie, what is all this? What are you doing?"

An odd, secret smile flitted across Meremptah-Sifti's beauty. "Do not concern yourself, Tal. This is between the princess and myself."

"I, I mean, I suppose—"

"Drop the *princess* crap, all right?" Barra said, taking refuge in her cynical mercenary act. She wished desperately that her daggers weren't buried beneath yards of purple linen. While she kept talking, she clasped her hands behind her and began hiking up the back of her dress little by little, bunching it up above her wrists, hoping that the Egyptians wouldn't realize what she was up to before she could get those weapons in hand. "We don't exactly have kings the way you do down here—it's more like my brother knows some guys who'll stand up for him in a fight, if he asks them nicely. Now, on the other hand, if he finds out his favorite little sister's been hurt down here in Phoenikia, you'll have about a million and a half screaming Picts running around down here burning towns and killing Egyptians and doing all kinds of—"

"Shut up." Meremptah-Sifti strolled toward her, the very image of nonchalance. "Simi, close the door and join us."

The demonist spoke for the first time, his voice surprisingly thin and querulous for such a robust-looking man. "All . . . *hrahkhakh*"—a racking cough—"all right." The door that he swung shut was constructed very much like the shutters, of crossing diagonal boards. Barra realized with sinking heart that this manor house was built like a fortress.

"I do apologize, by the way, for the unfortunate result of my invitation the other night. Who would have known he was so vain? And so determined, in holding a grudge." He smiled, and Barra's mouth went dry as sand.

The Governor said, "I should return to the feast, and let you two handle your business here."

"Well, thanks a bloody lot!"

"Don't blame him, Barra." Meremptah-Sifti turned to the Governor. He spoke as a parent does to an unruly child. "I think not, Tal. I think you'll be staying here."

"I don't much like your tone," the old man replied stiffly.

"It doesn't matter. Sit down."

The Governor sat down.

Barra said incredulously, "What are you *doing*? You're the bleeding Governor of the Canaan District! You don't have to do what he tells you!"

"Yes, he does."

"What, just because you're Ramses' bloody grandson? He was appointed by the Pharaoh himself—and I hear Ramses doesn't even *like* you! I hear he thinks you're a lazy, perverted pile of shit!"

"My, my, what a mouth you have." Meremptah-Sifti shook his head, smiling. "You know, you're so lovely in your gown and face-paint, I had almost decided to keep you for myself. But I could never bear your tongue, so"—he sighed deeply—"I suppose I'll give you to Chrysios after all. You wouldn't happen to recall where you left his arms, would you?"

Barra's whole body seemed to freeze solid, waves of chill radiating downward from the back of her neck; she couldn't move, could barely breathe.

"Chrysios?" the Governor sputtered. "That's the name of the man whose body was—"

"Yes, yes, be quiet," Meremptah-Sifti snapped. "I'm in the midst of explaining something to the princess. Now," he said, drawing himself up and crossing his arms, "it would be traditional, at this point, to simply murder old Tal Akhu-shabb and tell the guests outside that you'd done it. We caught you in the act, you see, still holding the weapon and wearing the blood-smeared gown."

The Governor began to rise. "Murder? Me? But, but Remmie—"

Meremptah-Sifti forestalled his protest with an uplifted palm. "Don't speak until I give you leave." He turned back to Barra. "But that would be wasteful. Waste not, want not. I'm going to let you live, Tal, and you'll never mention what happened here today. I'll even let *you* live, princess, at least for a while."

Barra had the dress almost high enough to get at the daggers. She said, "Why?"

In answer, Meremptah-Sifti showed her teeth that glistened in the lamplight and said, "Tal: dance. Do the chicken dance."

And the Governor, without a word, climbed to his feet,

crouched, doubled his arms, and began to flap them like wings. He shuffled grotesquely around the room, capering like an arthritic madman, his face gone purple and veins standing out in his neck.

Barra could only stare, tight pain growing in her chest. The folds of her dress dropped from her nerveless fingers. She said, "Stop." Against her will, her voice took on a pleading tone. "Stop him, you have to stop him!"

"No, I don't," Meremptah-Sifti said warmly. "I never have to stop. That's exactly the point. Tal: strip. Take off your clothes."

The Governor only slowed his dance so that he could pull at his clothing, never stopping, tears running down his face, pulling away his painted shift, exposing the scruff of grey hairs on his chest, his sagging old-man's belly and withered arms. Swelling showed high on his shoulder, where even if he were publicly bare-chested the mark would be covered by his formal pectoral, a dark blue-black mark on flesh still an angry red: a tattoo? He undid his breechclout and dropped it, still dancing. His pubic hair was grey as granite, and his genitals flopped limply, and Barra's vision began to blur with tears of her own.

Meremptah-Sifti, watching, had begun to massage himself through the embroidered kilt that he wore. Simi-Ascalon looked on, an expression of detached appreciation on his face, smiling a private smile and rubbing his fingers together.

Meremptah-Sifti said, "Tal: stop dancing and come here. Kneel before me." The Governor complied, and Barra's breath stopped in her throat.

The Pharaoh's grandson pulled aside the folds of his kilt to expose his erect penis, long and bulbous and the color of spoiled sausage. He looked not at the Governor, but at Barra, directly into her eyes, as he said, "Tal: suck on my penis."

In Barra's homeland, the Isle of the Mighty, they played a game that the Kelts had brought with them in their migration a century before Barra's birth. This game came to be known as Eirish Stand-Down, and its rules are fairly simple. It's played by two men at a time, who stand toe-to-toe. You punch your opponent as hard as you can. If he doesn't fall down, he wins. If he does fall, and then after he falls down he can't get up again, you win. You and your opponent trade blows until one of the two conditions prevail. A good match of Eirish

Stand-Down can last for hours, especially since it's traditional to down a mug of beer after each pair of blows. Barra, who as a child couldn't bear to be left out of any activity the boys were up to, grew up playing this game. She wasn't very good at it; small as she was, it was almost impossible to remain competitive against boys half again her height and twice her weight. On the other hand, it led her to develop a truly impressive two-handed haymaker.

Now, as the Governor bent his head toward Meremptah-Sifti's groin, her numb paralysis finally shattered into fury. She shrieked a bone-chilling Pict war howl as she sprang at the prince of Egypt and whirled herself recklessly around: her doubled fists exploded against his face. The blow lifted Meremptah-Sifti off his feet and dumped him on the cushions, shaking his head dazedly and struggling to rise.

A hard shoulder slammed into her back, driving out her breath and bearing her to the floor beside him—Simi-Ascalon had tackled her from behind. She squirmed around within his grasp and got a hand on his face, thumb digging for his eye while her other hand blindly sought the hilt of a dagger within the folds of her gown.

She got a glimpse of the Governor, still pursuing Meremptah-Sifti on his knees, and then the prince was above her, standing, veins bulging in his face, blood pouring from his mouth. Her hand found the dagger's hilt, Simi-Ascalon clutched her tight and tried to bite her fingers, and Meremptah-Sifti snarled, *"You worthless cunt,"* and kicked her in the head.

Stars shot through her vision as the blow unstrung her limbs. He kicked her again, and again, she tasted blood and vaguely felt her nose break as the room darkened around her. Meremptah-Sifti pushed Simi-Ascalon off of her and straddled her, his hard thighs crushing away her air, his fingers tangled within her hair as he slammed her head into the floor again and again and again and as the darkness closed in around her she thought disjointedly, *I thought he said he was going to let me live.*

CHAPTER FIFTEEN

The Sorcerer's Mark

The first vague stirrings of light within the darkness brought pain: face hurt, nose—no breathing here, only throbbing, mouth, taste of blood, ribs grabbing painfully—ah, that's a breath, she remembered what breathing felt like. Someone, something held her, leg and arms, head, everything constricted, no movement, only blind limbless writhing.

I think she's waking up. You shouldn't have beaten her so hard, you could have killed—

Shut up. Hold her. Watch out for her teeth.

Rape? Was that what was going on? She remembered rape. She remembered—

The road to Troy: eight days up the coast in a Penthedes freighter, off at Rhodes, a ferry to the mainland. Eighteen years of innocent bloodthirstiness and a pair of stone axes on foot through Thrace and into Lydia, spinning dreams of god-sired heroes, her breasts bound and her crotch stuffed. A mistake: the three deserters—Akhaian, she later learned: Mykenaians—were disappointed that she *wasn't* a boy. This was after they'd flung themselves upon her as she slept by the embers of her campfire. By this time, though, they'd already torn her clothes to shreds, and they shrugged and decided to go on ahead anyway. After all, there wasn't much a boy could have done for them that they couldn't get from her.

Princess, you must speak to me. You must tell me who else knows your pretty tale.

Give her to me, I can make her answer. It will take only a moment. This was a voice she half knew, simpering and thick as though speaking through a mouthful of drool.

I think not.

I demand that you give her to me!

*Idonosteus, we are not partners. You should never consider
yourself in any way to be my equal. Do not demand. If I
choose, you shall have her while she yet lives.*

While she yet lives . . . she remembered—

No question but she was lucky they were so brutal. They
used her for two days, there among the jutting rocks, while
they ate and drank all the supplies she'd carried for her
journey. She was unconscious for much of it, and when they
decided it was time to move on, she couldn't walk, both eyes
swelled shut, coughing blood with every breath. They gave
her a few parting kicks that broke another rib and left her for
dead. It could have been worse: they could have taken her
along.

Princess . . . The voice was chiding now, and half-wheedling.
Tell me. You must tell me who else knows the story.

She swam up out of the darkness enough to mumble,
"Sleep. Just lemme sleep. Ask me later."

Gibberish.

*Perhaps. Perhaps it is her native tongue. None among my
household will speak this—perhaps your servants?*

No. Just slap her a few times, wake her up more.

Mmm. All right. You do it; this will be a little treat for you.

Stinging hands sent her back into dreams.

It took her a year, all told, even though they made it easier
for her by staying together. A year to heal, a year to replace
her paired flint axes. A year to find a basalt blank that she
liked, of the proper size, to trim it down with her hammer-
stone, chipping, chipping, a constant *chik chik chik* that she
came to hear in her dreams. In Great Langdale, an experienced weaponsmith could produce a serviceable flint axe in a
few hours, one of basalt or granite in a day. She worked hers
for two weeks, refining the edge, smoothing the cheeks, rubbing them with a hunk of raw copper until they gleamed a
rich killing green. And then practice, learning the broadaxe,
learning the sinuous dance that let her slip shieldless aside
from spears and swords, and always, always practicing her
move, her own move, the one no one else used, the one which
no defensive reflex that a veteran learns will counter: that
whistling underhand arc, a speed move, useless to the big

slow men who depend on strength and weight to batter through an opponent's guard, no power behind it beyond the sheer momentum of the stone blade. Later in life, she'd use it to quiet a bear that stood on flagstones within a ring of buildings pressing back against a mob, she'd use it to gut a handsome Corinthian who'd offended the gods, but now she practiced, and hunted, and practiced, and traveled, and practiced, and prayed, and practiced.

It took her a year, all told, to find them.

Pain from someone's nose brought her swimming up through dark water. Something pressed on it, hard and twisting. Broken, it was broken, she half remembered—Loving Mother, what if she couldn't smell anymore, what if she was like—

She mumbled, "Leucas . . ."

What? What was that? Was that a name?

Hm. That's the Athenian, the big boxer. There's a question for you—where are the Athenian and the grubby Egyptian?

Grubby Egyptian?

No offense, Most High, but he is. He is. He must be seen—smelled—to be believed. He and the Greek are her partners. Where are they? More twisting, fire bursts showering behind her eyes. *Where are Leucas and Kheperu?*

"Where are Leucas and Kheperu?" she repeated numbly. Well, where are they, really? Weren't they supposed to be rescuing her right now, or something? Or was she on her own?

Tell me! I know you hear, I know you understand! Tell me!

She'd told the story only once, in eleven years. She never told her parents—either set of them—she never told her sons, neither the adopted nor the one she'd given screaming bloody birth to at the age of fourteen. She'd told the story only to Khemshi, a huge and gentle Nubian, a spearman in the Ptah Division, one long golden-drifting afternoon in the haymow of a stable in Pharos. They lay with limbs entangled, and his face had taken on an uncommon gravity as the tale had leaked from her, not in a steady stream but drop by drop, the way a pinholed wineskin gives up its contents.

" . . . And, you know, I only killed the first one. I wasn't quite as mad at him, if you must know. The other two are still alive, I'd guess. Right now they're likely skipping hand in hand through the forest and braiding flowers into each other's hair—if you receive my meaning."

The Ptah Division had marched less than a week later, to reinforce a beleaguered frontier garrison. Khemshi was killed on campaign above the Second Cataract in Kush. She'd heard, later, that the spear he took in the belly had not killed him outright, and in his three days of dying fever he'd asked for her. She'd picked him up to ease an interval when her loneliness had become unbearable; she had barely known him.

Her life was full of regrets and missed chances.

But never for lack of trying.

This time she struggled up into the light by her own will. Her consciousness once again inhabited her eyes, and she decided, finally, very deliberately, to open them.

Meremptah-Sifti's smiling face greeted her, blurred and twisting into twins and back again. Floating near his side was the bulbous jowly mass of Idonosteus.

She was tied, with what she couldn't tell, and someone who knelt behind her held her head—Simi-Ascalon, probably. She lay on cushions that would have been comfortable if not for the bound position of her arms and legs. This was still the room where she'd spoken with the Governor; as this realization came to her she also became aware of muffled sobbing that came from somewhere out of her line of sight. That, more than anything, told her that she hadn't been unconscious more than a few minutes: Tal Akhushabb was too tough an old bird to cry for long, even from the shattering humiliation he'd suffered. Soon he should recover at least a facade of dignity.

She squinted blearily at Meremptah-Sifti, whose mouth was swelling nicely, already showing traces of blue-black bruising. "I repeat," she said thickly, "you're a shitty host. And your face is a mess," *though I'm sure it's a sight prettier than mine right now.* "Who's a girl have to maim to get a drink around here?"

"Hmm." His aristocratic self-possession had entirely returned, and with it his superior smile. "We have no very great time to spend, Princess. Tell me now who knows your tale."

Barra sighed. With great effort she could force her swollen tongue to form clear words. "Well, let's see, mm, well, there's the Governor, Idonosteus, you—"

He cut her off by taking her broken nose between the first knuckles of two fingers and grinding it through a short arc. Her eyes glazed and blurred with tears, and she clenched her jaw against a yelp. Through the blur she could see Idonosteus licking his mouth. Fresh blood trickled across her lips.

Meremptah-Sifti sighed, "Let's try that again, shall we?"

When she could trust her voice again, she said, "You're not all that bright."

His eyebrows went up. "Oh?"

"If you'd been thinking, you'd have realized that I wouldn't tell anyone except the heads of the Great Houses or the Governor. Nobody else can do anything about you. And you'll kill anyone who knows."

He straightened up, nodding. "And where are your partners?"

She gave her best approximation of a shrug. "Hiding in the desert."

Idonosteus said, "What about your family?"

A frozen hand clenched in her belly.

"Family?" The word, in Meremptah-Sifti's mouth, dripped with malicious joy.

"Oh yes." Idonosteus' chins jiggled with the nodding of his head. "She lived with the Penthedes shipmaster and his wife. In fact, they are here tonight, at your invitation. . . . This is no doubt how she got past the guards."

"Mmm, well. So." Meremptah-Sifti reached down and gently stroked her chin, the line of her neck. His flesh felt warm and dry, and she couldn't shrink away and she didn't dare to bite him. "I imagine that we'll have your cooperation, then, won't we?"

"I . . ." Barra's voice rasped in her throat; she coughed to clear it. "It won't do you any good to hurt them. They're pledged to Agapenthes, and he'll revenge them if they come to any harm."

"Of course he will." Meremptah-Sifti's gaze drifted over her head as though he was deep in thought. "I suppose it really doesn't matter, much. Slight change, minor adjustment. Imm. We'll do it right now, I think. Everyone's here, everyone I need for a successful beginning. Sim, are you ready?"

The nervous, phlegm-roughened voice came from close

behind her. "I, well, I can be, I suppose. In half of an hour, less perhaps . . ."

"Very well. Idonosteus, you can be of service here again. Gather the Heads and such of their lieutenants as are most trusted and influential. Tell them that an attempt has been made on the Governor's life, and I must speak with them all immediately. Bring that fool of a garrison commander in here as well. Oh, and—get that shipmaster and his wife."

Idonosteus licked his lips, nodded, and scurried out.

"Sim: get your equipment and summon six guards, mm, just tell Haral to bring his five best men—he's over by the fountain."

"All—*hrakhakh*—all right." The gripping hands left her head and Simi-Ascalon stumbled out.

"Tal: stop crying."

The sobbing ceased abruptly. Barra could turn her head now; the Governor sat in a crumpled ball not far to her right.

Meremptah-Sifti pursed his lips. "Tal: from now on, you will believe that you take my suggestions of your own will. You love and adore me and want nothing in the world so much as to please me in every way."

The Governor did not respond, only looked up at the prince with bruised eyes.

"If, after I leave this room, this woman makes any attempt to escape, or even speaks, kick her in the head until she stops moving. And fix your clothing. Make yourself presentable."

The Governor busied himself with his clothing. Meremptah-Sifti once again smiled down upon Barra. "I'll return shortly. Please don't do anything that would make Tal hurt you. I think the old gentleman's actually fond of you, and he'd regret it later."

"What . . . what are you going to do with me? Fix me up with a tattoo like his?"

He gave her a mock frown. "Not at all. Am I not a man of my word? You will be given to Chrysios—although what he expects to be able to do with you, considering the shape in which you left him, I cannot say. No, the tattoo, that's a curious thing, that bit of magic. It only works if you ask for it. If you take it willingly."

He crouched on his haunches beside her. "The human will is extraordinary, isn't it? Perhaps more than anything else, the will is what makes us human; the ability to intend, to see a future and direct our thoughts and actions toward it. A powerful force, a potent force that can bend the course of history, and yet it is so easily surrendered. Sometimes with hardly even a thought. Sim's little tattoo, why, that's just another way of surrendering; it's like a slave's collar that won't close unless one fastens it around one's own neck."

"What future?" Barra asked softly, picking something from his rambling to keep him talking. "What future is it you're going after?"

"That can hardly matter to you," he said, standing again and striding toward the door. He finished the thought without looking back, ". . . since you won't be there to see it."

Helplessness clawed at her; she had to do something more than only lie here and wait to die; she had to fight, to hit back, somehow, no matter how petty or ineffectual it might be. She called after his retreating back, "Y'know what, you bastard? Everyone says your mother's a *whore*!" He kept walking, without so much as a twitch to indicate he'd heard her. "And I hear that you've sucked more than your share of—"

But he was gone from the room now, and the soft step behind her was the only warning she got before the Governor's kick exploded stars across her eyes and sent her spiraling back down into nothingness.

She had never been prone to nightmares, not even as a child, and so she had no recognition of this fog of shrieking apparitions that swam in and out of her vision, doubling and redoubling. Bruising claws dug into her arms and yanked her upright, and torchlight speared her eyes. Light pulsed within her head, flashing at the corners of her eyes in time with her heartbeat. Her head weighed tons, she struggled to bring it upright, and suddenly her throat ripped with vomiting as though a giant had leaped upon her belly. The spasm finally passed, and she hung strengthless in their grip.

Faces crowded in around her, and words wavered into comprehensibility and out again.

gabble *under the charm of the sorcerer, of course* . . . *Here, look here,* at gabble gabble . . . Hands ripped at her dress, the beautiful gown that her mother had made; tears leaked from her eyes as the cloth gave way, and clearly through the haze in her brain she heard the horrified gasps.

. . . *armed, you see? She nearly killed him* . . . gabble

daggers gabble gabble *barely caught her in time* gabble gabble gabble . . .

Some of the faces she recognized, vaguely, in a sort of distant blurry way—a fat man that she was sure she knew from somewhere, repulsive and quivering; a handsome Egyptian who was doing most of the talking: he frightened her, somehow, though she couldn't remember why. And there—there was Peliarchus, she knew him, she was almost sure that this grey-faced, stricken old man was named Peliarchus, and she loved him very much, but who was the woman he held in his arms, her face buried against the joining of his neck and shoulder? That was, was, was Tayniz, she foggily guessed.

I'm hurt, was her first clear thought, and she was obscurely pleased that it rang so true. *People've been kicking my head.*

Now the Egyptian was talking again; she guessed that what he was saying might be important, and so she gritted her teeth and forced herself to understand him.

". . . consulted with the Governor, and he agrees. My steward, Simi-Ascalon, was once a priest of Osiris, and is an expert in these matters. The Governor and the highest officers of the Canaan Division have been protected from this sorcerer's power—it is a simple charm, merely a moment's work, a tattoo that renders one completely immune. Now that this sorcerer has struck at the very heart of Egypt, in the use of this poor girl to attempt a bloody assassination, I feel that it is my duty to make this protection available to all of you. I am only sorry that my steward could not have done so earlier, in time to save your friend Othniel, Jephunah; or yours, Nephrol; or any of the dozens of unfortunates who have died at the inns, innocent victims of a wizard's vendetta against this city. But at least there is this comfort: all of you here tonight, along with such of your nearest and dearest that so desire, can be completely, almost painlessly, perfectly protected."

They clamored for it—at first, they still tried to hold their dignity, but even through her hazy eyes she could see the wide-eyed lust on their faces, the twisting elemental need like a baby's cry for the tit. They stretched out their hands, asking to be taken ahead of their fellows, ahead of their wives and children, as though in this last moment of vulnerability the sorcerer could come and slay all who delayed. So much fear, so much helplessness, weeks and months of creeping tension as the curses and the fires and the demons struck here and there at random throughout the city—how could anyone resist such an offer? A little mark on the skin: an end to fear.

Barra croaked, *"No . . ."*

None of the clamoring press could have heard her, but Meremptah-Sifti's head came around as she spoke.

She tried again, gathering strength and pushing for volume to cut through the surf of voices. "It's a trick! No! Don't—"

Meremptah-Sifti came to her, stood close before her until his smiling face filled her eyes. He cupped her chin with his strong dry hand, pressing closed her mouth against the unbearable weight of her head. "You never give up, do you?" he said softly, almost lovingly. "Do you not understand that you've lost? Now you must turn your attention to salvaging what can be saved from the wreckage." His smile spread like oil, curving maliciously. "Think of Peliarchus, think of his wife. Think of what could happen if they are not *protected* from the *sorcerer* . . ."

She inhaled a pale spark of anger and spat blood across his face. His eyes suddenly blazed, and a vein pulsed out from his hairline to his brow; his fist clenched and only tendon-popping self-control stopped its flight toward her face.

"Most High . . . Most High, please, lord, may I ask . . . ?"

Meremptah-Sifti turned, and behind him was Peliarchus, ashen and trembling, Tayniz leaning with stricken dignity upon his shoulder. Barra's heart plunged within her breast; she could not risk endangering them further.

Peliarchus said in halting Egyptian, "Please, lord, this girl is like my own daughter. If she is the, the helpless . . . tool of the sorcerer, then she herself is blameless, isn't she? What will you do with her? You won't . . . please say she won't be—"

Meremptah-Sifti smoothly swallowed his rage and lifted his hand to wipe his cheek and mouth. "This is not within my control. The Governor shall make the disposition; it is he who bears responsibility for the administration of justice. For my part, I can do no more than see to it that she"—he half turned back toward her, and smiled with the half of his face that his audience couldn't see—"receives that same special protection from the sorcerer. Beyond that, we must await the Governor's decision."

"Can I speak with her?"

"Of course. I do not know, however, if she will understand you."

Peliarchus stepped close. Barra could taste the fear on him. "Listen, Barra, Barra honey, they're going to help you. I, we, know that none of this was your fault, and I'll go to Agapenthes, he'll understand, and he'll talk to the Governor, and everything will be all right. All right? Everything will come right in the end, you'll see. I promise." He was trying, trying so hard to sound confident, but he was so scared. . . .

Barra's eyes filled with stinging tears, and the story swelled behind her lips, the story of what had been done, was being done to the whole city, but over Peliarchus' shoulder she could see the calm, close-lipped smile and one slightly lifted eyebrow of Meremptah-Sifti. She dropped her head and released her effort, and the world drifted away into fog once again.

. . . *Take her . . . workshop . . . until I arrive . . . may require . . . hours . . .*

Those bruising hands dragged her toward darkness, and she barely felt them.

"Stand aside."

Barra swam up toward the light once again. She'd been occasionally aware of what was happening to her—she knew that she was being dragged somewhere, but she had no idea how long they'd been dragging her, or where they were going, or even if they were still on the estate. Like some great sea creature, she'd surface only long enough for a breath, and then slip back down into the darkening depths.

"Stand aside." The first command had been in mellow, almost indulgent Egyptian. This one now came more forcefully in Phoenikian, as did its reply.

"I don't think so."

When Barra's eyes opened, she at first saw only what her captors saw: a loose semicircle of men in servants' dress of light belted chitons. Something familiar in their faces tickled her mind.

They seemed to be in some sort of cellar—at least, there were no windows. Barrels and sacks were stacked neatly around them, floor to ceiling, labeled flour, salt pork, apples, wine, beer, and on and on in Egyptian demotic. Two armored men half held, half carried her. Two others carried lamps. And the final two carried swords.

"You shouldn't be here. This is the prince's private stores."

One of the men in servant's dress shrugged unusually broad shoulders. "We're leaving, soon enough. And we're taking the woman with us."

The man who spoke was missing one ear, and a white streak in his hair was connected to a similar one in his beard by a long thin scar.

Barra's heart sang.

The leader of the guards looked over the men that faced him. They were ten to his six, but they were unarmed, while he and his men wore bronze cuirasses and helmets, greaves and bracers, and carried broad-bladed swords. The leader said, "You're mad. Get out of here before you get killed. The prince won't like it, us killing servants at his feast."

Kamades replied, "I said we're taking the woman, and I'm a man of my word."

"Look," the guard said patiently, "I don't want to hurt you. I don't even know you. But I've got my orders, and if you don't get out of our way, I'll cut you down where you stand and take my chances with the prince."

Kamades spread his hands, smiling, seemingly calm, but there was a certain gleam in his eye. "I'll wrestle you for her. One fall, winner gets the girl." The other Myrmidons also began to crack smiles and nudge each other.

The guard sighed heavily and looked exasperatedly at his fellows, as though to say *can you believe how stupid this guy is?* In the bare second that his eyes were averted, Kamades stepped up and grasped the wrist of the guard's sword arm with his left and unloaded a thundering right cross on the guard's cheekbone. The other Myrmidons were already in motion, no need for a signal of any kind, leaping upon the other guards.

Barra barely had time to gasp a single breath. The lamps crashed to the floor, one extinguishing and one wick still flickering in a spreading pool of oil. Kamades used his grip on the guard's wrist to swing the half-stunned man to the floor, dropped his knee on the man's chest, and in a single smooth motion drew his dagger and sank it into the guard's throat. By the time he could rise again, his men had finished the fight—the other, with sword in hand, had a cut throat that gurgled as the last of his life poured across the floor; the other four had never had a chance to draw. They were all facedown on the floor, being efficiently hog-tied by the Myrmidons.

Barra sagged against a wine cask, barely able to stand. "Loving Mother!" she breathed. "You guys are good."

Kamades flashed her a grim look; all traces of his earlier smile had vanished. "Who's hurt?" he said.

Only one voice responded—the Myrmidon who'd dealt with the other swordsman had taken a shallow cut under his arm. Two others retrieved the unbroken lamp and lit it from the guttering wick of the other before stamping out the spreading flames.

"How . . ." Barra gasped, "how did you find me? How did you—"

"Not now," Kamades told her curtly, then turned away from her and began snapping orders while he gathered up the sword and belt of the man he'd killed and wrapped them in cloth. In seconds one of the Myrmidons had stripped, to offer his chiton to Barra, who only now was becoming coherent enough to remember that she was naked except for the pair of empty knife scabbards still strapped to her thighs. Another took blood from the floor and smeared it across his face, while a third tore his chiton into a strip to bind up Barra's hair in the guise of a bandage.

"What—?"

"You look bad," Kamades explained. "If anyone questions us, you and him got drunk and started fighting. He—the one with the cut—got hurt trying to break it up. I'm taking the pair of you to the stable to sleep it off until the party's over. Got that?"

Barra nodded dizzily. "Ay, surely. But what about your naked friend, there?"

"He'll stay here to watch the guards, make sure they don't get loose, and raise the alarm before you're well away."

She frowned. "You're going to let them live?"

His face kept swimming in and out of focus; she couldn't read his expression at all. "I can do my duty without killing them," he said. "So, yes, I'm going to let them live."

"But, but they'll *tell*! They'll tell it was you that helped me!"

"Barra, you are my guest-friend. I am doing what is right. I'm not going to hide from the consequences."

"Kamades—"

"Hush. Your form can pass for a boy's, but your voice can't. Let's go before we're missed."

Barra tried to fix in her memory the route they took up out of the manor's bowels, but her mind wouldn't hold the facts. While they went, Kamades explained in a low voice that he hadn't even known she was at the feast until the rumor went around that some redheaded woman had tried to kill the Governor. "But I didn't!" Barra protested weakly. Kamades shook his head. "It doesn't matter." He felt his obligation was clear: the only way to save her from execution, or so he'd thought, was to wait for her to be led to wherever they would lock her up and take her away from her guards. He and the Myrmidons had spread themselves through the chambers surrounding the shut-up room where the Heads had gone, and had followed the guards when they dragged her out.

Twice on their way through the feast they were stopped by armed men and questioned about the blood that painted their faces and clothes. Twice Kamades told his story, twice the guards examined Barra's bloodied, swollen face with incurious eyes, and each time the guards waved them along. Everyone seemed much more concerned with the swirling rumors of strange things going on in the room in which the Heads were cloistered. There was much debate about it—even the entertainers had stopped their pointless acts, and stood in little knots, conjurers with acrobats, singers with jugglers, talking mostly in whispers. Word was out that an attempt had been made on the Governor's life, but no one seemed to know what could be happening now within the house.

Barra knew, and the sick twisting in her stomach might have come as much from that knowledge as from the nauseous spinning of her head.

After what seemed endless stumbling progress, they reached the warm darkness of the nearest stable. Hand gestures from Kamades told four of the Myrmidons to search out the stalls, to make sure that there were no surreptitious lovers nestled within the straw. Seconds later, they told him that they were alone, and he turned to Barra. "We have a horse for you—I have a horse for you; she's mine. Take her—Glandys will saddle her for you. Take this." He thrust forward the cloth-wrapped sword and belt of the lead guardsman. "We can't help you beyond getting you off the estate; Lord Idonosteus has ordered us to stay with him tonight. After that, my duty is discharged and you're on your own."

"Kamades," Barra said, shaking her head, trying to rattle some clear thought back into it, "Kamades, you have to come with me. You all must come with me. You have to leave here now."

"No, we don't." Kamades' voice was cold as mid-winter in the northern fjords. "And we won't. We've been ordered to stay near the side of our lord. We obey. What I've done already tonight is dishonor enough."

"What is the *matter* with you? Why are you acting this way?"

"I believe that Lord Idonosteus regards you as an enemy, but you are my guest-friend. The danger you're in puts me in a place where I must choose between my duty to my lord and my duty to the God. I have . . . dishonored myself . . . to preserve the sacred bond of guest-friendship, but now my duty there is done. If I am ordered to hunt you down, I'll . . ." For the first time, his metallic tone faltered; his voice faded and he looked away. ". . . I will do it, Barra. I beg you to go, and may Zeus spare me that task."

"Listen to me!" she insisted, clutching at his chiton to hold herself upright. "You don't know what kind of man that fat bastard is! He doesn't deserve your service. Cutting his throat would do you more honor than taking his orders."

Kamades' face froze over once again. "You must go, now."

How could she explain? What words could tell all the truth in the little time they had? She ground her teeth in frustration. "You don't know what he'll do to you for letting me go. You have no idea what he's capable of."

"I have sworn my service to him. Whatever punishment he chooses, I'll accept."

"Loving bloody *Mother*! You and your bloody honor, your talk about guest-friendship and duty to the God and duty to your lord and I don't know *what* bloody all! If Idonosteus were here, right now, he'd be ordering you to cut off my head so he can fuck my corpse in the neck! And he'd make you watch him do it."

Kamades' eyes went wide and hot, gleaming in the lamplight. "Then you'd better be gone before he gets here," he snarled.

Barra's temper flared inside her head, sending sparks

shooting across her vision. "You thickheaded son of a goat's asshole! Why won't you listen? I'm trying to save your *worthless bloodyfucking life!*" Her battered mouth cracked with her shout, and she tasted fresh blood.

Before Kamades could snarl his reply, distant yelling came from the direction of the manor house. Kamades cast a desperate glance over his shoulder. "I think we've been found out. Can you ride?" His voice held a note of sudden care that tore at her chest.

Barra nodded. "I think so."

He led her to his horse's side and helped her up into the high-built saddle. "Her name's Andromakhe. Steer with your knees. Now go!"

Barra found looking down from this new height to be more than a little dizzying. She gathered the woven-rope reins in one hand, and with the other reached down to touch Kamades' face. "I'll see you again."

His eyes met hers, and they were far warmer than his tone. "I hope not—unless it is by my will, not my lord's order." He spun away from her. "Glandys! Othoön! Cut the girths of every saddle! Lalcamas, open that door and bar it behind her when she goes. Come on, snap!"

The broad doors swung back. Barra leaned forward to wrap her arms about Andromakhe's neck, and kicked her hard in the ribs. The mare sprang forward, scattering a crowd of approaching guardsmen, and galloped off into the night. They'd be on her trail in minutes, saddles or no. She thought she could hear, among the startled shouts and cries that accompanied her passage, faintly behind her the deep growl of Kamades still snapping orders. She told herself that the sharp sting in her eyes came only from the wind.

The ride was a bouncing, jouncing nightmare; every beat of Andromakhe's hooves pounded another spike into Barra's brain. She hung on grimly, arms locked around the mare's neck. Bare moments after she'd burst from the stable, two broad spears of torch-bearing riders had curved out after her, swinging wide to cut off any escape. The wind had shifted, now bringing high clouds in from over the sea, and the declining moon cast huge hill-shadows across her path.

In the dark, every hill looked alike, and shouts might carry to her pursuers. Finally, Barra had to coax Andromakhe to a halt; the mare stood, flanks heaving. Barra put both hands to her face, one on either side of her swollen nose, and suddenly pressed hard while pulling down. The pain made her vision swim, and completed the process that the ride had begun: she vomited convulsively. But after she wiped the last strings away from her lips, she was able to blow, painfully, a huge glob of half-clotted blood from her nose and then she could breathe through it again, just a little. Just enough.

After that, it took only a few minutes of judging the wind and riding back and forth. She knew she was in the right general area, and Kheperu's scent would stand out in a slaughterhouse.

She found it and rode upwind, following, she crested a small rise, and there they were; she dizzily prayed that the Mother might shower blessings on them like rain. She tried to greet them, but her throat constricted and she could barely croak a hail. They both came to their feet, uncertain; Leucas had his spear in hand and his shield in place, and Kheperu reached within his robe, but then the last wisp of cloud was swept away from the moon.

"Great Thundering God!" Leucas said. His shield and spear dropped by his side, and he sprang to her. "What did they do to you?"

She let herself collapse into his arms. He cradled her gently, while Kheperu took Andromakhe's reins. Leucas lowered her to the pile of blankets he'd been using as a cot. She said thickly, "The next time . . . the next time I tell you I want to go in somewhere by myself? You should just beat the shit out of me right then, save the other guys the trouble."

Kheperu knelt beside her, reins still in hand. "I take it things did not go as well as they might?" he said, but the mockery in his tone was only reflexive, almost loving.

"I'll hit you for that later, when I can move again. I am," Barra rasped, "really, really, *really* glad to see you guys." She clutched Leucas' arm with both hands, pulled on it as she tried to sit up.

"No, no," he said, gently pressing her back down onto the blankets, "you just lie there for a bit."

"I wish I could," she said, "but pretty soon the whole shit-cake Egyptian army is going to be hunting us. If we want to live through the night, we'd better find a place to hide."

CHAPTER SIXTEEN

Hostages

The pair of lamps sprouted flames that rose tall and still in the dead air of the cellar, twisting pillars of lampblack falling upward to the ceiling. The smell here was unmistakable: the blood that had poured from the curling cut across Haral Mesti's throat mingled with the shit that his dying convulsions had squirted into his armor. The unconscious men had been untied and revived; only the two corpses now lay here. Meremptah-Sifti stood with his sandals half an inch from the edge of the pooled blood, and looked down upon his dead captain. The prince held a handkerchief of white linen to his mouth, and every so often pulled it free and examined it to see if his swollen and split lips had stopped bleeding.

Idonosteus hovered nervously near the prince's shoulder, rubbing his sweaty hands together. Meremptah-Sifti ignored him, interested instead in the scar-faced man in servant's dress who stood holding the lamps. He appeared perfectly calm, perfectly relaxed, entirely oblivious of the pair of men-at-arms who held the stabbing points of their blades against his ribs, one to either side of him.

"You did this? *You?*" Meremptah-Sifti said in slow Phoenikian, mindless of the bad taste his milk tongue left on his lips.

The scar-faced man's eyes shifted, looking behind the prince to Idonosteus. The fat merchant must have given some sign, because now the man nodded in response.

"With men—the men I lead," he said, his words halting and thickly accented. "Yes."

"How many?"

The scar-faced man frowned. "Ten—one, there, watching," he pointed toward the stairs that led upward into the house. "Nine, and me."

Meremptah-Sifti murmured, "Extraordinary." He glanced

over his shoulder. "These are the pretend servants you brought with you yesterday, to my patio, are they not?"

Idonosteus' chins jiggled with his nervous cough. Meremptah-Sifti smiled secretly to himself at how much that preparatory throat clearing resembled Haral's; Haral, who lay at his feet here with his throat cleared for good and all.

"Y-yes, my prince, but, you see, I don't think—"

"Six men," Meremptah-Sifti mused, ignoring Idonosteus' panicked sputtering. "In full armor, with swords. Ten men in servant's chitons, armed with, what? Knives?" He shook his head. "Extraordinary. Haral was a good man, and his men are veterans. By all rights, they should have slaughtered you."

The scar-faced man shrugged blandly. "He feared to disrupt your feast, by killing servants."

"Yes . . ." Meremptah-Sifti nodded, chuckling. "Yes he would, wouldn't he? Poor Haral. If I had known of your skill, yesterday, perhaps I would have been more cautious in my dealings with your master. I had no idea how much danger I was in."

His chuckle expanded into a throaty laugh, and he turned back to Idonosteus; the blood painting his teeth and drying on his chin made his grin so gruesome that Idonosteus flinched back as though he feared the prince would bite him. "I hope you have a good explanation for why your bodyguards killed two of my men and let that little whore get away."

"I, well, no." Idonosteus shook his head hastily, having come to a swift decision to tell the truth. "I cannot say— they're Phthians, you know, and all Greek speakers are lunatic."

"Mm. I have heard this said before."

"She and I are guest-friends," the scar-faced man said calmly. "Guest-friendship is a bond that is sacred to Zeus. I could not stand by and allow her to come to harm."

"Zeus?" Meremptah-Sifti said disbelievingly. "What is Zeus, some Akhaian god? Some little hedge-god from halfway across the world? You fear this little unknown god so much that you throw away your life?"

The scar-faced man's gaze had a curiously occulted look to it, as though he didn't really see the prince at all. "I do not fear the God. I respect his law."

"But this is Phoenikia, do you see? Your little god has no power here."

The scar-faced man did not respond.

Meremptah-Sifti turned his face to Idonosteus and murmured, "Yes, he is mad; but mad perhaps in a very useful way."

Idonosteus licked his lips. "Un-until this moment, my prince, I, I would have said that he was completely reliable."

Meremptah-Sifti shrugged. "Perhaps he is." He directed his words once again to the scar-faced man. "You must have known you would be punished."

He shrugged minutely.

"Why did you not run away? Escape with her?"

"I am sworn to my lord Idonosteus' service."

Meremptah-Sifti shook his head in wonder, and then his face broke out into a broad smile, oblivious of the cracking of his lips and the fresh blood that flowed because of it. "I respect your devotion to duty," he said, with only a hint of mockery, "and, I think, your punishment should be . . . mm, deferred to some later date. Your name is, what, Kamades?" He glanced at Idonosteus for confirmation; the fat man nodded. "Meanwhile," the prince went on, "you and your men should be protected from the sorcerer, even as are my own men. Go now, gather your men, and take them to Simi-Ascalon."

Again, the scar-faced man's eyes flicked to Idonosteus, who nodded. The scar-faced man handed his lamps to the men-at-arms, and walked stiffly up the stairs.

"And I hope you won't mind waiting," Meremptah-Sifti called after him with a laugh. "I understand there's quite a line!"

Idonosteus chuckled at his shoulder. Meremptah-Sifti's smile vanished behind the bloodstained handkerchief as he took a step away, half turned, and laid a whistling slap across Idonosteus' face.

Idonosteus staggered back a step or two, hands up to his reddening cheek and tears filling his eyes. "Wha—?"

"This is your fault," Meremptah-Sifti said, his voice low and deadly. "Those are your men, you should have known what they would do. Idiot. I should open your guts right here beside my men."

"B-but, but my prince, how could I *possibly*—"

"Be silent, you contemptible toad. The sound of your voice brings vomit to my throat." He regarded his hand with distaste; his palm was moist with the sweat that had coated the fat man's cheek. With a shudder of disgust, he wiped it on his kilt. "You boasted to me of your thousand men, who know all of Tyre. I have the army to seal the city; she cannot get away overland. If she is not taken tonight, she will go to ground in the city. Find her."

He stepped close to Idonosteus, and leaned into his face until he could feel the man's breath upon his own lips. "You lost her. You'll find her. You would regret disappointing me in this."

"I, ah . . . I, ah . . . ." Idonosteus, now that he was recovering from the sting of the slap, looked at Meremptah-Sifti with a certain glow to his eyes. Far from standing up for himself like a man, he was licking his lips in anticipation.

Meremptah-Sifti grunted and turned away; he should have known Idonosteus was that type, he'd seen enough of them in his childhood.

Idonosteus said, "If she is not taken tonight, my men will comb the city—although, my prince, I have an idea that she'll find a way of avoiding such crude methods. She's shown herself to be exceptionally resourceful, and skilled in changing her appearance."

"Is this some childish attempt to excuse failure in advance?"

"N-no, my prince, not at all. I was only thinking that, well, perhaps it might be more effective to have a plan to, well, to draw her out."

"Mm?"

"This can certainly wait for morning—no need to alarm your other guests. But it seems to me that she lived in Tyre for a few years with that Penthedes shipmaster . . ."

"Hostages?" Meremptah-Sifti's mouth quirked upward. "The difficulty with a hostage is that if you don't kill him, you are not taken seriously; if you do, his value is lost."

"Not, not *necessarily*," Idonosteus said. "I have an idea."

Once Idonosteus explained his idea in detail, Meremptah-Sifti shook his head in open admiration. He slid an arm around Idonosteus' soft and flabby shoulders and said, "You have made me become grateful that I let you live."

CHAPTER SEVENTEEN

Stand Down

Barra woke to a dully painful pulling sensation, as though a none-too-gentle hand had taken hold of the end of her nose, and a strange unpleasantly tangy taste soured the back of her mouth. She opened her eyes to find Kheperu's greasy beard far too close to her face, and he was rubbing something onto her bruises that stung and made her eyes water.

She didn't have the strength to punch him or push him away, so she settled for saying, "If I could breathe through my nose, I'd probably have to kill you." Her voice sounded thin and weak, alarmingly so, even to her own ears.

Kheperu only smiled distantly and encouraged her to roll over. The bed beneath her was too comfortable; considerable encouragement was required before she was willing to move. On the floor next to the head of the bed was a steaming pot of some kind of watery greenish preparation, with what might have been bits of leaves and flowers floating on its thick and greasy-looking surface. Kheperu held out his hand. "Blow."

Barra grimaced. "It hurts."

"I don't care. Blow."

Barra shut her eyes and blew a burst of bloody goo from her nose. Kheperu caught it deftly and examined it with interest. "Good, good," he murmured. "You are coming along fine. Here, drink this."

He offered her a mug about a third full of some thick milky fluid. She drank it; the taste was vile enough that she was grateful for her impaired nose. She wiped her mouth on the blanket beneath her. "I've been asleep for a while, mm?"

Kheperu shrugged. "You'll be stronger when you wake up. By the way, you did a fine job setting that nose of yours—I think it'll be only a bit crooked, perhaps not at all. We'll know more when the swelling goes down."

"I wasn't trying to set it at all," she mumbled. "Where's Leucas?"

"Out. Keeping an eye on things."

"You've been taking care of me . . ." Clouds began drifting into her mind, gently lifting her and rocking her toward sleep. "I'd've thought you'd be long gone . . ."

Kheperu shrugged again, and his smile became distant and his eyes a little sad. "I should be," he said gently. "I should have left days ago, as soon as we were paid. But—well, where would I find another pair of fighters like you two? I must have *someone* to protect me; might as well be you. And I've become used to you."

"You . . ." Whatever had been in that drink thickened her tongue and made it hard to gather words at all. "You liar . . . y' lying prick, I know better. You . . . jus' wanna get *at* me . . . while I sleep . . ."

He chuckled softly. "That's right. Sleep now."

As hiding places go, this was a beauty. It was Leucas' idea; he had sat on the hillside with his chin on his fist, and watched Barra and Kheperu discuss what to do next. Clearly, Barra was in no shape to be racing around the hills dodging patrols—she was too dizzy and weak to walk very far, and could barely stay on the horse. She'd need at least two or three days before she could do the kind of strenuous traveling that might be required to get away from Tyre, and a week would be better. Kheperu was all for splitting up and losing themselves in some sleazy waterfront inns; Barra held out for staying together at the funerary caves. They'd argued it back and forth for a while, until Leucas had grunted and sat up straight.

"Let me see," he'd said slowly. "The problem with an inn is that someone might recognize us and sell us out, but the advantage is that we're in town, we can keep up with what's going on, and we'll know when is a good time to make a break. The problem with the caves is that we're low on supplies and we're out of touch, but the advantage is that it's unlikely we'll be seen there, and we'll all be together. Do I have this right?"

The other two had nodded impatiently, and he went on. "Then, why don't we go to an inn, in town, where we can stay together, but no one will come and go, so there's no way we'll be seen, and there's no one who'll sell us out?"

"Oh, right," Kheperu said with bone-deep exasperation. "And where will we *find* this magical place, hmm? Perhaps if we start now, we can *build* it, hey?"

Leucas had only shrugged apologetically. "Sorry—I was thinking of Lidios' inn, that's all. Doesn't he owe us a favor?"

With the curse openly displayed, no one would dare to so much as look through his doors—and Lidios did, after all, owe them his life twice over. Kheperu turned a purple that was visible even by moonlight. Barra grinned at him, though it made her lip split again. He snapped, "How come he never does that to *you*?"

"Because I've learned that when Leucas gets that 'Let me get this straight' tone in his voice, I should just shut up and let him talk."

They carefully helped Barra up onto Andromakhe's back, and slowly picked their way toward town.

Leucas walked along beside the horse, his arm around Barra's waist to hold her in the saddle against her occasional attacks of dizziness. The search seemed concentrated on the routes out of Tyre; careful movement, relying on the intermittent moon rather than torches or lamps, got them safely within the city. They unloaded the mules and tied the packs across Leucas' shoulders—it wouldn't be wise to leave animals tied outside what was supposed to be a deserted inn—and Barra dismounted, leaning heavily on Leucas' strong arm, and slapped the horse on the rear. "Go home, Andromakhe! Go on, go home!"

Leucas watched the horse gallop off with grim bemusement. "Kamades named his horse Andromakhe . . ." he murmured, shaking his head. Barra had told them the whole story on their way into town. "That man really knows how to hold a grudge."

Barra felt herself unaccountably bristling. "What do you mean by that?"

Leucas looked down at her with his gentle smile. "Andromakhe was married to the greatest hero of Troy. Every time he mounts up, Kamades is riding Hektor's wife . . . if you see what I mean."

Kheperu laughed; Barra scowled. She said, "I don't know if I like that, or not."

The streets were quiet tonight, and they encountered no one between the edge of town and the silent, darkened and sealed inn of Lidios.

Lidios had answered his door himself, and when the companions identified themselves he let them in instantly. He was horrified at the wreckage of Barra's face, and he insisted on getting her cleaned up and in a bed before he would let them so much as tell him what had happened.

Barra'd told him, after she'd been safely put to bed: "I won't lie to you, Lidios. We're in a whole shit pile of trouble. A sizable chunk of the Egyptian army is hunting us, and if they find us here, I don't doubt they'll kill you for hiding us."

The fat publican's face went utterly expressionless. "So?"

"I'm just trying to say I'll understand if you can't do this. If it's too much, tell me now and we'll find someplace else."

"Barra," he said seriously, "any other mercenary I've ever known would hold a blade to my throat and lock the slaves in the cellar. From you, though, that offer I take with deep offense."

"Huh?"

"How could you possibly even think that I'd count the danger?" He touched his chest; the soiled bandage that still wrapped it was faintly visible through his bed shirt. "I owe you my life—because my skill is with stew and beer, not with weapons and fighting, that doesn't make me a coward."

He stood up and smoothed his bed shirt over his massive belly. "You just lie there and get better, I'll take care of everything. 'S been too long since I've belted on my apron, anyway."

He went out, and as sleep closed in around her, she'd pulled Leucas close. "Keep an eye on him, huh?"

He frowned. "I'm sure he wouldn't—"

"Just watch him, all right? Can't trust, trust anyone . . . Now"—her eyes drooped and she yawned enormously—"now I gotta sleep . . ."

Over the next three days, Barra woke only long enough to take food and water and relieve herself. Then Kheperu would arrive at her bedside with another of his sleeping powders, which took away the pain in her head and pushed the world off behind thick clouds. Whenever she woke, there would be someone sitting by her side, sometimes Lenka, Lidios' loyal house slave who had some minor medical experience, more often Kheperu or Leucas; and sometimes Lidios himself, often smelling of the thick lamb stews he cooked, always smelling of beer or wine—he claimed that water was at a premium, since the only water that was safe to drink had to come from clandestine visits to the public wells after dark; Barra suspected that the lack of water was going a long way toward sustaining his courage.

It was in the first hour of daylight when the thunder of fists against a door tore Barra from sleep and shoved her upright in bed. *Just Demetor and the whiners,* she thought fuzzily, then: *No, that happened already . . . the poisoning, the fight. What in the name of the Loving bloody Mother—?*

Lenka stood near her bed, looking off toward the public house's street door, her face blank with sudden terror. Abruptly Barra remembered where she was and why she was here, and she fought with her tangled, sweat-damp quilts until she could struggle up out of the bed. She swept up her weapons and lurched toward the door; her fingers wouldn't seem to work very well, as she tried and failed and tried again to tie the belt over her bed shirt.

"Where are Leucas and Kheperu?" she snapped, leaning against the door frame and gritting her teeth against a blinding swirl of dizziness. *Curse that shit-eating Kheperu and his shitcake potions!* Lenka only shook her head.

Now the shouting from outside resolved itself into a voice, demanding entrance in bad, Egyptian-accented Phoenikian. Lidios was already there; she could hear his reply: "I'm under the curse! Go away! Do you want to die?"

"Open door or door will broken!"

Barra pushed open her door, and Lenka clutched her from behind. "Don't! You must go out the rear! You must go!"

Barra irritably slapped at her hands. "Like it would do any good." She gave the woman a good shove that sent her backward toward the bed. "Sit down and shut up." Barra pulled her broadaxe out of its scabbard, and huffed a little as she hefted it; it felt heavy as a barrel of beer.

From the outer room she heard Lidios again. "I beg you to go away! If I open this door, you will all die!" He sounded very certain of that, and when Barra peered out around the doorpost—through the deep gloom that filled the shuttered common room, its only light a dull orange pulsing from the hearthshrine—she could see why. Lidios crouched among the tables, well away from the door, and in the shadows to either side of it stood darker shadows, the barely visible forms of Kheperu and Leucas, and the boxer's hand was on the bar.

"No death fears us more than anger of prince. If red-hair girl not is here, we go. Open!"

The huge silhouette to the door's right lifted a shoulder in an eloquent shrug, and flipped the bar off its hooks. The soldier outside kicked the door open, tearing it out of Leucas' grasp and slamming it around into the waiting Kheperu, who let out a muffled grunt. The soldier jumped in through the doorway and threw his weight against the door, pinning Kheperu in place. He wore Meremptah-Sifti's red and purple painted on his armor and a supercilious grin on his face. He said in Egyptian, "Oh, hiding, are we?" In his hand he carried the small trumpet-faced bronze axe of the Egyptian army, and his day-blind eyes, in the gloom, didn't see Leucas at all until the Athenian stepped into the doorway.

The soldier yelped and sprang deeper into the room, to get fighting space; Leucas ignored him, reaching instead out through the door to grab the soldier's partner by the clavicle of his corselet and drag him inside. With a sound like rock hitting bone, a huge fist fell once; the man's head snapped violently back, and Leucas opened his hand to let him fall.

The first soldier, deep within the inn, Leucas silhouetted between him and the light and freedom outside, between him and the rest of his life, said in awed Egyptian, "Oh, my god . . ."

With a slight push from behind, the door swung shut, cutting off the daylight with the finality of an axe.

Kheperu said, "Yes, in fact, I *was* hiding. How impolite of you to notice."

The soldier whirled to run toward the back, but his day-blindness betrayed him and he stumbled into a table. Kheperu needed no more than this; he skipped nimbly toward him and struck his knee with a sharp blow of the staff. The soldier's leg buckled, and he dropped to the floor, wailing, until the hard oak smashed his lips and scattered his teeth about the room. A third stroke quieted him, and Kheperu said in Greek, "There's likely one more, watching the rear; perhaps there may be two."

Leucas nodded grimly. "I'll take care of it." He reached

into the shadows along the wall and brought out his man-length spear, its haft as thick as his wrist and its blade as long as his forearm. "You handle these two." He slipped out through the front door, and in the momentary light Barra could see that he carried the iron scimitar behind his belt as well. She shuddered in a brief instant of empathy for the soldiers in the alley behind.

Lidios cautiously straightened from his crouch among the tables. "It's over?"

"Nearly," Kheperu said cheerfully. His hand came out of his robe holding a long, narrow knife. "All that's left to do is kill these two and hide their bodies."

"*Kill* them? Don't—I mean, do you, I wish you really—"

"Lidios, please. You can't keep them here—what will you do when the next group comes to search? If we keep them somewhere else, they'll get loose eventually, or be found, or starve to death. If we let them go, they'll tell, and you and all your slaves will be tortured to death. Besides, you told them if they opened the door they'd all die." Kheperu spread his stubby hands, and his teeth seemed to shine yellow in the gloom. "Do you want me to make you a liar?"

The fat innkeeper's mouth opened, then closed again; he wiped his hands on his apron and looked around at the floor. "Always cleaning up someone's teeth when you're around," he muttered distractedly. And he wandered off, barking at his slaves to quit cowering in the storeroom and bring him a broom.

At this moment Kheperu noticed Barra leaning on the door frame. He smiled. "I was just now coming to wake you up. I think we should be leaving."

Barra looked down at the huddled shapes of the two unconscious soldiers. She wondered where they'd come from, if one of them had a girlfriend he really loved, if the other might have a favorite horse, or a dog. She wondered who'd be crying for them when they didn't come home tonight. *That's the bloody trouble with this whole stinking* sceon tiof *business,* she thought. *Even when it's not working, you're wondering what you'd be seeing if it was.*

Kheperu said, "What's wrong?"

Barra began to speak, a rasping sleep-clogged croak. She coughed hard to clear her throat and spat on the floor. Kheperu's logic was unassailable, even though it turned in her stomach like a blade. "I'm tired of this business," she said softly. "I'm ready for another line of work."

"What?"

"Nothing," she said, stronger. "They were warned. Kill them."

Behind her, Lenka gasped. Barra ignored her.

Kheperu picked up the ankle of the soldier Leucas had felled, and started dragging him toward the back door. The soldier stirred and groaned, lifting a hand to let it fall back limply. "You want to help?"

Barra shook her head. "I . . . better get started packing up."

"Since when are you squeamish?"

Faintly, through the back door, came a hoarse cry of alarm that was cut off by the vivid *sluutch* of a blade tearing through a man's belly so that his bowels spilled to the ground. Someone sobbed in Egyptian, "Oh, shit, shit I'm really hurt, I'm hurt . . ." and the heavy barley-sack thump of a falling body was followed by a crunch of metal on something hard, like a skull.

Barra flinched—she couldn't help it, and she knew Kheperu had seen it. She shook her head. "Just kill them, all right? Then come help me pack. We've got to get out of here."

Kheperu and Leucas washed the blood off themselves using the last of the previous night's water. The dead soldiers were safely stashed in a refuse heap three doors away. ". . . That's why it was Meremptah-Sifti's men, rather than regulars, who came here," Kheperu was saying, as he strapped on the tight-fitting armor of the portliest of the three. He had already shaved the stubble from his cheeks and chin, and tied his beard into military braids. "They'd already have the tattoo to 'protect' them. What I don't understand is why they'd still be searching for us. What harm can we do him now? He owns this city already—why, from what you've been telling me about things out there, Leucas, I'd have to say that he controls this city more completely than any tyrant has ever held a city before. What good does he get from all this time and effort of searching? What makes us so special to be worth this? What does he get?"

Barra had quietly bound her breasts tight—to pass as a boy yet again—and tied off bundles of clothing and weapons while listening to Kheperu's nervous post-fight chattering. Now she said, "He gets me."

Kheperu snorted. "No offense, my dear, but I hardly think you are worth—"

"You weren't there," she said flatly. "You didn't see him, or hear him talk. He won't stop until he gets me. Just take my word for it. That's why I'm leaving. Like I should have done a week ago. Let the cocksucking bastard spend his life searching for me."

"Hmm," Leucas said. "This may be hard."

"Why?" Barra said. "With a hood up to cover my face—and as long as you remember to keep your knees a little bent and your back hunched—no one should question us. We just need to stay away from anyone else in red and purple."

Kheperu twirled for them, like a girl showing off a new skirt. "How do I look? Like one of the new masters of Tyre?"

"You'll see" was all Leucas would say. "You'll see."

Soon all three were ready to leave. Barra paused at the alley door to clasp forearms with Lidios. The publican licked his lips, and released one of Barra's arms so that he could mop pale sweat from his jowls. "You be careful," he said hoarsely. "And if you're ever back in Tyre—"

"I know," Barra said with a smile that bent her swollen face painfully. "Stay the bloody fuck away from here."

Lidios chuckled wanly and hugged her. "I owe you more than silver can repay. You have the freedom of this house forever." He pressed her close. "I hope you make it."

"We will. Remember—anyone who comes asking after those three men? They were here, you let them in so they wouldn't break down the door, they looked around, then left. That's all you know, right?"

"Right." He released her and stepped back. "May Zeus guard your path."

Barra took a deep breath. "May the Mother stand behind you and smile on every pot."

Lidios held the door for them as they shouldered their bundles and slipped out into the blazing Tyrian day.

You'll see, Leucas had said. Barra saw. On the streets of her adopted city, everything that came before her eyes tied another coil around the knot in her guts.

She saw the pinched faces and fearful eyes of Tyrian freemen when they looked upon Kheperu in his livery.

She saw the instant outward respect he got from Egyptian regulars, and their expressions of relief when he had passed.

She saw the slamming of doors and latching of windows that preceded them down every side street.

She saw little children watch him with wide, numbed eyes. Some of them screamed and ran. Their mothers stayed silent, their faces filled with hopeless, empty defiance.

At the beach, ships were drawn up gunwale to gunwale, barely space for a skinny man to slip between them; a man could walk the length of the beach deck to deck, without ever touching the sand. Carelessly unshipped oars made untidy, bristly stacks between the deck benches. The sand inshore was piled here and there with mounds of cloth and spices and goods from across the known world, some still guarded by sweaty, nervous crewmen, most standing abandoned and forlorn, left to the beachsiders, the gulls, and the flies.

Also on the ships this day were people. Hundreds upon hundreds of Tyrians, some with bundles of possessions, some clutching children close by their legs, stood anxiously among sailors and marines from every foreign port. They crowded onto the decks, shading their eyes to look out to sea, many standing up on the benches for a better view. Far out on the sea, a small spot on the endless expanse of shimmering greenish blue, the crew of a merchant ship pulled desperately at their oars. There was no wind; the hammering of the oarmaster's drum came frantic over the calm waters. For a while it seemed that they might escape, but no one on the dockside cheered. A murmur would ripple through the crowd, from time to time, that was always accompanied by flickering glances at the scattered pairs and trios of soldiers and men in bloodred and purple, skating glances, long enough to read an expression but too short to truly meet the eyes. No one was willing to meet their eyes.

Out on the water, a pair of slender dark warships fairly skipped over the sea, closing rapidly on the slower merchantman. Soon fire arrows trailed their sooty smoke in arcs over the water; shortly after that the warships overtook her, and the long spiked boarding planks swung down to lodge in the merchantman's deck. The planks swarmed with soldiers, and the cries and screams came clearly to the shore. In minutes the warships were curving away, pulling back for the city, leaving the merchantman burning, a pyre for its fallen crew.

Leucas looked down at Barra. "Any ship can enter. None have managed to get away."

Barra nodded grimly. "Then we'll have to go overland."

On a bright, wide side street not far from the Market, another silent crowd was gathered. Barra turned aside from their path through the city toward the northern road to Sidon; she insisted on knowing what was going on.

Leucas shook his head. "You don't want to go in there."

"What's happening?"

The Athenian's rumble was barely audible. "It's a rape."

Barra's eyes widened. "How do you know?"

"I have been about the city, these three days. I've seen this before."

Now sobbing, high and thin, a child's voice, the sobbing that remains after screams have failed, could be heard among the rough grunting and low, coarse laughter. Barra looked at the backs of the people, down the street.

"Why are they just standing there? Why doesn't someone do something?"

"Because a man who wears Meremptah-Sifti's colors—or the armor of an Egyptian regular—can do anything, in this city."

Barra turned toward the crowd, her battered face set as stone, her hand beneath her cloak on the head of her broadaxe. Leucas caught her shoulder. "Don't go there."

Barra shook him off. "I have to see for myself."

"No, you don't. What'll happen, you'll go there, you'll see some man pounding his hips into some boy, or girl. Maybe the child's mother lying dead in the dirt nearby. In broad daylight, in the middle of the street. You'll try to kill him; you'll likely succeed. Then the ten or fifteen Egyptian soldiers that are holding the crowd back will kill you."

"Maybe," she answered grimly. "Or maybe that crowd will stand with me."

"Barra, no. Watch them," he said, taking her shoulders and gently turning her, holding her so that she faced them.

Even as he turned her, a sound like a gentle breeze came to her ears, though the air was still. Then the sound came again, and this time she saw it, the sigh that moved the crowd gently as though it were some softly creeping beast. Barra's stomach suddenly spasmed, and she had to turn away. Even Kheperu looked pale.

Leucas' voice was as bleak as she'd ever heard it. "Why do you think they're *watching*? Why do you think they're not running away to lock themselves indoors and hide? Those soldiers, they don't hold the crowd back to protect the *rapist* . . ."

"That's sick," Barra said, swallowing a thin burning trace of vomit. "That's sick."

Kheperu murmured, "You'd perhaps be surprised how many men share my tastes—or worse—within their hearts, lacking only the courage to give themselves permission to indulge them. They may have to pretend outrage, later, to salve their conscience, but they won't have to hold themselves responsible—they can say, within their hearts, 'There was nothing I could do to stop him.' "

Barra stared at the crowd; another sigh, stronger now, rippled through it. "And not all of them are men," she said thickly. "Let's get out of here before I throw up."

A full company of Egyptian infantry sealed the north road out of Tyre, politely but firmly turning back all who tried to leave. Any who tried to duck around them and strike out despite their orders were easily taken by the cavalry that backed them up, ten two-horse chariots. No attempt was made to capture these fugitives; their flight would be stopped, each and every one, by a spear in the back or a hatchet blow to the head. By the time the three companions had made their way there, the gently rolling coastal plain to the north was dotted with corpses left lying in the sun, most surrounded by squabbling rings of vultures, arguing over which gets the eyes and which the tongue. Farther out, dim in the distance, two encampments were visible, one straight north near the coast and one far to the northeast, nothing between them but open, rolling hills. Even if it were possible to organize something like a mass rush for the hills, Barra could see no chance of escape. They didn't even bother coming up to the soldiers themselves; they just faded back and let the current of the crowd carry them into the city once more.

"How could he have done this?" she asked. "In just two or three days . . ."

"Simple, really," Kheperu told her. "He controls everyone who has the power to resist him."

The companions worked their way in a wide arc through the outskirts of Tyre, even though Barra foreknew it would be useless; the city was clearly sealed. She wondered, as they walked, how long Meremptah-Sifti could get away with this. A long time, certainly; it would take months, perhaps a year or more, for the rumors to get around to other ports, as traders failed to appear on their usual routes, and traders who didn't call at Tyre began to expand their territories. Barring some unusual event to the north—say, a disastrous loss in battle by Hattiland, who then would call upon its ally Egypt for reinforcements—that would bring a large army marching through, Ramses might never learn what his grandson was doing, up here on the Phoenikian coast. The Governor was the author of all official reports regarding events in the Canaan District, and Egypt had troubles of her own.

Meanwhile, the population would continue to grow. Tyre was already crowded, straining its wells to support the people who lived here now—this was why so many inns and private homes had their own rain barrels. Every caravan that came to Tyre would add to its numbers, as would every trade ship. Even thinking about this made Barra's breath run short; the crowds becoming thicker, spreading to fill every street, every house . . . The gods take it ill for men to live too closely pressed together; they strike the densest cities with sicknesses that kill and kill and kill until the gods judge that the crowd has thinned enough; and they send madness, too, that bends the minds of even honest, sober men toward bloodshed.

Leucas walked beside her, his back bent and head jutting forward, scanning any crowd for faces that might be even vaguely familiar, so that the companions might be able to turn away before they were recognized. Kheperu made himself strut a bit, playing up his Lord of the City act, but his face showed pale strain and he rarely spoke; whenever another man in the prince's colors came into sudden view, he'd clench his jaw and his fists, and breathe deep, trying to hold on to his courage.

Barra tried to distract herself as they walked, tried to think of other things, of spring flowers in Great Langdale, of the

sun sparking fire off the white limestone that faced the tomb
of Khufu, of the sunrise sacrifice on the Horns of the Bull
in the midst of the thousand-chambered hall of Knossos;
but somehow each attempt spun into some wild fantasy of
revenge, of retribution on Meremptah-Sifti. In one she led an
army of howling Picts against his estate; in the second she
stood before Ramses the Great and denounced his grandson
to his face; in the third, the prince himself was tied between
the Horns and it was Barra who stood before him, saluting the
sun with the double-faced golden axe.

The platform rose in the eastern quadrant, on a field not far
from the edge of the city, along the road crudely known as
The Tongue, since it led from the city toward the funerary
caves. The field was ringed with bored soldiers, drinking and
dicing and joking among themselves, but making very sure
that the mass of people there remained orderly, and within
the field's confines. Many persons in that crowd wore the
clothes and head wraps of white linen, rubbed with ash until it
is a mottled grey, that are the marks of mourning. There was
some small traffic from the city into the field and even less
returning.

Three liveried soldiers of the prince stood on that platform.
Two of them had scribe's tablets and pens; the third held in
his hands whatever item they were offering for auction:
sometimes weapons, or jewelry, or cups of precious metals,
more often rugs, or large squares of brocade, sometimes only
the painted cerements, the funeral wrappings cut from a
corpse.

As each item was lifted to the sun, wailing keens rose to
meet it, high shrilling voices of men and women who saw
again items they'd buried with their own hands, in the graves
of their loved ones. And there were curses, too, low-voiced so
that the soldiers could not hear, invocations to Ba'al-Berith to
avenge the disturbance of mortal remains; the less pious
whispered pleas to Great Mouth. Sometimes two different
families would each believe they recognized the same piece;
the bidding became tragic, as well as shameful.

Not all the bidders on these items were bereaved; many,
here and there, were clearly well dressed, cynical merchants
and agents of merchants who saw an opportunity for easy

profit—the same sort of men that will cut purses on a sinking ship.

The companions watched in silence from the rear of the crowd, until a woman in ashen linen spotted Kheperu, took in the colors of his livery, and clawed through the crowd toward him. "Lord, oh, lord!" she screeched, her hands extended in supplication. Kheperu stepped back, but she threw herself at his feet and caught the hem of his purple kilt. "Please, lord, please, in the name of whatever god pleases you," she sobbed, her voice half muffled from pressing the kilt's hem to her lips. "Great Mouth swallowed my husband only five days ago, lord! I have . . . I have no . . . I have nothing to pay for his cerements! They were sold, lord, and my husband . . . My children, I had to . . . *Please*, lord, can you . . . ?"

Kheperu swallowed, and looked a plea to Leucas, and to Barra. Barra, mindful that maintaining Kheperu's disguise was their only hope of evading capture, slowly shook her head; that tiny motion cut her like knives. She and Leucas began fading back toward the city's edge—others were taking notice, heads turning toward them. Kheperu nodded his resignation. He looked down at the sobbing woman and harshened his voice. "Leave off, woman!" he rasped. "Soil my kilt and I'll have you whipped!"

"*Pleeease!* I beg you, don't let my Thomi wander freezing forever!" Broad streaks of tears washed away the ash that clung to her face, and her eyes were raw. "I'll do anything! *Anything!* I'm still young, men desire me, please, please lord I'll do anything . . ." She tore open the front of her mourning-shift, exposing small breasts that quivered red and helpless. "*Anything!*"

Kheperu recoiled, horror twisting his face. She clutched at him again, and he kicked free. "Leave off! Let me go!" He got loose and hustled to rejoin his companions. Behind him the woman writhed in the dirt, wailing, "Please! Please!"

They hurried back into the city; the woman's screams faded behind them.

Barra shivered uncontrollably, though the late-year sun was warm. "I can't take this anymore," she said. She found the cool brick wall of a nearby building to lean against and put a hand over her eyes. "We can't run, and we can't hide, and I can't stand it. I have to do something. We have to do something about this." Leucas stood beside her and silently laid his huge warm hand upon her shoulder.

He squeezed once, and said, "We'll find a way."

Kheperu paced circles before them, clasping and unclasping his hands, wiping his brow, tugging at his beard. "Find a way, yes, oh, certainly. Neither of you is thinking. You're just *feeling*. Think! Don't you see what's going on?"

Barra said grimly, "This whole city is being raped."

Kheperu snapped his fingers. "Pah! That's nothing, an amusement. Why do you think they're selling those grave goods over there? It's not the money, that's not why they're opening the caves—that's peripheral, you understand?"

"You've always been the clever one," Leucas said heavily. "Just explain."

The Egyptian took a deep breath, and rubbed his jowls; he frowned, as though saying this would hurt, as though putting it into words would make it irrevocably real. "The few shekels they can earn from selling grave goods are hardly worth the effort of digging them up. This is a *sideline*, do you understand? They're opening the caves anyway, may as well make a bit of silver here and there, selling off what's left after their real treasure has been taken away."

Barra and Leucas both frowned at him, uncomprehending.

"You do not see, only because you close your eyes," he sighed. "What they're after is the *cadavers*—why do you think your bloodyfucking Simi-Ascalon has his bloodyfucking workshop right there among the caves?"

"Chrysios . . ." Barra breathed. Leucas had turned decidedly pale.

Kheperu still talked as he paced nervously before them, but Barra was lost in tales of her childhood. In the Isle of the Mighty the bards still sing of Bran the Blessed, who with his brothers led the men of the Isle against Matholuch the Red at Tara; Matholuch, who held the Cauldron of Rebirth. In the hour of his defeat, he filled the Cauldron with the corpses of his men and they rose to fight again, soulless, shambling, and unkillable. Of the great host Bran had led, only seven men came home. That endless army of corpse warriors had haunted Barra's nightmares as a child—now they filled her daylight mind. The shivering, that had subsided while listening to Kheperu, came back with a vengeance, full-fledged trembling. She hugged herself tightly, leaning against the cool-shadowed wall, and wished there were some way for her to get warm.

". . . And remember," Kheperu was saying, "Chrysios had been dead only a day or two; any Tyrian of reasonable means would be able to afford full Egyptian necromantic rites . . ."

Leucas and Barra only watched and waited for him to finish; from experience they knew that Kheperu, once going, needed no further encouragement.

"Do you see? You felt the strength of Chrysios, and the toughness of his skin. Imagine if his corpse had been properly prepared—it is the difference between skin, and leather; between cutting fresh meat and meat that has been smoked and dried. . . . These corpse-fighters like Chrysios—chryseids, if you will—they will be very tough, indeed. Tough beyond tough."

"But who would he attack with these fighters?" Leucas said, frowning. "Why create an army of corpses? What would he do with them?"

Barra said grimly, "Whatever he wants to."

"That's not a very good answer."

"It's the exact truth," she said. "Believe me. When he loses interest in Tyre, he'll be able to go anywhere, do anything, take any city. He can do what he's done here to—to anywhere."

"And," said Kheperu, "I do not believe there is any way to change it."

"We have to find a way out of town," Barra said. She thrust her hands under her arms to stop their shaking. "We have to get a message to the Pharaoh. It'll take an army to stop him now."

"Yes, well, and . . ." Kheperu said slowly, uncomfortably. He turned away and looked at the street near his sandals, and dug beneath his armor to scratch. "I think you may have to do that without me."

Leucas said, "Of course we'd never ask you to go into Egypt again—"

"It's not that." He tugged on his beard, and his expression was one of actual pain. "I've been thinking I might give myself up."

"What?" Barra barked, taking a sudden step forward.

Kheperu matched her with a step of retreat. "I do not see any profit in fighting the wind," he said, and spread his hands.

His face reddened in a way Barra had never thought she'd see: a blush of shame. "One might as well strike at the tide, or attack a mountain. I think I should get on the winning side while I still have the chance."

"And what about us? What about *me*?" Barra snapped.

"Please, Barra, if I planned to betray you, I'd hardly be telling you this now. Perhaps if I can establish my usefulness to Meremptah-Sifti, I can persuade him to give over his search for you. Or, at least, misdirect the search in such a way that you'd have a better chance to escape."

"I have used many low names for you, Kheperu," Leucas growled, "but coward was never among them."

Kheperu wrung his hands until the knuckles popped. "Listen—please try to understand. This is not my city, these are not my people. I am a mercenary—as are we all. You two seem to have forgotten that, but I haven't. I want to *live*. Meremptah-Sifti has outplayed the sharpest traders on the Middle Sea; he holds every stick, and I don't think his grip can be broken."

Barra examined him, the smooth round chubbiness of his cheeks, glistening now with sweat, the oiled braid of his beard, a look of defeat she'd never seen before in his beady dark eyes. She said, "I understand. You should understand, too, that if I do get away, if I get to Egypt and get to Ramses, this will have been the worst decision you've ever made. You follow?"

Kheperu nodded miserably. "But, you see . . . I really do not think you have a chance."

"I understand something else, too," Barra went on. "I understand that you didn't have to tell us. You could have simply made up some excuse to slip away, and never come back—that would have been the smartest thing, the most practical thing. You could have gone three days ago."

Kheperu looked away. "If, well . . . you're hurt, you see. I had to know you are all right. Blows to the head . . . they can be very dangerous." He turned back with a forced smile. "Look what it did to Leucas . . ."

No one laughed.

Barra reached out to him, took his arm. "I told you, I understand. Now, listen, I want to ask one thing of you. One favor."

"Ask?" Leucas growled. "We should ask? I think we should kill him. Now, while we have the chance."

Barra never took her eyes from Kheperu's face, though her words were directed at the giant Athenian. "Can you? Look at him. This man we've come to know so well—better even, maybe, than we wanted to. That we've fought with, and drank with, and laughed with. You think you can look him in the face and take his life?"

"Well—"

She knew better than to wait for an answer. "This is the favor I want, Kheperu," she said. "I want you to come and eat with us—we'll go to that grill court in the Market near Xuros' inn. We can talk about what to do next. Maybe we can come up with something that'll change your mind. All right?"

Kheperu swallowed, and nodded.

Barra looked over her shoulder. "Leucas?"

The boxer scowled, and huffed, and finally shrugged. He shook his head, surrendering. "Whatever you say, Barra."

Most of the Market was deserted, or nearly so, eerily empty stretches of dirty flagstones between the very few tentstalls that remained open for business. Footsteps scraped loudly over the whisper of the sea breeze; the only voices to be heard were held to mutters, from knots of men looking sidelong; and even these mutters trickled away to silence when the companions approached. Signs of activity began to appear only when they came near the central plaza, where they'd fought the bear—Barra counted days blurrily in her head. Was that twelve days ago, or thirteen? She couldn't remember; it seemed a lifetime.

Perhaps three quarters of the businesses were open, around the plaza; the merchants here seemed to feel safer, where they were in plain view of so many people, than did those in the narrow and twisty byways deeper within the Market. And, perhaps for the same reason, there were more citizens as well—even in a state of siege, or occupation, or whatever this was that Meremptah-Sifti was doing to this city, people must eat and drink. Some even continued their normal routines, as though by pretending that nothing had changed in Tyre, they could make it so. The plaza couldn't be said to be full, exactly, but there were enough people there to obscure the exhibit, on display in its center.

Leucas' great height allowed him to see it first; even hunched over as he was, he stood a head taller than either of the other two. He said, "Something new in the agora."

Barra and Kheperu had been walking along in silence, both staring at Leucas' stiffly uncommunicative back; now they both stopped and strained to see around it. Barra said, her voice weary, "Well, what is it?" She wasn't at all sure she could stand any more ugly sights today—and, now that she was paying attention, it seemed that an uncomfortably large number of people simply stood and stared thoughtfully into the middle of the plaza. After what she'd seen this day already, it took only this to kindle a sickly twisting dread within her chest.

"Looks like some kind of a cage," he replied slowly. "Set up on a little platform with guards around it. Meneides guards." He straightened, lifted himself up onto his toes and stretched his neck; then as he took in the view he seemed to shrink, to fall in upon himself, and when he looked back down and met Barra's eyes, his face was pale as the sand on the beach, save for the scars that crossed his shattered nose and bridged his cheekbones and brows: these flamed red. "There are two people in it."

A weight settled upon Barra's shoulders, the bodiless hand of some god crushing her into the earth. She struggled to hold herself straight, to make herself move forward over the flagstones that paved the plaza. Kheperu touched her arm, said something; Barra shook him off and kept walking.

As she passed a pair of men, she overheard one say to the other: "Well, it looks like rain's coming. Huh, if the weather's bad enough, they might live for a tenday."

"No—too old, I think they—" The second man never had a chance to finish this thought, for Barra wheeled on them and grabbed the nearest by the front of his robe.

"What's that mean?" she snapped, pulling his face close to hers. "What's that mean, if the weather's *bad*?"

"Hey, I, uh, listen . . ." he sputtered, waving his hands as though he wanted to push her away but was afraid to touch her.

Barra's eyes blazed, and she whispered a snarl: "Talk to me, you shit-eating prick! What's that mean?"

"There's a, a, an old couple, an old man and his wife, they got them in that cage there," he stammered. "They say they're keeping them there with no food nor water until some girl—some girl they're hunting for—gives herself up. So I figured, I figured, if it rains a lot, they might be able to get enough water to live for a while, that's all, catch it in their mouths or something. That's all, I swear!"

Her hands opened; his robe fell from her fingers. She rocked back on her heels. "A cage. Open. Open so everyone can watch . . ."

Leucas and Kheperu had caught up with her by now. She looked up at Leucas and said, "Everyone can watch them die." The Athenian and the Egyptian both could only stare; Leucas' hands twisted into fists, then relaxed, helpless. He said, "Don't do it."

He reached for her, but she spun and dodged away into the crowd. "Wait!" Leucas called, and Kheperu, too, surging after her, but she was too agile and far too quick.

And then she came in sight of the cage, and it was open-worked, with head-size spaces between cedar poles bound together with ropes, and within it were Peliarchus and Tayniz.

She stopped, panting harshly, wordless growls rasping under her breath. Townsfolk nearby edged away from her, slowly, so as not to attract her attention. The guards around the cage all faced outward, toward the plaza, eight of them in quilted armor painted with the sigil of House Meneides, spears grounded and shields in place upon their arms. They scanned the crowd, their faces full of serious self-importance, each deeply aware of the gravity of his task.

They were looking for her; she knew this, but she couldn't stop herself drifting closer.

Tayniz lay huddled in Peliarchus' arms; he knelt, grimly holding his head up. The cage floor was littered with garbage, dark and slimy bits of what might have been fruit, much of the cedar of the cage was stained with it; some of the towns-folk had been amusing themselves by throwing stuff at her parents as they sat caged there. Probably the guards had put a stop to it—it wouldn't do to have the townsfolk's cruel amusement provide food for these two who were intended to starve to death. Both wore only torn and dirty bed shirts, showing plainly the filth and bruises on their skin.

The afternoon sun struck hard upon everyone there, but hardest of all upon Peliarchus; he sat so as to give his wife

what shade he could, and beaded sweat glistened upon his
bare scalp.

And there was something else, there on the floor of the
cage, something grey and furry and still, not a body, too flat
for that: a pelt.

A pelt. The skin of a wolf.

Barra's mouth stretched wide, and her vision blurred and a
trembling took her hard, shaking, shaking so she couldn't
move, except her eyes, she looked up to Peliarchus' face, to
her father's eyes, meeting her gaze, he saw her, he recognized
her, he pushed aside his wife, and he came to his feet and
pointed at her and shouted:

"There she is!"

His bed shirt fell away from his shoulder, and she saw the
angry mark there beside his throat, the swollen redness that
surrounded the tattoo, and from somewhere beyond the world
a howl began that came ripping from her throat, pinning her
there on the plaza, motionless, screaming, howling, mind-
lessly wailing out her unconquerable pain. She saw the guard
come toward her, felt him grab her arm, but she couldn't pull
away, couldn't move, couldn't think, until from behind her
she heard the bark of Kheperu, "Barra! *Catch!*"

The simple order struck through her paralysis, and she
turned . . . the small bronze axe looped gently through the air
toward her . . . the guard's grip held hard her right arm, she
couldn't pull it free, but Barra was that rare warrior for whom
both hands are right and she deftly snatched the axe from the
air with her left hand and buried it between the startled eyes
of the young man who held her . . . it stuck in the bone as he
fell twitching away and she let it go, reaching behind for her
own axes of honest stone, she remembered now that she still
wore them pushed behind so that they were covered by her
cloak and the scream of rage and pain twisted into a war howl
as she threw herself toward the other guards.

Arms caught her from behind, arms irresistibly strong,
lifting her up, pinning her axes against her legs, and she
struggled and fought and screamed and kicked, but the arms
carried her away, charging through the crowd like a maddened bull as she screamed, *"I'll kill you! I'll kill you! I'll kill
you!"* in her native Pictish; only Peliarchus, of all the folk in
that Market, could understand her, and he was unable to care.

* * *

They paced slowly along an anonymous alleyway, side by side, as night drifted into the sky. Kheperu now wore most of Barra's cloak, to cover his livery; Barra kept only the hood, cut away and tied under her chin to conceal the telltale red of her hair. Leucas walked straight now—his back ached from being held hunched all day. Since that mad, headlong rush to escape the guards in the plaza, none of them had spoken.

They came to a small dung yard, a heap piled within it not much smaller than the one in which they'd found Mykos. As they passed by, a small door in one of the surrounding buildings scraped open; an old woman shoved it wide with her hip and stepped out to slop a couple of piss pots onto the heap. Flies lifted off in a buzzing, iridescent cloud, and its fringes gleamed with scarabs. The old woman caught sight of the companions, pushed a straggle of grey hair off her face with the back of her wrist and gave them a gap-toothed grin. "Not much here to eat, boys—and girl," she said, "but whatever you find, it's yours. You can pay me later." Chuckling, she slipped back in through the door, and Barra heard the heavy thunk of a bar settling into place.

"Hmpf," Kheperu mused, eyeing the dung heap thoughtfully. "How is it we always manage to skip our day meal?"

Leucas shrugged. "Maybe your prince will feed you," he muttered in a bitter undertone.

Barra moved away from them, silently sliding into the dung yard; beyond the heap, she'd spotted a spray of green in the fading light. She skirted the heap, and on the other side, pushing its twisted, stunted way up between the flagstones, was a young tree. It couldn't have been more than a few months old—it barely reached her chest—and its leaves were pale and sickly, but someone, in one of these buildings, must be caring for it, or it would have been uprooted long ago. The flags were scraped in a small ring around it, not clean, but cleaner than the rest of the dung yard. Barra crouched before it and ran her fingers over the roughening texture of its maturing bark. How long had it been since she'd touched a living, growing tree? She couldn't guess, not now, not here. She gently touched the leaves, pale and almost translucent, their shape that eldritch blend, midway between a human hand and the paw of a wolf.

A wind howled in her mind, roared like an angry sea; a wind from long ago and beyond the edge of the world.

She looked up to find Leucas and Kheperu standing over her. "You see this? You know what this is?" Her voice came out rough and thick; these were her first words since the scream in the plaza.

Leucas frowned, puzzled. "It's an oak," he said slowly. "Isn't it?"

Barra nodded. "It's an omen."

Kheperu snorted. "Oh, really, Barra, please—"

"It's an omen," she said stolidly. "Don't argue with me. How did she know I'm not a boy?"

"I, well, the shape of your face—"

"Shut up. She said, she told me that whatever I find, is mine." Her fists knotted until the knuckles popped. She straightened, and her expression of grim determination reached only to her eyes: her eyes burned like offering pyres to the god of war. "I tell you this. I'm not running, not anymore. I am not going to Ramses to tell on his grandson like a whining child. I'm going to beat him."

"Barra, really, I think you are a bit—"

"Shut up." She grasped the top of the little oak in her right hand, and took her axe in her left, and her voice rang like an iron bell. "I swear, by the life of the Mother that runs through this sacred oak, and by the power of her wedded Grey Lord that drives this weapon, I will whip Meremptah-Sifti cringing from this city. He is a dog, and as a dog will I whip him."

Kheperu and Leucas looked at her, then at each other, at the dung heap and the little oak. Finally, Kheperu took a deep breath and broke the silence.

"One should be cautious with oaths, I mean, really—"

"And you," she said, her voice level and calm, her axe pointing directly at Kheperu's long nose, "Kheperu, you will either help me do this or I will kill you right now. I will cut you down where you stand. Will you help?"

The Egyptian looked affronted. "How in the name of every living god do you expect to do this?"

"That's not your problem. Are you with me, or are you dead?"

"Barra, I've been thinking over my position . . ." he began uncomfortably.

"Yes?"

"Well, you see, much as it pains me to admit it like this, I . . . hmpf. Well. I do not care about this city. I do not care, really, about nearly any of the people in it. Meremptah-Sifti can, so far as I'm concerned, do what he likes with them. It's what he's done to *you*, Barra. That cage, in the Market—and to kill poor Graeg—!" Words failed him for a moment; he could only shake his head. "I'm with you."

"Leucas?"

"How can you ask?" the Athenian rumbled. "You know that I am always beside you. No matter what."

"All right." Barra tucked her axe back behind her belt. "Let's go."

"But—" Kheperu said, "what are we going to do?"

Barra smiled. The clouds that had hung within her mind all day had begun to break even as she'd made her promise to the gods. Ideas began to hum and shimmer behind her eyes. "I said it'd take an army. I've got an idea where we might be able to find one." Her smile widened, and it was not a happy smile; in the fading day her teeth gleamed and the light in her eyes became feral. She reached out and clasped the shoulders of her two companions. "That cage, there in the Market, Peliarchus and Tayniz, that tattoo, and, and Graeg—that was Meremptah-Sifti's best shot. He can't hit me any harder than that. He hit me with everything he's got, and I'm getting up again. I'm awake, and winding up."

She let go of her friends, and her fists tightened. "We'll see who's standing, at the end."

CHAPTER EIGHTEEN

Barra's Army

Down in the courtyard, Leucas measured his scimitar against the throat of the bull. The huge animal, drugged on honeyed wine, lowed contentedly. The flames of bonfires leaped up around it, painting its white flanks golden, and the two men holding its horns patted it and made comforting noises, and Leucas, with a solemn invocation to Athene, slit its throat.

The pouring blood was caught in a golden bowl, and the bull slowly knelt, going down on its front knees, and its rear legs buckled, and its front legs gave way, its chin coming to the flagstones, and finally, ponderously, it toppled to the right.

Up on the roof, among the green and growing plants of an incongruous garden, Barra knelt. Before her, on the roof, lay a small wooden trencher filled with hunks of dried clay. She spat on them, again and again, and ground the hunks together, mixing her fluids into the flesh of the Mother until they softened and combined into a paste. The keen edge of her throwing axe against the heel of her right hand drew blood, nine drops into the clay.

She gathered a handful and lifted it to the gleaming, grinning moon.

"Mother, my blood, Your Flesh. We are One. I am Your Mountain, it is my strength; I am Your Earth, and I endure."

As she spoke, it became true; this is Joining the Earth, the First Link of the ritual by which a Pict prepares herself for war.

In the deepening twilight after Barra's oath in the alley, the companions had gone straight to the home of Peliarchus. When they got in sight of the house, Kheperu had instantly observed, "This looks like a trap."

Barra and Leucas agreed; the house stood dark and unguarded, no sign of activity of any sort, and certainly
no appearance of watchers. Barra's response: "So what?
Follow me."

She led them around the corner of the house, into the
narrow right-of-way beside it, found the window she wanted
and knocked on its closed shutter.

Kheperu was horrified. "What are you *doing*?" he whispered urgently.

"Relax."

"But you don't know who's in there!"

"That's my room. It's the one where Demetor is staying."

"What if they're with him?"

Barra snorted. "Given the choice, how much time would
you spend in a room with Demetor?"

The shutters swung outward, and a man leaned out—the
startled, horrified look on his face when he saw the companions let Barra recognize him: it was the Kypriot she'd bullied
in the courtyard on the night of the poisoning. He turned
instantly red and put his hand to his mouth. "Shhh! Oh, great
Ba'al! *Shh!*"

Barra whispered, "How is King Demetor? Did he make a
full recovery?"

"Yes, well, yes, he's fine, but the courtyard is full of men—
they're *waiting for you*! They took Peliarchus and Tayniz—
your wolf . . ."

Barra silenced him with a firm gesture; she couldn't bear to
hear about this right now. "Let me talk to him."

The Kypriot stepped away from the window, and within
the room there was much whispering, and then came a
familiar whining moan that struck tears into Barra's eyes—
and then, blindingly, she realized that she had not imagined it.

She never knew how she got into the room; her next cogent
memory was of lying on a pile of rugs beside Graegduz, and
he was happily nuzzling her under her chin. The blankets, the
whole room, reeked of him—if not for her damaged nose she
would have smelled him instantly. The bandages on his
shoulder and leg were clean, and clearly new, and now
the tears did flow from her eyes and she clutched him to
her chest, and he was warm, and breathing, and stinking
in terrible need of a bath, and she told him so in her Pictish
baby talk.

She lifted her tear-streaked face, and the smile that brightened it brought answers from Leucas and Kheperu, peering in through the window, and from the Kypriot, and from King Demetor, who stood over her grinning into his snowy beard.

Demetor said, "When your father left, those men, why, they wanted to kill this wolf. I told them you'd placed him under my care, and I found myself a sword and ordered my men to fight to the death to protect him, and they decided they could do without. I told them this wolf had been hurt saving my life, and while I had life they weren't to touch him."

That pelt—why, they must have simply bought it, or stolen it from some shop in the Market. Just a jab, a stinging slap for her—they probably hadn't even guessed how deep a wound it would inflict.

Barra rose, and clasped forearms with him, and when she could trust her voice, she said, "May the Mother of All shower blessings upon you like the rain in spring."

"It was only my duty," mumbled the old king, a bit shamefaced but obviously enjoying himself. "I only wish I could have done the same for your parents, and I would have, y'know, I really surely and certainly would have, except that Peliarchus himself told me that everything was all right and I shouldn't worry, that they weren't going to be hurt or really even very inconvenienced—"

That had been the tattoo's magic talking, Barra knew; but there was neither time nor reason to explain that to King Demetor and his man. "You know what this is?" she asked, talking to her friends outside, her eyes alight.

"Let me guess," murmured Kheperu. "Another omen?"

"Best believe it," Barra told him. "I thought he was dead, lost forever, and here he is alive, and soon to be well. Saved by blades and boldness. It's an omen of victory."

"Victory?" Demetor said, obviously puzzled. "Over what? Against whom? I'm sorry, I've been a bit out of touch, recovering and all—that's thanks to you, y'know, and I can't tell you the depths of my gratitude—but it does keep one out of circulation. By the way, how was the Governor's feast? Sorry I missed it, I wasn't quite well yet. And, you know, you look like someone's given you a bit of a beating . . ."

"My lord." Barra once again firmly dammed the river of words. "I must ask you for a favor. You have done me so great a service in saving my friend that I don't want to demand this as a right, as guest-friend and all, but instead I only ask."

"Anything, Barra," he said firmly. "Anything at all. I owe you my kingdom, and my life."

"What I'd like," she said slowly, "is a private interview with your cousin Agapenthes."

His brows drew together. "Agapenthes? Why, certainly. I've been keeping out of his way while I'm here in Tyre—just between you and me and this wall, I don't think he likes me very much—but I should think he'd see me if I presented myself at his gate."

"Good," Barra said, nodding. "Great. Now, just one more thing before we go—"

"Now? You want to go *now*?"

"Oh yes, we have to. Tomorrow might be too late." She took a deep breath and rubbed her hands together, gave Kheperu an encouraging smile.

Kheperu coughed, and reached within the small purse that hung at his belt. "Yes, well. Up in the servant's quarters, on the second floor, there's a large box. This key will open it. There are just a few items that I'd like you to bring for me—carefully, casually, so as not to shake them up too much, or alert those men who are waiting out there . . ."

Down in the courtyard, Leucas busily gutted the bull, while the two handlers stripped back the skin, starting with the head and front legs. There was none of the laughter and cross-talk that normally characterizes such a task; a sacrifice such as this is a solemn occasion.

Up on the roof, Barra shook a powder out into the palm of her hand, a powder that comes from boiling the crushed leaves of a small shrub that grows in the Isle of the Mighty. Her pouch, containing this powder, she'd carried with her for years, since her last visit home; this powder's blue showed clear and vivid even under the pale light of the moon. When she judged she held exactly the right amount, she shook it gently over the moist clay, and kneaded it in, until the clay took on the color of a threatening sky. Slowly—a bit awkwardly—she unbound her long gleaming red hair, silver-black under the moon. It fell free around her shoulders, and she began to work handfuls of the clay into it, in long, sweeping ritual gestures. She built it up with the clay into a

fan above her head, with straight spikes descending like rain
scattered in the wind. A few dabs of powder on her clay-
moistened fingers drew spirals around her eyes and slashes
below her cheekbones.

"On my brow, Your Thunder, that is my voice. In my eyes,
Your Lightning, that is my fist."

As she spoke, it became true; this is Joining the Sky, the
Second Link of the ritual by which a Pict prepares herself
for war.

King Demetor had easily persuaded his men to lend the
companions their clothing, and after a bit of low comedy in
getting the old king safely out the window, the four of them
snuck off, looking for all the world like four Kypriots
creeping drunkenly toward the nearest brothel. Kheperu made
his preparations on the way; by the time the four of them presented themselves at the gate of the Penthedes compound, the
closed censer in his left hand leaked a minuscule amount of
sweet-smelling smoke, and he had concealed in his right a
folded paper packet that contained some brownish-grey
powder.

Demetor had a fine time, pretending to be a bit drunk ("In
my youth I performed the occasional dithyramb, here and
there, rather well, I might add—") and bullying his way in
past the Penthedes guardsmen. Whenever he was refused,
whether by a guard or a servant or the house steward himself,
he simply raised his voice, louder and louder, demanding to
see his cousin Agapenthes, until finally the four were allowed
in solely to shut him up. Barra's face was swathed in bandages, and Demetor merrily pretended that she was one of his
men, who had come out on the losing side of a brawl with
some imaginary Penthedes tough, and now he'd come to see
his cousin to demand restitution.

Agapenthes finally greeted them in an inner room, broad
and low-ceilinged, richly carpeted, layer upon layer of rugs
overlapping across the floor in a garishly contrived arrangement, and other rugs from Dilmun and Punt were hung about
the walls. He looked considerably less regal than he had at the
feast; his silver hair was tied back in a hasty horsetail, as
though he'd just awakened, although the strong scent of wine
that came even to Barra's damaged nose suggested that if he
had been sleeping, it hadn't been for long.

He offered warm, if somewhat wary, greetings to his cousin from Kypros, while Kheperu paced slowly around the room, watching the smoke from his censer to judge the air currents. A slow smile crept over his face when he saw that by standing just *here,* he could twist open the censer's ports and get both Agapenthes and Demetor in the path of the smoke. Barra and Leucas leaned away in their chairs, not so much that Demetor or Agapenthes would notice, only enough that they wouldn't breathe it: the incense in the censer was the same compound that Kheperu had used to beat the Myrmidons at dice.

"What is this?" Agapenthes demanded, and when Demetor went into his story about Barra's supposed fight, Agapenthes shook his head. "No, I mean this—this smelly incense. You— what are you doing?"

"I'm cleansing the room, my lord, of spirits and adverse influences," Kheperu said smoothly. "With all the rumors of magic and sorcery, I thought it best our little gathering be protected."

"I am *already* protected," Agapenthes huffed. "The prince's steward drew the mark of protection on my shoulder with his own hand."

Kheperu glanced at Barra; she gave him a tight-lipped smile and a tiny nod.

"And, here, see now, Demetor," Agapenthes went on, "this man's Egyptian—he's not from Kypros at all. Since when do you keep company with Egyptians?"

Demetor looked utterly blank. "Since, why, er . . ."

Barra closed her eyes and sent a swift prayer toward the Grey Lands.

"Well, since, you see, I'd been hearing about all this, all this, this magic and all, so I . . . hired this man to look after me, you know . . . protection from this sorcerer everyone's always talking about . . . and, well, that's it, you see."

Agapenthes nodded, and the cloud of suspicion cleared from his brow. Barra thanked her gods that he was drunk, and already a little woozy from Kheperu's smoke. He said, "Well, perhaps we can take some refreshment, and you can tell me of your trouble with my man."

Kheperu watched the pair of cousins while servants streamed in, bringing wine and bread and fresh goat's milk cheese. By the time the servants had left, Kheperu was satisfied; he nodded to Barra, and she gave him a tiny gesture of *get on with it*.

As Demetor began to once again trot out his invented story, Kheperu interrupted. "You may be too tired for this, Demetor. You're very tired. Agapenthes—he looks tired, doesn't·he?"

Demetor yawned. Agapenthes leaned toward him, concern painted clearly across his face. "Why, you look absolutely exhausted, cousin."

Kheperu said, "You'd best offer him a bed for the night."

"Demetor, we can deal with this difficulty in the morning. Won't you be my guest, sleep here this evening?"

"Why . . . why, Agapenthes, awfully kind—" He stretched, and yawned again.

"In fact," Kheperu said, "Demetor, you're about to fall asleep. You *are* asleep." Demetor's head dropped to his chest, and his eyes closed, and he made comfortable burbling noises into his beard. Kheperu grinned at Barra. "Told you I could do it."

"Then quit fooling around," Barra growled.

Agapenthes peered at the two of them drunkenly. "Do what? What have you done?"

"Nothing," Kheperu told him firmly. "Agapenthes, do you recognize me?"

"Erm, well . . ."

"I am Meremptah-Sifti."

The Head of House Penthedes squinted, frowning. "Most High? You seem different."

"I'm in disguise," Kheperu said irritably. "Agapenthes, stand up."

He stood.

"Spin around."

Slowly, with a certain graceful stateliness, the Head of House Penthedes spun himself in a circle. Again, Kheperu grinned at Barra, and this time, he spoke in Greek, so as to include Leucas in the conversation. "Want to see him dance like a chicken?"

"No!" Barra snapped. "That's not funny."

Leucas leaned forward, resting elbows on knees. "Does it bother you," he asked softly, "to use the same methods Meremptah-Sifti does?"

"Where I come from," Barra told him evenly, "that's called cutting a man with his own knife—and it's counted as quite a

coup." Leucas shrugged, looking unconvinced. She turned
her attention back to Kheperu. "What about his tattoo? Is that
going to cause a problem? When, say, we come across, well,
someone in particular that I'm not going to mention?"

"Perhaps; perhaps not. If my hold is good I can tell him day
is night and he'll see what I tell him to. On the other hand,
this spell fades over time . . ." He opened the paper packet
he'd carried in his right hand and swirled its contents into a
half-full winebowl. He gave this to Agapenthes to drink, and
the old man did so with pathetic eagerness to please. "This
potion is a more concentrated, potent form—its effects should
certainly last until sunrise; perhaps until mid-morning."

"I'm still worried about that tattoo. Is there anything you
can do to nullify the mark itself?"

"I don't know. There's no way to be sure without extensive
experiment. Probably the surest way is to kill Simi-Ascalon;
magics often die with their creators."

"Fine," Barra said. "I'm going to do that anyway. What
about the meantime?"

Leucas, ever practical, said, "What if we simply slice it out
of his flesh?"

Kheperu nodded dubiously. "That would probably work—
but it might not; I'm unsure about the actual mechanism
behind this spell. However, doing so will certainly break *my*
spell. Any sudden physical pain will wake him right up, and
then we will all be in a bit of trouble."

Barra nodded. She waved a hand at Agapenthes, who still
turned himself in slow circles. "Ask him how many men he
has under arms."

"Agapenthes, you can stop now."

"Thank you, Most High," he gasped. "I confess I was getting a bit dizzy."

Kheperu smirked. "Yes, well, whatever. Now. You will
answer all questions and follow all orders that come from this
person as though they come from me," Kheperu said, indicating Barra. He turned back to her. "Ask him yourself."

Barra switched languages, back to Phoenikian. "How many
men do you have that can be gathered, ready to fight, within
the hour? I'm not talking about houseboys, here; I mean veterans, blooded, with their own armor and weapons."

"Now? In the middle of the night?" He frowned, calculating. "Three hundred, perhaps. Or a bit more."

Barra's heart thundered. That was *three times* what she'd been expecting! She said to herself, *This could work*. "How many chariots?"

"Only forty—the garrison keeps the rest locked up for emergencies."

"Forty is plenty. All right. Get your messengers going. I want all three hundred men and forty chariots assembled in that big courtyard out there within the hour, with all their gear, and weapons, and horses. Oh, and wait," she said as he turned to follow her orders. "Is there a garden around here somewhere? Some place with a few plants and maybe a tree or two?"

"On my roof," he told her. "It's the best view in Tyre. I like to sit up there and have a bowl of wine or two at sunset—"

"That's good enough."

"And a bull," Leucas said.

"What?"

"I want a bull. His best bull."

"Leucas, in the name of the Loving bloody Mother—"

He set his jaw stubbornly. "Remember those cuts I took at Lidios' house? I still owe a bull to Athene for protecting me, and I'd be a fool to go into battle without paying up."

Barra sighed and said to Agapenthes in Phoenikian, "And your best bull. Have him brought to the courtyard, too."

"Of course. May I go now?"

Agapenthes' eagerness to please gave her a greasy, slightly sickly feeling in the pit of her stomach, but she told herself that this was no time to get squeamish. Plenty of time for that after the battle, while they bury and burn the dead.

As the companions watched Agapenthes scurry off, Leucas nodded toward Demetor, who now snored softly. "What about him?"

"Let him sleep," Barra said. "By the time he wakes up tomorrow, this'll all be over."

Down in the courtyard, Leucas wrapped the entrails of the bull in its skin, along with the fat from its thighs and belly; he tossed the bundle onto the central bonfire of sweet-scented cedar. The offering bundle crackled and popped in the flames, and the dark, rich-roasting meat smoke rose gently into the sky, drifting on a breeze westward, out to sea. Leucas' song followed it, his powerful bass voice surprisingly pure and sweet, in his hymn to Athene.

Up on the roof, Barra stripped off her Kypriot tunic and leggings and set them aside. Her nipples hardened instantly in the chill night air. Clad only in her breechclout, sandals, and weapon belt, she began to paint herself with the clay, spirals out from her nipples and waves across her belly, long curving stripes from her bandaged ankles to the curve of her hips.

"My breast is Your Waters, struck but never injured; my legs are Your Wind, swift and inescapable."

This is the Joining of the Sea, the Third and final Link in the ritual by which a Pict prepares herself for war.

"The Earth does not tire, the Sky does not clear, the Sea does not rest, until war is done."

Barra stood, and took the hilt of her broadaxe in her teeth; she must carry a weapon naked, never set it down or tuck it away, until the battle is done. She took the trencher, which was stained blue and still contained a handful of blue-grey clay, over to the largest of the pots that housed the green and growing plants around her. With her hands, she scooped aside the moist earth, and laid the trencher within it, covering it over once again in reverent burial.

"That's quite a spell," Kheperu said from behind her.

She hadn't known he was there, she didn't know how long he'd been watching, but she didn't startle at all. She took her axe in her right hand and turned to face him.

Any lingering doubts she might have had about Kheperu's loyalty or determination to see this through were instantly washed away: she was in the grip of the *sceon tiof*, and she saw that his commitment, once made, was unbreakable. She looked over her shoulder, down at the men gathered in the courtyard, at Leucas as he donned his armor, and she saw into the hearts of each and every one. The fear and dismay that had always accompanied the *sceon tiof* were absent, though; Barra was calm, and sure—and when any of these men fell, she would grieve for them as though they were her blood kin.

This she accepted; it was the inevitable price of fighting her war.

And the *sceon tiof* did not pass; it was no momentary, flickering thing, but it rested within her spirit and looked out through her eyes.

Kheperu wore his old robes once again, faded, stained, and patched, with many, many pockets, and beneath them his familiar armor of boiled leather. Those myriad pockets bulged with every bit of magic he thought could possibly be of use—he walked carefully, as he stepped toward her.

He said, "You know, I'd really feel better—more comfortable—if you'd put on some armor."

"Armor?" Barra said. The serene consciousness of the Mother's Love drew her lips into a thin smile. "I'm not even going to put on my shirt."

Kheperu had concocted a fantastic story about an impostor taking over Meremptah-Sifti's name and lands, with the connivance of Idonosteus and Simi-Ascalon, and they were now holding Tal Akhu-shabb, the Governor, hostage; the impostor must be brought down, and the Meneides punished, and the Governor rescued, and no matter how ridiculous the story sounded, Kheperu had no difficulty at all in selling it to Agapenthes, so thoroughly was he magicked.

He'd had a bit more trouble with Agapenthes' wives. All three of them had come screeching after their husband, swearing and moaning about the noise and confusion and snapping questions about what the drunken old fool thought he was going to do now, until finally Kheperu took pity on the stammering old man and offered the women bowls of wine that contained double doses of one of his sleeping powders, and breathed a heavy sigh of relief when they nodded off.

Agapenthes also had some difficulty in persuading his men. He stood on the back of a chariot and exhorted them in a penetrating—if somewhat slurred—voice of command. Kheperu stood beside him, just behind his shoulder, and whispered occasionally into his ear. More than three hundred men had answered the call; they clustered about the courtyard in ragged, undisciplined knots. They wore armor and carried weapons, but they seemed more interested in keeping close to the warmth of the bonfires than in chasing about and fighting a pitched battle in the dark; especially with all these Egyptians around—nobody wanted to get on the wrong side of an Egyptian axe company. Not one of them was unaware of what had been happening in Tyre over the past few days, they just didn't think that they should be the ones to risk their lives trying to fix it. The appearance of Barra at the edge of the rooftop, looking like some wandering spirit from a children's tale, didn't help matters any. Barra, watching from above while Kheperu fed Agapenthes his lines, shook her head. She would have traded the whole three hundred of them, chariots and all, for twenty-five Myrmidons who knew when to shut up and follow orders.

Finally, Kheperu hit upon the magic phrase to turn the tide of opinion in the proper direction: "Equal shares."

Equal shares. The phrase whispered through the untidy ranks; it was as though they'd learned that some god would stand at each man's side, an almost superstitious shivering of awed semi-belief. Would Agapenthes really let every fighter share equally in all the loot? It was unheard of!

Kheperu shrugged, and made Agapenthes seal the promise with an oath by the witness of Ba'al-Berith.

The shout that went up from the courtyard warmed Barra's heart.

She went in, and made her way downstairs to where Leucas was dressing in his armor. He took a long, long look at her, frowning, squinting, then finally he nodded. His only comment was, "You be careful. Whatever magic that is, it won't work as well as bronze plate." He shrugged. "On the other hand, it won't itch and make you sweat."

The greaves were already strapped about his shins, and the interleaved bronze plates of the corselet about his chest. He strapped on the girdle, to protect his loins, and then tied back his long grey-salted hair into a pile on the top of his head, to serve as additional padding under the helmet. He lifted the great helm and regarded it solemnly, shaking his head at the ratty, bug-eaten look of its crest of horsehair. "I don't think I've been in full armor since Troy," he mused. "Should keep better care of it." He snugged the helmet over his head, sighed, and tapped the nasal, the long bar that extended from the helmet's brow down to the tip of his nose. "Makes me go cross-eyed. Blasted thing always gives me a headache." He slung his scabbarded sword across his back, stuck the iron scimitar through his belt, then got his massive shield, five layers of alternating ox-hide and bronze. He lifted his man-length spear of heavy ash, and said, "How do I look?"

The *sceon tiof* glowed behind her eyes, and made his every gesture shine with joy. Leucas was a huge man, already; with the helm's crest adding to his height and the corselet deepening his chest, he looked more than human. "Happy," she said. "You could be the very son of manslaughtering Ares."

One of his rare grins split his ruined face. "I admit, I'm looking forward to this."

Barra nodded. "Let's get started."

The fires began at midnight.

All over Tyre, buildings burned, lighting the clouds with an orange glow. Fifty men, ten teams of five, raced through the city torching skins of lamp oil and throwing them onto roofs, or through windows.

Roofs of Meneides warehouses. Windows of Meneides inns.

In some of these, there were guards, or watchmen, or guests sleeping off heavy meals and too much wine. The teams knew their lines; at each, shouts were heard: *"Barra Coll Eigg Rhum makes war! Let Egypt beware! Death to Meremptah-Sifti!"*

At approximately the same time, the Egyptian garrison commander was startled out of a sound sleep by trumpets of alarm and cries that the city was under attack from the sea. At the camps north of the city, breathless riders reported that sea pirates had landed south of the city; at the southern camps, the word was that Joshua ben Nun and his Habiru horde were attacking from the Lebanon, to the northeast, and forward elements were already within the city.

Every camp of the Canaan Division suddenly burst into the furious activity of a kicked-over anthill.

Barra watched it all from the roof garden, Leucas, Kheperu, and Agapenthes at her back. Down in the courtyard below the remaining two hundred–odd men were formed in ranks, surrounding the forty chariots.

Barra said softly, so that only Leucas could hear, "You know, the first time I went to war I was only eight years old. My brother—that's Llem, the High King—he said I couldn't go out hunting with the boys, that I wasn't old enough. My father was visiting from Eire and I told him about it, asked him what he'd do. He said, 'Fuck it. Go to war!' So I did. Painted myself up and marched into my brother's hall, where he was holding a big meeting feast with a bunch of northern chieftains, and proudly informed him that I was at war with him." She sighed, shrugging into the warm regard of Leucas' grey eyes. "Wasn't much of a war. There were exactly two casualties; I still sit on both of them."

"This one's a little different," Leucas murmured.

"Don't I know it."

They stood in silence for a moment, watching the growing flames that sprang up in the night like toadstools. "If Zeus sends no rain," Leucas said, "we might end up burning down the whole city."

Barra shook her head. "No. We won't. Tyre won't burn."

"How do you know?"

She looked calmly, deeply into his eyes. "I know."

Perhaps he saw something of the *sceon tiof* certainty within her gaze; perhaps he only wanted to believe her; at any rate, he nodded. "I understand the fires," he said. "We need to stir up the Egyptians and get a lot of people out on the streets so that we can move around without being interfered with. But why the announcement? Why give warning?"

Barra leaned on the parapet and looked out over the city. "Because we don't know for sure where Meremptah-Sifti is. He could be out at his estate, or here in town at the Meneides compound, or staying in the garrison, or practically anywhere. It won't take more than a couple of hours for the Egyptians to get things back under control; we don't have time to pick a place, and be wrong."

"I still don't understand."

"That's because you don't know Idonosteus." The *sceon tiof* insight she'd gained of the Head of House Meneides had given her this tactic, and there was no doubt within her that it would work. "He panics. He's smart, but he's weak; his nerve'll break. I have ten horsemen surrounding his compound, watching from all sides. I'm just waiting for him to get word of the fires. For him to get word that I'm the one doing it. Because the first thing he'll do is send a message to his master and beg for protection. Then we'll know where Meremptah-Sifti is."

"But they'll be warned."

Barra showed her teeth. "So?"

A clatter of hooves interrupted them. A strong voice shouted hoarsely from the street below. "My lord Agapenthes! Twelve riders and a light coach left House Meneides and galloped out of the city. Toward Karbas' home!"

"Southeast," Barra interpreted grimly. "He's heading for the estate."

"No messenger, then," Leucas said. "He's going himself."

"I suppose he's thinking he'll be safer out there. I told you he's weak."

"Twelve riders, though." His voice was freighted with grim meaning. "Twelve."

Barra knew what that meant: her worst fear had come to pass. "The Myrmidons are with him," she said flatly. "Kamades is with him. They saved my life."

More than that: she thought of the pure joy she'd felt, seeing Kamades in that cellar, and the stunning efficiency with which the Myrmidons had dispatched her guards. She thought of the throat-tightening purity of courage with which he'd faced an angry Leucas. It was possible that he'd fall in this war she'd begun; it was possible she'd find herself matched against him, to kill him or be killed herself.

Leucas, never one to waste words, snaked an arm around her shoulders and gave her a gentle, solemn hug. The smooth bronze of his corselet struck a chill into her bare flesh.

After a moment, she shook him off. "Kheperu—get Aga-penthes into a chariot and move 'em out. Let's go do this."

CHAPTER NINETEEN

Fun

Meremptah-Sifti listened with interest to Idonosteus' breathless tale, nodding and encouraging him with thoughtful questions. He reclined on a high couch, his hair unbound, his mouth still swollen and ugly with a purple-yellow bruise from Barra's fists. He winced, just a bit, with each sip of wine; this wine was resinous enough to sting his lips.

Idonosteus, by the time he finished his tale, was practically hopping with panic. "Well? So? Well? What will you do about this?"

Meremptah-Sifti shrugged languidly. "What do you suggest I do?"

"Well, you'd better, er, we . . ." he sputtered, then finally controlled himself. "My prince, I think you should send riders to the army immediately, tell them that we're going to be attacked."

Meremptah-Sifti shook his head dismissively. "Not at all. We have the Governor's personal guard here, as well as my personal retainers: over a hundred men."

"But, but she has *more*! Ba'al alone knows how many! They're burning Tyre even as we speak! Where could they have come from? She could have *thousands*!"

"It does not matter."

"What do you mean? How can you say this?"

Meremptah-Sifti twisted his battered mouth into a knowing smile. "I have been hoping for this." He pushed himself upright and swung his legs down off the couch. "Sim has moved his operations downstairs, since his workshop at the caves was discovered. I am well prepared for this occurrence."

"But, b-but still, my prince, shouldn't we have the army—?"

"No."

"B-but—"

Meremptah-Sifti suddenly stood, towering over Idonosteus;

Idonosteus cringed like a whipped slave. Meremptah-Sifti smiled, and decided not to hit him.

"No, if the army were here, it might frighten her off," he murmured with deep amusement. "Then I would have to go into Tyre after her. This will be much more convenient." He touched his mouth thoughtfully, running his fingertips over the swollen curve of his underlip.

"This will be much more fun."

CHAPTER TWENTY

Barra's War

The clouds had not yet stretched east to the mountains, and the rising moon still gave light for the march, illuminating the rolling ground enough for the horses to step confidently. The orange glow of burning buildings in Tyre faded behind them.

Barra stood beside Leucas in the chariot, wearing only her breechclout, her axes, and a long coil of rope that looped diagonally over her shoulder. The huge Athenian enjoyed himself immensely, driving again for the first time in more than five years. He handled the reins expertly, and chuckled with pleasure when the horses took his direction smoothly and eagerly. "Fine animals," he rumbled. "Greek-trained; they know all the right signals." Barra thought privately that it was more likely that the Greek style was derived from the Phoenikian, but saw fit to keep her mouth shut on the subject—Leucas was the expert, not she.

Alongside them drove Agapenthes, leading his men; Kheperu stood beside him, holding on to the chariot's rim with both hands.

There had been a good deal of laughter and back talk among the men when they'd left Tyre; it had now faded into expectant silence and harsh breathing. Barra pushed their pace as fast as she dared. "Remember," Leucas had said, "these are townsfolk, really—they're warriors only by a sort of accident. You can't expect them to run for an hour in full armor and be able to fight at the end of it." Barra's solution was to keep the pace at a steady jog, and rotate the men through the chariots—at their most crowded, each could hold four men. With this reduced force—numbering now, subtracting the men who still raced around and burned buildings, and the others spreading lies and confusions among the Egyptian camps, perhaps two hundred and twenty or thirty—well over half could ride at any one time. The battlefield she'd chosen would be small; better the horses should be tired and the men strong.

The fires and diversions had their desired effect. On the march toward the estate, they were challenged only once. A large group of horsemen had galloped toward them out of the south—an Egyptian patrol-in-force, investigating rumors of the Habiru invasion—and Barra had crouched low behind the chariot's wall while Kheperu explained to the officer in charge that this ragtag group was a force of Penthedes irregulars, heading out to reinforce the troops protecting the prince at his estate. Kheperu's reply had captured perfectly the nasal arrogance of the Egyptian aristocracy, and the moonlight bleached the stains from his robe; the officer waved them on and the patrol galloped away.

Barra's army marched on, footfalls and hoofbeats muffled by the grass. Conversation was muted, if any took place at all; to Barra's ears came only the hush of the west wind and the creaking of the chariots, the occasional snuffle of a horse and slap of reins.

In the Isle of the Mighty, when the men—and sometimes women—march to war, it is a great and festive occasion, with dancing and singing of songs, with much drinking and more fucking, a celebration of fragile life for the many warriors who will not return. Here in Phoenikia, war was a quiet, grave thing, and the men had no song to keep the dread from their hearts.

Barra didn't like it; to her, it smelled of disaster.

Barra squinted up at the manor house, where it squatted on top of the hill. At this distance, little could be seen of it save the tiny pinpricks of light from its windows. The moon, still fairly low over the mountains, let her see clearly the terrain and the waiting men. "He wants us," she said softly, near Kheperu's ear. "He hasn't even closed the shutters—he's trying to draw us in pretending we can surprise him."

Kheperu gave her a sickly smile. "It's going to work, too, I'm afraid."

"That's right."

She looked at Leucas. He nodded, and extended both fists clenched before him, then slid his shield into place in the grooves of the left side chariot wall and reached back to check that his spear stood firmly in its holder. He was ready.

She looked at the men around her. Their shuffling and snuffling had faded into expectant stillness as they'd caught their breath from the hour's hard march out here.

"I've told you," she said softly, so that only Kheperu and Leucas could hear, even though she spoke in Greek, "that the house up there is built like a fortress. I don't know how many men he has—there is at least one barracks that could hold, say, fifty men or even more. Remember that we don't have to beat them. We just have to get inside, get our hands on Meremptah-Sifti. And, for the Love of the bloody Mother, *don't kill him.* I don't intend to save Tyre only to have it destroyed by Egypt. Simi-Ascalon, Indonosteus—they're fair game. The sooner they're dead, the happier I'll be."

She took a deep breath and gestured toward the manor. "Now, I figure that his best defense is to hold his men inside the house, fight with arrows from the second floor and third, maybe sortie once or twice to keep us back from the walls. For our part, we have to get in close. We need to be fighting right up against those walls, which should produce enough confusion that we can get inside. I'm thinking the roof—you see that colonnade, there?" She pointed it out, ghostly in the moonlight. "If we can get up there, Leucas, you can toss me up onto the roof, just like you did at Xuros' inn. I lower this rope"—she patted the coil over her shoulder— "and all three of us are up there. We should be able to get in from the top— nobody should be expecting that."

"Why the roof?" Leucas asked, frowning. "The house may be built like a fortress, but it's not a fortress. If we get to the walls, we can force those doors, or the shutters on the windows. Why go to all the trouble of going to the roof?"

"Because," Barra said tightly, "that's where he'll be. If we go in from the ground, we'll have to fight our way up. He might be on the third floor, but probably he's on the roof."

"How do you know?"

She shrugged. "That's where I'd be."

Agapenthes was given his final instructions in an undertone by Kheperu, leaning with both hands on the old man's armor. "You must lead your men in close, and do not fall back. Keep them with you, shame them if need be, but bring them to the house and surround it, and break the windows and doors, and take the house. Those inside who do not resist, take prisoner. Take only the ground floor, do not go up into the house nor down into the cellar." Barra had decided this was safest; she didn't want Meremptah-Sifti killed by some Penthedes bully who got his blood up. This wouldn't stop the Penthedes men from running up and down those stairs looking for things to steal and people to kill—no leader has that much control over his men, except perhaps the late Akhilleus—but it should slow them down.

Kheperu ended his instructions with, "And, once the attack begins, follow no other order, from me or anyone else, until the battle is done." This risky command was given in hopes that it would prevent Agapenthes being turned by a shout from the real Meremptah-Sifti; Kheperu didn't know for sure whether it would work, but it seemed to be the wisest precaution.

"Oh, and"—Kheperu winced, and made a superstitious warding gesture against bad luck—"when the arrows come at you, keep your shield up."

The orders were given. No trumpet sounded, no shouts or songs rose toward the sky. The chariots were deployed in wings, to the right and left of the body of footmen, where they could respond swiftly to any sortie, except for the chariot of Agapenthes and his driver, and the chariot that Leucas drove, carrying Barra and Kheperu: these were in the center.

The army advanced, up the hill, toward the house, at a walk.

Blood thundered in Barra's ears, and she gripped the chariot's low wall with her free hand, more to keep herself still than to maintain her balance. She kept telling herself that Meremptah-Sifti couldn't have more than fifty or sixty men here, and if he'd sent riders in search of reinforcements from the Egyptians, they'd have a hard time time finding the necessary officers, who were spread out all over Tyre looking for raiders or fighting fires in the city, and even if they did find the officers, they wouldn't be able to get any substantial force here in time to alter the outcome, and that Meremptah-Sifti had some extremely fast-looking horses in his stable and so if things went badly she could steal one that just possibly might be able to outrun the Egyptian chariots.

She turned, into the trailing wind, and now they'd risen up

the hill far enough that she could see the distant fires, and she scanned the rolling ground for any sign of troops marching toward them—she had no illusions about how her little army would fare against Egyptian regulars. The orange-tinted clouds were reaching inland now, and the moon rose to meet them, and she had another thing to worry about: if the moon went behind the clouds, the only light they'd have to fight by would be whatever fires Kheperu could quickly set, which would be a stunning advantage to the archers within the house.

And she kept looking at the ornamental groves of olive and fig trees that they passed, these stands of trees that were scattered artistically about the grounds. The blackness within them was impenetrable, and any one of them could hold enemies lying in wait.

She looked around her at the apprehension, the stomach-knotting dread, that showed so clearly on the faces of the men who walked alongside the chariot. Which of them would live to tell this story? Who would take an arrow through the lung? Who would return home to his wife with a gangrenous stump where his arm had been? Who would scream for his mother as he lay on the ground and tried to stuff his bowels back inside his slashed belly? The *sceon tiof* couldn't show her that; it did show that they feared humiliating themselves in front of their comrades more than they feared death or injury; it showed the resolve, deep within each man, that if he was wounded he'd bear his injury bravely, silently, that if need be he'd die without a sound, so that he could be remembered as a warrior. It showed that not courage, but shame, would keep these men fighting in the strong encounter.

Leucas, glancing back, caught her expression. "I've seen that look before," he said.

"What look?" Barra shook herself free of the gaze that had held her, and shifted her grip on her axe.

"Your face, just then, could have been Agamemnon's, at Aulis. I saw him there, when he put his daughter to the knife for a fair wind to Troy," he rumbled thoughtfully. "I saw Diomedes gaze on his young companions, in front of the seven-gated walls of Thebes, and he too wore this look that you wear now."

She shook her head. "I've never led men into battle before."

"Well, actually," Kheperu said, "*you* are not really leading them, you know, if anyone could be said—"

"It doesn't matter," Barra said, interrupting him with a slice of her hand. "This is my fight, but it's going to be their blood that pays for it."

"It's hard, your first time," Leucas said. "Or so the poets say. Maybe there'll be a song about us, someday."

"About this?" Barra said skeptically. "This dirty little fight? I don't think so."

"You never know," Leucas told her. Then: "Look up there. They're coming out."

Above them, at the crest of the hill, the lights in the windows winked out, one by one, like fireflies dying in the cold. Out from the main front door issued a long file of men. In the moonlit distance, it was hard to tell if they were armed, or not. They came out onto the front lawn, and formed a ragged line, and stood, waiting.

"What's he doing?" Barra muttered. The army continued to advance while she counted them silently. Twenty-five men, perhaps thirty, that was all. What could Meremptah-Sifti be thinking of, to put thirty men outside the safety of the walls, to face two hundred? Some still trailed out the door, and none of them seemed in any great hurry to get into position. For a moment, she nursed a wild hope at her breast that Meremptah-Sifti, arrogant as he was, might actually come out to parley, to find out why one of his tattooed slaves had turned against him.

Then the breeze shifted, only for a moment, whispering from the east, and a chill understanding made Barra shiver. Bad eggs and rotting meat . . . "Smell that?" she said. "Those are—what did you call them?—corpse-warriors."

"Chryseids," Kheperu murmured, then suddenly his gaze sharpened. "You can *smell* them?"

"I'll explain some other time." She shut her eyes, briefly searching for some of the serenity the Rite of War had given her, but she found it nowhere within her. *Well,* she thought, *better they should be out here, against the army, than waiting for me inside . . .*

She opened her eyes. "Cry the charge," she said softly. "Kheperu, tell Agapenthes to cry the charge."

Leucas answered her with a laugh that thundered like a

happy Zeus. "We don't need words to cry the charge!" He snapped the reins against the horses' rumps. *"Hyah!"*

The horses surged ahead, leading the way, leaving the men behind, and as they saw this, the men of the army roared with a single voice and broke into a run.

The footmen overtook the chariots, tired as the horses were, and once again the army surged up the hill as a single mass. Agapenthes shouted something wildly about the impostors sending servants and slaves against them, because the chryseids wore no armor, only carried spears and knives, and then the battle was joined.

During the initial shock and crush, Barra was most concerned with keeping her feet in the bouncing chariot. Kheperu crouched below the chariot's walls, preparing some spell, and Leucas stood like a ship's captain holding the tiller in a storm. Hands clutched the chariot's rim, and Barra cut at them, feeling again the leathery shock as her axe failed to slice through the skin.

The army's war cries turned to shouts of alarm and dismay, when they found their weapons often failed to bite the skins of their opponents. The chryseids fought silently, delivering blows of tremendous power, driving spear points through the very bronze of the Penthedes corselets, ripping through the livers and unstringing the knees of many a man. Against enemies of such strength, the footmen's armor served little use, providing scant protection and slowing them to make them easier prey.

The chariot lurched, knocking Barra sprawling against Leucas' legs, as a lunging chryseid slashed his spear blade through the neck of the left-hand horse. It reared, screaming horribly, spraying blood that drenched Leucas and made the clay paint begin to smear on Barra's skin. Leucas gathered the reins in one hand, cursing, and then with a single smooth motion drew the bronze sword from his back and cut away the traces holding that horse to the chariot in one swift stroke. "Learned that trick from Nestor himself!" he roared with a laugh that spread his mouth within his blood-drenched face like an open wound.

He fought the reins as the other horse reared away from its injured partner, still driving for the house. A chryseid clung to the rim, and Barra got her feet beneath her and chopped a two-handed gape into its skull. The viscous milky fluid that served it for blood splashed across her face, and the chryseid stabbed clumsily at her with its knife, and she shouted, *"Kheperu! Help me kill this bastard!"*

"I'm right beside you," he snapped. "Don't shout." He reached toward the chryseid, his hand full of some black-tar substance that he slapped across the thing's snarling lipless face. "Stand back."

The tarry substance burst into brilliant white flame, and the chryseid lost its grip on the chariot as its flesh melted and its brain boiled within its skull. Kheperu held up his hand and examined both sides. "Must be sure none of it clings—that would smart quite a bit!"

Something *spangged* off Leucas' armor and dropped into the chariot's bed: an arm's-length shaft tipped with bronze and fletched with gull pinions. *"Arrows!"* Barra shouted, and soon the cry rose across the battle. Men cried out in pain as another flight struck among them. She looked around, searching for the archers—that arrow had hit Leucas in the *back*. There—pale grey in the moonlight, she saw a flight of gull-fletched arrows arching toward them from one of the ornamental groves; and another flight rose from a different grove, and she clenched her jaw. Meremptah-Sifti meant to crush them against his house, and let none escape.

Arrows showered thick as rain around them, the archers uncaring whom they hit. If a chryseid was struck, most arrows would bounce from its leathery skin; any that pierced it were yanked out or had their shafts broken off, and forgotten. A Penthedes man only steps from Barra threw his arms up, his spear tumbling away, as he clutched vainly at the arrowhead that stuck out through his eye; he crumpled to his knees and slowly pitched forward onto his face.

Then Leucas cursed and before Barra could see at what he swore, she found herself tumbling helplessly forward, over the front of the chariot to the ground, where she scrambled away from the screaming, struggling horse. The horse lashed out convulsively, and one hoof caught Barra a glancing blow across the hip that sent her spinning again to the ground. She got a glimpse of its sheared-through front leg and then Leucas rose to his feet and drove his spear through the guts of the chryseid that'd savaged the horse. The chryseid flopped on the spear point like a fish; Leucas roared and lifted it into the air. It clutched at the shaft, howling wordlessly, and Leucas whipped the spear like a staff sling and threw the chryseid tumbling high over a nearby melee—it landed among the struggling men and instantly came to its feet and attacked the nearest. Leucas' eye found Barra.

"Are you all right?" he bellowed. "Where's Kheperu?"

"I'll find him," Barra yelled, coming to her feet at once. "Don't let that horse suffer!"

Leucas stuck his spear headfirst into the ground and drew the iron scimitar, and Barra turned away. Kheperu she found almost instantly; he'd been crouching in the chariot when the horse went down, and had hit his head against the wall. "I'm all right," he insisted dazedly. He staggered a bit as he came to his feet, and he had to lean on Barra in order to stand. "I'm all right," he said again, his voice getting stronger. "We'd best get to the house and settle this business."

She plucked an arrow out of the folds of his robe; spent of its force, it hadn't penetrated the armor he wore beneath. She shook it in his face. "Stick close to Leucas! Try and cover behind his shield!"

Leucas had struck off the wounded horse's head with a single blow. Now he returned the scimitar to his belt and recovered his spear, and pointed off behind Barra. "I think we better run!"

She followed his finger with her eyes. From around the corner of the manor house pelted men wearing the quilted armor of the Egyptian Army, and the colors of the Governor's personal guard. Barra groaned; small wonder the arrows had flown so thickly! The bloody Mother alone knew how many men there were still inside the house. Chryseids, the prince's men, now the elite of the Canaan Division . . .

She whirled back to her partners, whom she had led here to die.

"Guess we'd best go that way," she yelled, pointing to the opposite corner of the house. She took the coil of rope in one hand and her axe in the other, and took off running hard for the colonnade.

Leucas thundered along behind her, his much longer legs nearly capable of pacing her, even carrying Kheperu; he'd said to Kheperu, "Hold these," and handed the Egyptian his spear and his shield. Kheperu, too startled to refuse, took them, and Leucas gathered him up in a bear hug and carried him in Barra's wake.

She rounded the corner of the house and pressed close to the wall, hoping that none within could see her. No one appeared to be up on the colonnade's roof, and when Leucas and Kheperu joined her, the Athenian was able to lift her high enough that she could get a grip on the edge of the roof and scramble up. So far their luck was holding; no one within the house seemed to know they were there.

The battle raged around them as she helped Kheperu up onto the roof beside her, and then they both held the rope for the armored Leucas. She paused a moment, to catch her breath once Leucas was safely up, and looked across the unbelievable carnage that spread throughout these grounds. The flagstones ran with black blood, and the grass was painted with it, and corpses lay strewn here and there like the dolls of a careless child. It seemed incredible that only a few days before she'd been here, on these very grounds, for the Governor's feast of welcome. She'd sat on the rim of that fountain, over there, where now a Penthedes man lay facedown and darkened the water with his life's blood. Agapenthes and his men struggled with the chryseids and the Egyptians close to the wall—and, even as she watched, an arrow struck Agapenthes in the thigh, below his girdle. Blood began to flow, and the old man shook himself like he was awakening from a dream.

Any sudden physical pain, Kheperu had said, *will wake him right up, and then we will all be in a bit of trouble.*

If Kheperu ever decided to get out of the mercenary trade, Barra decided, he could make a fine living as a prophet.

She bleakly pointed this out to him and Leucas. Kheperu looked stricken; even now Agapenthes began to yell at his men to fall back, or surrender. Leucas only shrugged and said, "I suppose this means we'll have to hurry."

Barra put her hand on his arm, and gave his stone-hard bicep a grateful squeeze. "All right."

She shook out the coil of rope. "I'll hold it in the middle," she said. "You keep both ends down here, so once I'm up there I won't have to waste time tying it off. There's a low wall around the roof up there, and there are torch stands sticking out of it—I can just throw the loop over one of those."

"Mmm, wait," Kheperu said, digging within his robe.

"You have something to say, or are you just scratching?"

"Here." He brought out two small pouches, teased them open; within each was a glass pot about the size of her fist, wound in linen that Kheperu carefully unwrapped. "This one, when broken, makes light—quite a blinding flash, actually—and this one makes thick smoke. Just in case you were right, and he's on the roof."

She snatched them out of his hands. "Great, that's great—" He flinched back from her.

"Be careful! They're fragile! You must protect them with your body—hold the rope in your teeth when Leucas throws you."

"What are you, crazy? I'm not going to carry these things up there!"

"Barra—"

She looked up at the roof and whistled piercingly through her teeth. "Hey!" she yelled in Egyptian to get their attention, "Meremptah-Sifti takes it up the ass!" and followed this with the two glass pots, one only a second after the other. They burst with a crash of glass and a hissing sound like a nest of cobras, and the flash of light flared across the sky. Voices cried out from above. "They're up there," she said. "Let's go!"

She stepped up into Leucas' finger-laced hands, gripped the rope, and nodded. He returned her nod, and bent his knees. So did she.

With an enormous surge he threw her into the air; she leaped with the throw and arrowed up over the lip of the wall. She tumbled onto the roof, and into a stinging cloud of smoke that hung near the deck; she popped to her feet and instantly looped the rope around one of the torch stands, before even looking to see where her enemies were. *"Come on come on!"* she yelled, and Leucas sprang to the wall and began to swarm up the doubled rope, Kheperu right behind him.

The smoke drifted in the breeze, beginning to clear already, and the flashpot still burned brightly, lighting the smoke from within, and she could hear Meremptah-Sifti's voice, that chilling Egyptian drawl, calmly ordering someone to "take the bitch." So he knew; he knew it was her on the roof. She hefted her axe and grinned into the smoke. Her nose was useless here, but she could follow the sound of his voice. It wasn't a conscious decision that sent her loping around the

rim of the roof; she didn't *decide* that she couldn't wait for
Leucas and Kheperu; she heard his voice and she went for
him in the instinctive blood lust that sends a wolf pack
against a stag. She stuck close to the upwind wall so that she
could see her footing, and was startled to hear voices shouting
from below: *"The Wild Woman! It's the Wild Woman, on the
roof!"*

Penthedes men, weapons down in the act of surrendering,
stared up at her uncertainly. She realized that with the flash
and the smoke, those below must have thought she'd trans-
ported herself up here by sorcery. Silhouetted against the
white-lit smoke, she shook her axe at them and howled,
"Fight! Fight, you sons of shit-eating dogs! *Fight or I'll come
for you next!"*

They swept up their weapons and threw themselves against
the Governor's personal guard below, and Barra turned once
again to go after Meremptah-Sifti. The smoke had now cleared
so that she could see shapes within it, moving uncertainly
toward the sound of her voice.

Then the wind gusted, and whipped the last of the smoke
away, and the men who crept toward her were Myrmidons.

Back beyond them, Barra saw Meremptah-Sifti, and beside
him the round form of Idonosteus. She howled again; faster
than thought she drew a throwing axe from her belt and
hurled it spinning for Idonosteus' head. And she screamed,
"No!" as the Myrmidon beside him threw himself into the
path of her axe.

It was the young one who'd been excited by the prospect of
action, the same one that Leucas had terrified into summoning Kamades, all those days ago. He covered Idonosteus,
and the axe struck him full on the breast and stuck into his
armor; he staggered back, blood welling around the pitiless
flint.

Meremptah-Sifti said, "I want them alive. Damage them as
much as you like, so long as they are still breathing."

Kamades, his face expressionless, nodded. "Take the
Akhaian first, then the Egyptian. Lalcamas: you and I have
the girl."

They closed on Leucas. He'd left his spear behind, since he
couldn't climb and carry it, and he'd lost his short straight
bronze sword somewhere out in the battle. He whipped the
scimitar around his head menacingly enough, but uncertainty

showed on his face—these were guest-friends, and an injury to them would be avenged by Zeus. This momentary uncertainty was all the Myrmidons needed; six of them leaped upon him together. He roared and cut one at the joining of the shoulder and neck, the keen iron slicing through bronze, but the other five bore him to the ground. Kheperu waded in behind them; he killed the wounded Myrmidon with a staff blow at the base of the neck, below his helmet, then he had three Myrmidons of his own to face. They forced him back, and he gave ground, blocking desperately with his staff against their stabbing spears.

Kamades and Lalcamas, the man who'd held the stable door for her to escape from this place, advanced on her, shields up to their eyes; Lalcamas held a spear low, by his thigh; Kamades held a sword.

"Kamades," Barra said, "call off your men. Remember what you said? You wouldn't obey the order to harm guest-friends, because those could only come from a madman! Remember?"

Kamades' expression never changed, and the *sceon tiof*, that lived now within her eyes, looked at him and saw nothing at all. No will, no choice, none of those things that make a man what he is, in himself.

Across the roof, still clear in the fading light from Kheperu's flashpot, Idonosteus smirked at her. "We decided he should be . . . decorated. Seems now like that was a wise choice."

From beneath the struggling pile of men, Leucas arose with a roar, a Myrmidon hanging upon each arm. The huge Athenian whirled and bellowed and slung one of those two men over the rim of the roof; the Myrmidon screamed as he fell, and hit the paving below with a thunderous crash that cut off his voice.

Kamades turned his head at the scream, only for an instant, and Barra broke past him, streaking for Idonosteus, her broadaxe up and a wild howl erupting from her throat. She was fast; no man could catch her at a run, but they didn't need to catch her. Even as Leucas' knees were unstrung by a spear shaft clubbed into his jaw, even as Kheperu went down beneath his attackers' pounding, Lalcamas cast his spear and struck her deep through the front of her thigh, the spear slicing through and tangling her legs, and she tumbled to the roof. He was to her in a blink of an eye, but that was too slow—she popped to her feet with the bulldancer's kip, feinted at his bare thigh to draw down his shield, and swung full force at his head.

She was no Akhaian, to be god-bound in the oaths of hospitality, and iron is not the only thing that will cut bronze. Her broadaxe sheared through the helm that he wore and opened Lalcamas' brain to the night sky.

She did not pause to watch his shuddering fall, but turned again to make for Idonosteus and something struck her shoulder with staggering force; her right arm went numb and limp, and her broadaxe dropped clattering to the roof.

She spun, and clapped her left hand to her shoulder and howled when she felt the lips of an open wound and the jagged ends of bone within. Kamades stood there, blood on his sword and no expression on his face. She drew her remaining throwing axe with her left hand—and remembered losing her breath at his courage as he faced Leucas and Lysandros in the apartment; and remembered his gruff commitment to save her life, no matter the cost to himself—and in that instant of hesitation, Kamades slapped the axe out of her hand with the flat of his blade and battered her off her feet with his shield.

Stunned, she could only lie there as he put his foot upon her throat and held his sword pointed at her eye.

Some few shouts and screams, not too many, still sounded from the grounds below; on the roof all was quiet.

Meremptah-Sifti strolled casually up beside Kamades, and looked down at her with mock concern. "Your little war is over, Barra Coll Eigg Rhum."

A glorious smile spread across his face like the dawn.

"I win," he said warmly. "You lose."

CHAPTER TWENTY-ONE

War's End

Kamades' foot pinned her to the roof. She didn't struggle. Meremptah-Sifti said, "Let me once again extend the hospitality of my home. You won't refuse me, this time, will you?" He turned to Kamades. "Take them down to the workshop. Tell Sim not to start on them until I finish up with this." His gesture took in the struggling men on the grounds around. "Do no more than restrain them until I get there; I want to watch."

Idonosteus sidled up to him and licked his lips. "*I* could go—"

"Stay with me. There will be nothing to see until I get there."

It took three Myrmidons to carry the unconscious Leucas in his armor, one holding his legs while two more took one arm apiece; another two had Kheperu gagged and his hands bound, and they kicked him stumbling along before them. Kamades took his foot from Barra's chest and knelt beside her. "I'm sorry I hurt you, Barra. I didn't want to, but you shouldn't have killed Lalcamas."

Barra's throat rasped from the screaming she'd done. "It's all right, Kamades, I know you couldn't help it."

The ends of her broken collarbone ground together as he lifted her in his arms, but the wound was still numb—it only made her dizzy, instead of faint with agony. He carried her gently, as a father carries an injured child. "I'm told this Simi-Ascalon is a fine surgeon," he murmured as he carried her down through the open stairwell. "I'm sure he can save your arm."

Her last view of the sky also held the silhouettes of Meremptah-Sifti, standing with legs apart, hands clasped behind him, looking proudly out over his handiwork, and

Idonosteus, standing identically, imitating mastery as he had imitated manhood.

Barra looked up into Kamades' face, searching it for any understanding of the reality of what was happening. She wondered idly which shoulder his tattoo was on. "He's not going to heal me, Kamades; he's going to kill me. Simi-Ascalon will torture me to death."

"Now, Barra, that's just not so," he said, sounding so much like Leucas that it hurt her chest.

The last two Myrmidons walked close behind him. Barra's mind whirled, racing through fantasies of escape—but Leucas showed no signs of awakening, he might be dead, Kheperu could do nothing, gagged and tied, and she was weakening rapidly, going fuzzy with blood loss and defeat. Kamades carried her across the third floor, archers turning curiously away from the windows to watch the procession, and down more stairs, deeper into the manor.

"Your hair looks funny, Barra," he said. "What did you do to it? I liked the other color so much better. And it looked soft."

"Kamades, I know you can't help yourself," she whispered, "but I hope you'll remember. Someday, when this power wears off, remember that I don't hold you responsible for this."

"For what?" he said, frowning. "No one will hurt you, Barra."

She understood now what was happening within him; he was spinning fantasies, to justify following these orders. He was making himself believe that since he was doing this, it must not be wrong—the only way he could justify hurting her as he had, was to believe that he was now carrying her to someone who would help her. Under the power of the tattoo, he was forced to do things which were against everything he believed in, and his mind was searching for ways to convince himself that these things were right.

He would go right on convincing himself while he watched Simi-Ascalon slice her and shred her into bloody death.

She looked at the others, the ones carrying Leucas, the two shoving along Kheperu. They had the same bland certainty that painted away all thought from Kamades' face. And again, she understood: getting Kamades to accept the tattoo would have been easy. Idonosteus would have just told him to. Then, he would pass the order along to his men; they would obey unthinkingly.

Ironic, that the magic only enforced behavior they already practiced.

Barra turned her head painfully to look at the two who brought up the rear. "You understand what's going on, don't you?" she rasped. "You know the dishonor you bring upon yourselves."

One of them—the young one who'd saved Idonosteus by leaping in front of her axe, he had a rag stuffed into the gap in his armor to stem the bleeding—said hesitantly, "The only dishonor I fear is disobedience."

"What are you, *dogs*?" she snapped in sudden anger, and would have gone on at length had Kamades not gathered her head to his corselet and clamped a warm, dry hand over her mouth.

"Don't abuse my men, Barra," Kamades said reproachfully. "If you don't promise to leave them alone, I won't let you talk at all."

They passed through several rooms on the first floor; in one of them, Barra's rolling eyes caught a glimpse of the Governor, sitting morosely on the floor, alone in a corner. In nearly all the others were any number of soldiers and servants of Meremptah-Sifti; of course he had sent the Governor's personal guard into the battle and held his own men back.

Finally, Kamades looked down at her and said, "Do you promise not to say anything against my men?" When she nodded agreement with her eyes he released her mouth.

"All I want," she gasped, gritting her teeth against the grinding of broken bones that she could hear inside her head, "all I want, Kamades, is a favor from you. We're guest-friends, and I'm going to die—"

"You're not going to die," he insisted, but as they descended into the cellar, where he'd risked his life and the lives of his men to save her, he sounded a little less sure of himself, and a slightly puzzled frown came over his face. The other two, who'd been bringing up the rear, now carried lamps they'd lit from the ones on an upper floor. They looked at each other, also frowning.

"Listen, Kamades, whatever happens, you and I both know

I'll never see my home again. But, at the house of Peliarchus, my foster-father, there's a bundle, a . . . a packet. I want you to go there, please, get it, make sure it's sent on a ship to Albion."

"Well, why . . . I don't know—"

"Please, Kamades." She clutched at his armor with her working hand, and tears welled in her eyes. "I'm begging you. I have two sons, one of my own and one a little Akhaian boy that I adopted—and that packet, that's my letters to them, and if you could just write something, to let them know how I died . . ."

She heard the sounds of shifting stones, a heavy scraping with hollow, echoing undertones; some sort of underground door was being opened, here in the cellar, and a wash of air, a breeze warm as human breath, spread a stench around her that she instantly recognized—that mingled black decay and chemical reek could only have come from the demonist's workshop. There was an overlay of burning cedar that hid the worst of it; she clenched her teeth grimly against the gagging rebellion of her stomach, and kept her eyes on Kamades' face. She was getting through to him, not much perhaps, but she thought she saw answering tears in his eyes.

"Please," she whispered, "I don't want to die alone and unknown in a foreign land. Don't leave my sons to forever wonder what happened to me, to look for me at Midsummer's and when I don't come, think it's because I've forgotten them. They'll think it's because I don't love them . . ."

"I . . . Barra," his voice was husky with emotion, "Barra, I swear, I wouldn't bring you here if, if I thought you'd come to any harm. Please—"

Now they descended along steps cut into living rock, and the stone that bounded these stairs to either side showed faint reliefs carved beneath the layers of lampblack. Barra clutched at him again. "Promise! Promise me!"

A single tear rolled down Kamades' cheek, a jewel more precious to Barra than any stone, slowly moistening the creased scar down to his beard. Somewhere, deep within him, she was getting through, some understanding was coming clear. He said solemnly, "You have my word."

The shackles were of bronze, strongly bolted to the rough, unpolished wood of the table. Their edges were sharp, cutting into her ankles and scraping her wrists alongside the bandages that still covered the hyaenae-bites. Against her back she felt the grooves carved into the table, channels that led to three different drains drilled through the table's surface. She hadn't struggled when they bolted her down to this table, even after she'd seen the rich brown stains and blackened flecks of decayed flesh that covered it; with a broken collarbone and a stiffening gash through her leg, she could hardly hope even to hurt someone before they brought her down, let alone escape. Lying flat and still on this table was the only way she could keep the growing pain tolerable, although the blood that trickled from her thigh and her shoulder and into the channels of the table made her flesh crawl, like it was a trail of ants marching down her back.

Simi-Ascalon's workshop was a natural cavern, like the one at the funerary caves, that had been subtly enlarged with skillful stonework. Small tripod copper braziers stood about the cavern, holding pyres of cedar to both light the room and combat the horrible stench. Shadows shifted across the rough stone folds of the walls. This place was larger and better furnished than the one at the caves, lacking also its hasty, improvised look. Simi-Ascalon's workbench was much bigger here, a long well-carved table that bent in the middle to follow a natural corner of the rock, and shelves rose above it, so high that the uppermost would be out of reach of even a very tall man; it was crowded with boxes and scrolls and bottles and implements of every description. A ladder rested against one end of them.

Four worktables held the center of the room; one of them was empty. Next to Barra, Leucas was bolted facedown on his table, and Kheperu, on the other side of him, had given Barra a look that pulsed with some sort of undetermined significance as they shackled him facedown as well. They hadn't bothered to remove Kheperu's robes—none of the Myrmidons had wanted to touch them, and Simi-Ascalon assured them that he'd cut off the clothing himself. The Myrmidons had stripped Leucas of his armor, and now beside her, Barra could see his naked, scarred back slowly rise and fall.

He was alive, then. Another tear leaked from her eyes. *Thank you, Zeus, Athene, whoever it is that watches over him. If we are not to escape this, though, I beg you not to let him wake up.*

Leucas moaned and shifted a little bit, and his eyelids fluttered, then he relaxed back into unconsciousness.

On the other side of the cavern, where Barra tried not to look, were bodies—cadavers, corpses. They were stacked in untidy heaps like shipbuilder's planks, some in roughly pyramidal piles, some leaning up against the walls, five, seven bodies deep; men, women, even boys and girls. Hundreds upon hundreds of them, stacked on the walls in a cleft in the cave that receded into darkness: the dead of Tyre, brought here piled in wagons, no doubt. Now that there was no longer any need for secrecy, the less-comfortable workshop at the caves had probably been abandoned. Barra tried to keep her face turned from there because that was where Simi-Ascalon worked, but the sucking void that was his spirit drew her through the *sceon tiof*; whenever she glanced toward him that blackness grew once again within her mind, drawing her down like a ship caught in Kharybdis.

He was working on one of the corpses, where it stood against the wall, incising designs in its leathery flesh with some kind of gouging tool like a chisel. She glanced at him, unable to stop herself, and his hand twitched and he cursed in fluent, accentless Phoenikian. He stood, and threw down the chisel in disgust. "More warriors, he says. Always more warriors. How am I supposed to work under these conditions? Does he think this is *easy*? You there—Kamades, is that your name?—stack this one with the others, that pile, over there."

Kamades rose; unlike the other Myrmidons, who were clustered nervously near the stairs, he'd been squatting beside Barra's table. Silently he complied, and as she watched him, Barra's eye caught something that she'd missed before: leaning against the wall, half concealed by the stack to which Kamades carried the stiff corpse, was one that stood without arms, and with its split head bound together by soiled linen. She let her eyes drift closed and sent a prayer to the Mother that Meremptah-Sifti had forgotten his promise to give her to Chrysios.

Simi-Ascalon said, "And you! You stop that, stop that *looking* at me. I don't like it."

Barra opened her eyes and glanced toward him. "You mean like this?" Darkness sucked at her, but she ground her teeth and pulled with her right arm against the shackle. The hideous pain of the ends of her collarbone grinding together anchored her against the pull of his void, and she held her gaze on him, and he stepped toward her, his face twisting.

"Stop it!" His voice took on a querulous whine; as he came close, Barra could see the thick makeup on his face, the paint he used to cover the decay of his flesh, and he smelled—even through the stenches of this room, that were fading now as she became accustomed to them, she could smell the acid sweat on this man, the animal musk: fear.

It made her smile.

"I'm tired of it," he said. "I don't like it. I told Remmie he should have killed you before. It feels like, like I don't know what. Like something's *crawling,* inside my skin. Like you're *doing* something to me."

Within her mind, winds tore at her, driving her spirit toward him, but she wrenched her shoulder and clung to the pain. "All I'm doing," she ground out through her clenched teeth, "is *seeing* you. I'm seeing you, for what you really are. If you don't like it, you should have been something else."

His fist flashed out and cracked her across the cheekbone, she tasted blood—and Kamades came at him from behind. "That's *enough*!" he shouted.

Simi-Ascalon whirled in surprise, and Kamades grabbed him by the shoulders and shook him like a rag. "You're supposed to be *helping* her! You're supposed to be healing her!" He lifted the demonist off the ground; Kamades' face was red as an open wound, and his eyes bulged in fury. "Hit her again and I'll kill you!"

"No, you won't," Simi-Ascalon said hastily. "Put me down, and don't touch me again. You others"—he snapped toward the other Myrmidons, who had started toward their captain— "don't move. None of you move."

Kamades' face went blank; he released Simi-Ascalon, and the demonist dusted himself off and recovered his composure. The other Myrmidons stood like statues.

"Now, you will stand where you are, all of you," Simi-Ascalon said, his lower lip jutting out like a pugnacious little boy's. "Don't move until I say. Don't speak. You and I, Kamades, we'll have some fun later. I'll pay you out for putting your hands on me. I think I'll flay you and wear your skin as my new robe. Or something."

Kamades stopped moving; he stood like a statue beside Barra's table, but she could see the veins twist beneath
the reddened skin of his neck—and, just peeking out of the
collar piece of his armor, the black-ink rim of the tattoo that
held him.

"And now for you, you, you *cunt!*" Simi-Ascalon spat.
"You want to see what's going to happen to you? Is that what
you're looking for?" Down, far down deep within his swirling blackness, Barra saw a little boy, faceless, nameless,
playing alone, always alone, hurting things, pulling legs off
frogs, putting hot coals into a cat's rear, hurting himself,
cutting his hands, scraping his face with broken glass. This
wasn't his past she was seeing—it was his nature. He felt it,
he felt it again as she watched him; his face contorted into a
snarl and he writhed convulsively, like a man covered by
fleabites that he can't scratch. "Stop it! I didn't like it in the
Market, and *I can't stand it now!*"

He sprang to the workbench and started throwing things
off the shelves, digging for something, finally coming up with
an octagonal bronze rod as big around as his wrist and as long
as his arm. It was studded with bits and pieces of metal, cast-
ings of hieroglyphs bolted to it. He waved it at her, his eyes
shining with anticipation, his mouth slick with saliva.

"First, I *fuck* you with this, you see it? You understand
what it's going to *do* to you? Then, after you're good and torn
up inside, I leave it in there, you see, and I heat this end in a
brazier, until the whole thing gets red-hot. See? That's why
your boyfriends are face*down*, see? You take it in the cunt,
they get it up the ass! And that's only the beginning! You
want to see it all? Keep looking!"

A sound came from Kamades' throat, a horrible low growling moan, and tears streamed down his face, but he could not
move, could not even blink. Barra wrenched her shoulder,
again and again, grinding bones, holding on to the pain, glar-
ing at him, her eyes locked upon his void. He snarled, "Or
maybe I'll dig your eyes out, first!"

"It doesn't matter," she whispered. "It doesn't matter at all.
I have seen you, Simi-Ascalon. I know what you are. You felt
me at the feast; I can feel you now, whether I look at you or
not. You can take my eyes, but you'll have to kill me to take
the sights I already have."

"I, I would, I would, but Remmie wants me to wait—"

"You're such a frightened little man." Barra managed a forced sneer, contemptuous through her pain.

"What?" He lifted the phallus like a club, like he would beat her with it; his eyes bulged and his face colored with blood.

"You just about crapped in your robe when Kamades grabbed you," she said. "I bet you didn't think he could do that, under your tattoo. You're finding out that your power isn't good for much after all, and it's scaring the shit out of you. You're afraid of Meremptah-Sifti, you're afraid of Kamades—shit, you're afraid of *me*. All your power, and you can't even make one sad-ass wounded Pict girl shut up."

"I can—I can shut those eyes. Don't you doubt it."

"Yeah? What'll Kamades do while you try?"

"Nothing! My power—"

"Is shit. You can't make him do *anything,* really. He just does what you tell him because he's used to following orders."

Simi-Ascalon's eyes bulged as though they would pop from his head, the skin around them turning black with apoplectic rage. "All right," he said, no longer talking to her. "So I will. I can apologize to Remmie later. Things got a little out of hand, that's all. He always forgives me. So—" He chuckled under his breath, and the flesh of his face began to sag as he relaxed. "Kamades, you like her so much, you kill her."

That shivering moan grew louder within Kamades' throat, but he still didn't move.

"You can move," Simi-Ascalon said irritably. "Oh, hurt her a little first—stick your hand into that wound, there, or something."

Kamades' eyes bulged almost like his master's, but he couldn't stop himself: his dirty hand, covered with salt sweat, found the sword-cut and the ragged bone within it. Agony burst white fire into Barra's brain, but she didn't cry out in pain, not quite—this was what she'd been waiting for. She screamed, "Kamades, I love you! Kiss me!"

Simi-Ascalon said, "What?"

Kamades looked down at her, puzzlement suddenly written across his face.

Barra pleaded with her eyes. "Kiss me once before I die!"

He leaned down, tears streaming, to kiss her, and Simi-Ascalon shouted, *"No!"* and Barra lunged up convulsively, ignoring the shattering agony that blazed from her shoulder, and sank her teeth into Kamades' shoulder where it joins the neck.

Right into the tattoo.

Kamades howled from the sudden pain, and blood spurted salty and metallic into Barra's mouth, but she hung on, biting down, shaking her head from side to side like Graegduz worrying a piece of meat off a stag.

Simi-Ascalon sprang to the table, beating at Kamades with the huge jagged bronze phallus, screaming, "No! Get away from her! Get away!" and Kamades shoved himself back from the table with a mighty heave—but he left a chunk of skin behind, in Barra's mouth. He staggered back, hand clutching his shoulder to stem the blood, and his face cleared.

He bent to a fighting crouch, and veins stood rippling out on his forehead and around his eyes, and he moved toward Simi-Ascalon with the slow, lethal grace of a hunting cat.

He said, "Now, Simi-Ascalon, give me another order."

The demonist looked from him to Barra, horror plain as paint on his face. She spat the bloody hunk of skin out onto the floor and grinned fiercely through the gore on her lips. "Go ahead," she said. "See what it gets you."

Kamades sprang at him, but Simi-Ascalon ducked aside and darted around Kheperu's table, still holding the phallus like a weapon. Kamades drew his sword. "You won't leave this room alive," he said.

"Myrmidons!" Simi-Ascalon shrilled. "You can move! *Kill Kamades!"*

They moved slowly out of their statue-like freeze, hands grasping blindly at their sword hilts, tentatively lifting their short spears and sliding their shields into place, and a number of things happened very nearly at once.

Kamades, still unconvinced that Simi-Ascalon's power would prevail over Myrmidon honor, pointed his sword at the demonist. "Take him!" But even as he spoke, Simi-Ascalon snapped, "Ignore all orders but mine, and *kill him now!"* The Myrmidons advanced on Kamades, weapons coming hungrily free; they fanned out into a shallow arc, still the consummate professionals. Simi-Ascalon drew breath to order them again, but yelped in surprise instead, as blinding white fire rose hissing from the shackle that bound Kheperu's left wrist to the table. Simi-Ascalon stared across the table at it with open-mouthed incomprehension and while his eyes were held there, on the other side of the table, a small round ball of black tar flicked from Kheperu's right hand and bounced to the floor, unseen by all but Barra, coming to rest between Simi-Ascalon's feet.

The splintering, moaning crackle of wood being ripped apart drew Barra's eyes away from the smoking tar ball, and she shouted for sudden joy: the scars on Leucas' naked back had turned crimson as every muscle bulged out in knife-like definition. The table beneath him creaked and shuddered and moaned in protest, and one of the shackles around his ankles squealed and shrieked as it tore free of the wood. Barra shouted, *"Now, you bastard! Now you're deep in the shit!"* and her shout was nearly buried beneath the rolling thunder of Leucas' basso laugh.

In the next moment:

Kamades slid under the stab of a spear and drove the man stumbling back with a sharp kick in the guts; he ducked behind Barra's table, where only two of his men could come at him, one to either side. Even as he did so, Simi-Ascalon looked down, horror growing on his face as he realized what was smoking between his feet. He said, "Ah-ahh . . ." and the rest of his speech was obliterated by Leucas' roar of berserk battle joy as his other ankle tore free of its shackle; with a titanic splintering sound the table beneath him broke into pieces and Leucas rose from the wreckage, shackles still on his arms, head-size hunks of wood to which they were bolted still attached.

The sight of naked Leucas, upright and angry, gave the Myrmidons pause. He looked more god than man, and no one was eager to engage him. Leucas didn't wait for them; he roared, "Come on, then! Cowards!" and waded into them, battering to right and left with the huge hunks of wood shackled to his wrists. The Myrmidons scattered; they hadn't been ordered to fight Leucas, and they couldn't get past him to come at Kamades. Simi-Ascalon could have easily amended his orders, but he had problems of his own.

The tar ball at his feet smoked and sizzled; in one rush of recognition, he had realized what it was and now he tried to leap away from the coming explosion, but his single second of frozen realization had been one second too much: with a breath-stealing *whoosh* the tar ball detonated into a huge globe of eye-burning white fire. His robes burst into flames; he staggered back, beating at the flames that licked up his clothing, the jagged bronze phallus clanging on the stone as it fell from his hands.

Kamades, the perfect soldier, had never lost sight of his real objective, of the key to victory; freed by Leucas of the need to defend himself, he sprang like a lion onto and over the tables and launched himself through space to slam his powerful body into Simi-Ascalon and drive the demonist stunned and bleeding to the floor.

The Myrmidons, occupied with Leucas, couldn't find their target, and couldn't get themselves together to handle the whirling, roaring, pounding boxer. A couple of them saw Kamades now, though, struggling to hold Simi-Ascalon down, and turned away from Leucas to come at him from behind. Barra stretched up agonizingly from her table and shouted, *"Kamades! Kill him if he doesn't call them off!"*

Kamades' fist thundered down onto Simi-Ascalon's face once, and again, and the demonist ceased to struggle; he knelt on Simi-Ascalon's chest with his sword at the demonist's throat. "Call them off or die right now."

Simi-Ascalon shouted desperately, *"Stop!* Don't move!"

Barra shouted, "Leucas! Hold it!"

The Athenian stopped and looked around; he still held a semiconscious Myrmidon struggling weakly in midair with one hand, and his other was drawn back to punch. When he saw that the best of the Myrmidons were no longer moving, he let the man go. The Myrmidon collapsed bonelessly to the floor. Leucas said, "Oh. Sorry."

Everyone looked at each other for a long moment.

Kheperu said into the sudden silence, "Could someone get this damned shackle? I can't reach it, and I seem to have burned the shit out of my hand."

And it was over.

Soon Simi-Ascalon was tied up and gagged, and Kheperu was free, and Leucas worked on freeing Barra. The Myrmidons still stood where they had been at the instant Simi-Ascalon had given them their last order.

"How long have you been awake?" Barra asked, as Leucas pulled the bolts out of her shackles.

He shrugged. "A while. Since before you and him started talking." Another one of his rare smiles lit his wintry eyes, although this was a weary one. "I was waiting for what seemed like a good moment."

"Well, you picked it. Any earlier, the Myrmidons would have killed you; any later, they would have killed Kamades."

He shrugged again. "Luck."

"And you," Barra said, looking over at Kheperu, who now sat up on his table and thoughtfully rubbed salve onto his burned hand. "When did you palm the fireball? And you did the shackle with that same gunk you burned the chryseid with, right?"

Kheperu nodded. "I palmed both back up on the roof, while I was pretending to be unconscious. I must say, though, you did a fine job yourself. I really didn't expect to get a chance to use it effectively."

Leucas drew the last bolt, and Barra sat up, wincing and holding her arm very still. "Nothing much," Barra said. "I just never gave up, that's all. Neither did you, either of you."

"Need I remind you?" Kheperu said. "We're an awfully long way from being home safely."

Kamades still stood over Simi-Ascalon. Even though the demonist was now bound and gagged, Kamades kept his sword near the man's throat. Kamades' armor was painted with his blood, that still leaked from the bite wound on his neck.

He said, "What shall we do with this garbage? Will he make a hostage?"

"We don't do anything with him until we get a bandage on your neck," Barra said.

Kamades flashed her a grin. "You could use some bandages yourself, Barra."

Leucas pulled things off the shelves over Simi-Ascalon's workbench until he found some relatively clean cloth. Kheperu bandaged Kamades while Leucas packed Barra's shoulder with folded linen and tied her arm tightly to her chest, shaking his head all the while. "What did I tell you about magic?" he murmured. "Your Pictish battle-magic is all real nice and all, but you should have been wearing armor."

Barra winced at the pressure on her arm, and thought privately that her battle-magic had served her very bloody well, thank you. "Next time," she said hoarsely. "Next time maybe I will."

"Speaking of magic," Kheperu said, standing close by and pretending to be thoroughly interested with wrapping his burned hand with a long strip of cloth, "what was it you were doing to Simi-Ascalon there that got him so upset?"

"Looking at him," Barra said innocently. Truthfully. "That's all. Who knows why it bothers him so much—" She glanced down at Simi-Ascalon; he writhed within his bonds and moaned into the gag, and she had to lean hard on Leucas' shoulder to maintain her balance. "He's probably just crazy."

"Mm-hmm." Kheperu nodded; it was clear from his expression he didn't believe a word of it. "First you can smell the chryseids from far, far away. Now you can drive men mad with a glance."

"I told you before," she said, sliding down off the table and turning this way and that, to check the range of motion she could use without causing her shoulder to scream with pain, "I'm just full of surprises. Now let's kill this piece of shit and get moving. We've got some unfinished business on the roof."

Kheperu stared at her, dumbfounded. "Are you mad? There is still a *battle* going on up there! Or, worse yet, it might be over, and the soldiers returning to the house. You can barely walk, let alone fight. We are unarmed."

Barra said, "But we have the Myrmidons. They have weapons, and we can get some of our own."

"We have a hostage," Kheperu countered, and he gestured toward the darkened cleft in the wall. "And I'd wager that we have a way out of here, as well."

"We're not going to use him as a hostage. We're going to kill him."

"Barra—"

She blazed with sudden anger, and she thumped Kheperu's chest armor with her good hand, even though it hurt her shoulder enough to shoot stars through her vision. "If I thought you'd let him live, after what he was going to do to you, I'd kill you *myself!*"

Leucas rumbled, "I don't much like this idea of killing a helpless prisoner."

Barra wheeled on him. "Maybe if you go over there and look at that, that *thing* he was going to jam up your ass, you might change your mind. Kamades?"

The Myrmidon captain's face was as grim as his voice. "I don't have a problem with this."

"Do it, then."

"All right."

Simi-Ascalon screamed, but his voice was tied within his mouth; and struggled, but his limbs were bound with belts; and begged with his eyes, but found no mercy on any face around him.

Kamades, in his very matter-of-fact, businesslike way, stuck his short straight sword into Simi-Ascalon's belly, slicing upward with a back-and-forth sawing motion as though he were carving a roast, until the blade found the demonist's heart and cut it into a furious crimson fountain.

Barra watched it all, watched the abyssal darkness of his spirit dwindle, recede, and finally fade to nothingness, leaving only the stocky corpse of a Phoenikian-looking man dressed as an Egyptian seshperankh. She nodded to herself; she had a strong feeling that this simple cut of a sword had left the world a much better place. "Take his head," she told Kamades shortly.

It took two strokes of the sword. Simi-Ascalon's head, mouth still tied with the gag, bounced on the floor like a child's rag ball.

The Myrmidons, who had stood and watched this without volition, unmoving, living statues, suddenly staggered and gasped and looked as shattered and stunned as a sleepwalker awakening in the noonday sun of an unfamiliar town. Even the one that Leucas had dropped to the floor pulled himself unsteadily to his feet. Not a face among them looked less than stricken as they comprehended what they had almost done under the demonist's spell.

Several of them extended their hands to their captain; one even threw himself down to clutch Kamades' knees and beg forgiveness. He shook the man off and gruffly brought them to order, and then the screaming began.

Wild, howling eldritch screams echoed in the chamber around them, scaling up from a deep-throated roar to a shrill ear-piercing falsetto and back again. Everyone cringed and

covered their ears—in that small, stone-bounded room the
screams were deafening. After the first instant of shock, Barra
found the source of the screaming.

It was Chrysios.

The armless thing that had been Chrysios writhed on the
chill stone of the cavern's floor, screaming beyond breath,
halting, sobbing shrieks of unendurable agony. And now a
few within the stack of cadavers began to move as well, scattering the stiff corpses around them like branches before a
wind, staggering and falling and rising again, tearing at their
own flesh with their fingernails, ripping back hunks of it over
the bone and arching their necks to scream and scream and
scream.

Barra didn't stop to count them—in the condition she and
her allies were in, one or two could be too many. She had to
shout at the top of her lungs to be heard over the deafening
shrieks. *"Let's get out of here!"*

She found no argument among her companions; they all
scrambled for the stairs. She caught up the demonist's head
by its long braided beard and ran with the rest. Her wounded
leg betrayed her as she tried to race upward, buckling suddenly, but strong hands were there to bear her up: on one side,
Leucas, and on the other, Kamades.

They boiled out of the stairwell into the pitchy cellar, lit
now only by the faint reddish glow from the braziers in the
cavern below. The Myrmidons shifted the heavy block of
stone that closed it, and blocked away the screams, and suddenly there was no light in the cellar at all. Barra said, "Er,
does anyone have a lamp?"

No one did, and certainly no one was interested in going
back down to the workshop to get one. Kheperu said, "One
moment—this is surprisingly difficult to do in the dark."

A few long, dark breaths later that familiar horrid smell
permeated the cellar's air, and Kheperu's *tekat-neha* began to
glow, providing enough illumination for them all to find their
way up to the house above, and to find and light lamps of
their own.

They went in close order, the Myrmidons clustered around
them with weapons drawn as though Barra, Leucas, and
Kheperu were prisoners; but the deception proved unnecessary: no one paid any attention to them at all. A chorus of

screaming chryseids surrounded the manor house, hammering blindly at the walls with their bare fists. More screaming wails sounded out from around the grounds, and within the house all was confusion, panicked soldiers and servants rushing from door to door and window to window, trying to understand what was going on or to find a place to hide. In some rooms the soldiers struggled with Simi-Ascalon's hyaenae, the nightmare dog-things, cutting again and again at their unliving flesh. These rooms the companions passed hastily.

Kheperu nodded, mostly to himself. "His magic is dying with him," he murmured distractedly, as though he spoke while taking notes, "but the life in his chryseids comes from the gods, or from demons—it is his *control* of them that has died."

They came to a doorway that Barra remembered, and instead of passing by to the stairs, Barra said, "Wait here for a minute." She held out Simi-Ascalon's head to Kheperu. "Hold this."

He took it, and she slipped into the room. There, collapsed into a corner and sobbing upon his arms like a brokenhearted boy, lay Tal Akhu-shabb. He didn't look up at Barra's approach; even as she crouched beside him, he only moaned, over and over again, "What have I done? How could I be so weak?"

She touched his arm. "Governor . . ."

He lifted his head and startled back from her with a gasp, pressing himself against the wall. "What are you?"

"I'm Barra, Governor, ah, Briseis—the girl from the feast. Do you remember?"

He squinted at her, trying to see that lovely young girl beneath the clay-spiked hair, and the painted face that was now streaked with sweat and blood, blood that caked her mouth and chin. "There was a girl," he said uncertainly. "She tried to warn me . . . but it was too late . . ."

"I know what he did to you, Governor. It wasn't your fault. You couldn't help yourself."

Fresh tears streamed from his eyes. "I, I did things . . . I allowed things, even ordered them . . ."

The *sceon tiof* was still with her, and it lent unanswerable conviction to her words. She saw within him and knew that everything she said was true. "Your only fault is that you trusted a man who is unworthy of you. You understand? You were *magicked;* you could not have done any other thing than what you were told. You are a good man, who has been betrayed."

Hope blossomed within his wounded eyes; he almost dared to believe her. "Who . . . who are you, really?"

"I'm the girl . . ." she began, then bared her teeth. "I'm the girl that's going to give Meremptah-bloodyfucking-Sifti a bloody good spanking. If you want, you can come and watch."

The view from the roof was a fever nightmare of carnage. Bodies lay everywhere about the grounds, and chryseids staggered drunkenly around them, ripping limbs off corpses, biting into bellies, attacking each other or simply writhing on the ground and screaming at the moon. The survivors of the Penthedes army had run away when the corpse-warriors had gone mad, as had most of the surviving Canaan Division contingent; the chryseids no longer made any distinctions between friend and foe. Some of the hyaenae had escaped from the house and ranged about the battlefield, tearing randomly at living and unliving alike. Every now and then a human-throated scream would join the chorus, as the body of a chryseid savaged turned out not to be quite so dead after all.

The companions had been able to hear Meremptah-Sifti's curses from the floor below. Kamades and Tal Akhu-shabb led the way up the stairs.

The prince of Egypt stood at the retaining wall, shouting, "No! Stop it, do you hear me! *I command you to stop it!*"

Idonosteus stood beside him, his hand out as though to reassure the prince, and he saw them coming up the stairs. "Most High—"

"Something's gone wrong," Meremptah-Sifti said. "This is *wrong,* this isn't *happening.*"

"Most High—" Idonosteus said more insistently, now tugging on the prince's elbow.

"I told you never to touch me," he snapped. "What is it?"

Idonosteus pointed a fat finger.

Meremptah-Sifti turned and snorted, seeing at first only the Myrmidons and the Governor. He looked annoyed. "Tal, I told you to stay downstairs. Go back down and wait until

I send for you. Kamades—as long as you're here, go and tell Simi-Ascalon that something's gone wrong with the warriors . . ." His voice trailed off as it registered on him that the Governor hadn't yet moved to comply with his order.

"Did you not hear me? I ordered you to go back downstairs."

Tal Akhu-shabb slowly shook his old grey head. "No, Remmie. I came up here to watch, and I'm staying."

Meremptah-Sifti looked thunderstruck. "Are you defying me? What is *wrong* here? Has the whole world gone mad? Kamades, take him with you when you go. If he resists, kill him."

Kamades took a deep breath, and sighed it out. "You're not really so much, after all. I think I'm enjoying this."

"What?"

Kamades barked, "Step to the outside," and the Myrmidons parted.

Barra stood there, Kheperu behind one shoulder and Leucas behind the other.

Meremptah-Sifti staggered as though his knees had lost their strength. *"What are you doing here?"*

Barra showed him her bloody teeth. "I came to get my axe."

It still lay on the roof, not far away. She stooped and picked it up with her good left hand, flipped it end for end and caught it again. She held it up at arm's length and sighted along its top, measuring Idonosteus' face. The Head of House Meneides let out a low moan.

Meremptah-Sifti still thought he was caught in a dream. "This is *impossible*! Sim has done this a hundred times! He wouldn't *dare* fail! You can't be here! You can't be doing this!"

Barra said, "Kheperu?"

Kheperu gently tossed the demonist's head so that it bounced across the roof and rolled brokenly to stop at Meremptah-Sifti's feet. The prince looked down, and his hands clutched convulsively at the air, and he gasped *uh—uh—uh,* as though he'd forgotten how to breathe. He fell to his knees and cradled Simi-Ascalon's head in his arms, bundling it to his chest like a baby, and he screamed, *"Noooo!* Ahhh, gods, no!"

Barra looked on him with the *sceon tiof,* as tears streamed from his eyes and he lifted a sobbing face to the sky. There had been some deep connection between them, that went far beyond master and servant; she couldn't see what it was, but seeing Simi-Ascalon dead, holding his remains like this, wounded Meremptah-Sifti in some way so fundamental that it left a sickly taste in Barra's mouth. She turned away from him and fixed her gaze upon Idonosteus.

He backed away from her. "You don't dare harm us," he said hastily. "Shed one drop of the prince's blood and the whole might of Egypt will fall upon this city like an avalanche."

Barra paced toward him. "That protects *him*; what's it do for you?"

"Kamades," he said desperately, "stop her. I order you to stop her!"

Kamades shrugged. "I quit."

"You can't!"

"I have. We'll find a worthy lord to serve, somewhere else."

"But she'll kill me!"

"That's right."

Idonosteus turned his sweat-slicked face back to Barra and licked his lips, still retreating before her. "I'll pay you. A mountain of silver, gold, anything! I'll give you anything!"

"All right," Barra said. "I'll take your life."

He fell to his knees and clasped his hands before his face, squeezing fat tears from his eyes. "Please! I'm begging you! Please, please don't kill me!"

Barra stood over him. Fury filled her, but the cold determination that battled it was what found its way into her voice. "You're worse than Meremptah-Sifti. You're a disgusting little toad—that's an insult to toads. Even a toad will stand and fight to defend its nest. You sold out your own, Idonosteus. You sold us all, and you put my parents in a cage in the Market, and now you're going to die."

"But, but they're not *hurt,* they're all right, it's not like I *killed* them . . ."

"Look around you," Barra said. "Look out there. A hundred men died tonight, and more. How many more were burned on their ships, or were cut down as they tried to flee the city? Every one of those lives is a debt you owe, and this is the only way you can pay up. And you know? It's not even all that, so much, in the end. It's not so much for what you've done, as for what you *are*. Kind of like Simi-Ascalon over there. The world will be a better place without you in it."

She drew back the axe.

He screamed, *"Pleaaaaaa—"*

She buried the axe in his skull, and wrenched it out again with a sound of splintering bone. She stood over his corpse panting, and sweating, and in tremendous pain.

Eventually, Meremptah-Sifti recovered his composure, kneeling there on the roof, with the head of Simi-Ascalon upon his lap. Kamades and the Myrmidons had accompanied the Governor downstairs, to try to organize the surviving soldiers and servants. Leucas and Kheperu remained up on the roof with Barra, and the corpse of Idonosteus.

Barra leaned on the wall, in nearly the same place where Meremptah-Sifti had stood to watch the battle. He said from behind her, "What now, for me? What am I to do?"

Barra turned to face him. "Whatever I decide. Understand? You'll do exactly what I tell you to."

He still knelt on the roof with the head in his hands, but his features had returned to their aristocratic mask. "And if I don't?"

Barra shook her axe at him; she hadn't cleaned it, and splinters of Idonosteus' skull and bloody fragments of his brain spattered across the prince's face. He flinched helplessly, and lowered his head in shame.

"If you don't, I'll probably just kill you and take my chances with Ramses."

He said, his face still lowered, "You know, in the end, we're not so different, you and I."

Hearing this, Kheperu snorted, and he translated for Leucas, who shook his head.

Barra, though, nodded thoughtfully. She said, "You know the difference between us? Why you lost? It's this: all you had was slaves." She looked straight at Kheperu, and at Leucas. "I, on the other hand, have *friends*."

Kheperu gave her a tight little smile, and there was a faint gleam in his eye that might have been a hint of a tear; then he turned away to translate this for Leucas as well.

"So you beat me," Meremptah-Sifti said. "You won, in the end. How does it feel?"

Barra looked out across the bloody battlefield, and listened to the screams of the chryseids.

"This isn't winning," she said softly, painfully. "I beat you, but didn't win."

Then she brightened, and looked back at him, and said in a stronger voice that held a touch of a grin, "You sure as bloody death *lost,* though, didn't you?"

CHAPTER TWENTY-TWO

Barra's Peace

Later, during the weeks of her convalescence, Barra would often wake screaming from nightmares of being shackled once again in the reeking cavern beneath the manor house, and having her mouth tied shut, or having no teeth, or Kamades not being there: having no escape while Simi-Ascalon approached with the bronze phallus. She'd sit up gasping in the darkness, clutching the warm down of the quilts on her own feather bed, in her room in her foster-parents' house, and wipe the freezing sweat from her face, and slump there to wait for Kheperu to bring new cups of cold willow-bark tea to lower her fever.

Sometimes in the cool evenings, when her fever would recede, she engraved a new entry on the mental stone of her Suicide Table: *Take a job in your home town.* She calculated that she'd likely not survive another one.

Sometimes, when the infection in her shoulder made the fever worse, she dreamed of being dead, her blood replaced by milky oil, walking again beside the battered armless corpse of Chrysios.

Sometimes, too, as the fever finally broke, and her collarbone began to knit, the Mother answered her prayers and sent her dreams of the fires, instead.

Grey dawn over the battlefield.

The crows began to flutter down among the dead, and vultures wheeled on the wind high above. Flat clouds the color of slate roofed the world.

Barra sat on the ground, and watched the corpses burn.

Agapenthes had been found, wounded but alive, and he had sent back to Tyre for priests of Ba'al-Berith to perform the funeral rites for his fallen men. Initially, the arriving priests had been horrified at the idea of putting the corpses on pyres and burning them—this was a custom of the barbaric West. The survivors' stories had quickly changed their minds; Barra guessed that cremation would be very fashionable in Tyre for some years to come. The hundreds of corpses from the workshop below had been sent piled in wagons back toward the funerary caves; word would be sent out, and any that were claimed by friends or relatives could be returned to their crypts.

The rest would be burned, even as these fallen soldiers, Penthedes and Egyptian alike, were being burned.

The priests still resisted, until Agapenthes made his offer of one shekel per man. At this, they huddled together and conferred among themselves, and soon a delegate returned to inform the exhausted old man that such rites could be devised—for three shekels per corpse. Eventually, a price of two was settled upon, and the priests went efficiently to work with their improvised rites, counting silver in their heads; this was Tyre, after all.

Each man had his own small pyre. Meremptah-Sifti's olive groves had been cut down to make them, and they burned quickly, scattered across his grounds like the cook fires of a mighty army. The oily, resinous wood snapped and crackled and poured thick black smoke into the sky. Sometimes the wind whipped blinding plumes of it across Barra's eyes.

She sat on the ground and breathed it in, never blinking, as tears ran down her face.

The big bonfire in front of her, the one she looked at more than the others, was by now very nearly burned out. At one point it had towered high, licking the starry night sky with its crackling flames. Now it only smoldered here and there, and blackened bones showed everywhere among the ashes, and skulls answered her stares with lipless grins.

Barra had sat in this very spot, Kheperu on the ground beside her, and Leucas standing with folded arms behind, while she'd watched the chryseids, led by Chrysios himself, form themselves into a wailing line and march toward the huge bonfire, and one by one throw themselves screaming into it, and writhe shrieking among the flames as the blaze consumed their very flesh.

Chrysios had found her, after he'd staggered from the cavern by way of the underground cleft. Barra was still on the roof, and Chrysios fell to his knees on the flagstones below. He'd had some perfunctory repairs made to his face—he could speak, barely, with much drooling and slobbering and repeated attempts to find words that his shattered mouth could form—and he explained that Simi-Ascalon had had no time to do a better job; Meremptah-Sifti had been pushing him mercilessly to create new corpse-warriors. With a line of milky tears leaking down his torn cheeks, he had begged a boon of his victorious enemy.

"You mus' des'roy uz," he begged, with difficulty. *"You canno' know the agony . . ."*

"It's a tough life," Barra had said, her mouth twisting with revulsion.

"Pleazz," he said. *"I did no' choose thiz . . . Thiz was done do me againz my will . . . Ih hurzz, hurzz un'il you can' belee . . . belee . . . you can' unnerssann how ih hurzz. I can 'eel each wound . . ."*

He writhed on the ground before her, the straps that held his head together coming loose.

Barra said, "You can feel each wound? That's what you're telling me? Every one?"

"Where you cu' me, be'ween my legs—I can s'ill feel ih . . . hurzz. Hurrzz. Others . . . they feel their organs ripping ou' from their bodies, feel uh s'raw tha's in their gutz . . ."

"The other ones can feel the straw they were stuffed with? Inside? And they still feel their . . . and the rest?" Barra looked away, imagining against her will how it would feel to walk in agony like that, and know that you are immortal, and that your pain will only increase.

"Pleaz . . . Fire . . . need. Burnnnn . . . pleaz burnnnn . . ."

Barra could only nod.

Chrysios had struggled to his knees, and his improvised mouth worked agonizingly to make one last sentence intelligible. *"Burnnn mee, and I forgi'; forgive you, forrrgivvve you for killinnng me . . ."*

Barra looked down into his parboiled eyes, and remembered that she'd once found him handsome. Her gorge rose, and she hurried away from the edge of the roof, so that he wouldn't see her vomit.

And so he got his fire, he and those like him. There were rumors, in the days that followed, that not all of the chryseids burned themselves, that some still roamed the streets of Tyre in the night, when they would not be seen for what they were, and stood near to the homes where they once lived and called in soft, despairing voices for their loved ones. But these were only rumors.

Many of the unliving hyaenae had escaped into the night; they would be hunted by packs of nervous men for weeks to come.

Barra had watched the burning of the dead, and felt cleansed in her spirit.

All the dead were burned, even Simi-Ascalon and Idonosteus; vile though they had been, they received cleansing pyres that would send their spirits with some honor into whatever lands they might tread.

The gods pass judgment only on the acts of the living, and dishonoring the dead never goes unpunished.

After some consultation with Barra and the Governor, Agapenthes (as the sort-of general, willy-nilly, of the winning side) decided to accept, on behalf of the citizens of Tyre, compensation from Meremptah-Sifti. This was arranged to take place some days later, after Barra was able to be up and about again. She wasn't well; sickness had settled into her lungs, she coughed a great deal and tired swiftly. But her fever had broken, and she insisted on being present nonetheless. Long experienced in scribing contracts, and thus having detailed knowledge of the proper forms of Egyptian official communication, Barra herself dictated the letter that Meremptah-Sifti wrote to his grandfather.

In that letter, the prince described how he had been duped and magicked by his steward Simi-Ascalon, who would certainly have raped Tyre and would perhaps have made of himself a power that even Egypt might fear, with his army of animated corpses. This letter described how Simi-Ascalon had taken Tyre and how only the heroic actions of Leucas Deodakaides of Athens, Kheperu of Thebes, and Barra Coll Eigg Rhum of Great Langdale had stood between Tyre and utter ruin.

In "gratitude for my timely rescue" he wrote that he was donating all his Tyrian holdings to the people of the city, to be administered by Agapenthes of House Penthedes. The letter also asked for an immediate loan of one hundred thousand silver debens—each deben contained silver equivalent to about three Athenian weights—to "compensate the good citizens of Tyre for the horrible suffering my treacherous steward inflicted upon them," which he would repay from his personal holdings as soon as he could return to Egypt to sell them off.

"One hundred thousand!" Meremptah-Sifti had said. His fist clenched, and the reed pen snapped. "This will *pauper* me!"

Barra had shrugged, and looked across him to the Governor, who also stood behind him, reading the letter over his shoulder. She said, "I think the prince here could have been hurt in the battle against his treacherous steward, maybe even *badly* hurt."

The Governor put on a mock frown and touched a finger to his pursed lips. "You mean the unfortunate incident that cost him, oh, let's see, perhaps his left hand? Ramses will be most upset—but, of course, still grateful that the life of his grandson had been saved. Don't you think?"

Meremptah-Sifti looked from one to the other, and decided that despite their bantering tone, they were both deadly serious. He drew another reed pen from the case, dipped it, and continued to write.

"This is not over, between us," he muttered. "This will never be over, not while you live."

Barra draped her left arm across his shoulders—though the infection in her shoulder had begun to subside, her right arm was still bound immobile to her chest—and she leaned down so that she could speak directly into his lovely face. "You've got that backward, Remmie. This won't be over while *you* live. And the only place in the world that's safe for you is right here in Tyre. Of course, here in Tyre, everybody either thinks, one, you're a dummy who got taken by his steward or, two, you're a rotten prick who got his ass whipped by three rag-tailed mercenaries. You're a joke. I don't imagine you'll be staying."

He shook her arm off as though her very touch were loathsome. "Don't think that I fear you. Don't think I can't find you."

"I don't want you to fear me, Remmie," Barra said. She

summoned all her energy, to force a tone of solid conviction into her voice. "I want you to forget all about me. That way, when I catch you someday outside this city—someplace in Egypt, maybe—it'll come as a nice surprise. If you can find me, I can find you. And I will. My gods have a law concerning murderers."

The prince gazed up into her eyes; the swelling her fists had left on his chin was gone, and the bruise nearly faded; he was again heartbreakingly beautiful. "When I first heard of you—when I heard the tale of your capture of Idonosteus' bear—I knew that our destinies would tangle. I thought of you as a gift of fate. I thought that you would be mine."

"Not bloodyfucking likely," she said tiredly.

"If we had met—"

"Don't even try," she told him. She shook her head. "If I'm a gift to anybody, maybe it's to some of these poor bastards in Tyre, don't you think?"

After a moment, Meremptah-Sifti once again bent his head to the page, to write at her command.

The Governor frowned, and stroked his snowy braided beard. "I wish there was something else, something more we could do to you, Remmie. I don't suppose there is any way to punish you as you deserve, but I wish . . ." His voice trailed off wistfully.

Barra shrugged and drew her broadaxe. Though to her weakened arm it felt heavy as an anchor, she flipped it into the air, caught it again. "Want to see him dance like a chicken?"

The Governor frowned at her and began to shake his head, but as he watched the image in his mind, his eyes lit up.

Lysandros—Murso, or whatever name he chose—must have slipped away on the night of the battle. He, Barra figured, was as guilty as Idonosteus; she added his name onto her mental list, right behind Meremptah-Sifti's. *Someday,* she promised him in her heart. *Someday, you murdering bastard.*

Agapenthes threw a grand feast of celebration, for the victory that freed Tyre, and put on games in honor of his fallen men. He could well afford to; in addition to all of Meremptah-Sifti's holdings, Agapenthes had now merged House Meneides and all its possessions into House Penthedes. Idonosteus' sexual tastes had, unsurprisingly, left him without heirs. Agapenthes had been, even before this, the wealthiest man in Phoenikia; now his wealth rivaled the great fortunes of Babylon and Knossos.

Barra attended in a place of honor, along with Peliarchus and Tayniz, Kheperu and Leucas, Demetor and the Kypriots. It was an all-day affair within the Penthedes compound, and at intervals it spilled out into the streets, with drunken dancing and singing and scattering of gifts. The occasional fight was let run its own course, without interference. The Governor had wisely pulled the entire Canaan Division out of Tyre, and ordered the garrison commander to keep his troops indoors; the uniform of the Egyptian army would be unpopular here in Tyre for some time to come. As for the soldiers of Meremptah-Sifti, none could be found. Here and there burned pieces of bloodred and purple livery were discovered, but no one would ever admit to having worn it.

The days of Meremptah-Sifti's domination of Tyre faded into the past, a half-remembered nightmare for most; for some—some battered children, some widows, some cripples— it would fade more slowly, if at all.

At the feast, Agapenthes and Demetor both got staggering drunk, and ended up in each other's arms, swearing eternal friendship above and beyond the blood ties that bound them. Kheperu vanished periodically, for an hour or two at a time, to return with a gentle smile on his lips and, often, the arm of a prominent Tyrian about his shoulders. Leucas took part in the games, winning both the boxing and the weight-throw, taking runner-up in wrestling, and placing third in the spear-throw. Barra watched the games enviously, especially the runners; she was sure, that if she hadn't been injured—and trying, even now, to cough up her lungs—she could have placed high, even against the men, perhaps even beaten them all. She'd been nursing a secret dream to compete in the Trade Games at Knossos in the spring, and run against the fastest men in the world. She tucked away choice bits of meats and cheeses to take home to Graeg, whose leg was healing nicely.

She looked around the feast for Kamades, and the Myrmidons, but they weren't there. Kamades had been to see her a few times during her fever, but he had seemed uncomfortable: he hadn't said much, nor had he stayed long.

Peliarchus and Tayniz sat quietly at the feast, and ate little. A cloud seemed to hang over them, darkening their faces, and once Barra noticed, she pestered them until Peliarchus told her what he was upset about.

"I can't seem to get over it," he told her, running his finger over the now-powerless tattoo beneath his shirt. "Sitting in that cage, waiting for you to appear. I *wanted* them to catch you, Barra; I can't believe—I don't care what magic it might be, I can't believe it would make me want to hurt you. Great bleeding Mouth. If you listen to Agapenthes over there, he broke the spell over him by a heroic effort of will and led his men to glorious victory."

"Mm, well," Barra said, "not that I'd accuse the lord Agapenthes of being less than truthful, but he's a bloody liar. He came out of it at the same time you did, the same time everyone else did—when Kamades killed Simi-Ascalon. And as soon as he did, he dug down under a pile of dead men and hid."

Peliarchus only grunted.

"And seeing you at the feast, when they held you like that and showed you to everyone," Tayniz said. "Your poor face— I've never been so frightened in my life. I have nightmares about it."

Barra turned her head, looking away to where Kheperu chatted up a blushing Penthedes cupbearer. "I have nightmares of my own, now and then. They'll stop, in time."

"And this is the sort of thing you do all the time?" Tayniz asked. "How can you bear it?"

"It's not usually this bad," Barra told her. "Sometimes, it's kind of fun."

"I remember when I first met you," Peliarchus said. "I think you were about eight or nine years old, your whole body covered with freckles 'cause you weren't old enough to rate summer clothes, and the whole month I was in Langdale you followed me around and pestered me to teach you Phoenikian. Looking back on it, I guess I have to say it's a good thing I'm such a soft touch."

Barra didn't need the *sceon tiof* to tell her what her foster-parents needed to hear. She reached toward them, and took a hand of each. "I really love you, you know. You are the parents I always wanted, when I was little. I dreamed about having a mother who'd take care of me, and a father who didn't live across the Eirish Sea and I . . ." She blinked back sudden tears. "I'm just really lucky, that's all."

"We're the lucky ones, Barra," Peliarchus said. "And every person in Tyre today would agree with me."

Tayniz snuffled, and wiped her eyes, and said, "And what about this Kamades? He came to see you three times. Is he married?"

Days passed, and Barra's lungs gradually began to clear, and her strength began to return.

Word had trickled through the House Penthedes backstairs gossip that Agapenthes had sold the apartment block where the Myrmidons kept their household to the Jephunahi, who were evicting all the tenants and converting the apartment block into a fortified warehouse for spices, oils, and wines. Hearing this rumor, Barra had sighed, "I'd better go talk to Kamades." Leucas and Kheperu had insisted on accompanying her; in Kheperu's words, "Anyone who takes orders that well cannot be trusted."

On the walk to the apartment, Kheperu had badgered her until she reluctantly began to talk about Kamades. "It's not that I want him as a lover," she said. "Not really at all. I mean, he's very attractive, in a weathered kind of way, but—"

"Kamades, I love you! Kiss me!" Kheperu snickered.

Her shoulder itched fiercely beneath its bandages, reminding her that punching him would likely hurt her more than it would him. "That was *tactics*," she said severely. "Don't laugh—that kiss saved your life, too."

Kheperu acknowledged this with an acquiescing bow.

"He's just so serious," Barra went on. "If I wanted to get married, I'd give him some real consideration. But I don't think he'd be a lot of fun at parties."

"So why," Leucas rumbled, "are we going to see him?"

Barra grimaced. "I feel bad for him. I feel responsible, you know? I'd bet it was rescuing me at the feast that made Idonosteus have him tattooed—tattooed because he's too useful to kill. That feast was when he found out that Kamades couldn't be trusted." She shook her head. "He found out that Kamades couldn't be trusted to do something rotten and dishonorable just because he was told to."

"And you killed one of his men."

"That's got nothing to do with it!" Barra flared. "That son of a dog just about *gutted* me!"

Leucas only shrugged. The Myrmidon he'd thrown from the roof had broken a leg; he'd broken the heads of a couple more down in the workshop. The other Myrmidon, the one Leucas himself had killed, had been named Glandys; and Leucas' face would fill with blank pain whenever he thought of him.

Nothing more was said on the subject. Barra made Leucas and Kheperu wait in the street while she went up alone.

The Myrmidons had little gear beyond bedrolls, armor, and weapons; everything was well packed away when Barra was admitted to the apartment. Kamades was silently policing the rooms, to make sure his men had left no trace of their passing. When Barra entered, he acknowledged her uncomfortably, and went back to his inspection.

"Kamades," Barra said, coming close to him, but his cold reserve stopped her from taking his arm. She let her hand fall, defeated. "Where will you go now? Back to Phthia?"

He glanced at her, then went back to examining the dust at the base of a wall, and shook his head. "We can never return. We will find some new lord to serve, one with some honor of his own, perhaps."

"You know," Barra said slowly, "you never told me why you left Phthia in the first place."

Now he regarded her, his mouth a grim line. He spoke softly, so that his men would not hear. "I suppose it doesn't matter. You have seen me disobey, and abandon my lord in danger, even to allowing his death—no further dishonor could lessen your opinion of me."

"Lessen? Kamades—"

"Neoptolemos, the son of Lord Akhilleus—after Troy, when we returned to Phthia, he had the rule, and our service. But"—his face twisted—"but he wanted us to return to the farms our fathers worked, we whose trade was war, we who had known no other life for ten years, but war. His father had made of us warriors; we had no skill with land. We met among ourselves, and elected one man to go to the lord Neoptolemos, and ask him if we mightn't find some other employment. Neoptolemos, he has a temper, and when . . . this man . . . presented our suit, he was angered. He shouted that we were disloyal, for questioning his orders, and that if we wouldn't be farmers, then we should be gone. This is why we cannot go back to Phthia."

"He sounds like a jackass to me," Barra said.

Kamades frowned severely. "He was my lord. I should never have questioned him."

"It was you?" Barra said. "You were the one who went to him?"

Kamades looked away. "That was the seed of rot; that is when I started down this path of dishonor."

"Loving bloody Mother!" Barra exclaimed. "Kamades, you are more in need of a drink than any man I've ever met! I know a place—"

"Barra," he began, misery showing plainly on his face, "I must apologize to you. I think I have led you on."

"Hah?"

"I know that I approached you . . . ah, as a man does a woman, and I do find you desirable, really I do, but . . ."

"But . . . ?" Barra led, hoping that her rush of relief didn't show on her face.

"But, Lalcamas—I know you couldn't help it, it was in battle, but every time I look at you, I see his poor dead face, and, and well, he and I, we were friends, we were boys together. And my men are my responsibility, and I lost Glandys as well; it is my fault they are dead, my fault for having taken service with an unworthy lord . . ."

"Don't think about it," Barra said. "So, what you're saying is, that you just don't think you can get involved with me, is that it?"

"Barra, I'm sorry—"

"No, no," she said, acting like she was putting up a brave front, while underneath she was so relieved that her knees had gone weak. "Can we still be friends, do you think?"

Kamades looked dubious.

Barra said, "There is this publican, who owes me his life, you see? His name is Lidios, and he told me the other day that I have the freedom of his house for as long as I live. That means, I can take you and all your men there and get you so drunk you can't see, and it won't cost me a copper shekel."

"You would do that? Even though . . . you and I don't . . ."

"On one condition," Barra said. She scratched at her

bandages thoughtfully. "You have to promise that we won't talk about Tyre at all. All I want to hear about, all night long, is Akhilleus and Patroklos, Diomedes and Odysseus, Agamemnon, Menelaos—nothing but the Siege of Troy."

Kamades thought it over, and slowly he sighed, and allowed himself a gentle smile. "All right."

As she took his arm to lead him out, she murmured, "And, I've heard that the silver mines at Laurium, just down the coast from Athens, have been raided pretty hard over the past two years or so. The Twin Princes might be looking for some good men to keep order down there . . ."

"Oh, really?"

As her shoulder healed and her cough faded, Barra took to a habit of long walks in the hills around Tyre; now that winter had come, the days were shorter and cooler, and if one doesn't mind getting wet in the occasional thunderstorm, the walking was very pleasant. Graegduz went with her on these walks, limping at first but soon running with all his old speed after hares and snipe, and she was always armed—she wasn't fool enough to believe that Tyre was any safer than it had ever been.

Sometimes she walked for hours; sometimes she'd just find a comfortable hillside and sit, or throw rocks, or strengthen her arm with some halfhearted axe practice. But always, always looking out over the dark, straggling greens of the bushes that clung to a precarious existence among the sand and rocks, always looking into the desert and dreaming of home, of the lush grassy hills and dense, impenetrable forests of the Isle of the Mighty.

Leucas and Kheperu found her there, sitting on a stone outcropping and chucking rocks down the hill. Graegduz ranged the dry watercourse beneath her, nosing for hedgehogs among the rocks.

Leucas crouched beside her; on the other side, Kheperu plumped down and dangled his feet down the rock face, kicking his heels against it like a child.

Kheperu said, "He's healing well," indicating Graegduz, who seemed to have discovered something in a sheltered cleft; he happily skipped back away from it, and darted in again. "I'm glad of that. And I was curious about your shoulder."

Barra shrugged. Six weeks had passed since the battle; the season had advanced nearly to the Turning of the Sun. The wound was still covered with the remnants of a ragged scab, that Barra picked at when no one was looking, and her shoulder was still sore, and weak, but soon she'd be fully recovered.

"We've been thinking," Leucas said, "of moving on. Tyre is expensive."

She nodded, still not looking directly at either of them. They'd elected not to wait for the caravan from Egypt that was even now on its way with the hundred thousand silver debens; by arrangement with Agapenthes, they'd taken their shares out of Meremptah-Sifti's household goods. In addition to some fine clothing, and household implements of silver and gold, the companions had received five of Meremptah-Sifti's beautiful mares, three geldings and a dazzling white stallion. Barra had spent most of her share buying the spare horses from her friends; they'd make a princely gift for Idomeneus, king of Crete, when Barra went there for the Trade Fair in the spring. A gift like that should get her bumped up from the merchant quarters of the palace at Knossos to the royal chambers—then she could *really* do some business. Kheperu and Leucas, on the other hand, finding themselves cash rich, had been living high for this whole past month of Thirisin: throwing parties, buying expensive gifts for their expensive whores, gambling almost endlessly. Barra had known for days that the two would be ready to go pretty soon: they were running out of money.

Leucas said, "We wanted to know if you'd be coming with us."

Barra looked down at her fingernails. Under the forced inactivity of her wound, they'd grown out, and Tayniz had tended them, and her calluses had begun to fade. Her hands were slowly beginning to look almost ladylike. She said, "I lied to you, Kheperu."

"Really?" The Egyptian seemed more interested than surprised. "When?"

"That night. In Simi-Ascalon's workshop, when I said I didn't know what it was that was driving him so crazy."

"Oh?" he encouraged her.

She sighed. "I have a power, I guess. It only began to develop recently. It's a Pictish thing, called the *sceon tiof*. It comes and goes; I never really know if it's going to work, or not. But when it does work, well, I can look at someone and know them, like I've known them all my life."

"Hmpf," Kheperu murmured. "You have so many little secrets, Barra."

She could hear the frown in Leucas' voice. "You mean you can know their past, like a diviner? Or know their thoughts like a god?"

She shook her head. "Neither one. It's like, I don't know anything about them, except what kind of person they are. It's like when you look at a brother, or a friend you've known for twenty years, you don't think about things that have happened to them, but you just have a sense of what it is that makes him who he is, what makes him unique, I guess. You *know* him. I never wanted to be able to do this. In fact, I've been worried sick about it."

"An interesting ability," Kheperu said, squinting at her narrowly. "Why do you fear it?"

Barra grimaced. "Just imagine—imagine that every time you go into battle, you're fighting your best friend. Every time I see a man with this power, I see him like, like a beautiful sculpture—I see that there is no one else like him in the world, and if I kill him, I'm taking something away from the world that can never be replaced." She shook her head again, exasperated. "It's not even that. I don't even have words for it, really. I still, even now, feel bad about Idonosteus."

"It didn't seem to bother you at the time."

She turned and looked into his eyes. "I've been thinking about retiring. I probably would have quit before this, but Meremptah-bloody-Sifti would have . . ." Her voice trailed away.

"Let me see if I have this straight," Leucas said. "You're wanting to retire because it, kind of, *hurts* you when you fight. But you didn't quit before this, because . . . it would have hurt you *more* to watch what was happening to Tyre, and to your parents, and everything else. Have I got this right?"

Barra nodded. "But now it's over."

Kheperu smiled knowingly. "It's never over, Barra. Why, even now, a pair of Kena'ani kings are in Tyre, hiring mercenaries to defend Jebusi. It seems the Habiru are gathering their tribes together for another round of conquest, and you know what they're like. You've heard, no doubt, what they did to Jericho?"

"Yes," Barra said slowly. The massacre of every living creature in the fortified town of Jericho had been a campfire tale for at least ten years. "Yes, I have."

"It seems to me," Leucas said, "that you don't have to quit. Maybe you only need to be more careful who you work for. The way I see it, the only thing that's really changed is that you've found out that there are some things more important to you than money."

"Bite your tongue!" Kheperu snapped.

"Let's say, *as* important," Barra said. She got up, and whistled for Graegduz. "I said I'd been thinking about retiring. I didn't say I was going to. Jebusi is a good destination—overland, so we don't have to worry about storms at sea, and it takes us to the fringe of Egyptian control."

"And you'd be helping people defend their homes," Leucas said with a wise smile. "Maybe you're less of a mercenary than you've always thought, and more of a hero."

"I don't think so," Barra said. "You'd best believe I wouldn't do this work for free."

"So wait," Kheperu said, rising beside her. "If it's not an excuse to quit, why'd you finally tell us about this seeing thing of yours?"

Barra smiled. "We're friends, aren't we? Maybe I'm getting tired of keeping so many bloody secrets." She clapped Leucas on the shoulder, and almost did the same to Kheperu—she stopped herself barely in time, remembering that out here there was no water with which to wash her hands. "Besides, I can't quit now. I have just enough money for a down payment on another ship."

Leucas said, "*Another* ship?"

"You have a *ship*?" Kheperu screeched.

Barra looked down to where Graeg scrambled up the rocky sides of the watercourse toward them, and she bit her lower lip. "Well, one," she lied. "I'm a part owner. Just a little one, for short coastal trips . . ."

The beach at Tyre was no longer packed with ships, but a fair number came and went, sticking close to the coast to ply their routes, risking winter storms for the greater profits of the winter trade. The storyteller squatted on the beach, bent back resting against a sun-warmed hull, cloak wrapped tight around and hood up to keep old bones warm, perhaps, or to shade a pale face from the sun.

This was the fourth straight day the storyteller had been here, on the beach, telling again and again *The Rescue of Tyre*. Children and beachsiders knew the story, some almost by heart; often children would imitate the storyteller, sitting cross-legged on the sand and chanting along with the lines of the tale. Sailors from the calling ships often clustered around, listening intently; they'd heard confusing rumors about what had happened in this city, but this storyteller seemed to have the whole truth, and was able to tell it in a bewildering variety of languages.

". . . And with the mighty crash of the thunderbolt, Barra appeared on the roof, for the barbarian gods that love her set her down there to win the war. She cut her way through the prince's bodyguard with swift ease, her axe whirling as though it held life of its own and danced for its joy in the battle. And then Kheperu the Cunning cast a mighty enchantment that broke the spell of the treacherous steward," was the point the storyteller had reached on this particular day, when Leucas and Kheperu appeared on the beach, walking thoughtfully to the back of the crowd that listened so intently to the story.

The storyteller looked up and caught Leucas' eye, and went on with a wink: "And then Leucas, a man like the god-sired heroes of old, whose like has never been seen since Herakles the Mighty was set upon Olympus, crushed the great stones of the wall to powder with a blow of his fist . . ."

Leucas turned to Kheperu and murmured in a low voice that no one around them could hear, "Every time she tells this story, it gets bigger and bigger."

Kheperu shrugged, smiling. "She's right, though; if we want to command the top rates, it'll help if people have heard of us."

"I only wish she wouldn't exaggerate so. It's embarrassing."

On the beach, surrounded by her rapt audience, Barra went on, ". . . when warlike Odysseus and Diomedes the spear-famed scaled the god-built walls of Troy in the pitchy night to steal the Palladion from the very Temple of Athene, it was but a poor foreshadow of the valor and skill of the three heroes of Tyre . . ."

I'd call this success, she thought, smiling to herself as she spun out her tale. *I'd call this being happy.*

EPILOGUE

Dear Antiphos and Chryl,

I hardly know where to begin. It's certainly been an eventful few weeks. There was a little bit of difficulty with my last job, here in Tyre, but everything has turned out well, in the end. My shoulder is healing nicely. Here's a good rule for you: never turn your back on a man with a sword, even if you're pretty sure he won't hurt you. If you're wrong, it's a nasty surprise.

That mercenary captain I told you about—my admirer—has left with his men for Laurium. I'm not going with him. His name, again, is Kamades. When you two boys travel down here, if you're ever in need of help in the vicinity of Athens, go to Kamades. He is one of the finest men I have ever known, and you can trust him with your lives.

I wish I could give you similar advice about Tyre, but if I were you, I'd trust no one here but your Uncle Peliarchus. I've had about enough of this city, and I'm glad to be leaving.

King Demetor—he's the one from Kypros, you should remember from the last packet—he visited here in Tyre, and he had a little trouble again, and we saved him again, and actually, he's a pretty good old man. He's another one you could always come to, if he's still alive. If you tell him you are my sons, he'll give you the palace and all its furniture.

It looks like I'll be traveling with Kheperu and Leucas for some time to come. We had some testing times, here, and I've learned that these two are as brave and trustworthy—and as skillful—as any men alive. Leucas turned out to be a lot smarter than I originally thought, and Kheperu is a lot more honest—down deep, anyway. I

*think someday I'll even bring them back to Great Lang-
dale, so you can meet them.*

*I suppose what it is I want you most to know is this:
wherever you go, find the best men and women there are,
and do your best to be their friends. You can never have
too much money nor too many friends, that's what I say. It
can save your life.*

*I can't make this a longer letter; I have a caravan to
catch. Give my love to everyone, and mind Coll, and do
your lessons. I still think I should be able to be home for
Midsummer's. Tell Llem that I should be in a prime position for negotiating new tin contracts at Knossos in the
spring; I've found a bribe that I know King Idomeneus will
love. If your grandda Ouendail should visit, tell him I hit a
fella with the haymaker he taught me, maybe twenty years
ago, and got my face busted for my trouble. And Coll. Tell
Coll that she and I will have a lot to talk about, when I get
home. A lot.*

I love you both very much.

Take care,

Mother

*P.S. I'm sorry there's no gifts with this letter; I'm a bit
short of money right now. However, I've got a job, coming
up: there's this people called the Habiru, and they're getting together to attack a big city called Jebusi, under their
old general Joshua ben Nun. They're kind of a queer
people, from what I hear. The story is, they carry their god
around with them in a box, can you imagine? I don't know
that this is true, but I do know they have decided that their
god has given them Jebusi to be their own city.
Adonizedek, the Jebusite king, is hiring lots and lots of
mercenaries, so I'm going to go and help him defend his
city. These bloody Habiru don't even know the real name
of the place; they call it Jerusalem.*

Sounds like easy money to me.

The adventures of Barra
and her companions
continues in
Jericho Moon,
available from Roc Books
in April 1998.

Prologue

The storyteller sat cross-legged on a thin cloth pallet stuffed with straw; a shallow bowl holding a scattering of silver coins lay on the sandy flagstones near the storyteller's bony knees. An enormous wolf drowsed alongside, his head resting on massive paws. Only the clink of silver coin would prick open the wolf's eye, and his low growl was more than enough to discourage those who might think to take a coin, rather than leave one.

The storyteller's pallet rested on the fringe where the Market of Tyre, the centerpiece of the Phoenikian mercantile empire that stretched from the Indus Valley to the Pillars of Herakles and beyond, bordered upon the protected beach where the Phoenikian sailors—the greatest sailors the world had ever known—drew their longships up onto the land to unload their exotic cargo.

This same storyteller had squatted here for months, now, through a long and bitter winter, and had told endless variations of a single tale: How the Three Heroes of Tyre—Leucas of Athens, Kheperu of Thebes, and the barbarian princess Barra of far-off Albion—had saved the city from a mighty sorcerer of ill intent. Passing sailors would stop to listen, and sometimes drop a coin in the bowl, and they had carried the tale with them on their journeys across the sea; caravan guards did the same on the overland routes. It was a good story; it told well, and better yet, it was mostly true.

But even the best story grows stale with time, and now fewer children than ever gathered around to hear it, and of men, fewer still. On one chill spring morning with the waning moon still high in the sky, in a mist that billowed in from the sea, there was only a single listener, an older, hard-looking man wearing the hooded burnoose of an inland Canaanite. He squatted before the storyteller, and listened with squinting attention, nodding to himself as familiar parts of the tale came around; the parts where the magician Kheperu burned a thousand men with the flame from his fingertips, where Leucas broke stone walls with a blow of his fist, where Barra disappeared and appeared again with the flash of a thunderbolt, and fought with a magic axe that danced in her hands like a living thing.

A coin rang faintly in the bowl, and the man asked the storyteller, "And if a man wanted to find these Three Heroes of your tale, how would he do that?"

The storyteller looked down at the bowl in amazement: The coin this man had dropped was no silver shekel, but a disc of solid gold. She looked back at the man with a mercenary gleam in eyes the unsettling blue-green color of a stormy sea.

"Shit," Barra said, "for that kind of money, I'll introduce you myself."

Dear Chryl and Antiphos,

Well, it looks like we'll be heading out to Jebusi after all. This ought to shut up Kheperu's eternal bitching about how poor he is; he is absolutely the whiniest man I have ever met. Leucas, of course, never complains about anything, but he was getting pretty antsy, too.

Neither of them trusts me, is what it is. I mean, the king of Jebusi is paying five shekels a day—which is a bloody good wage around these parts, what with all the Trojan veterans driving the price down, not to mention the deserters from the Hittite army now that the Phrygians are carving them up in every battle—but it's a flat rate, no shares of loot involved. Sure, it's easy work (I don't think even the bloody fool Kelts would attack a city jammed full of mercenaries) but there's no future in it. At five shekels a day, it'd take me years to build a new ship; when you figure in living expenses, I'd never make it.

I kept telling them that if we held out for better, something better would turn up. As usual, I was right and they were wrong. It seems the prince of Jebusi was out riding where he shouldn't be, and he got captured by one of these bandit tribes, the Manassites, up in the hill country south of Beth Shean. The king down in Jebusi is offering a reward—a hefty reward—to anyone who brings him back. Now, this is the kind of job I like: We grab the prince, take him home, and stroll back to Tyre with saddlebags full of silver.

I know it sounds a little tricky, but don't worry. These Habiru—that's what the locals call the bandit tribes up in the mountains—can be dangerous when they all get together, but otherwise they're nothing much. Kheperu, bless his clever little heart, knows all about them. Apparently these same tribes caused some trouble in Egypt a few years before Kheperu was born, until Ramses kicked them out of the country. There was a rumor, last fall, that they were getting together to start another war, but that turned out to just be the usual donkey gas.

So, tomorrow we head out along the caravan road toward Beth Shean with some extra horses and a few scraps of this prince's clothing—the fella who told us about it had a whole bundle of them. I figure Graegduz and I can sniff him out once we find the right camp. Finding him is the hard part. After that, I don't figure we'll have much trouble at all.

Give my love to your grandma, as always, and tell your Uncle Llem that once we save this prince, I'm putting together a terrific scheme to cut the Phoenikians out of the tin trade. Why should they make all the money? It's our bloody tin. Keep doing your lessons—I guess I don't need to remind you how expensive it is to support an Egyptian tutor—and while you're at it, get after Llem to come and sit down for a lesson or two. After twenty-five bloody years as High King, don't you think it's time he learns to read? Then I could write straight to him. And if your grandda should visit from Eire, tell him I miss him, and I'm planning to stop by Tara on my way if I should make it home this summer. I'll have a few stories that even you haven't heard, I think.

Take care, and behave yourselves, and with the Goddess' favor I'll see you in summer.

With all my love,

Mother.